STONE COLD NOTES

THE SEASONS CHANGE

JULIA WOLF

Proofreading: My Brother's Editor

Editor: Word Nerd Editing—Monica Black

Photographer: Xram Ragde

Cover Design: Kate Farlow

To the weirdos, the introverts, the quiet ones, and anyone who never fit in: this one's for you, babe.

CHAPTER ONE

WREN

THIS WOMAN THOUGHT I WAS DUMB. Really and truly stupid. And there was a chance she was right. I couldn't transfer a call for the life of me. Being it was a pretty vital part of my job as a receptionist, I understood the tone she was taking with me. That didn't mean I liked it.

My new coworker, Natalie, tapped her coffin-shaped, matte-black nail on the phone's buttons. "You can't hang up on them. You know that, right?"

I kept my face straight, working hard not to blush, but it was a lost cause. My cheeks were on fire with embarrassment...and a little bit of anger. Contrary to what I'd shown, I had more than three brain cells.

"It wasn't on purpose. I haven't used a phone like this before. I'll get the hang of it quickly."

Her smoky eyes narrowed. Actually, all of her narrowed. Arms crossing on the curved, high surface of my desk, her tattooed shoulders bunched below her gauged ears, her shiny lips pursed.

"I won't babysit you," she hissed.

"I don't need a babysitter," I replied.

Someone to actually train me on my first day would have been lovely. Natalie, the person who had been assigned the task, had no interest. She'd shown that from the moment I'd arrived this morning, throwing me to the wolves without so much as a *'the bathrooms are down the hall, bitch.'* And that was fine. I really was a fast learner, I just hated making a fool of myself.

The phone rang, and Natalie watched me with raised eyebrows. Stomach in my throat, I pressed the answer button and spoke into my headset.

"Good morning, this is Wren. You've reached Good Music. How can I help you?"

I thought that sounded professional. I'd practiced it in the mirror last night and on my subway ride this morning. I just had to remember to switch over to 'good afternoon' when the time came.

The person on the other end asked to be transferred to someone in engineering. I put them on hold and sucked in a breath. Natalie hadn't blinked once during this process. When I successfully made the transfer, I exhaled, and she finally allowed her eyelids to lower.

"There. Even a trained monkey could do it." She smirked like she was clever and not spouting trite idioms.

I tilted my head and widened my eyes. "How long did you say you had this job before your promotion?"

She stilled except for her eyes. They scanned me up and down, then a slow smile spread on her shiny lips. "Well, damn." Her nails flicked in my general direction. "I didn't expect you to have claws. Look at you."

I wondered if I should have apologized. The last thing I wanted was to make an enemy. I kind of hoped to be at this job for a while. But I hadn't counted on someone like Natalie.

"What's up with all the animal comparisons? Am I a monkey or a kitten?" Guess I wasn't apologizing.

Her face reddened, and I thought I was done for. Three hours had to be a world record for the shortest time holding a job. I wasn't even sure Natalie had the authority to fire me since she was only one step above me in the food chain, but I shouldn't have been taking chances—not on my first day at a job I desperately needed. I still couldn't quite believe I'd landed it in the first place, but that was beside the point.

She burst out laughing, tossing her head back with glee. "Oh, shit. Maybe I do like you." Leaning over my desk to peer down at my outfit, her lips pressed together in a curved line. "You came in here looking like a lost little preschool teacher. I didn't think you'd last a day. Now, I'm not so sure."

I'd dealt with mean girls my whole life, but I had hoped that legacy wouldn't follow me into the workplace. At what point did we grow up and get over it all? I was beyond ready for today to be the day.

I squared my shoulders. "I'm not going anywhere. I need this job."

Her amusement was tempered slightly by my declaration. "That's good to know. We have way too many girls who work here solely to meet rock stars. If I was involved in the hiring process, I'd throw in some music questions. Like, what's your favorite band, Wren?"

"I don't know. Foo Fighters. Blue is the Color. I like the White Stripes too."

She rapped her knuckles on the desk. "See? That's a good answer. None of those bands record here. If you'd said The Seasons Change or Blossoms and Bones, I wouldn't have hired you." She fluffed her glossy mane of finger waves. "But it's not my decision. I'm just the one who has to work with the thirsty chicks they hire to sit at this desk."

Good Music housed recording studios and some rehearsal spaces for artists signed to Good Music Records. Since GMR was a massive label with multiple smaller labels under its umbrella touching on every genre of music out there, the studios were bustling day in and day out. At least, that's what I'd been told. As the receptionist manning the front desk, I saw everyone who entered the building. So far, it had been relatively quiet, but it wasn't even noon. According to Natalie, musicians were night owls. The building never closed, and recording sessions often went overnight.

"That's not me, I can promise you that. I'm here to work, not drool over musicians."

"Good." Natalie nodded. "I'll hold you to that. Because some of these idiots think flirting is their job. If you show them even an ounce of interest, they'll have you bent over a copier faster than you can say 'I love your music.' Trust me, keep it professional or you'll regret it."

She looked me over again, beginning at my sapphire-blue pleated skirt, which hit midcalf, up to my plain, long-sleeved black T-shirt. Her gaze swept over my small mouth, medium nose, and oversized brown eyes. She paused on my hair. Everyone did. It was light copper, thick and shiny—the only truly memorable part of me.

"Well, as long as you're not throwing yourself at anyone, you probably won't have a problem." She added a smile on the end of her barb, I guessed to soften the blow. I already knew a rock star wasn't going to walk in and sweep me off my feet without her driving the point home.

My phone rang again, and Natalie watched me like a hawk while I handled the call. When I was about to press a button, she hissed, and my finger froze midair. Reaching down, she jabbed a different button, successfully transferring the call for me.

"Ugh. I'm sorry. I'll get this soon." My cheeks were flaming hot again. I hated being bad at something that should have been simple. My college diploma did not prepare me for this.

She came around the desk and perched a hip beside my phone. "Honestly, no biggie. To tell you the truth, I hung up on the owner of this whole place on my second day. Saul freaking Goodman got my dial tone. And let me tell you, he did not find the humor in it."

With that whiplash of a confession, Natalie ran through the phone system like she was talking to a child, and it was exactly what I needed. By the end of her lesson, I had pretty much caught on and felt fairly confident I wouldn't hang up on anyone. For the most part.

She left me alone, retreating to her cubbyhole of an office at the rear of the lobby. She handled the main administrative work while I greeted everyone who came in, handled phone calls, and did anything else that was asked of me. Natalie was right, a trained monkey *could* do this job. It was a stepping stone for me. My first big girl job post-college. The key to exiting struggleville for good.

A few people came and went over the next couple hours. A tall man with sunglasses on, taking long, confident strides across the shiny marble floor, really caught my attention, and I put on my best smile to greet him.

"Good morning. Welcome to Good Music," I singsonged.

His steps slowed. He brought up his hand and pulled back his sleeve to check the chunky watch on his wrist. "It's afternoon now." Then he walked over to my desk, propping an elbow on it. "You're not the girl who was here the last time I was in."

"I'm not. This is my first day." I rubbed the goose bumps on my arms. I was terrible at speaking to men, but this was part of my job. "Good afternoon. Can I help you with anything?"

He pushed his sunglasses to the top of his head, revealing crystal clear blue eyes. "I don't think so. Not now at least. I always need help with something, though. I'm Adam. What's your name?"

My heart thrashed wildly in my chest. And it was from more than nerves. I had to swallow down a thick lump to answer him. "I'm Wren." My lips strained to keep the smile plastered on my face.

This beautiful, famous man in front of me took no notice of my wobbly smile. "Wren? Like a little bird? That's cute."

Little Bird.

"No." I shook my head harder than I should have. "Just Wren."

He canted his head, still interested despite my sharp rebuke. "Ah...you have one of those rad, unique names that probably got you teased by the idiots you went to school with, huh?"

I nodded, swallowing hard again. "Yes. I really don't like nicknames."

"I feel you, Wren. Although, I still say Little Bird is cute as hell, like you." He tapped his blunt fingertips. "How's your first day going?"

My chest was in knots. Sweat beaded at my hairline. I was about thirty seconds from vomiting. "It's going great." That was all I could wrench out of me.

His brow lowered, and he leaned in, his voice low and conspiratorial. "You're nervous. Is it the job, or am I doing that to you?"

From the way he raked his pretty eyes over me, it seemed like he hoped he was the cause of my shaky answers and sweaty palms. And he was, in a way, but not directly.

For once, I willed my phone to ring, but it remained silent. *Traitor.* And Adam Wainwright, lead guitarist for The Seasons Change, seemed to be in no hurry to leave. He was enjoying the sight of me quite literally quaking in my boots.

"A mixture of both, I think," I squeezed out.

His mouth opened to reply, or flirt, or tease, but another man entered the building behind him, and the gust of icy wind from outside pulled both our eyes in that direction.

Callum Rose was impossible not to recognize. Bass player for The Seasons Change, his rockabilly style would have been distinguishable without his towering height and shoulder-length blond hair. Callum didn't so much stride as he did saunter, his hands tucked snugly in a fitted leather jacket, the chain hanging from his belt loops bouncing softly on the side of his leg.

Black spots danced in my vision. If he spoke to me, I would faint. There was nothing I could do to stop it. I should have prepared for the possibility of seeing him here, but I hadn't. And the reality of seeing Callum in person was far beyond any feeble preparations I could have made anyway.

"S'up, man?" Adam greeted him. Callum tipped his chin and rolled a toothpick along his lips like a character from a James Dean film. His blue eyes swept over me like I was a piece of furniture.

And then...he kept going, passing us both without even a slight pause, to take the elevators up to the third floor. Adam snorted at my vacant expression.

"Don't bother with pleasantries with good ol' Cal. He's a man of very few words." Adam's brow lowered, and his sparkling blue eyes locked on me. "You can save the sweet for me. I can't get enough of it."

Sucking in a ragged breath, I forced my lips to curve. "Does that line work for you often?"

Chuckling, he patted the desk with both hands and took a step back. "Oh, you have no idea. See you soon, sweet Wren."

As soon as he was gone, I folded in half, looping my arms under my thighs, and sucked in deep breaths that only mildly calmed my racing pulse. It was the stinging in my eyes that was the true problem. If I cried on my first day at work, I'd never be able to live it down. Even if no one saw me do it, I would know. And that was...no.

I wouldn't cry over Callum Rose. I'd done enough of that three and a half years ago. The man who made me fall in love with his words then broke my heart when our eyes first met. I had been as invisible to him then as I was now.

My eyes dried. My spine stiffened. Everything was fine. I had a great new job. My family was healthy and taken care of. My outfit was cute, despite Natalie's obvious disdain. I'd just been flirted with by a rock star.

The phone rang, and I answered with my cheeriest greeting.
I managed to transfer the caller without hanging up.
Everything was definitely fine.

I READ THE EMAIL AGAIN. For no reason other than it curbed my boredom. I didn't know why, couldn't explain it to myself, but I was tempted to respond. I'd been tempted since it landed in The Seasons Change's inbox a few weeks ago with my name at the top.

We'd been on the road since the summer, playing in every venue that would pay us. And by pay, I meant a couple quarters and a chewed-up piece of gum scraped from the bottom of a table. But we were hungry enough—literally, sometimes—we'd take those two quarters and rancid gum and treasure them like gold doubloons.

We were traveling in our junker of a van, across the middle of America, where everything was flat for miles and miles and miles. A lot of the same. But this email, it was different. It perked up my tired brain, and I took an interest.

I read it again.

Dear Callum Rose,

Hi!

I know you'll never see this email, so I'm going to be completely honest and forthright. I wonder how many other emails to your band's fan account have started the same way? Do other girls use this address as a journal entry?

Well, not to be cliché, but I'm not like other girls. I don't plan to pour out my sob story in a stream of consciousness. I have questions! Like I said, I know you'll never see this email, so the answers I seek will probably forever be floating around in the ether, but that's okay. I've accepted my fate.

I saw The Seasons Change play the Swerve Festival last weekend. I had never heard your band before then, but I have become obsessed. Of course, I love Iris's voice, but I adore the style and sound of your music as a whole. I have done a deep dive on the internet to find out everything I can about the four of you. Specifically you, though.

Did you know they call you Stone Cold on the forums? They say you never show any expression on stage, or...I guess, off either. People were speculating all manners of things that made you that way, but I won't repeat their armchair psychology in polite company.

I didn't tell them, but I think they're wrong. I don't think you're cold, and I saw plenty of expression while you played. You bit your lip when you were really concentrating. You tracked Iris around the stage, and when she stood in front of you to sing, you responded with your eyes. Your emotions might be micro, but they're there. I saw them easily, even while being shoved around by sweaty boys in the pit.

Callum, are you shy? I think we might be kind of alike. My mind is a busy bee and my thoughts are all over the place (as you might have noticed in this email), but in person, I'm shy and I...I guess I shrink. Do you do that too? It's hard to be this way. Is it hard for you? Or do you like being alone in your own world?

I could be way off base. I'm probably projecting my own personality onto you like a complete weirdo. But if I'm right... well, it's nice to know I'm not alone. I'm happy you're able to get on stage and make magic, even though it probably feels like physical pain to have all those eyes on you.

Well, I guess I'll never hear from you. I promise not to make this a thing by constantly emailing. This was a one off I'm sure I'll regret as soon as I hit send.

Here I go anyway!
Your faithful fan,
Birdie

Yeah, I was going to reply. I was curious, and it wasn't often I felt that way. I wasn't looking for a pen pal. I didn't know that I was looking for anything. But I guess that was the thing. I couldn't predict what was going to happen, but I wanted to find out.

Adam peered over my shoulder. "What's that?"

There were three rows in the van and four of us, but he somehow always ended up beside me unless he was doing the driving. Adam played lead guitar and did what he needed to on stage. Off it, though, he was all golden retriever energy.

I slid my phone in my pocket. "It's nothing."

For someone like me, who didn't easily make friends or form connections, Adam was a shock to the system. I'd gotten used to him over the couple years I'd known him, but he hadn't gotten used to me. If he had, he'd understand I needed time to myself to feel sane.

"Sure. Keep being boring, Callie."

"Don't call me Callie," I shot back.

"Iris calls you that," he protested.

From the driver's seat, Iris, our lead singer and peacekeeper, held up her middle finger. "Some things aren't for you, Adam. Just accept it."

Rodrigo, our drummer, bobbed his head and tapped his hands on the dashboard to a beat only he could hear. Adam climbed over the seats to invade his space instead. Roddy was a lot more receptive to the intrusion.

I took my phone back out and tapped out a reply.

Birdie,

You might be surprised how few emails a band that plays town carnivals and rundown clubs gets. You also might be surprised to know I run TSC's social media. I do a piss-poor job of it, which is why it's taken me two months to reply.

I didn't know they'd nicknamed me Stone Cold, but that's pretty accurate. I don't mind.

You might be projecting, but you're not fully wrong either.

Don't shrink, Birdie. Whatever you do, don't do that.

Did you regret it?

Callum Rose

Dear Callum,

Excuse me if I don't play it cool. I should be mad it took you two months to respond while I'm replying within minutes of your email, but I'm not. It might be another two months before you reply again, or it might be never, but it seems important not to waste a second on my end.

I am mad you didn't answer my questions! I guess you sort of did, but not really. That's okay. Can you tell me which part I'm not fully wrong about?

I don't know what it is about you, but I'm fascinated. Where are you now? Are you touring or are you home? Which do you prefer?

I've barely left home, so I think I'd like to be on tour, but I'm not sure yet. I have a document saved on my computer of destinations I plan to go to one day...hopefully when I graduate. What's the best place you've ever been to?

Do I regret what?

Xoxo,

Birdie

I took my time replying again. But I did read her emails on a constant rotation. This person, this stranger, caught me off guard. The Seasons Change wasn't big by any means, but we had fans, and our fandom kept growing. That meant there were girls hanging around after our shows. I'd gotten more than my fair share of questions and prying, but none interested me.

Not until this girl behind the screen. Birdie.

So, I wrote back from the creaking bed in a cheap motel room we'd splurged on for the night.

Birdie,

I watched the sun rise at the Grand Canyon last week. Like you, I wanted to play it cool, but it was impossible. Those minutes in that place were the best I've experienced so far.

TSC is touring. Always touring. I don't really have a home to go back to at the moment, so I'm cool with touring. The van gets cramped and our pits stink it up sometimes, but I still like it.

Traveling's in my blood. I grew up in a family of musicians/grifters. The Traveling Roses did as much singing as they did pickpocketing. I kicked the thieving habit, but I like to keep moving.

Are you still shrinking? I hope not.

Do you regret your first email?

Callum

Dear Callum,

Two weeks! That's a lightning-fast response. I was certain my 'xoxo' scared you off. Those were strictly platonic hugs and kisses, just so you know. I'm sure you have girls throwing themselves at you constantly, but as we've established, I'm not like other girls.

Stinky pits? You've ruined any romantic illusions I had about what it's like to tour. Although, I'd probably love it anyway, especially if it came with Grand Canyon sunrises. I just added that to my list.

The Traveling Roses? I found a few articles about your family! I bet the pic I saw of a little blond boy with dirt on his face is you. One day, when we're better friends, I need to know more!

On a serious note, no, I don't regret my first email. I never expected a response, but the two emails I've received from you have been the highlight of my life. I know that sounds pathetic, but I've lived a very small life and this feels bigger than big to me.

I don't know how not to shrink. I think about what you said as I close in on myself, but I can't stop it. I want to, though.

You never told me which part I wasn't wrong about.

Xoxo platonically,

Birdie

Little Bird,

Highlight of your life?

How old are you?

Callum

Dear Callum,

I should lie, but I have a dreadful habit of telling the truth. I'm 17 and a senior in high school. I know you're 21 and you're going to say this is all sorts of inappropriate, but I swear, I don't have designs on you. I just like your emails and feel like we could be friends if we were the type to make friends. I don't know. My stomach is sick right now because I have a feeling I won't hear from you again.

    Your platonic friend,
    Birdie

I almost deleted her email, but I couldn't bring myself to. Seventeen should have been too fucking young for me to be entertaining even a conversation, but I believed this girl. And she was right. If we were the type to make friends, I could see that happening.

But that wasn't what this was, and she seemed to know that. I didn't know what it was, but I didn't want to stop writing to her. Not today. We'd see about tomorrow.

    Little Bird,
    You're right. I wasn't going to reply. I shouldn't. But I have a bad habit of doing the wrong thing. The thing about being on the road is there's a lot of downtime. I get bored and tired of my own thoughts. Your emails are entertaining.

    You were wrong about some things. I don't shrink like you. I'm just not there, you know what I mean?

    Glad you don't have designs on me. That would be a mistake. If you're going to choose one of the band members to have a crush on, it should be Iris or Adam. Rodrigo's cool, but he's the marrying kind. Not your kind.

    Callum

Dear Callum,

Hi. Hello. After a month, I didn't think I would hear from you again. But here you are. Did I say hi?

Does your band know what a terrible social media manager you are? A month to reply to a fan is beyond the pale. They should fire you.

Speaking of the band, thanks for your attempt to foist me off onto one of the other members. That's kind of you. Unfortunately, I'm a weird one who doesn't really get crushes. I go from zero to hopelessly in love in a heartbeat. There's no in between. This has only happened once, when I locked eyes with a boy named Karthik Singh in 9th grade. He had the deepest brown eyes I've ever seen (yes, still to this day, none have compared). I followed him around like a puppy for two years until he finally kissed me. One kiss was all he could spare. It was a perfectly nice kiss, but I fell out of love with him by morning. So maybe the kiss wasn't as nice as I thought...

I don't think I would get tired of your thoughts ping-ponging around in my head.

Where are you right now?

Your almost-legal friend,

Birdie

Karthik Singh could die.

That was my first thought after reading her email.

It alarmed me, but after a lot of introspection, I determined I felt some twisted sort of protection toward this little bird. A girl like that, who wore her heart on her sleeve, needed protecting. I grew up surrounded by criminals, so I knew firsthand how cruel the world could be. It wasn't my role to protect her as her half-assed pen pal, but instinct was instinct. The leftover caveman in me beat his chest and pounded his club.

I wrote and rewrote my reply. The first one would have gotten the cops called on me. I took my time, but not too long, formulating something that sounded more level headed than I felt.

Little Bird,

We're in Alabama, making our way into Georgia, then we'll drive to Florida. I grew up hearing Alabama accents, so in a roundabout way, I feel like I'm home whenever I hear people speaking when we stop.

Karthik Singh sounds like an awful person. It's a shame you devoted so much time and energy into following him. There had to be a more worthy candidate.

You did say hi.

Callum

Dear Callum,

Holy granola! Do you have an Alabama accent?

Karthik Singh is an adequate person. There are probably several girls available to sing his praises. There might have been someone better for me to follow, but you're right, I was blinded by his pretty eyes. I think next time, I want to be the one who's followed.

By the way, don't think I didn't notice my threat to narc on you to your band improved your response time. Three days... wow, you must have been waiting by your phone for my email. Sad, really.

What part of you is stone cold? Is it just on stage or...?

I hope you're seeing great things and you'll tell me all about them next time.

Your constant pen pal,
Birdie

Little Bird,
How can granola be holy?
I do have an accent. I think. I can go for days without hearing
my own voice, but I believe it's still there.
When you stop shrinking, someone will follow you. Let's
hope it's someone you want as your shadow.
No threats needed, Little Bird. I told you I like your emails.
We're in Miami now. It's hot and loud. Colorful in a way
nowhere else is. I like it. We're staying in a rental apartment
attached to a bigger house for three nights. The owner is a tiny
old Cuban woman who has plied us with food since we got here.
She was trying to speak with me this morning. I didn't answer
her and hurt her feelings. I know that, but I'm not going to do
anything about it. That's me. Stone Cold.
What kind of name is Birdie, anyway?
Callum

It was there, in Miami, months after her first email, it really struck me that we were friends. We didn't know a lot about each other—I'd been purposely keeping my distance from knowing her specific details—but it didn't matter. I knew this girl, and she knew me.

But hadn't she known me from the very start?

CHAPTER THREE

WREN

ONE WEEK AT GOOD MUSIC, and it was like I'd always been here. No more hang ups, I usually remembered to switch from 'good morning' to 'good afternoon,' and Natalie rarely looked at me with suspicion.

She did hiss at me a little when Adam Wainwright stopped at my desk to flirt with me again, but she cooled off quickly, citing Adam would 'flirt with a pig if it had a dress on.'

I wasn't too sure I liked Natalie.

A weekend at home with my family had fortified me for my second Monday on the job. I wore my blue skirt again, with a white top this time—one I would never dare wear at home because it would be stained in an instant. I felt good. Professional and put together. Nothing pig-like about me besides my big, round butt.

The clack of Natalie's heels on the marble floor signaled her approach. She stopped behind my desk, adjusting the strap of her bag over her shoulder before crossing her arms.

"I need you to stay a little bit longer. Studio 3B placed an order for food, and it's coming within the next hour, but I have an appointment and can't wait for it."

My stomach clenched. I'd been looking forward to going home. "Can't the delivery driver take it up to them?"

Her eyes rolled so hard, I wouldn't have been surprised if they'd made a full loop in her skull. "Don't be lazy, Wren. We don't allow anyone outside the company to enter the studios. You've signed an NDA, but Joe Schmo from the pizza place hasn't. What's to stop him from recording the session?" She huffed. "Think, please. *Jesus.*"

There was really no other answer I could give besides yes. We both knew that. And though I wanted to get home more than anything, disaster wouldn't strike if I left in an hour instead of fifteen minutes.

I just wish Natalie would fully commit to being a villain if that's what she was going for. She was nice and funny during half our interactions, which made her switch to a bitch-monster particularly whiplash-y.

"That's fine. I can stay tonight." My voice came out more meek than I'd intended, but that wasn't something I could control.

"Good." She squeezed my shoulder. "And try not to flirt with the band, even if they're coming onto you, okay? It's just really not a good look."

Luckily, my burning face was all the response she needed. Natalie strutted out of the lobby in her pencil skirt and swing coat. A blast of arctic wind slapped me when she opened the door, cooling my hot cheeks.

Minutes ticked by as I waited. Upstairs, the studios were still filled with musicians, but most of the support and administrative staff had already left for the day, so it was quiet in the lobby.

I held out my phone and snapped a picture of myself making a funny face with my cheeks blown up and my eyes bugging out. Then I texted it to my great-aunt with a bunch of emojis. She'd get a kick out of it.

Forty-five minutes later, the delivery driver dropped off three large bags of food and a tray of drinks. Balancing them carefully, I rode the elevator to the third floor, pretending my stomach wasn't tied in a hundred knots.

As I approached studio 3B, I wondered if I should knock or just go in. My hands were really too full to let myself in, so I—

My train of thought stopped as a tall, tall man strode toward the same destination from the opposite direction. His eyes were on the ground, so I could look at him for a moment, but only a moment since his long legs ate up the short distance between us.

He pulled open the studio door, nearly hitting me with it. He hadn't even noticed me standing there helplessly. If he had, he'd chosen to ignore me.

"Excuse me?" I forced the words out loud and clear. He stopped, his back to me, head cocked to show he was listening. "Can you hold the door for me? I have your dinner order."

There was a pause, and my mind jumped over a hundred conclusions straight to the one where he'd let the door fall closed without a second thought.

Luckily, he pushed the door open wide, his long arm bracing it. As I passed him to enter the studio, my shoulder brushed his chest, and I gasped. His head jerked at the sound, and for a fleeting beat of my heart, his eyes raised to inspect me. It was over as soon as it had happened. Callum's icy eyes glanced away, then he moved out of the way entirely, letting the door snick closed at my back.

I was suddenly in a roomful of rockers and had never felt more out of place and conspicuous. They must've been on break from recording, because they were all sitting around on the couches, feet kicked up on the coffee table in the center, laughing about something.

The woman with ribbons of midnight hair streaming down her shoulders noticed me huddled against the wall first. Her smile grew bright, and she stomped on the floor with excitement. Iris Adler, the lead singer of The Seasons Change, was twice as pretty in person. Even in baggy sweats and no makeup, she didn't have to try to be the prettiest woman in the room. She simply was.

"Oh, look, an actual angel has arrived," Iris announced, hopping to her feet.

Every head turned in my direction. Adam stayed in position, slouching on the couch with one leg slung over the arm, but a slow, mischievous smile spread on his lips. Callum was across the room, arms crossed, leaning against the wall. It was Rodrigo Chavez, the muscular drummer with soft brown eyes, who took pity on me. He took the drink tray from my shaky hands and motioned for me to follow him.

As I placed the bags of food on the coffee table, Adam shifted to sit with his elbows on his knees.

"Hi, Wren," he cooed. "If that food is as good as it smells, I think I'm gonna love you forever."

I couldn't help but give him a small smile. From our limited interactions, I'd surmised he was somewhat of a jackass, but a harmless, charming one.

"Since I didn't make it, that love would be misplaced, but I hope you enjoy it anyway." I straightened and tucked a lock of hair behind my ear.

Adam chuckled and stole a fry from one of the Styrofoam containers. "Have you met everyone yet?"

"I'm sure I've greeted them all." I caught myself fiddling with my skirt and quickly snapped my hands to my sides. That felt awkward, so I clasped my hands in front of me. That felt unnatural, but I made myself stop fidgeting.

Adam barreled over my discomfort, making a round of introductions. "Iris, meet Wren. She's the ray of sunshine at the front desk."

Iris had just taken a big bite of a veggie burger, so she covered her mouth with one hand and waved to me with the other. Adam continued, pointing out a producer and sound engineer, who were both digging into their food. They hardly spared me a glance, but that wasn't new for me.

"Roddy, this is Wren." Adam tossed another fry into his mouth, and my stomach grumbled. I was hungry, and the smell of their dinner wasn't helping.

Rodrigo nodded, bracing his ankle on his opposite knee. "Nice to meet you, Wren. You weren't working here when we recorded our last album, were you?"

"No." I tucked my hair again and nearly slapped my hand away to stop the nervous tic. "I've only worked here a week."

He nodded. "Didn't think so. I distinctly recall the last woman being surly some days and all up in my grill other days. That's not you."

"Wren has never been surly a day in her life." Adam whacked Rodrigo's arm with the back of his hand.

"I'm sure I have at least one or two days." My chin trembled with the effort it took to continue this conversation and not melt into the floor.

Adam's grin warmed on me. "Speaking of surly, that quiet bastard over there is Callum. Callum, say hi to Wren."

As if in slow motion, Callum's head turned, and his gaze landed on me. Not on my face, though. It seemed his focus was on my hands, which were ringing the life out of my skirt.

Then, even more slowly, he spoke in a smooth, deep, southern drawl. "Hi, Wren." It came out sounding more like '*Ha, Rin,*' and I instantly loved the way he said my name.

Except no. I couldn't love anything he did. He was a beautiful rock star, and I was the plain girl with the big butt who sat at the reception desk. One he passed every day without ever returning my quiet greeting.

"Nice to meet you." I thrust the words from my throat. His gaze was still on my hands, so I allowed the fabric to unfurl and flattened my palms to my sides. Lips curving into a lopsided smirk, his shoulders jerked once, then his attention shifted to a window, and I was set free.

"You should hang out," Adam said. "We have enough food to feed a legion. Stay a while, have dinner with us. I want to get to know the girl at the desk."

A balled-up napkin hit him in the chest. "Leave her alone," Iris said. "She's just trying to do her job."

I tucked hair that was already tucked and shifted from foot to foot. Everyone was staring at me again. I probably should have left, except my ballet flats suddenly felt more like lead boots.

"Aren't you off the clock?" Adam asked. "Isn't it, like, illegal to make employees work more than a certain number of hours?"

The engineer huffed a laugh, slapping his jean-clad thigh. "You're fucking funny, kid. I've been locked in this room for twenty hours during a marathon recording session. You were there. You know this for a fact."

Adam nodded and shot me a sheepish grin. "But Wren is an office girl. Rules apply, don't they?" He moved into my space, making my heart kick up a notch. Adam Wainwright was handsome and famous. Being flirted with by him sent me sideways. I didn't know what to do with myself. He probably knew that. The Seasons Change was a newer band, but Adam had been famous long enough to be well aware of the effect he had on women. Especially women like me who weren't used to attention.

I shifted again, moving to the side, one step closer to the door. Callum came into view, and to my shock, he was watching my interaction with Adam with keen interest. His deep, cold pools were narrowed and focused, not quite on my face, but on me. His attention was more disorienting than being flirted with by a beautiful rock star.

"Um…" I stopped myself from tucking my hair for the hundredth time, "I don't know about laws or rules, but my workday is over. Thank you for the offer, but I have a long commute home, so I need to get going."

"Come on, Wren. You're too young to be acting like a responsible citizen. Stay a while."

I shook my head. "I really can't." If my feet didn't weigh a thousand pounds and Callum Rose wasn't burning me to the ground with his steady, unyielding gaze, I would have darted from the room to put an end to this back and forth.

Adam opened his mouth, most likely to argue, but it slammed closed at the low, commanding southern drawl coming from across the room.

"Let her go, Adam."

Adam whipped around to look at Callum, and Callum answered him with a cold, blank stare and a faint shrug. I took the opportunity to move my leaden feet and make my escape.

Rodrigo sprung from his seat and opened the studio door for me. "After you, Wren. Thanks for the food. Sorry shit got weird. It happens from time to time."

A light laugh bubbled out of me. "You're welcome. And don't worry about the weird. I don't mind it."

"Then you're always welcome to come sit in and watch us work, if you're into that." He patted my shoulder before I could sputter out a response. "Have a good night."

The following day, Adam stopped at my desk just before it was time for my lunch break. "Hey." He pushed a small succulent in a vibrantly painted pot toward me. "This is an apology."

"Hi." I picked up the tiny pot and fingered the green leaves. "You don't owe me an apology, but thank you. This is really cute."

"Like you."

His brow lowered, and he leaned on his elbows, bringing his face closer to mine. I'd gone home last night sure I'd been imagining his interest in me. Then I'd chalked up the possibility that he might have been flirting with the fact that I was the only available woman around. There was Iris, of course, but from what I'd seen on the internet, she was most definitely taken.

And here he was again, bringing me a plant and calling me cute. This evidence was undeniable.

"Thank you. Again." My giggle was wobbly and nervous. "All of this is unnecessary."

He cocked his head, shooting me a crooked grin. "Let me decide that. I was a pushy ass last night when you just wanted to get home. The fact that Callum had to speak up really hammered that point home. Don't let me off the hook."

"Then I accept your apology and this adorable succulent." I placed it beside my computer and flashed him my best smile. My lips barely trembled. "It's already brightening up the space."

He grinned wide, pleasure seeping into his crystalline blue eyes. "Again, like you."

That made me snort a little laugh. "Holy granola, such lines, I swear."

"I'd never use lines on you." His long fingers tapped the surface of my desk. "I know I'm probably going to get you in trouble if I keep standing here talking to you, and I don't wanna do that, but I'd like to hang out with you. There's a party I'm going to Friday night. What do you think?"

My eyebrows raised. "Think about what?"

He laughed. "What do you think about coming to the party with us? I know you said your commute is long. I'll send you home in a car service when you're ready. Or, you know, you could crash at my place."

I sucked in a sharp breath. At the invitation. The implications. All of it. "I wasn't expecting that."

"Is that a yes? Callum'll come too for your protection."

I rubbed my lips together. My first instinct was to say no. I had obligations. And wild nights of partying weren't something I did anymore. Okay...well, I'd never really done them, but even less now. But it didn't have to be a wild night. And he was promising a car home. I was definitely ignoring his sleepover invitation. It wasn't even close to being an option. My great-aunt Jenny was always telling me I was allowed to be young. That I should be young. But still...

A party with Callum Rose.

"It's a maybe."

With a wide, triumphant grin, he backed away from the desk. "You're rad, Wren. Just sayin'..."

"That wasn't a yes," I rushed out.

He held his hands up. "I didn't hear no, so I'm taking it as a win. See you later, cutie."

He sauntered to the elevator with a skip in his step, his whistle echoing off the lobby walls. I definitely hadn't said yes, and if Adam knew the reason I'd said maybe, he probably wouldn't have been whistling.

Natalie appeared out of nowhere a minute later, nearly shoving me out of my seat. "Go to lunch." She picked up my succulent, rotating it around in her palm. "Cute, but make sure not to clutter up your desk. Not a good look."

"Don't worry." I grabbed my purse from the drawer where I'd stashed it. "I won't. See you in an hour."

She covered the desk for me every day, and every day, she acted like the most put-upon person on earth. I had decided not to let it get to me and took my full hour even if I didn't need it.

I'd packed my lunch but stopped at a café a block from the studio to buy a mocha. Though it was winter, the sun was shining bright, and the temperature was just warm enough for me to sit on a bench in the park and people watch while I ate.

The line for coffee was longer than expected. After I'd been waiting a minute or so, the hairs on the back of my neck rose as someone got in line behind me. I glanced over my shoulder and nearly swallowed my tongue when I locked gazes with Callum.

I whirled around to face forward out of instinct, but I couldn't just pretend I hadn't seen him. He was right behind me. Probably closer than he should have been. If I hadn't been wearing a scarf and coat, I might have felt his breath on my neck.

I turned around fully, tucking my chin in my scarf. That wasn't going to work, since he was almost a foot and a half taller than me, so I tipped my head back to meet his gaze.

"Hi. You probably don't remember me, but—"

"I remember you, Wren," he drawled. *Rin.* God, I loved that too much.

"Okay." Hearing his voice still felt like a kick to the solar plexus, but I wanted more of it. "Are you getting coffee before you head to the studio? I can always grab it for you."

"That's all right." He nodded at my lunch bag in my hand. "You're on your break."

The line moved, so I stepped back. There were still three people between me and the register.

"Yeah, I am. But I wouldn't mind."

He stared back at me but didn't reply. Like this, face to face and up close, I noticed things about him, details I stocked away in the cavity of my chest reserved for all things Callum Rose.

His cheeks were flushed. Probably from the cold. And it looked good on him. Made him more human. Almost touchable. He wasn't impervious to weather.

The pools of his eyes weren't as opaque as they'd appeared from far away. I could see subtle flecks of lighter blue and a tiny bit of yellow and gold. Like pebbles in the bed of a clear, glacial stream.

The tops of his hands were slightly chapped, and the skin was rugged looking. Knuckles slightly scarred. A fresh cut on his right hand.

Beneath his thick, golden stubble was a dark bruise on his jaw and a cut on the opposite cheekbone. Looked like Callum Rose had been in a fight recently.

After ordering, we waited at the end of the counter for our drinks. I was at a loss for words, and Callum didn't seem to be interested in speaking. But it hadn't escaped my notice that he'd chosen to stand right beside me, the sleeve of his leather jacket brushing my wool coat. That had to mean something.

"Adam invited me to the party you're going to Friday."

Callum startled, the hand that had been on the way to his face freezing in midair. "He did?"

"Mmhmm. I haven't said yes yet but—"

"Say no." He moved in front of me, heat blasting from his hard glare. "You're not going to any party Adam is going to."

My stomach plummeted so fast, I had to bite back bile. "That isn't...um..."

"No," he said again.

"Why?" I whispered. I shouldn't have pressed it, but if he was going to be an asshole, I wanted him to fully own it.

"The parties Adam and I go to aren't for a girl like you." He reached around me and grabbed his cup from the counter. "Take your coffee, Wren. Go eat your lunch. Forget about this."

His cheeks were flaming red. Not from the cold this time. Was he burning up at me?

"What does that mean?" I asked.

He shook his head again, hard enough to cause a lock of his blond hair to swoop down on his forehead. He brushed it back roughly while scorching me with his heated gaze.

"The answer is no."

Then he turned on his heel and stalked out of the shop. Like he was angry at me. Why? For thinking I might be associated with him in public? I didn't understand, not really. My throat felt swollen. It was almost impossible to swallow.

I wasn't sure why I was surprised. At one point, I had thought I'd known Callum better than anyone else in my life. Better than anyone in *his* life. But letters can lie. Words on a screen that had meant everything at the time weren't relevant anymore. Besides, the last email I'd read from Callum had been over three and a half years ago. I'd changed since then. Obviously, so had he.

I ate my lunch in the park, barely tasting it. My mocha scorched the roof of my mouth. I tried to sort out my feelings, but I couldn't decide if I was hurt or angry, so I let it go. It didn't matter. I had other things—other people—in my life who were far more important than an arrogant rock star.

Four and a half years ago

Dear Callum,

Hmmm...you're right. That is pretty stone cold. But the fact that you noticed you hurt her feelings and told me about it means you did care. Maybe you didn't know how to make it right? Or didn't feel capable. Or maybe you're just an a-hole. Time will tell!

Birdie is a nickname everyone calls me. I've never gone by my real name. It's Wren, btw, but no one calls me that. It's Birdie until the end of time.

Granola is holy because I say it is! I don't know, it's just something I say. Get used to it!

An Alabama accent! Jeez, maybe one day I'll actually get to hear you speak.

Tomorrow's my birthday. Eighteen and only kissed once. I'm determined to find a date for prom and get kissed on the dance floor. The only problem is, I'll never ask a boy, and I'm pretty sure I'm invisible. But we'll see.

Where are you now?

Your friend,

Birdie

Little Bird,

I missed your birthday by a week. You should have given me warning. You know how fucking bad I am about writing back.

Happy birthday anyway. I feel slightly less like a child predator writing to you now.

I am an asshole. No need to sugarcoat it. A stone-cold asshole.

Holy granola is extremely cute. Never stop saying it.

Wren, huh? I like Little Bird. That's who you are to me. And you're my friend now, is that right? My little bird friend.

You don't need to kiss anyone just to do it. Keep it to yourself until you find your shadow. That's coming soon. You're not invisible, it's just...no one's seen you. Do you get that?

My voice...yeah, maybe one day.

We're staying with Rodrigo's family on their farm in South Carolina. They're letting us camp out and use their bathrooms to shower. It smells like cow shit everywhere, but it's peaceful. I like it.

Callum

CHAPTER FOUR

CALLUM

THE LONGEST I'D EVER GONE without speaking a single word was fifteen days. It wasn't on purpose, not at first. Two or three days had passed before I'd realized, and then I'd wondered how long I could go. I was around people. I was constantly around people back then. On the road, backstage, after-parties. It was just...no one expected much from me. Or nothing, really. And that was what I gave.

By day fifteen, I panicked. Silence had become too comfortable. I walked outside the venue we were playing and screamed the alphabet at the top of my lungs. Just to make sure I still existed. That I could be heard when I wanted to be.

Right now? I wanted to be heard.

I latched onto the back of Adam's shirt and yanked him down the hall, away from the studio and prying ears.

"What are you playin' at?" I gritted out.

His eyes flared with innocence. "Dude, I have no idea what you're talking about. You're going to have to be specific."

"Inviting that *girl* to one of Benson's parties." I crossed my arms over my chest. "I told her no."

Adam sputtered, laughing me off like he always did. He didn't take anything seriously. That worked for him. He was a twenty-six-year-old man-child. I'd known him since I joined the band when I was nineteen, and he hadn't changed one iota. The money got greener, the parties better, the girls more plentiful, but Adam remained constant. A free-wheeling fuckboy.

"You can't tell her no. I was the one who invited her."

"Can and did." My molars ground together. "What are you thinkin'?"

"I'm thinking Wren is cute. She says things like 'holy granola,' for fuck's sake. She's my type. A little plump, sweet perfection. I could spend the next couple weeks flirting and buttering her up, but why waste my time? I'm taking her to Benson's. If she's into it, I'm golden. If she's not, I'll send her on her way in a car. No harm, no foul." His eyes narrowed. "Why the fuck do you care? I gotta say, this is kinda out of character."

"I don't want her there."

This was something I wouldn't budge on. I rarely went out, never indulged in drugs or had debauched nights of trashing hotel rooms and being captured on film by the paparazzi. Adam and I lived opposite lifestyles, except one thing:

I liked to watch, and he liked to show off.

No surprise Adam was an exhibitionist. He used to bring random groupies back to the van we all traveled, slept, and basically lived in, and fuck them, whether we were all in there or not. And it wasn't some subtle fucking. It was skin-slapping, moaning, dirty-talking, ass-banging, filthy sex.

Roddy and Iris would run for the hills, and I did too at first. But one time, the girl asked me to stay. Adam gave me the nod, so I did. I watched. I got harder than I ever had in my life.

And a kink was born.

Since those early days, we'd grown up some. The minivan had been traded in for sex clubs and the occasional swinger party. But Adam still liked to fuck with an audience, and my voyeuristic tendencies had flourished.

We didn't do it often, but it was enough to call it a habit.

A habit I had indulged in more than once at a Benson Martin party. It had been a long time since I'd been to one, but the scene never changed. It was a den of iniquity where voyeurs and exhibitionists came to play.

Adam rubbed the back of his neck, his brow pinching. "Can I ask why you don't want her to go? You don't think she's cute?"

"She's fine, but I can say with absolute certainty she's not into what you are."

Wren was more than fine as far as that went, and it was true, Adam did have a type. He liked his girls thicker than average, with girl next door faces and soft attitudes. Wren fit that to a T. But like recognized like, and this girl was shy. She was no exhibitionist.

He cleared his throat. "What *we* are."

I tipped my chin. "Sure. What we are. You know she'll turn right back around once she sees what kind of party you've taken her to."

"She doesn't have to do anything she doesn't want to do." He squared his shoulders, preparing to go to battle over this. "You don't get to decide this. I'm not backing down."

"Did she say yes?"

He hesitated, tucking his hands in his pockets. He was already backing down. Hedging his bets, so when he inevitably admitted defeat, he could pretend he'd never expected her to say yes in the first place. "Not yet. But she will."

Iris stuck her head out of the studio door. "Hey. If you're done with your Girl Scout meeting, it's time to actually do some work. Get your asses in here, honey bunnies."

We fell in line easily, dropping our conversation to follow Iris's orders. There was magic in her 'honey bunnies' that made Roddy, Adam, and me want to do her bidding. Since the day she marched up to us after one of our very early shows and told us she'd be a better lead singer than Adam, she'd been our leader, caring yet firm. She kicked our asses when we screwed up in rehearsals or performances, and even though I'd always shied away from authority figures, it had never bothered me.

I passed by her on my way into the studio. She squeezed my arm.

"Callie," she cooed.

"Irie," I answered back.

"You good?"

"All good."

"Good." She slapped me in the center of my back, propelling me forward.

The Seasons Change were in the midst of recording our third album. We spent the last week writing and had started to put it all together this week. It was a shit show. Iris and Adam did the bulk of the writing and melodies, while Rodrigo came up with the beats. I was mostly a silent contributor until I had a strong opinion, then I voiced it in one way or another.

I knew sounds.

Not just instruments, but nature, animals, fabric brushing fabric, wind rustling trees. Being silent most of the time had attuned me to the world around me. I wasn't waiting with bated breath to jump into a conversation. I often checked out in social situations. When the world became too big, I narrowed it down to the rustling of a plastic bag blowing in the wind.

A therapist would have a field day with me. But I grew up as a Traveling Rose—and we didn't do therapy. We also didn't do public school, taxes, land ownership, rent, or vaccines. It wasn't something to brag about, just a fact.

The upside to my head being full of sounds was I could listen to a song and have an instinct for what was missing.

We weren't at that stage yet. Adam and Iris were bickering. The producer had his own opinions that didn't mesh with Iris's vision. Roddy kept leaving the studio to make calls or got distracted by texting, which was pissing Iris off.

There was a lot of pressure on us. The dreaded follow-up album to a hugely successful one—would we sink or swim?

Hours passed, recording and listening back to the shit we produced. No one was happy. I was at the window, losing myself in the view of the city sky rather than tuning into the tension at my back, when she showed up.

The girl from downstairs with the copper hair and memorable eyes.

"Hi, I have your dinner order."

She barely spoke above a whisper, and even that was strained. I gave her credit, though. If I didn't know the people in this room on a bone-deep level, I wouldn't have been able to force myself to walk inside and announce my presence.

I turned to watch her place bags on the table in the middle of the room. Rodrigo, ever the gentleman, had taken the drinks from her and thanked her profusely.

Her oversized, owlish eyes flicked to me, then away just as fast.

"Is there anything else I can get you?" She had an accent. It was soft, but there was no mistaking a Jersey girl.

Adam was sprawled on the couch, his arms draped over the back. "Come sit and listen to the shit we just recorded. Tell us how shitty it is."

"Um…" Somehow, her eyes went even wider.

Iris snapped her fingers. "Actually, yes. It would be fantastic to have an unbiased pair of ears. Can you give us five minutes, Wren?"

She tugged on her top, straightening it over her round hips. I tried to picture her, bent over for Adam, her flesh giving way to his. Would she moan loudly when he pounded into her? Would her inhibitions fall away when she was turned on?

Something stirred in the pit of my stomach. Something ugly and snakelike. Almost violent. It slithered around as my feet moved me without intention, until I was standing over Wren, who'd settled on the couch a safe distance from Adam.

He frowned at me, a crease carving deep between his brows. "Sit down, dude. Don't be creepy."

I hated being called out like that, and he knew it. But he was pissy from earlier and this was how he expressed it. Fuckboy.

Wren sucked in a breath when I took the cushion beside her. The sound felt better than most. Dulcet. Like worn flannel on a winter night. She scooted closer to Adam, and the snakes in the pit hissed.

The song started, and the girl listened. I watched.

Small hands were folded in her lap, over the soft pudge in her middle. Each of her nails was a different color. Her legs were short, and the couch was deep, so her feet didn't touch the ground. Her feet were small too. Encased in black ballet flats with little bows in the front, pale skin lined with blue veins peeked from the top. I wondered if her toenails were rainbow too.

She held still, barely breathing. Her breasts rose and fell with shallow breaths, and I got caught there. They were full, softly round, and flaring out to the sides. Much more than a handful, even with how big my hands were.

Those snakes writhed, and I pressed on my stomach, ready to set fire to the pit to end this silent war.

The song cut out. Her hands splayed on her thighs, fingertips digging in. Everyone turned to her, including me, even though I knew she had to hate it. I would have.

Her mouth trembled. "I liked it."

Iris pushed the bags of food aside and perched in front of her on the coffee table, narrowing her eyes. "But did you love it? Did you feel like it was missing something? Missing everything? Would you want to hear it again?"

"I don't know." Hair tuck. Lip bite. Cheeks flame. "The chorus was...well, the chorus is the part I always remember, you know? Even when I can't remember the rest of the words. And this one...um..."

Iris propped her chin on her fist and smiled at the girl. "It wasn't memorable, was it, honey bunny? You're right. God, you're absolutely right."

"I'm not an expert. Don't...don't take my opinion for more than it's worth. That was just my first thought, so..." she trailed off, glancing toward the door.

Adam laid his big hand on her shoulder. "You did good, Wren. So good. Now we have a direction. We can fix something if we know it's not working. Honestly, I was ready to scrap the whole fucking thing."

"Don't do that," she rushed out.

Iris laughed. "We won't. Adam's just a drama queen. It's been a rough day. We're all about ready to set fire to the studio and walk away." She eyed me. "Except Callie. He's as cool as a cucumber while the rest of us are losing our minds."

Wren gave her a wobbly smile. "I'm glad I could help even though I don't feel like I did anything." She scooted forward. "I need to go, so, if that's it...?"

Iris let her by after a profuse thank you, and Wren headed for the door. Adam followed her into the hall. I watched. He was going to try to talk her into the party. After I told him not to. After I said I didn't want her there. After seeing how uncomfortable she was in this room of a few strangers. He wanted what he wanted, reality and consequences be damned.

Anything they were saying to each other was lost on the other side of the soundproof door and walls. The room was filled with bags crinkling, tearing plastic, squeaking Styrofoam, crunching, chewing, swallowing. Dinnertime.

Adam ducked back into the room. Not smiling, but not frowning either. He grabbed dinner and didn't look my way. That was fine. As long as she hadn't said yes, all was well and we didn't have to talk about it.

Four and a half years ago

Dear Callum,

What was your first kiss like? Now that I'm 18, I feel like we can talk about these things.

I don't know if I want to wait on my shadow. First of all, I'm not sure that's ever going to happen. Secondly, shouldn't I be experienced so I can kiss him right if the time ever comes?

On that note, I bought a prom dress. I still want to die when I think about going alone, but I've missed out on so many things because I'm afraid. This is my only chance to go to prom. So I'm going. I'm not shrinking. Are you proud of me?

Holy granola, a farm! A Southern accent! Oh, that's perfect.

I'm a Jersey girl, so yeah, I have an accent. I'm sure it's not as pretty as yours.

Where are you now?

Your brave boss babe,

Birdie

Little Bird,

My first kiss was in a dark movie theater. A friend of a friend decided she wanted to kiss me, so she did. I didn't like it, and I didn't want it.

When your shadow finds you, you'll be perfect for him. He won't mind if your lips are unsure. So don't waste it, Little Bird. Trust me.

I am proud of you. It's hard not to shrink, just like it's hard not to disappear.

We're traveling up the East Coast. We'll pass through New Jersey tomorrow. I'll look for a little bird out the window. I never drive, so I can look the whole time.

Next time you write, tell me all about prom. I never went, so I want to know what it's like.

Be good.
Callum

Dear Callum,
I'm sorry it's been so long since I last wrote. I just...didn't have the heart to write back.
Can we not talk about prom? Can we forget I ever mentioned it?
Please tell me something good. Anything. About the farm or Alabama or your band.
Birdie

Little Bird,
No, no, no. Did someone hurt you? Was it Karthik fucking Singh? Tell me now, and I will bury him. You don't even have to tell me what happened. I will destroy that kid. Tell me, Little Bird. Let me make it better.
Don't hide from me. Give me all the ugly. I'll take it and carry it for you.
I'm proud of you. Don't shrink. No matter what happened, don't shrink.
Callum

Dear Callum,
Maybe I'll tell you one day. The fact that you want to go to battle for me has made me feel better already. Your email made me smile for the first time in weeks. I'm sorry I hid from you after prom. I won't do it again.

Can we get back to our regularly scheduled program? Tell me where you are. What are you doing? Did you see me when you drove through New Jersey? Wouldn't that be something if you drove right by me? I'm telling myself you did.

Thanks for being my friend, Callum.

Your humbled and devoted pen pal,

Birdie

CHAPTER FIVE

WREN

BY FRIDAY, I had made up my mind. That didn't mean I wasn't nervous, but I was determined enough to override it. I was twenty-two. I could go to a party without guilt. I *would.* I might not have fun, but that was beside the point. Life was for experiencing, not hiding.

Callum arrived at Good Music before Adam. I thought he was going to stride right by my desk, but when I offered him a quiet good morning, he stopped and stared, holding me in his jeweled gaze.

His jaw was tight. Tense. Working at grinding his teeth to dust. That couldn't have been a good habit.

I held up the little plant Adam gave me earlier in the week. "Do you know anything about succulents? I don't, but I really don't want this one to die. It's cute, right?" He wasn't reacting in any way, so I forged on. "It's against my instincts not to water it. You water plants, don't you? That's just what you do. But not succulents. They hold water in their leaves. That's why they're so plump. And I just—"

He lowered his head, and without a backward glance, walked away. Not even a blink or a middle finger. Callum Rose walked away in the middle of my sentence.

At first, I was stunned, my jaw flapping like a fish on dry land.

Then, a giggle burst out of me at the absurdity of the entire situation. What kind of person walked away in the middle of a sentence? Without saying a single word? Who did that?

My eyes burned and my nose tingled as my laughter died down, but I refused to acknowledge that feeling.

A cold blast of air and Adam Wainwright's cheerful gait distracted me from my rude dismissal. He was smiling before he got to my desk. Before I could even greet him.

"Good morning, cutie," he cooed at me. "Are you gonna say yes to me today, or are you gonna break my heart?"

"I'm going to say yes."

I was even more determined to go now. Spite was a powerful motivator. Callum Rose didn't want me at his fancy party, so I'd show up and stay until the last straggler left. I'd shut the damn thing down to show him he didn't get a say in what I did.

Adam pumped his fist. "I thought I'd have to do some more coaxing and sweet-talking." He nodded a few times and grinned down at me. "Holy shit, this is gonna be lit."

"No coaxing necessary." I straightened my spine. "I have to go home after work, so I guess I'll meet you—"

He smacked his forehead. "Of course you do. I'll send a car for you." He slid his phone across the counter. "Type in your address and phone number. I'll make the arrangements."

I felt slightly guilty for getting Adam's hopes up. I wasn't interested in him romantically, and that wouldn't change. I wasn't even going to the party because I wanted to spend more time with him, although I certainly wouldn't hate it. But I typed in my number and address like a good little girl and bit my lip when he winked at me.

After years of hiding away, being flirted with by a rock star didn't feel so bad. Even if he was the wrong rock star.

The drive from my great-aunt Jenny's townhouse in Queens to the sleek, modern high-rise in Manhattan went faster than I expected. Faster than I wanted. Too caught up in all the scenarios that could happen tonight, I'd barely watched the scenery.

I took a deep breath when the driver opened the door and then placed my hand in his so he could help me step out of the SUV. That was a good thing too. I'd worn heels tonight, and I was more of a ballet flat kind of girl.

I'd bought a sexy dress during my lunch break on Wednesday, so heels were necessary. And even I could admit the extra three inches they gave me boosted my confidence. So had the Veronica Lake finger waves in my hair and perfect wings of eyeliner at the corners of each lid. Great-Aunt Jenny had said I looked *va-va-voom*, and well…maybe I did feel a little of that.

Adam was waiting for me just inside the lobby doors. When he saw me, he pushed outside to meet me. His eyes swept over me, stalling on my bare legs for a beat before he ended on my face.

"Why do I know for certain there's something delicious under your coat, cutie?"

If only he knew every time he called me cutie, I thought of the brand of clementines I bought at the grocery store. Then again, I *was* round and small, so maybe it was purposeful. I almost giggled at the thought.

I tucked my hand in his offered elbow, and in the pool of light spilling from the lobby, plucked up a little bravery.

"That's because there is," I replied.

He chuckled and tugged me a little closer to his side. "Oh, we're going to have fun."

All that bravery came crashing to the floor when we entered the lobby and a tall, glowering man stepped from the shadows. Callum fell into step with us on the way to the elevator, flanking me on the opposite side. He didn't greet me verbally, but I guessed his scowl said it all.

"Tell me whose party this is again." The silence between the three of us was too much, even for me.

"Benson Martin." Adam leaned back on the wall beside the elevator, watching me from under hooded eyes. "He's…uh, rich. I'm not really clear on what he does to make his money, but he has a lot of it. He's generous with it too. Always throwing the best parties with the best weed."

I wasn't too sure that constituted generosity, but whatever.

"No weed," Callum declared. I turned my head, finding him closer than I thought. Right beside me, his forehead creased with consternation. Why did he always seem so angry with me? It was maddening. Yet, I was tempted to drag my thumb over the line between his brows to smooth it out.

Adam's vicious chuckle caught my attention. "Oh? Dad's laying down the law, huh? I think sweet Wren gets to make that call."

They exchanged a long look, and I was more than relieved when the elevators slid open. But then I was trapped between them in a small box, so that wasn't much fun either. I fiddled with the buttons on my coat while my heart sat firmly in the center of my throat, pulsing madly. Adam had placed his hand on my shoulder while Callum was a foot away, his arms crossed, glaring with heated intensity.

If he was psychic and could reach inside my mind, he'd know I was thinking about how different he was to his emails. He wasn't the person I'd gotten to know over the year and a half I'd been so deeply devoted to his words on my screen, I couldn't even look at another boy. I didn't crush, but I did fall in love. One moment, he was Callum Rose, quirky, shy rock star. The next, he was threatening to hunt down whoever hurt me on prom night. And I was his. I thought irrevocably, but I'd been wrong. Nothing lasted forever.

The elevator opened directly into the penthouse. Security checked our names at the entrance. An opaque, black curtain that looked like it had been installed for the party divided the entry from the rest of the apartment.

Adam rested his hands on my shoulders. "Ready to take this off?"

"Oh." My hand rushed to a button. "Yes. I guess I shouldn't walk around in my coat all night." I shrugged it off into Adam's waiting hands while Callum stood in front of me watching. Always watching.

I tipped my chin up, and he brought his down, raking his gaze over me. My black, sleeveless wrap dress dipped low on my cleavage, gathered in the center, and draped over my legs. The length would have been obscenely short on a taller woman, but it stopped just past mid-thigh on me. Daring, for sure, but I wasn't in danger of flashing my lacy red panties. Not unless I wanted to.

Adam hung up my coat on a discreet, tucked away rack, then he placed his hand on my lower back and guided me through the curtain. Once on the other side, I wondered if he was the white rabbit and I'd followed him down a rabbit hole. It certainly felt like an entirely different world. Wonderland, except more debauched.

The smell of incense and spice hit me first. Sultry music filtered through the air. Below that was a din of conversation and clinking glasses. There were performers on mini platforms. Barely dressed women rolling their bodies like waves. One woman wore leather straps for clothes and slowly and sensually swallowed an impossibly long sword.

"Oh. Holy granola." My face was hot. My chest too. Even my toes were on fire.

Adam leaned in, brushing my hair from my ear. "Not what you were expecting?"

"I don't know what I was expecting."

"We'll have fun," he promised.

Through this, Callum observed me carefully, his arms folded across his chest like a bodyguard. He'd left his leather jacket with my coat. He wore a close-fitting, pale blue button down, the sleeves rolled to his elbows, and dark blue jeans with a chain hanging at his hip. Tonight, his normally unkempt hair was tucked neatly in a bun at the base of his head.

He looked nice, but I didn't think he'd care for me to tell him. He certainly hadn't said anything about my appearance.

"Did I mention how utterly delectable you look?" Adam placed his hand on the small of my back, guiding me deeper into the party. "I don't think I can keep calling you cutie. Hottie is more like it."

"Her name is Wren," Callum muttered from my other side.

Adam rolled his eyes. "Dude, no kidding. This is called charm. Girls like when you compliment them and shit. Maybe try it sometime."

I snorted at the two of them. "Wren is good. Hottie is weird."

A man in a leather mask with a zipper over his mouth carried a tray of drinks by us. Adam scooped two up and handed one to me.

"I have no idea what this is, but..." he took a sip of the pale pink cocktail, "it tastes like lowered inhibitions and good times. Cheers, Wren."

I clinked my glass with his and turned to Callum. He only stared at me, not making a move to tap my glass, so I took a step closer and did it myself.

His mouth flattened. His eyes danced over my face.

"Cheers, Callum," I whispered.

He sucked in a deep breath, his nostrils flaring. "You should go home, Wren."

A ridiculous laugh burst free. "I'm not familiar with that toast. Is it one that was passed down as a family tradition?"

His eyelid twitched, and the very corners of his mouth curved slightly. "The night is young. It's only goin' to get crazier here."

"Who says I don't like crazy?"

We were in a room filled with people, but our tones were so low, it was like it was only the two of us. This party didn't seem to be anything like I had been expecting, but I wasn't running scared. I may have been pretty inexperienced, but I wasn't a prude. Once I'd gotten over the surprise of the sword swallowing and skimpy outfits, it became background noise.

"You don't want this kinda crazy," he promised. "Go home like a good little girl."

I shook my head. "Not a little girl."

Adam slid his hand around my waist from behind. "Stop trying to steal my date away, Rose. Next time, bring your own."

The three of us skirted the edge of the vast room, stopping in front of each performer. There were others doing the same, couples and small groups. Adam greeted a few of them with a nod or handshake. The men were friendly enough to all three of us, but I flushed under the extra attention I was paid. Like I was Adam's prized pony or something. I wasn't Adam's anything.

My pink drink was just ice when another man in a leather mask—or maybe the same one—passed by again. Adam grabbed us both a new one, and I sipped while a man in a leather thong and motorcycle hat spun perfect pirouettes in front of me. We didn't stay there long. I got the strong sense Adam wasn't so into his performance. Although, he did proclaim he'd look just as good in that costume, and I kind of believed him.

Before we got to the next platform, a man with silver hair and arms covered in tattoos held his hand out to Adam. "Wainwright, pleasure to have you again." He nodded to Callum. "Rose, long time no see." Then his eyes lit on me. "And who have you brought tonight? A ripe little peach by the looks of it."

Subconsciously, I shifted closer to Callum. I felt his gaze on me as Adam greeted the man whose eyes traveled over me like a road he planned on driving down very soon.

"This is sweet Wren. Her first time at one of your parties, but I think she's gonna like it," Adam said. "Wren, this is Benson, our host."

"Ah, a virgin." Benson Martin rubbed his hands together. "My favorite. It's my absolute pleasure to have you here, Wren. If Adam and Callum don't tire you out, come find me. I'd love to get to know you better."

I didn't know what to say, but Adam was good at the whole small talk thing. He and Benson traded stories while I glanced around the party. If we were in a normal living room, the furniture had been cleared for tonight. There were several leather settees and benches, but no couches or coffee tables.

A pair of chains with leather cuffs attached hung from the wall above one bench. A man in a sleek suit and woman in a bright red body-con dress were checking them out, tugging to test their sturdiness, I guessed. She rubbed his chest, and his hand slid to her ass, giving it a squeeze followed by a firm slap.

I jumped, and beside me, Callum chuckled.

I was pretty sure I hadn't stopped blushing since walking into this place, but my cheeks had worked up a furious heat imagining what they were talking about. The plans they might be making. Fighting for the hottest part of my body was the place between my thighs, though.

"Ready to go home yet?" he drawled.

My eyes flicked to his. "I'll let you know when that time comes." I shook my head. "You don't have to stay with me."

"I know I don't." But he was going to, if only to make me uncomfortable.

Adam broke away from Benson, and we continued our path around the room. The next platform contained two performers, a man and woman, both in tiny thongs. They were dancing and touching, no parts were off limits. His hands skimmed her breasts and cupped between her thighs. She dipped back, and he dragged his tongue from her belly button to her throat.

I liked this one. I liked it a lot.

I must've squirmed because Adam's hold on my waist tightened, and he tugged me into his side, brushing his lips along my cheek. "It's hot, right? Do you like watching, Wren?"

"I-I don't know. Maybe I do," I stammered.

"Callum likes watching too." He pressed his lips to my temple. "I'm more of a man of action, but I don't mind letting other people watch."

"Oh." I pressed my lips together. They felt like I had just rubbed peppers all over them. Tingly and hot, almost unbearably so. All of me felt that way.

He laughed. "Yeah, oh. You still good, cutie?"

I forced a grin. "Back to cutie again?"

He booped my nose. "You banned hottie."

Callum groaned right behind me. His chest skimmed the back of my head, and beneath the sultry incense, I could just barely pick up his clean, pine scent. It was such a contrast to the stronger smell, there was no doubt it was coming from him.

Wow, after all this time, I knew what Callum Rose smelled like. My eighteen-year-old heart would have exploded if I'd found out back then. It was hard to separate myself from those old feelings when it came to him, but I was trying. And he was helping me along by being a stone-cold asshole.

The man on the stage lifted the woman into his arms, her legs wrapping around his waist. He cradled her on one forearm while his hand molded to her breast. Her spine bowed, and he slowly rotated them in a circle. Her eyes were closed, and her lips were parted in rapture. They weren't having sex, but they were doing something close to it.

My breasts felt swollen inside my bra, and my panties were shamefully damp. I'd watched porn before, but it was nothing like this. Two beautiful people lost in each other, their desire a dance of writhing bodies and tangled limbs.

I tipped my head to speak to the looming block of ice at my back. Only...he didn't look so frozen when our eyes connected. Callum's cheeks were flushed beautifully, and his chest rose and fell just a little bit faster than normal.

"I think I like watching too."

His eyelids lowered to half-mast. "Turn around, Wren. Look."

I did as he said. Something had changed on the platform. Intensified. The woman's hips were writhing against her partners, and he answered her with powerful thrusts.

I gasped, and Adam chuckled. They weren't dancing anymore. They were fucking, right in front of us. And not just us. At least twenty pairs of eyes were on them.

"They're having sex," I pushed out.

Adam laughed again. "Hell yes, they are. It's hot, right?"

I was hot, like I'd spent the day in the sun. What was happening on stage was volcanic. I was embarrassed even though I knew I had no reason to be. By the way they were focused on each other, it was obvious the couple didn't care they were being watched.

"Yeah. It's really hot." I was surprised by how hot I found it. My thighs pressed together, and I caught myself panting softly.

"Are you okay?" Callum asked from behind me.

"She's fine." Adam trailed a finger along my cheek.

Callum shifted to my side, scanning me with detached interest. When he reached my chest, I sucked in a shallow breath. His eyes darted to my face, and I tried to give him a reassuring smile, but I couldn't hide the tremble in my lips.

"Are you okay?" he asked again.

"Yeah," I breathed. My hand came to my chest, tracing the heated bare skin of my cleavage. "This is...new to me, but I'm not uncomfortable with watching."

His eyes narrowed. "You're not?"

"No. It's..." I licked my suddenly dry lips. "It's like really sexy art. And I think they *want* us to watch."

His nod was sharp. "They do. They get off on everyone seeing them."

"Then why do you want me to leave? If they like it and I'm comfortable...?"

"Because, *Wren*," he dipped his head closer to mine, "this is only the beginning of the evening. Much more than watching happens."

The man on stage captured my attention again when he swung his partner around in slow circles, her hair hanging loose down her back. Her hips moved like rolling hills, fluid and smooth, meeting his every thrust.

Adam turned my chin toward him. "Come on, Wren. Let's sit over there so we can relax and see some of the other performers too."

He pulled me to a leather bench to the left of the platform and down onto his lap. I sucked in a breath, pulling in my stomach, as if that would make me lighter. His arm banded around my middle and tugged me against him until my back was flush with his chest. My overheated body sank into his like a piece of chocolate melting in the sun.

Callum took a seat on the bench facing ours. In the back of my mind, the part that wasn't scrambled from the activity happening around me, I thought this seating arrangement was strange. Who put two benches directly across from one another? Neither Adam nor Callum seemed to take an issue with it, so I didn't bring it up.

Around us, people mingled and drank. The shows on the platforms became more sensual and some outright sexual like the pair we'd been watching.

Some couples and trios had claimed the other seats scattered around the room. Nearby, two women were relieving each other of their clothes while a man seemed to be directing them. Several other partygoers stood around them with drinks in their hands, observing them like they were another show.

"What kind of party did you bring me to?" I breathed.

Adam's big palms skimmed my stomach and hips.

"Whatever kind you want it to be, Wren. You're in charge."

"You don't have to do anything." Callum's words should have been reassuring, but he said them with a razor edge, so they sounded more cutting than anything.

"She knows that," Adam shot back, giving my thigh a squeeze.

Choosing to ignore Callum even though he made it next to impossible, I rested the back of my head on Adam's shoulder. "Do you usually have sex at these parties?"

"Mmm." He cupped my jaw, tilting it back. "Yeah, that's kind of the point. But that's up to you. It's all up to you."

I swallowed hard. This was...not me. It had been ages since I'd had sex, and even then, it was fumbling in the dark. It was one thing to watch others, but it was entirely something else to participate. Even if I was turned on and my core ached with a building need. Callum's eyes were on me while I began to panic just a little. His fingers dug into his knees until the tips turned white.

I saw why he hadn't wanted me here. Why he thought this kind of party wasn't for me. It wasn't, not really. I wasn't a girl who could get naked in front of strangers and let a man have his way with me. I didn't even know why I was still here, except I couldn't bring myself to leave.

What I did know was Adam's hands felt good as he stroked the outline of my curves with appreciation, and Callum's angry eyes felt even better.

If he asked me, I'd be in his lap in a heartbeat.

"I don't know if I want that, but I'll stay," I said.

Adam's mouth hovered over mine. "We're going to have so much fun, cutie."

And then he kissed me.

CHAPTER SIX

CALLUM

SHE SHOULDN'T HAVE BEEN HERE.

She wasn't like us. A good girl like Wren didn't belong in a place like this, full of depravity.

Adam wasn't a bad guy, but he wasn't good either. He covered that up with his bright, big smile and easy manner, but there was darkness in him he hadn't exorcised.

I didn't know if I was better or worse. I'd accepted I wasn't normal a long time ago. Years and years. I made bad decisions, but not rash ones. No, my badness was calculated.

Wren wasn't like us. She might have thought she could dance on the dark side tonight, but this wasn't for her. No matter how good she looked cradled in Adam's lap, her soft, round, petite body in perfect contrast to his long limbs and taut muscles.

Wren had surprised me by seeking me out each time she became uncomfortable. Not Adam. Me. She didn't seem to like me. Could barely look at me. Yet her instincts pushed her in my direction for protection. Assurance. Comfort. I was the last person anyone would think to seek those things from, but for Wren, I was the first.

And now, she was on Adam's lap, and my friend looked like a king. A cat king who'd eaten a hundred canaries. Touching her, whispering secrets in her pretty ears—and she couldn't rip her damn owl eyes off me.

The slithering snake deep inside me had transformed into something out of Greek myths. A chimera. My serpent had a lion's head, and it was roaring and clawing as Adam leaned down to touch his mouth to Wren's.

I liked to watch. More than liked, I got off on it. Tonight was different, though. There was no pleasure in watching Adam with Wren. The feeling it gave me was ugly and visceral. My gut knotted with fury at the irrational yet undeniable feeling he was stealing from me.

Mine.

I was on my feet the moment his mouth met hers. Her hands were in mine before she had a chance to respond to his kiss. She was straddling my lap by the time Adam had registered she was gone.

I hadn't known I was going to move. Hadn't known I was going to do any of it. But now that Wren was in my arms, I wasn't giving her back.

"What the fuck?" Adam hissed from behind her. "What are you doing?"

Wren's hands landed on my shoulders to stabilize herself, but I had a vise grip on her. She wasn't going anywhere until I allowed it.

"What *are* you doing?" she whispered breathlessly.

"I think you look better over here." I pressed on her hips. Her legs split even wider, her center molding to my steely erection. The hem of her dress rode up to the tops of her thighs, and I tugged it down, covering her from view, but not before I saw a flash of red lace.

My attention flicked to Adam. His mouth had fallen open. His eyes were scanning my hold on Wren. He appeared more perplexed than angry.

"I want this one."

His gaze jerked to mine. "What?"

I moved Wren's hips in short rocks. "I want her," I replied.

He wanted more of an explanation, but it was that simple. I'd never once wanted any of the women he'd fucked in front of me. I'd never touched them or even spoken to them. If I offered direction, I only spoke to him. This...this was new. Out of character. His brow pinched with what seemed like dawning understanding of the gravity of my move.

"Do you want to stay here?" I asked her. "In my lap?"

Her mouth fell open, and a little pant escaped. She was rocking her own hips now, just enough for us to feel each other.

"I—" She blinked. One of her hands drifted to my jaw. The tips of her fingers trailed over my scruff. "I don't know."

"You don't want to leave." I should have formed that as a question, but I didn't want to give her another chance to deny me.

Wren smelled good. Better than I ever would have thought. Like green apples and fresh water and the summer sun. Ironic since we were in the thick of winter.

She felt good too. My fingertips sunk into the give of her waist, and her thick, supple thighs encased my hips. Her pillowy tits skimmed my chest, and like the rest of her, they were warm and soft.

"I don't know," she repeated.

But she wasn't leaving. Her hips kept moving. Her fingertips continued to stroke my jaw. That was the only place she touched, and it was more than enough for now. It was overwhelming, but not in a bad way.

"You'll stay." I cupped her nape, squeezing hard enough for her to pay attention and give me a little nod. "Good, brave girl." She whimpered and seemed to go almost boneless against me.

Over her shoulder, Adam shook his head. He leaned forward, bracing his hands on his knees, like he was ready to pounce and snatch her back.

I buried my face in her hair, inhaling her summer scent, and she let out a faint gasp. Her thighs tried to close, clamping tighter around me. My cock had been at attention for most of the night, but the noises she made when I touched her turned it to an aching, steel mast threatening to punch through the zipper of my jeans.

"You're mine now," I rasped against her neck. Her pulse fluttered under my lips. "I have you."

"I don't...I don't—" She was flustered, but her need overrode that. Moving with me, responding to my touch like she'd been wanting this for ages.

Without intention, I took her fluttering pulse between my lips, sucking gently. Her skin was so smooth, it felt like silk under my tongue. Her breathy pants hit my ear, sending a wave of insanity straight to my straining cock.

Her cheek pressed against mine. She sucked in a sharp breath as I moved her back and forth over my length a little faster than before.

"Callum," she moaned quietly. Only for me. Not a show for anyone else, though I sensed more than a few eyes on us. I owned her reaction, her need. This was about the two of us. "What are you doing to me?"

"You like this." Again, not a question. To hear her deny it, even though I knew the truth, would be too much. A bridge way too fucking far.

"I like this," she agreed so very sweetly.

"Yeah, you do. Jesus, fuck, you're a good girl, Wren."

My palms moved to her ass, taking two handfuls, holding her tight against me. I thrust upward, her panties and my jeans separating me from where I wanted to be. It was an exercise in frustration, but I couldn't stop. Not now.

Her moans picked up, and so did her rhythm. Rocks turned to sensual rolls. She clutched at my shoulder and my hair, keeping her cheek flush with mine. My mouth nipped at her jaw and ear, the only places I could reach. I wanted to explore more of her, to taste her skin, but she needed me right where I was, that much was clear.

"Callum, you—" Her head fell back, and her lips parted. She pressed down hard on my cock, driving me to the same brink she was on.

"Use me." I squeezed her ass, and my eyes fell shut. "Take what you need."

And she did. Wren rubbed herself on my cock until she had to dip her head down and muffle her cries against my neck. This soft, surprising girl was coming in my lap, her limbs shaking, body quivering, and I was holding her through it. She mewled my name like a sweet little kitten, and that was it for me. I'd been holding back all night, keeping myself away from her, ignoring the ache behind my zipper, but hearing my name from Wren's lips was the end of it all.

My cock jerked against her hot center, and my fingers dug into her ass so hard, she whimpered, but that only made me come with more force. Hot cum spilled from me, seeping into my underwear and jeans like I was fourteen years old again.

"That was perfect," I rasped. "You made me come so hard. It's never been like this."

She made a noise that sounded like a purr as she nuzzled me and pushed herself deeper into my hold.

A minute passed, maybe two. Wren's hot breath on my skin soothed me into a stupor. She was limp against me, her short nails scratching my scruff, the other hand working up the back of my hair. I wasn't one for cuddling and afterglow, but I didn't mind this. Not with her.

Somewhere, a glass shattered, startling her. She sat up abruptly, and her big, round eyes flew open, growing even wider as she took in the party that had been going on around us the whole time. We weren't the only pair who had gotten lost in one another, not by a long shot, but there were a few eyes on us anyway.

Wren whimpered. "Oh my god." She scooted back, trying to extricate herself from my hold. "What did I—?"

Already, she was filled with regret and horror. That had to be a world record. Especially since I'd barely touched her. We hadn't even kissed.

"You're fine."

Her eyes squeezed shut. Her nose wrinkled. It would have been cute if she hadn't been so distressed over being with me. That made it hard to take.

"I'm not." She worried her bottom lip with her teeth, refusing to look at me. "I need to go home now."

"Okay." I helped her slide the rest of the way off my lap then stood up so I could steady her shaky legs. "I seem to have made a mess of myself, so I need to go too."

"You don't have to. Don't let me take you from your party."

Bending down, I spoke low into her ear. "I came in my pants like a pubescent boy. I'm not stayin' here another second. Let me walk you out."

She swallowed hard. "Okay."

With my hand around her waist, I escorted Wren through the party, which had turned into something of an orgy over the past half hour. Adam was nursing his heartbreak over losing Wren with two women crawling all over him. He didn't notice us pass by, but from the jump of Wren's muscles, she had noticed him.

We passed through the black curtains and into the real world. Wren tried to flee as quickly as possible, but I caught her elbow.

"Wait."

She turned to me with wide, glassy eyes. "We don't have to have a big talk right now. In fact, I'd prefer if we didn't. So, I'm just going to—"

"Your coat." I held my hand out toward the coat rack. "Don't leave without your coat."

"Oh." Crimson suffused her cheeks. "Of course. I'm not really thinking straight."

I slipped her coat from the hanger and held it out for her. After a moment's hesitation where I thought she might not allow me to help her, she slid her arms into it, and I pulled it onto her shoulders, then I spun her to face me again. Her hands shot up to curl around my wrists, but I ignored her and methodically slid each button through the fabric until it stopped under her chin.

"Don't forget your coat either."

I raised my eyes to hers, and she looked away, sucking in a deep breath, her gaze trained on a spot near the front door. Did I make her nervous? Even after she came in my lap?

"Thank you," I muttered.

In the elevator, I sent a message to my driver that I was on my way out, then slipped my phone away. Wren was leaning against one wall, while I was propped against the other. She was trying not to look at me, but she'd also chosen to arrange herself so we were facing each other. Every second or two, she'd brave a glance, then study my feet. I never took my eyes off her. She made me curious. I wondered what was going on inside her head.

Neither of us spoke. We kept up a silent game of cat and mouse eye contact until the doors slid open to the lobby and my hand once again returned to Wren's back, guiding her outside.

My driver opened the back passenger door for her. Just before she climbed in, she faced me.

"I hope you know I won't become a stalker now, after…that." She pointed skyward, toward the penthouse. "I won't make it uncomfortable for you at work or anything. Don't worry about that."

"I wasn't worried," I replied swiftly.

"Okay…well…" she tucked her hair, "I'm sure it's happened before, but that's probably one of the pitfalls that comes along with being handsome and famous and a wonderful conversationalist."

Her round, amber eyes glowed. I stared back, surprised she was joking with me.

"Sarcasm suits you," I said.

She shaded her eyes with her hand. "Does it? My mother always told me it was the lowest form of humor. Plus, I was only being sarcastic about two of your three attributes."

A blast of arctic wind had her tucking her chin in the collar of her coat. I nodded to the car.

"You should go home."

Something sparked in her eyes. They were her biggest tell, broadcasting every single one of her emotions in high definition.

"I'm actually going to listen this time." She climbed into the back of the SUV, stopping me from closing the door at the last second. "Am I taking your car? Be honest. I'll get out right now and take the subway."

She was taking my car, but there was no world in which I would allow her to ride the subway tonight. Even if it was something she did every other night. That hadn't been on my watch. This was.

"Take the car, Wren." I took her cold hand in mine and bundled it into her lap. "I'll take care of myself."

Her gaze lowered to where my hand still covered hers. "Thank you for taking care of me."

I yanked my hand away, and her fingers curled into her palms. Giving me credit for taking care of her after I'd used her body to get myself off was bordering on obscene. I'd done the opposite of take care of her. "You shouldn't have been here."

I shut the door on her startled face and glistening eyes, waiting in the same spot until the driver pulled away and carried Wren into the night. She'd soon be safely at home. Away from stone-cold monsters like me.

Four Years Ago

Dear Callum,

Do you know what today is?

I'll wait.

Did you remember? It's been one year since I wrote my first email to you. I won't say it's our anniversary because that might freak you out, even though it kind of is. Or did our friendship begin the first time you wrote me back?

In the last year, we've exchanged 32 emails. 32! I never thought we'd get past 1. Did you think we'd get past 2?

I think we should try to double our emails this year. You've been writing me back faster, so I'm confident we'll make it. Besides, it's hard for me to go more than a week without hearing from you. I start to feel a little panicky. I guess it makes sense that in a year, you've become important to me. I hope that doesn't freak you out either.

Here's the sad thing, Callum: not much has changed for me in the last year. I got older, slightly wiser, I finished high school, and I'm in college, but that's it. I'm still living with my shitty parents in an even shittier apartment—no, wait, reverse that. My parents are definitely shittier. Still a once-kissed virgin. I haven't been anywhere. I still shrink.

What about you? What's changed in the last year?

Will this be the year I get to hear your voice?

Your favorite pen pal,

Birdie

Little Bird,

Yeah, I was confident we'd get past 2 because I knew you'd write me back. I never suspected I would continue to reply to you, though. You're something of a surprise. Probably the biggest in my life.

I'm writing back to you the same day you sent this. Couldn't miss our anniversary, could I? I've never celebrated an anniversary. I'll probably have a drink and watch Adam make very bad decisions. The drink makes it a special occasion.

Don't worry about change, Little Bird. You're smart. You'll make it happen.

You're only a once-kissed virgin because your shadow hasn't come to claim you yet. Don't rush things. That day will come.

In the last year, I've set foot in almost every state. I read 28 books. I've improved as a bass player. I still disassociate. I'm as stone cold as ever. I haven't spoken to my parents in three years. I turned 22. I made a new friend, and she's a little bird.

I don't know if I want you to hear my voice. You like me this way. You probably won't if we ever meet.

Happy anniversary.

Callum

Dear Callum,

Holy granola, are you kidding me?!?

If we ever met, I'd be so awkward, you'd immediately block my email address and never write to me again. I was thinking maybe a phone call, but that makes me want to die because—you're going to laugh, so brace yourself—I've never spoken to a boy on the phone before. Maybe a voice memo? Or you could call at an appointed time and leave me a message.

Okay, you're right, this is a terrible idea. We'll forever be pen pals.

Except, one day, I might want to meet you. And I know I'd like you because I already know you're not stone cold. So, even if you just stared at me, I'd know it wasn't because you hated me.

Do you have any idea where your parents are? Are they still The Traveling Roses? I still can't believe you were raised completely off the grid by hippie musicians. Who else can say that? I just have Donna and Gene, who should attend some parenting classes and AA meetings. Their dysfunction is so boring!

(BTW, I am not making light of your trauma, I swear. I am trying to make light of my own)

You know, Callum, I'm beginning to think this shadow person you keep mentioning doesn't exist. I keep checking, and no one is following me.

Your shadow-less friend,

Birdie

Little Bird,

The shadow's coming. You're too special for someone not to see that. You really fucking are. Don't forget that.

I don't know if my family is still playing music and grifting all over the country. I haven't run into them on my travels with TSC. But I can't see any of them ever changing, so yeah, they probably are.

Make light all you want. I like it when you do, but I hate that you understand what it's like to barely exist to the people who brought you into the world.

I could do a voice mail. Maybe. One day, Little Bird. One day, I'll do it.

And then, maybe one day we'll meet. I'd like to be capable of meeting you.

Give me some time.

Callum

CHAPTER SEVEN

WREN

"MOMMY..."

One soft whisper in my ear, and my eyes flew open. I immediately regretted it, though. I wasn't hungover, but my room was way too bright, and the sunlight stung my tired eyes. I'd gone to bed with closed curtains, but they hadn't stayed that way.

"Mommy!" Tiny hands gently patted my cheeks, and I opened my eyes more carefully. Round, amber eyes—a shade lighter than mine—and an upturned, button nose filled my vision. My favorite way to wake up.

"Hi, baby buddy." I smoothed my hand over my son's wild, copper curls. "Is it time for me to wake up?"

"Wake up time," he replied, tugging on my blankets. "Come on!"

"Are you hungry?"

He shook his head. "No. I ate already."

"Did you?" I grabbed his hand, which was still just a bit sticky from his breakfast, and nibbled on his finger. "Can I eat you then? I'm starving."

He dissolved into giggles and denial. I pulled his thirty-pound body into bed with me so I could tickle his tummy and grab a few snuggles before he ran away. Ezra was sweeter than most freshly turned three-year-olds I'd met, but he still contained a fully charged battery run by miniature Tasmanian devils. He would lie next to me and give me the cuddles both of us required to start our day right, but only for so long. Then he'd be out of here, charging up and down the stairs, running in circles around Aunt Jenny's cats, Lyle and Lovett, and cooking up plans to overthrow kingdoms and governments. That was, until seven thirty every night, when he passed out as soon as his head hit his pillow.

"Ezra! I told you to let Mommy sleep." Great-Aunt Jenny rushed into the room, her cheeks rosy. "Sorry, Birdie-girl. Your child is a slippery one. I figured you could use some extra sleep after your exciting night, but the second I turned around to wash some dishes, little Houdini made his great escape."

Ezra climbed onto my chest and tucked his head under my chin. "I missed you," he cooed. This kid could've broken my favorite vase right in front of me and gotten away with it if he used that voice. The most dangerous part of him was he knew he had me wrapped around his pudgy finger. Three-year-olds should never wield that much power.

When I was nineteen and pregnant, alone, depressed, and so distraught, some days, I didn't think I'd survive to see the next sunrise, it would have helped more than anything to view a snippet of what life would be like as a mother. Not that it was easy. It wasn't, and that was okay. Loving this boy, *my* boy, made those early days fade away. I lost a lot when I got pregnant with Ezra, but none of them were more monumental than what I gained. It took me a while to see that, but once I realized it, that sureness seeped into my bones, and I never doubted it once.

"It's okay." My fingertips trailed up and down his back. "I'm not that tired. I should get up anyway."

Jenny leaned against the doorframe. At fifty-four, she hardly fit the image of a great-aunt, but she was the youngest of my great-grandparents' children by ten years. A true 'oops' baby. She was my mom's aunt, but they were only six years apart, so they grew up more like cousins.

When I was a kid, and I guess even now, I wished Jenny had been my mom. She was the cool aunt who traveled and dated and always wore beautiful clothes. She'd been married young to a police officer who was killed in the line of duty before their second anniversary. She never had children, but she'd taken a special shine to me from the start. She said it was because I was the only one of her nieces and nephews who'd inherited the Macallan copper hair like her.

Whatever the reason, she took me in, no questions asked, when I was pregnant with Ezra, and had supported me in almost every way since. Thanks to money from her late husband, I'd been able to attend college too.

She still traveled and dated and wore beautiful clothes, but now, she had a twenty-two-year-old and a preschooler to come home to.

"Good, get up and tell me every single detail." Her eyes narrowed on me. "You don't look much worse for wear, so it couldn't have been too fun."

Ezra was beginning to get restless, but he stayed put when I wrapped my arms around him and gave him a gentle squeeze.

"It was interesting. We'll have to talk during n-a-p time."

Jenny's eyebrows popped up. "Oh boy. If something happened that's not appropriate for little ears, it must be delicious."

Ezra raised his head. "What's delicious?"

I grinned at his parted rosebud lips and excited eyes. This kid didn't miss a single thing. "Your cheeks are what's delicious." I growled against his cheeks, giving him a gentle nibble. That got him going, flailing to get off me and dart from the room.

Jenny slowed him by grabbing his arm. "Go take a shower. I'll guard this miscreant with my life." Her voice faded as my son pulled her down the hallway and rattled on about the castle he wanted her to build for him with his wooden blocks.

After I rolled myself out of bed, I ducked into the shower. Under the warm water, I turned my mind back to last night. It hadn't been a dream, even though it had felt like I'd been in a trance. The whole evening had been otherworldly, but the moment Callum Rose tugged me into his lap, I was someone else.

I was seventeen again, breathless with excitement after witnessing a stunning performance by the most beautiful man I had ever seen. I was eighteen and enthralled by the man behind the screen. I was nineteen and so head over heels, I would have given myself to Callum Rose if he'd asked.

The reality was, I was a twenty-two-year-old single mom who'd dry humped my teenage fantasy in front of a lot of people. I cringed at myself, but only a little. I'd been at a sex party after all. If anything, I probably should have been embarrassed I didn't get naked and swing from a chandelier. Dry humping had to be considered tame in that crowd.

I scrubbed my scalp hard in hopes I could cleanse my brain a little too. My mind was far too jumbled to even attempt to make sense of what had happened last night.

Once I dried off, I threw on an oversized sweater and a pair of leggings and made my way downstairs with a basket of laundry tucked under my arm. Ezra leaped up from his place on the carpet with Jenny and dashed to the basement door.

My child had an obsession with dark, spooky places. A few months ago, he'd figured out when I came downstairs with the basket, I'd be going to one of those dark, spooky places, and he made sure to tag along.

He trailed behind me on the creaking steps. To tell the truth, I hated coming down to the basement, so it was nice to have company in the dank, cold space. Plus, Ezra gave absolutely no fucks about spiders and other creepy-crawlies. He'd chase them down or shoo them away for me without blinking. When he was two, I'd realized he was hardcore the moment he giggled as a spider the size of a half-dollar crawled all over his arms—because he'd picked it up.

"What should we do today?" I asked as I tossed laundry into the washer.

"Playground," he suggested. He always suggested that.

"How about a candy factory instead?"

He guffawed. No way was he falling for that old trick. "No, playground!"

"Have you checked the weather? Isn't it cold enough to turn your lips blue?"

Ezra rolled his eyes when he thought I wasn't looking. I swore, he only put up with me because I supplied him with applesauce squeezers and the occasional donut. Otherwise, he would have been out of here.

"No, Mommy. I wear a *big* coat and gwoves on my fingers."

I knew which battles to pick, and this one wasn't one of them. Ezra needed to run and run fast so he didn't tear down the walls of Jenny's townhouse.

"All right. Let's make a deal. We'll go to the playground while the laundry's in the washer. If your lips don't turn blue, I'll take you again after your nap."

He crossed his little arms and considered my proposition as if we hadn't made the same compromise a dozen times before. After a good thirty seconds, he nodded, taking me up on my deal.

We bundled up and walked hand in hand to the little park down the street. Jenny's neighborhood had seen better days, but the sense of community couldn't have been bought for all the money in the world. We knew most of our neighbors by name, and no one blinked at me being a young, single mom. Ezra was accepted just as easily as a kid from a nuclear family in the fancy burbs.

Mr. Sulaimani at the bodega always had a lollipop for him no matter how many times I protested, and he made sure to check in with me too. When I'd been in college, he'd insisted on reading the papers I wrote for English classes and would give me a bar of chocolate when I got an A.

Auntie Jackie—our next-door neighbor who wasn't related to us in any way—dropped everything to babysit Ez when Jenny wasn't available. She didn't even let me pay her and loved my kid like he was her blood kin.

There were times over the last three years I'd felt like there were eyes on me. I didn't know what it was exactly, just an awareness of someone else's presence from time to time. But I hadn't been afraid, and I still didn't know if I was imagining things or the feeling was from living in a close-knit community where business didn't remain private for long. Either way, I had gotten used to it and barely noticed the feeling anymore, though it was still there, lingering.

Life wasn't easy, but it was good here.

After thirty minutes of swinging, running, and throwing himself off the playground equipment, Ezra and I stopped at the bodega on the way home for a cup of hot chocolate. Mr. Sulaimani helped Ez open a cherry lollipop while I went to the back to get his drink.

I was pumping the creamy hot chocolate from a carafe into a thick paper cup when someone slid next to me, leaning their elbow between the coffee pots and soda machine.

"Hey, mami. Is today our day?"

My stomach dropped. There were a lot of things I loved about our neighborhood, but Edwin Cruz wasn't one of them. He was a few years older than me, handsome in a slimy way, with perfect edges in his hair, a sparkling diamond in his ear, and a slit in his eyebrow. His heavy, cloying cologne coated my nose and made my eyes water like pepper spray. I backed up a step to try to remove myself from his sphere.

"Sorry, no." I hated myself for apologizing. Edwin had been asking me out for the last year and he always took my 'no' as 'not right now.'

He reached out and ran a hand over my hair, smirking at my answer. "Come on, Wren. We'll have fun together, you and me. I'm a quality guy. You just got to give me a chance."

I shook my head even as my lips lifted into a tremulous smile. There was something about this man that made me slightly afraid to be truly firm with him and tell him he gave me the damn creeps.

"I don't date. You know that." That wasn't a lie, but even if I did date, a man like Edwin would be the last I'd ever choose. I didn't know what he saw in me that he liked—maybe he thought I was vulnerable and easy—but I didn't see anything in him that interested me. He was too pushy—and way too smooth.

He kept touching my hair, not taking even an ounce of a hint. "We don't have to leave the house, mami. I'll be your man and take real good care of you. You won't want or need anything else."

Ezra came tearing down the chip aisle with Mr. Sulaimani on his heels, holding his lollipop up like he was the Statue of Liberty. "Mommy, where's my choco?"

Edwin dropped his hand from my hair and crossed his arms over his broad chest with a disgruntled, "Hmph." Mr. Sulaimani crossed his arms over his chest and gave him a dark look. I'd never seen that expression on him, but he appeared downright murderous.

I showed Ezra the cup in my shaking hand. "Here it is, baby buddy. Let's go home. It'll be cool enough to drink when we get there." I grabbed his hand and pulled him back in the direction we came. Mr. Sulaimani called after us when I laid a dollar down on his counter and didn't stay to chat, but I kept going.

Once we were outside in the daylight, I breathed easier. I didn't think Edwin would actually hurt me, but he made me uncomfortable enough. I sometimes wished he'd fall into a sinkhole and never return. He could live a perfectly happy life on the other side of it, just not anywhere near me.

Ezra and I were back home in a minute, warming up and changing out the laundry together.

"Mommy, Bob Ross now?" he asked as we trekked upstairs from the basement.

"Sure. Do you want to paint along with him?"

His eyes lit up. "Yes! I wanna paint trees!"

I got Ezra set up with his smock and easel and turned on an old episode of *The Joy of Painting* for him. Bob Ross had randomly become Ezra's hero, and I wasn't mad about it. I'd prefer to hear about happy accidents from a man with a gentle voice and terrible perm than watch a zillion episodes of *PAW Patrol.*

Jenny and I sat at the small dining room table, which was only feet away from the living room, because three-year-olds and paint could be dangerous.

"Give me the tea, Birdie. What happened?" Jenny cupped her mug of coffee between her hands and leaned in close, eager to hear all about my night.

"Um...well, it wasn't really a regular party."

She tilted her head. "Of course it wasn't. I imagine famous rock stars don't exactly go to keggers. Was it at some chichi place?"

"Yeah, I guess so. It was in a penthouse apartment." Jenny gripped my arm, already excited where this story was going. She had *no* idea. "I guess I expected that. What was surprising were the performers."

Her eyes lit up. "Oh, was it someone famous?"

"No." My cheeks flooded with heat. Not from embarrassment, but from the memories of watching that man and woman dancing and then fucking on their small stage. "They were...erotic performers. I think to get everyone in the mood."

She looked at me like a deer caught in headlights. "What the hell, Birdie? What kind of party did you go to?"

I cupped my mouth and whispered. "A sex party."

Her mouth fell open. "And did you—?"

"No." I shook my head hard. "Absolutely not."

She released a long sigh. "I didn't think so, but—"

"I didn't have sex, but there was grinding."

Her hand flew to her chest. "Who the hell were you grinding? Adam?"

I shook my head again and chewed on my bottom lip. Jenny knew all about my emails with Callum. She was the one person I'd ever been able to be completely open with. When my heart broke over him, I cried on her shoulder. When he appeared in the lobby on my first day at Good Music, we freaked out together. Since she knew all about my loaded feelings for him, he was probably the last person she imagined I'd ever hook up with— especially since he had no clue I was the little bird he'd written to for all that time.

"Adam kissed me, but, um…Callum yanked me off his lap and said he wanted me." I buried my face in my hands. "And then I kind of writhed all over him like…well, not anything like myself. I don't know, he felt so good, and I forgot where I was. We were in a room filled with people, and I just…didn't even think about that."

When I peeked between my fingers, Jenny stared back at me with wide eyes and a gaping mouth. I'd stunned her. Then again, I'd stunned myself.

"We didn't even kiss," I continued, needing to get it all out. "I'm not sure he likes me. But when he took me and said he wanted me, god…" I still couldn't believe that had happened. He kept telling me what a good girl I was. How perfect I was. How hard I'd made him come. No one had ever spoken to me that way, but his praise had coated me with carnal bliss.

Jenny had pulled herself together a little, but she still looked how I felt—like she'd stepped into an alternate universe where everything was almost the same but tilted just enough to make it entirely different.

"I don't quite know what to say." She fanned her face and looked at me like I was a stranger. "Wow, so there was grinding, and then…?"

"We both came," I rushed out. "I made him come in his pants. *Me*. Wren Anderson."

Her head bobbed on her neck like a couple screws had come loose. "I never doubted you had that power, Birdie. I always tell you how gorgeous you are."

"You're biased because you love me and I have your hair."

I wasn't gorgeous. On a good day, I was cute or adorable. On a very, *very* good day, when I carefully did my hair and layered on makeup, I could pass for sort of pretty. I was a few inches too short, more than a few pounds too heavy, and my features were too disproportionate to qualify for more than that. And that was okay. I'd learned to accept that and like myself anyway.

Most days, at least.

"You're gorgeous," she insisted. "That's a fact. One day, you'll recognize beauty doesn't come in one model. But that's really beside the point, isn't it?"

"What is the point?" I was a pretty smart girl, but I was definitely flying blind when it came to sex parties, random hookups, and Callum Rose.

"Well, how did you leave it?" she asked.

I shrugged. "He put me in his car and sent me home."

"Hmmm…" She tapped her chin. "Did you tell him about the emails?"

"Of course not."

She snorted. "Of course not. And are you going to?"

I blew out a long breath. "I don't want to."

She leveled me with a hard stare. "That's not really fair to him, honey. You have him at a disadvantage. If you had been two anonymous pen pals, neither of you would know if you crossed paths. But that's not the case here. If you're going to continue—"

"I can't see that happening."

"Why not?"

"Because..." I held out my arms, gesturing to the toys, the boy, and finally, myself. "Because of who I am and who he is."

Her eyes narrowed. "You're starting to piss me off." It was true. When Jenny got mad, her Queens accent thrived. "You were you and he was himself last night. That didn't stop either of you. So, tell the man who you really are. Be fair. Maybe he'll surprise you."

"I know I should." I rubbed my forehead with my fingertips. "But it'll open a whole can of worms I'm not ready for, you know?"

She patted my hand, sympathy melting in her soft brown eyes. "I know, baby. I really do."

Ezra pulled my attention away to show me his masterpiece, putting the conversation to an end. He'd had a *happy little accident* with his paint water, so I had to stop fantasizing about my rock star crush and clean up the mess my little boy had made. If that wasn't a reality check, I didn't know what was.

Sundays were my shopping day. During Ezra's naptime, I bought our groceries for the week, using the solo trip to grab a little peace and quiet for myself. Jenny was always urging me to go out and basically get a damn life, but that wasn't me. I'd barely had one before my kid, not a chance I was going to make a big change now.

On the way home, I dawdled, peering into storefronts and pushing my wire cart filled with reusable shopping bags.

I stopped in front of a Krav Maga studio. I'd walked by it a hundred times, but never really looked in. Something about the pristine window and swirly script of the sign caught my attention.

There was a group of mostly men and a couple women gathered in a semicircle on a blue mat, watching a sparring match between two men in black uniforms with padded helmets on their heads. They were grappling and kicking, tossing elbows and trying to drag each other down to the mat. I winced every time an elbow connected, but I couldn't seem to look away.

What kind of crazy person would have willingly signed up for something like this? Not me, that was for sure. I didn't like pain, like most sane people.

When one man pinned the other down with his arm wrapped around his opponent's throat and his legs around his middle, my breath caught like I was the one being choked. I glanced at the people watching the fight, wondering if anyone else was concerned about the two people trying to kill each other. But no, they all seemed enthralled.

At least, that was what I thought, until I reached the end of the semicircle and found I was being watched. Callum Rose stood on the mat with his arms folded over his chest, his hair swept back in a low bun, dressed in the same black uniform the men currently fighting wore.

He wasn't watching the fight, though. My throat squeezed when our eyes connected through the glass.

His stare pinned me in place, even with the blast of cold wind that seemed to sneak between the fibers of my coat to torment my bare skin. I thought about leaving, but he held up a finger, bent to grab a gym bag from between his feet, and strode for the door.

Callum pushed outside and slung the bag across his chest. "Hello."

"Um...hi." I pushed my hair off my face with my gloved hands. "Don't let me take you away from your murder-fight thing. I was walking home and stopped to watch and you're here."

He bowed his head. "I *am* here." He crossed his arms, and his eyes bounced from my cart to me. "I was gettin' ready to leave anyway."

My stomach was doing somersaults, more than it ever had in his presence. I was babbling like a ninny and making a fool of myself. I needed him to go back inside and pretend he never saw me. It didn't seem like he was taking the psychic messages I was sending him, so I probably needed to speak before things got too awkward.

"All done murder-fighting?" I pushed out.

His mouth quirked. "For now. There's no tellin' what will happen later."

"Do you often have spontaneous murder-fights?"

His head cocked, and he looked at me like a puzzle. "You know it's not really called that, right?"

"Yeah, I do." I giggled, but it sounded more like a gurgle. "Well, I'm heading home. I have groceries that need to be put away."

"Okay." He nodded like he'd come to a decision. "I'll walk with you."

"Oh. Okay. All right." My brow pinched as I really took him in. "Where's your coat?"

He tugged on the strings of his hoodie. "This is all I need."

"That isn't true. It's twenty degrees. You need something more than a sweatshirt."

His nostrils flared as he exhaled heavily. "You're worried about me?"

"I would worry about anyone who wasn't wearing a coat in this weather."

One corner of his mouth tugged up. "So, I'm not special?"

"Of course you're special." I pushed my cart forward and tucked my chin into my scarf. "Your fans would be devastated if you were taken out by a perfectly preventable case of pneumonia."

I had no idea what I was saying anymore. This man flustered me, and I didn't understand why he was walking down the cracked, uneven sidewalk by my side. He had to have somewhere better to be. If not murder-fighting, then signing autographs and trashing hotel rooms as rock stars were wont to do.

"Would you be devastated?" he asked.

"If you died from pneumonia?" He nodded. "I...I guess? Can we change the subject, please?"

"Sure." He tucked his hands in his hoodie pocket and walked in silence. His long legs were easily twice the length of mine, but he kept my pace, staying right beside me. His arm brushed mine every other step, which had to be purposeful. If he wanted away from me, he could go. Instead, he was actively coming closer.

"Why are you here?"

He cocked his head. "Here?"

"In Queens. Why are you in Queens? There have to be hipster Krav Maga places in Manhattan."

"There probably are." He rubbed his jaw and stared straight ahead. "But I live close by, so I don't know why I would go to Manhattan."

I stopped walking, and he noticed immediately, pulling to a stop and facing me. "Is there something wrong?" he asked.

"You live close by?" He lived close by? Callum Rose, my first love and teenage obsession, lived in the same borough? "Why?"

He gave me that puzzled look again. "Why what?"

"Why do you live here?"

"Why do *you* live here?" he countered.

"Um...well, my great-aunt Jenny has a house a few blocks over and I live with her, so...that's why I live here."

His eyes were so pretty. It hurt me down to my guts to keep looking at them, but the idea of turning away churned my stomach even worse. They were so blue, they glowed. Like northern lights or something. They shouldn't have been real, not on this street corner, in this city, on this planet. Getting to know Callum from far away all those years ago had muted him. I had known he was beautiful, but up close, he took my breath away.

His head dipped, and he reached down to open one of my grocery bags. "You should get home. Your popsicles will melt."

"That isn't an answer, you know."

"Mmm." He rubbed the golden stubble on his chin. "It's true, though."

"It's twenty degrees, remember? I think the popsicles are okay." I closed the bag, and my cheeks warmed, despite the cold. "Anyway, it's silly to eat popsicles in the winter, but I—"

"You should go home."

I huffed at his firm tone. "You keep saying that. You seem to like to tell me what to do."

He gazed off down the road, his jaw ticcing. "Maybe I do," he said softly. "I wish you would listen."

As pretty as his eyes were, I wasn't sold on this version of Callum. When he'd just been the man behind the screen, he hadn't bossed me around or interrupted me. A part of me wished I had been able to keep him locked away as a memory.

I reached out and touched his arm. He went completely motionless.

"I think I'll take you up on your advice. But I don't need an escort, so I'll say goodbye to you here." I let go of his arm and wrapped my fingers around the handle of my cart. "Bye, Callum."

He let me go with a simple nod. When I turned the corner a block away, I glanced back and found him in the exact same position, legs braced wide, arms crossed, following my every move with his eyes.

I gave him a little wave, even though he was giving me murder eyes, and continued on my way. When I was completely out of his sight, and he was out of mine, I finally took a deep breath and tried to calm my thrashing heart.

Everything was fine. That had gone just peachy. I was new to dealing with men I'd spent an evening dry humping, but I was pretty sure that had gone as well as to be expected.

I could have told him I'd once been his little bird, but since we wouldn't be hooking up again, and The Seasons Change would likely be done recording their album soon, it seemed like an exercise in self-destruction. My memories of him might have been tainted by the true blue, live-and-in-technicolor version of him, but he could keep the ones he had of me.

Because that was all we were: memories of people we used to be to each other.

Four Years Ago

Dear Callum,

Do you date? How does that even work? Are you ever home long enough to take a girl on a date?

This line of questioning isn't out of the blue, I promise.

There's this guy I was paired with in my earth science lab. The only reason I sat beside him was because I missed my train and was late for class and it was the last seat available. Not that I need to explain myself, but since you know me, I'm sure you're surprised I ended up beside a boy.

Anyway, his name is Will, and he has floppy brown hair and dimples. Kind of the opposite of Karthik Singh, which is a good thing, believe me. He doesn't seem to mind that I'm mostly mute around him, and he told me he likes my hair (I almost vomited right then and there). Well, he asked me out, and I said yes.

Why?

I don't even know if I like him, but jeez, I should be dating, right? I can't just wait for this mythical shadow, can I?

Since you're older, and hopefully wiser, I'm hoping you have advice for me. What do I do? How do I act? Do I even want to go out with him? Help me, Callum!

Your neurotic friend,

Birdie

Dear Callum,

Hey. Hello? It's been two weeks. I wanted to make sure everything's okay. I've gotten used to hearing from you more often and I'm sad not seeing your name in my inbox.

Just in case you're wondering, the date went fine. We went to a movie so I didn't have to talk a lot. And then we had ice cream and sat side by side on a bench to eat it so I didn't have to figure out how much eye contact was too much eye contact.

He kissed my cheek and gave me a hug. I'm pretty sure he had an erection, which...I don't know, is that normal?

The sad thing is, other than the errant erection, he was perfectly nice, but I was so preoccupied with worries over you, I couldn't really give him my all.

Can you just write me back? I really miss you.

Xoxo,

Birdie

Dear Callum,

Hi?

I miss you. A month is too long to go without speaking. If you're done being my friend, please just tell me so I don't have to wonder.

BTW, I went out with Will one more time and told him I don't see us going anywhere. I don't think I'm in a place to give my heart to anyone now. Not when it's already out of my hands.

Just let me know you're alive, okay? Please?

Missing you,

Your Little Bird

Little Bird,

I'm sorry, I'm here.

I'm a dick, okay? I have no other explanation.

I don't know what to say except I'm fucking glad you ditched that guy. What the fuck are you thinking going out with a guy who rubs his dick on you on the first date? You gotta wait for your shadow. That guy isn't it. He isn't it at all. You're worth ten times more than that.

Don't think for a second I don't want to be your friend. You're important to me. You keep me sane and connected to what's real. I'll try real fucking hard not to drop out of your life again. Promise me you won't waste your time on half-baked dickfaces with stupid hair. I need that promise from you.

To answer your question, I don't date. Don't even know if I know how.

I missed you more than anything. Tell me you're okay.

Callum

CHAPTER EIGHT

CALLUM

ADAM WAS WAITING FOR ME OUTSIDE GOOD MUSIC. As soon as he laid eyes on me down the block, I stopped walking, and he closed the distance, shouldering me into the brick wall at my back. I had known this confrontation was coming. I'd put it off as long as I could. Seemed my time was up.

"What the hell was that Friday night, and why have you been avoiding my calls all weekend?"

I couldn't read if he was angry or confused. Quite possibly a mix of both.

Adam and I didn't fight. We had a twisted symbiotic relationship that required each of us to bare parts of ourselves we didn't show to anyone else, but we weren't best friends. We didn't clash because we didn't have anything to clash over. There had never been any stakes between us. Adam was laid back about most things, and I avoided attachments and getting in too deep, even with my bandmates.

No stakes. Nothing to fight for.

But Wren? I would fight over her. There was no way he was going to have her. She was too good for either of us. Too sweet and soft to be corrupted by our *habit*.

"I don't want her with you," I answered.

Scoffing, he shoved a hand through his hair. "Yeah, I got that message."

"Then why are we still talkin' about it?"

His brow furrowed, and his eyes rolled around in his head like he was close to having a seizure. "Are you for fucking real, man? You pulled the girl I'm interested in—"

"Don't use present tense. You *were* interested. That's done."

He jabbed a finger into my shoulder. "You, asshole, pulled the girl I was very clearly interested in off my lap and had her riding your dick in seconds. You have literally never expressed interest in a girl in front of me, and definitely never this particular girl. I'm gonna need more of an explanation than you're giving me, because right now, it feels like I've walked into an alternate universe."

Icy wind whipped my hair into my face. I pulled my leather jacket a little tighter around my chest, almost laughing at the memory of Wren being concerned about me only wearing a hoodie and dying an untimely death from the cold.

"I told you, I wanted her."

He scrubbed his face with both hands and growled in frustration. "I noticed you used past tense."

I lifted a shoulder. "I wanted her Friday night. I haven't thought beyond that."

I very much wanted her still. The question remained whether it was mutual.

His eyes narrowed as he leveled me with an assessing stare. "But if I still want her, then what? I can't go for it?"

The pit of snakes in my gut writhed in a sickening flurry. I swayed on my feet, and my hands curled into tight fists. If this motherfucker thought for one second he was going to lay a hand on Wren, he was sorely mistaken.

"She's not for you, Adam."

Even if I didn't exist, Wren wouldn't be for Adam. He meant well. I understood that. But he fell in and out of love at the drop of a hat. At least, his definition of love. From what I had gleaned in my lifetime, deep, real love wasn't so easy to shake off. But when Adam was done with women, he was like a dog after a bath, tossing them off his back like pesky drops of water in his fur. A girl like Wren deserved a lot better than that.

He took a step back, turning his head to the right to scan the sidewalk. I leaned against the brick, waiting for him to come at me again. He could challenge me all he wanted, I wasn't backing down.

He turned back to face me, his nostrils flaring. "Tell me what it is about *this* girl."

"Does it matter? I'm not backing down or giving her up to you."

"It matters. I want to know why the hell you're acting so out of character, and yeah, I'm gonna need to know what your plans for the girl are. I don't know her well, but I like her, and I don't want you fucking her up."

His accusation was an icy dagger to my chest. He had no reason to believe I would fuck Wren up other than his perception of the kind of person I was. I had never hurt a woman. I had never dumped, cheated, or misused them. *He'd* done those things. Not me.

"I would never hurt her."

That was the truth. Beyond the truth. It was a statement of fact that had been written in the stars. I would hurt myself before I hurt that girl.

"I know." He heaved a sigh and squeezed his eyes shut. "Fuck, I know, man. I'm just so…I don't know, perplexed by this whole situation, and you're not giving me anything to go on."

"I don't know what you want me to say. I wanted her. She liked being with me. No one got hurt. You found a couple new friends to spend the evening with."

The corner of his mouth hitched. "That's the only reason I'm not more pissed at your breach of bro code. Melissa and Andrea were pure delights and all too happy to nurse my broken heart."

I straightened, giving him the laugh he wanted. "All's right in the world." I plucked a toothpick from my pocket and rolled it between my lips.

"I guess it is." He cocked a head toward the studio. "My dick is about to snap off from the cold. Let's go in. No doubt Iris is frothing over us being late."

We entered Good Music side by side, both of us focused on the empty front desk. My chest tightened at the absence of the timid, cheery greeting I'd come to expect when I arrived every day.

"Where is she?" Adam's head swung back and forth, like he'd find her hiding behind one of the oversized planters.

She appeared from a doorway at the back of the lobby, hurrying toward her desk with a lime green mug in her hand. Her long, purple dress danced around her legs, and the lights seemed to follow her, glinting off her shiny hair like her own personal ray of sunshine.

She stopped in her tracks when she noticed us hovering near her desk.

Her mouth fell open in surprise, but she quickly schooled her features and forced out a smile. "Good afternoon." She set the mug down on her desk and smoothed a hand over her hair. "I stepped away for just a moment to get some water for my plant. I'm sorry I wasn't here to greet you."

She held up the small plant Adam had given her, and I swore he preened, puffing out his chest like a proud rooster.

"No worries, cutie. I'm glad you're taking care of your gift," he said.

She petted a leaf gently. "I'm trying. I have a black thumb, so it's going to take some luck for me not to kill it."

"Good luck. Better you than me. It'd be dead within a day in my care." He tapped her desk. "Are you good after everything that went down at the party?"

She sucked her bottom lip between her teeth. Her gaze darted to mine, then back to Adam. "We're fine. I'm good."

He tapped the desk again. "Rad. You're a good girl, Wren. Too bad tall, dark, and devastatingly charming isn't your type."

Adam swaggered off, leaving Wren giggling and me still lurking near her desk.

"Every two weeks," I said.

Her laugh fell away, and she canted her head in confusion. "What's every two weeks?"

"Last week you were wondering how to care for a succulent. I looked it up. You're supposed to water them every two weeks, after you allow the soil to dry out completely."

Looking away from her curious gaze, I shoved my hands in my pockets.

"Well, shit," she whispered. "Did I just kill my poor plant? The soil definitely wasn't completely dry."

I peered over the high top of her desk to her work surface below. The small plant was nestled between her computer and phone in a bright pot.

"If it dies, I'll buy you a new one. This one's too small anyway."

A laugh burst out of her. "By whose standards? I think it's cute."

I lifted a shoulder. "No standards, it just is."

A smile still played on her small mouth, and amusement lit her wide, amber eyes. There was no balance or symmetry to her features, yet they all fit on her heart-shaped face. She really was pretty, whether she knew it or not.

"Well, I'm not going to kill it, so it doesn't matter if it's too small." She tucked her hair behind her ear. "Don't you have to get upstairs? The rest of your band arrived a while ago."

"They'll be all right without me."

"Isn't the bass important?"

Resting my elbow on the desk, I leaned closer to her. "I'll tell you a secret, Wren." Her nose was smattered with freckles, and I wondered if they darkened in the summer. Did she burn in the sun? Probably. Didn't redheads burn easily?

She crossed her arms and rested on her elbows, giving me a subtle glimpse of cleavage. "Tell me, please. You have me curious."

Snapping out of my wandering thoughts, I focused on the woman in front of me. "The truth about recording an album is we spend ninety percent of our time talkin', writin', and riffing. They don't need me there for that."

"You don't talk and write and riff?"

I shook my head slowly. "I don't. I've written one song, but I kept it to myself."

The place between her pale brows pinched. "You don't want to share it?"

"I don't think so, no."

"You should." Her owl eyes were locked on mine, shining bright with something unsaid. "If they're having trouble getting the album right, maybe they could use your song."

"No." I took a step back, and Wren straightened, eyeing me warily. "See you later."

Wren lifted her hand in a wave before I turned and walked to the elevator. I stuffed my frozen hands in my pockets, staring at the numbers lighting up as the elevator rushed to the lobby to pick me up.

That interaction with Wren could have gone better, but knowing me, it could have gone much, much worse. I'd call it a win for today.

As soon as I walked into the studio, I was accosted by an angry woman.

"Nice of you to show up, Callie." Iris charged toward me, her cheeks flaming bright red. She was drowning in her pale pink sweats, but her presence was bigger than both of us combined. That was how she drew in crowds, even when we were the first opener for a shitty, has-been band back in the day. "You're never late. Why are you the last one here? I need you to be the one person I don't have to worry about."

Rodrigo waved his hands in the air behind her. "Hello. Responsible AF here. I'm never late."

Iris twisted around to talk to him. "That may be true, but you're only half here lately. Your big-ass head is up there in the clouds. Callum is the steady one in this band." She faced me again. "Like a glacier."

I didn't have easy relationships with anyone. It wasn't in my nature. But Iris and I came to an understanding in the very beginning. She left me alone while keeping an eye on me, and I did the same for her. Nearly six years of being bandmates, and I couldn't say we knew each other intimately, but I cared for her, and she cared back.

"Those fuckers are melting down." Adam raised an eyebrow at me from his place on the couch. He had a guitar in his lap but didn't really look like he was going to get to work anytime soon.

"I'm here. What do you need from me?" I asked.

She threw out her arms. "I need you to not be late again, all right? I got a call from Saul fucking Goodman this morning. He's been a monster since his child bride ran off with her bodyguard. I'm pretty sure he hates me since that bodyguard happens to be Ronan's best friend, as if I control his freaking dick."

Iris's boyfriend, Ronan, had been her bodyguard for a minute before he became a lot more. He showed up to our rehearsals and recording sessions sometimes, rumbled in an Irish accent, beat his fancy-suited chest to make sure none of us had eyes for his lady, and whisked her away. Iris seemed to like him, and he seemed to be enamored by her, so that was all I needed to know.

"What'd he say?" Rodrigo asked.

"What do you think he said?" Iris pursed her lips like she was sucking on a lemon. "Assholes gonna asshole, you know? There was a lot of 'time is money, young lady,' and 'if I don't have a hit single in my hands soon, you'll be in breach of contract.' Ronan tried to soothe me by calling them empty threats, but damn, boys. I really don't love having to kiss Saul's puckered and hairy asshole because we can't seem to get our shit together on this fucking album."

Roddy hopped up from his seat to give her a hug. The truth was, the lot of us could be spoiled and difficult, and sometimes we fought, but we'd been through thick and thin together. Nothing was going to change that. "I'm sorry I've been a bad bandmate. Give Saul my number. He can rant at me."

She hit her head into his shoulder. "We've gotta finish this week, guys. This is it. I need you here with me, focused and working your asses off. *Please*?"

Adam unfolded himself from the couch and wrapped his arms around them both. "You got it, Iris. I'll get my shit together."

I stayed rooted in place, but I nodded to myself. "I'm here. I'll be here."

Iris looked up from Roddy's chest and flashed me a watery smile. "Thanks, Callie. I know you're here. You're the best."

That was a major fucking overstatement, but I *was* here. I'd be here as long as they were.

Three and a half years ago

Little Bird,

Happy birthday. How does it feel to be in your last year of your teens?

If I was near, I'd take you anywhere you wanted to go. I really fucking hope you don't want to do something that requires balance or grace. As you know, my center of gravity is too high for me to have any chance. I would like it if you asked me to take you bowling or to make pottery. My long, spider fingers would be aces at both.

Tell me what you're wishing for on your birthday, Little Bird. Are you happy?

Did someone make you feel special?

I did get you a present. I wish I could give it to you in person, but I don't think I have the nerve.

So, here it is. I wrote you a song. The first song I ever wrote. I'm crossing my fingers you like it, even if it's shit.

<u>A Little Bird Said</u>
I'm stone cold in the dark
Waiting for something
Time stands mostly still
I thought it would happen by now
But it's all the same
Day after day

A little bird said
What are you waiting for?
The sun is out there
The day is bright now
Open your eyes and see that
Times have changed now

Oooh, delicate feathers

Let's fly together

I'm standing in the light
Watching for someone
The world is spinning
'Cause life has begun
But I haven't changed
I'm still the same

A little bird said
Are you trying to find her?
Your someone is right there
Shining like the waxing moon
Open your mind and see that
Change is coming inevitably

Oooh, delicate feathers
Let's fly together

I'm writing down notes
And reading her letters
Her words dance in my mind
My heart is melted ice
'Cause of the fire in her eyes
That I've never seen

Oooh, delicate feathers
Let's fly together
Into daydreams of you and me
Bright and stubborn and free
From the bonds of our tethers
And withstanding the test of time

Oooh, delicate feathers
Let's fly together
You and me
Oooh, you and me
Little bird

Happy birthday, little bird. You're on my mind. I hope all your wishes come true. If not today, then soon.
Callum

Dear Callum,
Thank you.
Thank you.
Xoxoxoxoxoxoxoxo
I'll write tomorrow when I stop sobbing. That was...
Okay, I'll write tomorrow.
Your grateful little bird,
Birdie

Little Bird,
No, don't cry.
Did I fuck up?
I'm sorry. Please don't cry.
Callum

Dear Callum,
My heart is brimming.
I've heard that idiom before, and I thought it sounded trite,
but god, it's true. It feels like you took a pitcher of affection and
warmth and care and poured it into each chamber of my heart
until it was overflowing.
You made my birthday great. Perfect. I don't even remember
the other stuff that happened. You made me feel special. All you.
You wrote me a song, Callum. A song of my own. I don't
know how to thank you.
If you were here, I'd probably stare at you for a while. I
wouldn't ask you to take me anywhere special. We could go for a
walk—you'd have to go slow because I'm very, very short—and
we wouldn't have to worry about eye contact awkwardness
because we'd be beside each other. I guess I should think of
something more exciting, but that's it. I want you to take me for a
walk.
Want to know something sad? My parents forgot my birthday.
When I mentioned it to my mom, she got defensive and angry.
Told me I'm an adult now, I shouldn't expect to be celebrated for
being alive. She said if I'm going to be ungrateful, I should go
live with my great-aunt Jenny in Queens since I clearly like her
more than my mom. My dad got in the middle, and for a second,

I thought he was going to defend me, but he backed my mom. He called me a bitchy little brat on my nineteenth birthday.

So, I want you to know how perfect your song was. It erased everything and patched me up so well, I barely even feel the barbs my parents threw at me.

Tell me how you are. Where are you? I want every detail.

Xoxoxoxoxo forever,

Birdie

Little Bird,

Fuck them. Go live with Jenny in Queens if she treats you right. There's no reason to stay with parents who don't appreciate and care for you. Family is only a word if it's not backed by feeling and action.

You aren't any of those things your parents said. You are the most thoughtful, sweet, and real human I've ever known.

I wish I could do a lot more than write you a subpar song, Little Bird. You deserve everything. I'm sitting here feeling stupid and helpless. And you want to go for a walk with me. Look at you, Little Bird. I tell you I'll take you anywhere, and it's a walk you request.

One day, when I get my shit together, I'm going to ask for your address and show up for our walk. Would you want that?

I'd walk slow for you. Tell me how tall you are. Are we going to look silly side by side?

I'm in Chicago for the next couple months. Adam, Rodrigo, Iris, and I are sharing a two-bedroom apartment in the basement of Adam's friend's house. I sleep in the van half the time just to get space.

How are you? Tell me the truth.

Callum

Dear Callum,

I'm okay, I promise. My birthday was rough, but I'm okay. Your emails are always a bright spot.

Sometimes I think about moving in with Jenny. But she's single and lives this fun, amazing life. She doesn't want a teenager with social anxiety cramping her style. And I'd have to transfer schools, get a new job, become a city girl...I don't think I'm a city girl. But I could be, I think? One day.

I'm only 5 ft. tall! We would look extremely silly together. Like I'm your child or something.

Would I like you coming to visit me? Are you kidding me, Callum Rose? I would die. You could drag my corpse around on your walk.

But there's no hurry. As much as I want to stare at you, I'm scared of messing things up between us. Aren't you?

BTW, why have you never asked for a picture of me?

Your freakishly short friend,

Birdie

Little Bird,

I guess we're never going to meet because I don't want to live in a world where you don't exist.

Move to the city, Little Bird. Have adventures. Don't shrink just because your parents aren't good enough to even know you, let alone call themselves your family.

Last night, I slept in our van, and I guess I forgot to lock the door. This morning, I woke up next to a homeless man who introduced himself as Crazy Leon. He'd let himself in while I was asleep. So, yeah, the city is rad as hell.

I don't need a picture of you, Little Bird. It never even occurred to me to ask. I'll see you when I can look at you in person. Okay?

I like knowing you're short, though. You'll come up to my chest.

Promise me not to die when I show up at your door, and I'll start working really hard on getting my shit together so we can make it happen.

Callum

CHAPTER NINE

WREN

WHEN I SAT DOWN AT MY DESK TUESDAY MORNING, my baby succulent had disappeared and been replaced by one twice its size. Its pot was glazed ceramic and very pretty, a pale shade of blue. I would have liked it if I wasn't stumped by its very existence.

Natalie's heels clacked as she approached from behind me. "Good morning," she singsonged.

"Good morning." I bent down and shoved my purse and coat in the compartment under my desk. When I straightened, Natalie had picked up my new plant, rotating it in her hands to inspect it.

"Do you not remember me telling you not to junk up your desk? Did you interpret that as 'replace the small plant with an even bigger one'?"

"No." I smoothed a hand over my lilac sweater. I'd felt cute when I'd left the house this morning, but in the face of beautiful Natalie and her flaming red swing dress and crimson lips, I felt myself shrinking.

Don't shrink, don't shrink, don't shrink!

"No, I didn't interpret it that way, and I don't see this pot as junk. If it's a problem, though, I'll take it home."

Natalie lowered her long, thick lashes, staring at me through slits. Then she waved me off and rolled her eyes. "It's fine. Just keep it tucked under the counter so no one else sees it." She pointed one of her dagger nails at my sweater. "This is pretty, but didn't you just wear it last week?"

My hand shot up to my scoop-neck collar. "I might have. Is there a rule about how often I can wear my clothes?"

Her painted lips tipped into a not-so-friendly smile. "No rule, per se. But if you ever want to be more than a front desk receptionist, you really need to look the part. Of course you have limitations given your height and…other things, but you manage to make yourself look cute." She clapped her hands together. "We should go shopping. What are you doing next weekend?"

My eyes widened. She had taken me so off guard, I couldn't think of an answer fast enough to get out of her invitation. "Um. I don't have concrete plans, but I have a son, so—"

Her mouth formed a perfect, cherry O. "Oh my god, I had no idea. How old?"

"He's three."

"No way." She tossed her perfect curls behind her back. "I have a three-year-old niece. She lives in California, so I never get to see her. Bring your baby shopping with us. I'll love up on him and play with him. It'll be perfect."

I should have been better braced for Natalie's whiplash, but I didn't think there was any getting used to her drastic change in moods from one second to the next.

"Ezra loves to play. Shopping, not so much."

Her eyes drifted to the side, and she bit her lip. "You're right. Holly isn't really down for watching me try on clothes either. Nix the kid. We'll do a playdate another time."

With her decision made, she clattered away on her high, high heels, and I slumped back in my chair. I had no idea what had just happened. I didn't really want to spend time with Natalie outside of work, but she hadn't given me the opportunity to tell her no. I supposed that was one way to get what she wanted. Maybe I needed to take lessons.

Callum was standing outside of my regular coffee shop. I stopped in my tracks when I spotted him, tall and lean, huddled in his leather jacket that couldn't have provided him nearly enough warmth. As soon as our eyes connected, he pushed off the wall and sauntered toward me.

I had twenty seconds to remember how to breathe. There was a time I used to dream about Callum walking toward me this way. In those dreams, I ran into his arms, and he wrapped me up tight. We'd breathe each other in and stare at one another in disbelief. We'd marvel that the person behind the screen was real. Solid. Perfect. But I'd screwed up everything before that ever happened, and now...now I didn't know what we were.

I sucked in a breath and tucked my frozen hands in my pockets.

"Are you stalking me?" I asked.

The corner of his mouth hitched. "What would you say if I was?"

I lifted a shoulder. "It depends. Are you stalking me so you can find the perfect opportunity to get me alone and murder me, or are you just run-of-the-mill obsessed with me?"

His blue eyes sparkled with secrets and amusement. "You'll have to wait and see."

"Are you being ominous on purpose?"

He shoved his fingers through the side of his long hair. "Maybe mysterious."

"What if I told you not to follow me?"

"I was here first, so you can't claim I followed you, Wren."

Rin. There'd be a time when hearing him say my name in his soft Alabama accent didn't weaken my knees, but today wasn't that day.

"Why are you here then? It seemed like maybe you were waiting for me."

He nodded. "You're right. I was. I enjoyed standing in line with you last week. I'd like a repeat of that."

I snorted a light laugh. "A repeat of standing in line? Are you going to be mean to me again?"

His lids lowered, but his eyes never wavered from mine. "No, I won't be mean to you. I didn't think I was being mean last time. It wasn't my intention."

My feet itched to run. Even after what happened at the party on Friday, I believed I could slip out of Callum's life without telling him I was his disappearing little bird. With every encounter we'd had since, that belief faded, and I was faced with reality. I had to tell him. And I would.

Just...not now. This conversation wasn't suited for a public place.

"Okay. Let's go inside and be nice to each other then."

The line was even longer than last time, but instead of lurking behind me, Callum stood next to me. He didn't speak, and neither did I. His arm stayed in constant contact with mine, and there was no denying it was purposeful.

Customers were taking second and third glances at Callum as they came and went. He lowered his head, locking eyes with the ground, but he was impossible to miss.

"Do you hate it?" I murmured.

His head canted toward me. "What?"

"The stares. Everyone's looking. If they haven't figured out who you are, they're wondering."

He paused for a moment and brought his eyes up to my face, scraping them over my features slowly. "I don't love it, but I'm adept at ignorin' it. People stare, but they usually leave me alone."

Probably because he'd perfected that stone-cold expression of his. With his height, his stark features, and the *fuck off* snarl, he was more intimidating than inviting.

"You don't have to be here with me, you know. I can bring you coffee to the studio."

He brought his hand up and trailed his rough thumb along the rounded curve of my jaw. "I'm not really here for the coffee."

My heart rattled in its cage like a can on prison bars. This man had no right to say something like that to me, and yet, here he was, being his blunt, Callum Rose self.

"The pastries?" I quipped. If I didn't make light of this, I'd cry over what I'd lost with him. We could have had this. It could have been real. But now we were living in the calm before the storm that wiped us completely off the map.

He rolled his head in the direction of the well-lit case holding a wide selection of baked goods. "They're not so bad. I have a massive sweet tooth."

"Oh yeah? Which one are you going to choose?"

"You choose for me. I trust you, Wren."

Oh, that was a dagger to my conscience. I couldn't keep standing here with him, letting him say things like he trusted me and not tell him the truth. Or at least make a solid plan for telling him the truth. Jenny had been right—it wasn't fair to Callum to be kept in the dark. Even if he never spoke to me again, I had to do it.

We ordered our drinks, I picked out a chocolate muffin for Callum, which he seemed to approve of, then we were back outside again. I was heading to the park to eat my lunch, and he had to get back to the studio.

But neither of us hurried off. I scuffed my heels on the sidewalk, and he stared down at me. I was trying to work up the nerve to ask him to meet me somewhere this weekend to talk, but he spoke first.

"You haven't mentioned the plant. Did you like it?"

It took me a beat to understand what he meant. "The oversized succulent that mysteriously appeared on my desk this morning?"

He nodded, intent on my face.

"Of course I liked it. It was a surprise, though, since I already had a nice little plant."

"Too little," he said flatly.

"By your standards. That doesn't make it fact, you know." I dug my teeth into my bottom lip to hold back a smile. I never thought I'd have such an easy conversation with this man while I looked up at his bright, blue eyes with the winter sky behind him.

He shrugged. "I wanted you to have it. That's all that matters."

"Well, thank you." I almost brought my hand up to touch him, but my arm suddenly weighed a thousand pounds and I couldn't seem to lift it. "What did you do with the one Adam gave me?"

"It's gone. I got rid of it."

My nose wrinkled. "You threw away a perfectly good plant? That's a crime, Callum. You can't do that."

"I did."

"You shouldn't have."

His eyes flared for barely more than a breath, then went calm like a fathomless sea, peering back at me without a wave or whitecap in sight. If we weren't standing in front of a coffee shop on a crowded sidewalk, I would have taken my time studying the sharp planes of his cheeks, the softness of his mouth, his hair glinting with gold in the sun. Callum Rose was starkly beautiful. Everything about him broke my heart a little more.

"Okay. I should go so I have time to eat lunch."

"Okay," he echoed. "I won't be here tomorrow. We have to finish the album this week, so I'll be locked in the studio."

I nodded. "Makes sense. So…this might have been our last time waiting together."

"No." His hand flexed by his side. "No, definitely not."

One last look, and he dropped his gaze from mine and strode with his head down in the direction of Good Music. My teeth dug into my bottom lip as I drank in his long gait, the shape of his ass in his jeans, his hair tucked into his collar, and every other detail I'd been starving for three years ago. I couldn't quite grasp who this raw, real version of Callum Rose was, but I was beginning to think I liked him.

My chest ached with the very real possibility he wouldn't think much of me anymore once I told him who I really was.

Three and a half years ago

Little Bird,

Things are happening for TSC.

We're playing the Swerve Tour again this summer, and not on the tiny stage behind the port-a-potties you saw us on. We'll be in front of the toilets this year.

This week, we're headed into the studio to record a demo. There's someone from A&R at Good Music coming out to see us play live. I don't lean toward optimism, but I'm feeling hopeful. It's strange. I didn't think I cared whether TSC took off, but now that it might be happening, I'm finding I fucking want it.

I'm working my way toward you, Little Bird. I haven't slept in the van all week. I talked to a stranger. I got a haircut. I'm close.

Here's me being as honest as I can be: I'm more afraid of meeting you and ruining it than not getting the record deal. Does that make sense to you?

How are you? Any thoughts on moving to the city?

Callum

Dear Callum,

Of course you're going to get a record deal. I knew TSC was going somewhere when I watched you behind the port-a-potties. And now look at you guys, in FRONT of them! You're going places.

Haha, but for real, I'm so proud of you and the band. Even if it falls through (which it won't), I'm proud, because you guys have worked your asses off.

Here's me being honest back: I'm so freaking scared of meeting you and losing you after, I don't know if I can go through with it. And that's so stupid because I think about you every day. All I want is to deepen our connection, but I'm still hesitating.

You know me. I feel closer to you than everyone in my life aside from Jenny. If I lose you, I don't know what I'll do. How do I get over that fear, Callum?

I'm okay. My dad threw away my $200 textbook two days ago because I didn't remember to start the dishes after dinner. I have to figure out how to scrape up enough money to buy a new one. Jenny will help if I ask, but I hate to ask. The city seems like such a far-off dream now. I don't know what I was thinking even considering it.

I hope Crazy Leon doesn't miss you too bad now that you're not sleeping with him in the van.

Your neurotic friend,
Birdie

Little Bird,

I wish I could make you understand there's nothing you could do to make me not want to know you. Do you get that? You are pretty much everything.

I'm scared too. For the same reasons as you and a thousand others. This is the exact wrong time in my life to even attempt to move you and me to real life, but I can't go another year and a half without knowing what your presence feels like.

Can you, Little Bird?

I would offer you the money for your book, but I know you won't take it. If you change your mind, please tell me. I'm not rich, but I've saved everything I've earned and can easily spare $200. Or more if you need it. You want me to put a hit out on your dad? I think I can afford it. Or I'll do it myself for free. If that man touches you in any other way than fatherly kindness, you won't be able to stop me from showing up.

I heard this new song on the radio yesterday and it reminded me of you. I rarely connect with lyrics, but this song put me on my ass. Have you heard "Hold My Girl" by George Ezra? Give me a minute, Little Bird.

Callum

CHAPTER TEN

WREN

EZRA JUMPED UP FROM HIS chair at the kitchen table to throw himself at my legs. "Pretty, Mommy!" he shrieked.

I picked up my boy, relieved his face wasn't covered in something sticky that might have transferred onto my pants. It looked like eggs and toast were on his menu for breakfast this morning. My black trousers and emerald green cardigan were safe for now.

"Why thank you, angel face. You're rather dashing yourself." I booped his nose, making him laugh. "Are you, by any chance, a real, live prince?"

He shook his head, sending his curls into a frenzy. "Nope. I'm a painter like Bob."

I smacked my forehead. "Duh, of course you are." I wondered if Bob Ross was a hero to any other three-year-olds. Maybe in 1982. "You have the same hairdo as Bob. I should have known."

Ezra proudly reached up and tugged on his frizzy ringlets. "You like my hair?"

"You know I do. I'm jealous I don't have curls too."

He touched my hair so gently and reverently, I could have cried. "You have pretty hair too, Mommy."

I didn't know what I'd done right to get a son like this one, but it must have been something huge. He'd been born sweet and had only grown sweeter.

"Oh my gosh, thank you so much. I'm going to tuck that compliment in my pocket and take it out later when I need a little pick-me-up." I plucked the air and put my hand in my pocket, sending Ezra into another fit of laughter. Fortunately, my sense of humor did well with three-year-olds.

Jenny walked out of the kitchen, drying her hands on a towel. "You do look nice, babe. Did you put in a little extra time with the curling iron?" Her brow went up, and it wasn't exactly in a kind way. She was more than a little annoyed with me for not coming clean to Callum yet.

"I did. My sort-of boss, Natalie, seems to always have something to say about my appearance. Meanwhile, she looks like she stepped off the set of *Mad Men*."

Jenny rolled her eyes. "She sounds like a piece of work, and not someone you should compare yourself to."

"Believe me, there's no comparing."

I set Ezra on his feet and kissed his forehead. He promised to be a good boy at preschool and made me promise to be a good girl at work. Jenny gave me a pointed look at that promise, which I mostly ignored. After bundling up, I grabbed my bag and blew another kiss to Ezra, then I hurried out the door to make a dash for my train.

I stopped short at the idling SUV and the rock star leaning against it. When his eyes locked on mine, he opened the back door and held out a hand.

"Holy granola," I murmured.

I slowly walked down the rest of the steps to the sidewalk, unsure if this was real.

"Uh...hi?" I croaked.

"Good mornin'. Are you ready to go to work?" he asked.

I exhaled a slow breath, forming a cloud in front of me. "Yeah, I am." Stepping off the sidewalk, I peered into the empty back seat, then at Callum. "Are you taking me?"

His nostrils flared slightly. "Yeah, Wren. I'm takin' you to work. Climb in. Your nose is red already."

My gloved hand flew up to cover my nose. "Well, okay. Thank you, Callum." I had to step up to get into the SUV, and Callum braced his hand on the small of my back, giving me a little push. He climbed in after me and closed us in the warm space. The driver pulled away from the curb as soon as we were settled.

I turned my head to look at Callum. "Your nose is red too. Your cheeks too."

He shifted so his back was against his door and he was facing me. Taking my gloved hand in his, he rubbed it on his cheek. "Warm me up then."

I liked it. I let him continue using my hand, wishing I wasn't wearing the glove so I could really feel his skin. He was like a cat, rubbing against me, almost purring. He didn't try to stifle the pleasure he was taking from the simple stroke of leather against his cheek. He watched me with curious, unabashed eyes.

"You really are stalking me, aren't you?"

"Maybe." His brow crinkled. "What makes you say that?"

I huffed a laugh. "You showed up at my house this morning and I don't remember giving you my address."

His head cocked, and he pressed his cheek against my hand a little harder. "All it took was a little digging. You're not hard to find, Wren Anderson."

"Again, with the ominous."

His mouth pulled into a smirk, and damn did it look good on him. "Do you mind that I picked you up?"

"No," I answered immediately. It was sort of scary how little I minded him picking me up. "You didn't go out of your way though, did you?"

"No. I live pretty close by. If you want, I'll give you my address so you can stalk me back." He placed my hand back in my lap and took out his phone. "I'd like your phone number, Wren."

"You didn't find that in your Google search?"

He only stared at me, waiting, so I rattled off my number. My phone chimed in my purse a moment later. I dug it out and found he'd texted me a picture he'd just snapped of me.

"This isn't very flattering," I said.

He studied his screen, two lines forming between his brows. "I don't know. I like watchin' you when you don't notice."

A laugh burst out of me. "You keep saying creepy things like that and I'm going to believe you mean them. Do I have to check my bushes?"

"You don't have any bushes, unfortunately. I checked."

I grinned at his dry delivery. Callum Rose was funny. I was surprised by how comfortable I felt with him while a hot poker swirled in my belly. One should have precluded the other, but that wasn't the case. Being around him was easy and painful at the same time.

"How's the recording going?" I asked.

"Yeah, I don't know. It's happenin'. That's all I know."

"Aren't you there for it?"

"Kinda. I'm there physically."

I chewed on the corner of my bottom lip and considered him. I knew what I'd say to my old friend, Callum, but I didn't quite know how to respond to this man beside me.

His finger drew a straight line down my leg. "Did you like what we did at the party, Wren?"

I jerked my head back at the sudden change in our conversation. "What?"

"Watchin'." His palm settled on my knee, engulfing it in his big hand. Long fingers curled into the soft flesh on the inside of my knee, pulsing to a beat only he could hear. "Did you like watchin' the other people?"

I started to tuck my hair behind my ear, but he caught my hand, squeezing it in his. Then he let go and tucked my hair himself, tracing the shell of my ear with the tip of his finger.

The knot in my throat only allowed me to nod.

He dragged that finger along my jaw. "There's a private club I go to sometimes. You can do anything there, but I go to watch. Will you go with me Saturday night? No Adam. Just you and me."

"Um, well…" I needed to think. I should have said no. There was no way I could get any closer to him without telling him who I was. I was a wimp and had hoped to avoid this topic until the end of time, but even I knew that was beyond the pale.

"Don't say no." He cupped my jaw and tilted my head back. "I'm only askin' you to watch with me, Wren. That's all. I'm not askin' or expecting any more than that."

"Do you even like me?" I blurted out.

He flinched at my question. "What makes you think I don't like you?"

Because of things I can't talk about. You shouldn't like me. You probably hate your little bird—and that's me. I'm the girl who ghosted you. I'm the girl who didn't show up when you needed her. I'm the girl who's been lying to you for the last couple weeks.

"Well, that's the impression you gave in the beginning. Like my presence annoyed you and you were angry about me being at that party. I guess I'm a little confused."

Twin lines formed between his brows. "I'm not good with people. Or words."

I huffed at his nonanswer. "So, you weren't annoyed with me? You do like me?"

His icy fingers slid through the side of my hair, and for a moment, he squeezed his eyes shut. "I'm not annoyed by your presence. And I may not be good with people, but I do think I've made it very obvious I like you. I've been stalkin' you, for Christ's sake."

I burst out laughing. It couldn't be helped. Callum's deadpan sense of humor shot me straight in the funny bone. I shouldn't have been laughing. I was in a giant pile of trouble. But holy granola, I really liked this man. Callum let a slow smile spread across his face, revealing his slightly crooked and perfectly charming white teeth.

"Is that a yes?" he asked.

"It's not a no. But can we table that for a week or two and maybe get to know one another?" *Give me a chance to come clean.* "I know it doesn't seem like it, given my behavior at the party, but I'm not normally like that."

"I know." There was more sureness in those two words than I contained in my entire body.

"You do?"

"I do. We'll table it." He tipped his chin. "You'll come over to my place. I'll feed you dinner. If you say no, I'll be forced to use the copy of the key I made to your townhouse and drag you out with me."

I giggled, but he'd uttered his threat so seriously, half of me almost believed him. I must have been a little mental, because the thought of Callum so desperate to be in my presence he'd commit a literal crime to have me, turned me on so suddenly, my thighs clapped together.

"Okay. We can skip the kidnapping. I'll come willingly." And I would tell him when I got to his apartment. Even if it hurt and he kicked me right back out, I wouldn't delay it a second.

"Good girl." His mouth spread into a grin. "Although, I'd been kinda lookin' forward to the kidnapping. I think you'd look cute all bound and gagged."

The flood of heat between my legs practically made me moan. What the hell was with me? A normal reaction to what Callum said would probably involve jumping out of a moving car, not getting turned on. It had to be because of our history, not because I'd been transformed into a kinky monkey.

His grin spread even wider, and a finger skimmed my hot cheek. "You liked that, didn't you?"

I blinked slowly and let myself smile back at him even though I was confused and embarrassed by my reaction. "I don't know. Maybe I did. At least the idea of it. I think my aunt would be a little put off if you actually dragged me from our house all tied up."

His chuckle slid over my skin like warm silk. "I'll have to remember to make sure there are no witnesses."

"I wonder if you know how incredibly creepy you sound."

He lifted a shoulder. "It doesn't bother me very much. I don't talk like this with anyone else. Does it bother you?"

"No." I didn't hesitate. "It should, but it doesn't."

"Who says it should?"

"Well…society, I guess. Threatening to kidnap women if they don't do what you want is sort of frowned upon."

With a long exhale, he leaned his head back on the rest and dug his fingers into the sides of his scalp. "Somethin' you might wanna know about me, Wren. I grew up outside the confines of society with a bunch of criminals. Conformin' to rules doesn't make sense to me, but I do it for survival. I don't like it, and I don't believe in it."

I sucked in a little breath. "You don't believe in laws?"

"I don't care about laws. I'm not gonna hurt anyone, not unless they ask for it. But when I'm in the privacy of my home, or my car, I'd like to be able to drop pretenses and just be myself. If I say somethin' that scares you, tell me. But think about it first. Is it scary because you feel it, or is it scary because it's different than what you grew up believin' is right?"

I didn't have an answer, and he didn't seem to need one. He kept his eyes closed, and a look of contentment relaxed his sharp features. I settled beside him, twisting my fingers together as I tried to predict his reaction to me spilling the truth.

A warm hand landed on my fidgeting fingers. He had turned his head, observing me while I fretted.

"Stop, Wren."

I swallowed and moistened my lips. "Okay."

His lips quirked. "Thank you."

He closed his eyes again but kept his hand on mine. As the minutes passed, tension seeped from my muscles and I relaxed beside him. If I could have tucked this moment into a capsule and hidden it away in my coat pocket, I would have.

But the car pulled up in front of Good Music all too soon and reality set in when I saw Natalie sashay into the building.

"I can't get out here," I rushed out, panicked. I tried to take my hand back, but Callum kept it firmly in his grip. "Please. If my coworker sees me with you like this, she won't approve. And I know you don't care what people think, but this is my job, and I do care."

He let go of my hand to cover my mouth. "Quiet." He leaned forward to speak with the driver. "Take us a block down and let us out there."

Please, I added mentally.

The car lurched forward, but he kept his hand over my mouth. I wrinkled my brow and flashed him the dirtiest look I could muster with a half-hidden face. He chuckled but he made no move to release me until the SUV pulled up to the curb again, this time near our coffee shop.

Callum slid out first and held a hand out to me. I wanted to protest and not let him help me, but the step down was high, and I wasn't dumb enough to cut off my nose to spite my face. The trouble was, once he had my hand again, he didn't let it go.

"This defeats the purpose of us not arriving together in the car. You can't hold my hand."

With a sigh that sounded utterly annoyed, he released me. "Is there a rule about bein' seen with musicians who record in the building?"

"Not that I know of. But it's a very new job, and I'm trying to make a good impression. I need to be strictly professional while I'm at work."

"Do you like this job?"

I nodded. "I do. It's my first big girl job post-college. It's not a forever kind of thing, but I'm enjoying it."

"Good." He stopped at the door, gripping the handle, and let his eyes trail over me from bottom to top. Then he took a toothpick from his pocket and rolled it between his lips. "Good," he murmured, and this time, I wasn't so sure if he was talking about me or the job.

Callum left me at my desk, and Natalie didn't appear to tell me what I was wearing made me look like a homeless hag, so as far as I was concerned, the day was starting off without a hitch.

Three and a half years ago

Little Bird,

I know you're scared. I am too. But we're coming to New Jersey this summer on the Swerve Tour and I want you there. I need it. I attached a ticket and a backstage pass for you.

It's a month away. You have time to think about it. That's all I'm thinking about. Seeing you. Maybe hearing your voice. Feeling your vibe. Confirming everything I know about you.

Don't you want that too?

If it's too much to do more than meet, that's okay. You can say hi, and I'll say it back. If you want to leave after that, I won't stop you. I know I'll want to, but I won't.

It's a step, Little Bird. A step we're ready to take, even if we're both petrified.

Tell me what's on your mind.
Callum

Dear Callum,
I don't know what to say. I almost wish the concert was tomorrow so I didn't have a month to obsess. But then, I'm kind of always obsessing about you.

I'm sorry if I shouldn't say that. I know we always dance around those types of feelings. But it's true. You have become the center of my universe. What would the earth do without the sun? Excuse my dramatics, but I don't want to fade away, nor do I want us to fade.

I want to say hi to you. I would kill a man to hear you say my name (I'm talking an evil serial killer, not just an ordinary, innocent man, mind you). I want all the same things you do.

I'm so scared I won't be what you expect or need.

What if we're not compatible in person?

What if what makes us special is confined to the notes we send?

Tell me what's on your mind, Callum.

Yours,
Birdie

Little Bird,
You're on my mind.

We're traveling up the coast of California, spending long, sweaty days playing for crowds that are growing each time, and even longer, hot nights cooped up on a tour bus with another band. I'm never alone, and the only thing keeping me sane is knowing I'll be seeing you.

Keep me sane, Little Bird.

Be the light at the end of this exhausting tunnel.

I don't want to dismiss your fears, but fuck, Little Bird, do you think I'd still be emailing someone I didn't connect with on a level I never thought possible? I don't know what that will mean in person, but I know I will always need you in my life. Nothing will take that need away.

Tell me you'll come, Little Bird.

Callum

Dear Callum,

You made me cry.

I want to believe you. I know you mean it, but it's so hard for me to believe someone truly feels that way about me.

I'll come. I can't promise more than a 'hi,' but I'll come.

I'm so proud of you. I know it isn't easy for you to be surrounded by all the noise and people, but you're doing it, and your band is going somewhere huge. I know it.

But also, tell people to back off and leave you alone if you need that. Stay sane for me.

Tell me where you are and what you see.

Your scared shitless girl,

Birdie

CHAPTER ELEVEN

WREN

THERE HAD BEEN A CAR waiting to take me to work every single day and bring me home in the evening. Only, I was alone in the back seat. The driver informed me Mr. Rose's schedule differed from mine, but he wanted to make sure I was comfortable and safe during my commute.

My heart actually hurt when he told me that.

It was Saturday now, and I couldn't avoid telling the truth any longer. I felt the burden of it on my shoulders. Each day that passed, it became heavier and heavier. Jenny had been right. None of this was fair to Callum.

Ezra sat on my bed with a massive stack of books while I rushed around like a mad woman. I couldn't decide what to wear. Somber was most likely the right choice. I was feeling like I was about to walk in front of a firing squad. If I owned a hairshirt, that probably would have been suitable. But since I wasn't John the freaking Baptist, I had no idea where one would acquire such a thing.

"Whatcha doin', Mommy?" Ez asked.

"Going crazy, baby angel. What are you doing?"

He held up a board book about Picasso. "I'm reading. This art is crazy."

I peered at the picture of *Le Reve*. "Do you know *le reve* means *the dream*?"

He giggled and jabbed at the portrait of the sleeping woman. "She's havin' a dream?"

I tickled his chin. "Or maybe she *is* the dream, like you're Mommy's dream come true. The light of my life." I poked his side. "The syrup on my pancakes. The butter on my bread."

Squealing, he rolled to his stomach, locking his arms over his sides. "The peanut butter and jelly!" he shrieked.

I kissed his shoulder and grinned at my happy boy. "Yeah, that's right. You're the peanut butter to my jelly." Straightening, I put my hands on my hips. "Now, jelly, can you help Mommy decide on what to wear tonight?"

He sat up and scanned the pile of clothes I had thrown on the opposite side of the bed. "Are you leavin'?"

"Not until you go to sleep, and I'll be here when you wake up."

His face scrunched for a second, and my heart plummeted. Ezra was pretty go with the flow. Then again, I rarely went out, and pretty much never at night. He shrugged and reached for a book, and I blew out a heavy sigh of relief.

Jeans. I'd wear jeans and a cute top with a cardigan. On the very off chance Callum forgave me, I wanted to look presentable in case we actually got to the dinner portion of the evening.

This would be okay. No matter what happened tonight, I'd be coming back to a safe home, an aunt who loved and cared for me, and a son I lived and breathed for. That was my mantra for the rest of the evening, until Ezra was tucked snug in his bed and Jenny stood by the front door with me.

I blinked back tears as I smiled at her. "I don't know how to do this."

She squeezed my shoulders. "Just blurt out the truth. Get it over with the moment you see him. Answer any questions he has and accept the feelings he might have toward you. It'll all be okay, Birdie."

"Promise?" I asked meekly.

She clucked her tongue. "I can't promise you something I have no control over. But you need to do the right thing even if it hurts." Her lips pressed against my temple. "I won't wait up, just in case it goes really, really well."

With a laugh, I walked out to the SUV waiting to bring me to Callum's apartment. The trip was under five minutes. Not even long enough to let me catch my breath. I couldn't get over how incredibly close he lived to me. What were the chances? If I had started my job at Good Music a month or two later, I might have never run into him.

Maybe this was fate stepping in, giving us closure. Except this didn't really feel like closure. The fissure in my heart from the day I'd said goodbye to Callum had been cracked open wide the moment he strolled past me in the lobby without giving me a second glance. And it had only grown wider.

Shadows worshiped Callum. He stood outside his building, waiting for me in the bitter cold. Light illuminated him from the back while darkness claimed his front, dancing over the sharp corners of his jaw and sliding down his straight nose. He stepped forward, and even more darkness moved in on him, until all I could make out was the glow of his blond hair and the broad hand reaching to help me out of the SUV.

"Hi." My heart thrashed like a wild beast in my chest. My stomach churned.

"Hi, Wren." *Rin*. Oh, how I'd miss hearing that.

I swallowed, holding myself together. "You're not wearing a coat." He had that leather jacket on that made him look like he'd stepped out of a James Dean film. It was sexy and made my knees weak, but it wouldn't stand up to a New York winter.

He pulled me toward his building, my hand tucked firmly in his. "You're worried about me again?"

"Anyone would be. It's freezing, Callum. What if you get frostbite and lose a finger? You'll be kicked out of the band and become destitute."

"No, I'd be okay. I'm really good at picking pockets."

I jerked my head to look at him. He was smiling kind of softly at me. "You won't be so good at it without a finger or two."

He opened the door to the brightly lit lobby, allowing me to enter ahead of him. "You've got me," he murmured as I passed.

I shivered even though I was bundled warmly in my coat and scarf. "I do?"

The doorman at the front desk nodded to Callum and gave me a halfway friendly smile.

"Good evening, Mr. Rose. Madam." He tipped his hat. "Have a lovely night."

I barely got a wave in as I was led past so quickly, I had to jog a little to keep up. Callum's growl was low, but I didn't miss it.

"Mmm." His arm pressed against my shoulder as we waited for the elevator. "I'll have to think of a new profession besides pickpocketing and playin' bass once I lose my fingers."

I craned my neck to look up at him. "I would suggest basketball, but you probably need all your fingers for that too. Honestly, you should just wear a coat and gloves."

"You're really cute when you're concerned." He brought my gloved hand up to his cheek and rubbed it in tight circles. "I'll just borrow your heat."

"No. I need it. You can't have it."

"Don't be greedy, Wren. I'll share anything of mine you want."

I laughed. "Except your body heat because you have none. I can feel your cold cheeks through my leather gloves. That's never a good sign."

The elevator doors slid open. "Come on." My hand was still in his, and he didn't seem to want to let go. And I was okay with that. Since I knew all of this was on borrowed time, I let myself live a little fantasy, just for a while.

As the elevator rose, Callum's gaze locked on me. He was studying me unabashedly. It didn't exactly make me uncomfortable, but it wasn't something I was used to. My skin tingled and felt a size too small. My free hand fidgeted with my buttons, then my collar, the one he held itching to move.

"Thank you for sending the car all week. It's been really nice."

"You shouldn't be riding public transportation. It's not safe for a woman on her own."

I would have rolled my eyes if he hadn't sounded so earnest. "I've been riding the subway since I was a teenager. The worst thing that ever happened to me was stepping in a puddle of vomit. Everything else is just background noise."

His hand tightened, and the elevator door opened. His arm shot out to keep the door open, but he didn't budge. "Do men speak to you? Do they say things?"

"Of course. I saw a guy catcall a grandma last month. I mean, she was well kept for eighty, but she was still eighty. She had a headful of white hair and a face full of wrinkles. Not to mention her orthopedic shoes." Oh jeez, I was rambling.

His brow furrowed. "What does that mean?"

"It means it's not a big deal. It's part of being a woman in a city. It happens. I ignore it." I stepped out of the elevator and tugged him with me. "Stop worrying about me."

He took my face in his cold hands. "If I told you to stop worryin' about me, would you?"

"No." I had years of experience thinking, dreaming, and worrying about Callum Rose. It would take more than a simple order to unlearn such behavior.

"Then don't ask me to stop worryin' about you, Wren. I'm going to. And I'm going to keep sendin' a car to take you to work, so don't fight me."

I didn't fight him then and there because…well, after tonight, I really doubted he'd care about my transportation. He'd probably rue the day he ever answered my first email, if he didn't already.

"Okay," I whispered. "I won't ask."

With a sharp nod, he led me to the end of a sleek hallway dotted with only a couple doors. I'd barely taken in the surroundings before he swept me into his apartment and unbuttoned my coat. He was meticulous, slotting each button through its corresponding hole carefully, all the way to where they ended mid-thigh, then he slid it off my shoulders and hung it in a small closet by the front door. His own jacket was haphazardly hooked on the doorknob.

Callum placed his hand on the center of my back, ushering me deeper into the apartment. My mouth went dry as I tried to formulate what I was going to say. As if I hadn't thought about this nonstop all week.

His apartment was stark. Barely furnished, nothing on the walls, almost no color. There was a low, gray couch with a glass coffee table in front of it. A stand holding a row of guitars was propped beside a black console table with a small TV on top. The windows were almost floor to ceiling, but they were covered in those temporary paper blinds builders put in new houses. The floor was covered with a plush, creamy carpet.

"How long have you lived here?" I asked.

"Three years," he replied.

My gaze swept over his as I searched for anything personal. I guessed the instruments counted, but there was nothing else. We were standing in a sea of white, gray, and a speck of black. "Wow. It looks like you just moved in."

His mouth twitched. "I don't spend a lot of time here. Things aren't important to me and neither are homes. It's a place to sleep."

"Says the rich musician," I murmured. When his eyebrows raised, crinkling his forehead, my hands shot to my mouth to cover it. I was supposed to be here to confess my sins, not insult my victim.

He bowed his head and released a low chuckle. "You aren't wrong." His phone chimed from inside his pocket. He took it out and tapped a hurried message. "Our dinner's here. I hope you like Thai."

"I—I do." I was supposed to be coming clean, not actually eating dinner. What was I doing? My palms were itchy and sweaty. My mouth was so dry, my tongue kept sticking to the roof.

"Good. I don't like anyone comin' up here, so I'm goin' to the lobby to get it." He touched my hair. He was always touching my hair. "Stay here. Snoop around if you want. When you're done, please feel free to find what you'd like to drink in the kitchen."

My giggle came out choked. If I sounded nervous or suspicious, he didn't react, leaving me in his apartment. For someone who grew up with criminals, he was far too trusting. I mean, I could have stolen his underwear and sold it to his crazed fans for a mint...if I were that type. Which I wasn't.

My thirst overpowered my need to snoop, so I headed to the kitchen. It was more of the same in this room: cream, gray, black, with a dash of stainless steel in the mix. The cups were easy to find since the cabinets had glass fronts. I filled it up at the sink and drained it quickly.

The sole splash of color in the whole apartment caught my eye. A tiny potted plant sat in the corner of the icy white marble countertop. I recognized the painted pot immediately and cradled it in my hand.

"You didn't throw it away," I whispered.

Callum had taken Adam's plant home with him. My heart tripped over itself, and I sighed. Of course he had done something sweet and adorable. That only knotted my stomach up tighter.

A small piece of folded paper fluttered to the ground after it became unstuck from the pot. Stooping down, I picked it up and placed it on the counter. Then I read my name written in messy scrawl on the outside.

Callum had left me a note?

I exchanged the plant for the paper and unfolded it before I could overthink what might be inside.

All the breath left my lungs, his words punching through my chest.

Little Bird,
Don't shrink. I know.
Callum

CHAPTER TWELVE

CALLUM

MY APARTMENT WAS SILENT WHEN I WALKED BACK IN. Squeezing my hand into a fist, the plastic handles from the take-out bag dug into my fingers. She'd either found the note or she hadn't. Anticipation hummed in my veins.

The kitchen was empty. I left the take-out bag on the counter and ventured into the living room. Wren was perched on the edge of the couch, holding a piece of paper in her shaking hand. Her wet eyes searched mine.

"You know?" she rasped.

I lowered my chin. "Yeah. I know."

Her small mouth fell open, but she quickly closed it. "I was going to tell you tonight. I've been rehearsing all the things I wanted to say. I forgot them as soon as I got here, but I promise I was going to tell you. I've been hating myself for not saying anything, but I just—"

"So tell me." I crossed my arms over my chest. "Tell me what you were goin' to say, Wren."

She shuddered. "I really like how you say my name."

"I like sayin' it."

Her chest rose and fell as she took deep breaths. I watched her. She fascinated me, up close like this. After so many notes passed back and forth between us, being in the same room was still a novelty. An addicting one.

"How did you know it was me?" she asked absently, rubbing her cheek, barely looking at me. "Did I give myself away? I didn't think..."

I blinked at her. She was more adorable than I'd imagined she'd be. When she panicked and got shy, her cheeks lit up like cherries.

"How many five-foot-tall women named Wren who live with their great-aunt Jenny in Queens and say 'holy granola' with a New Jersey accent do you think there are?"

She'd dropped so many hints, I had wondered a couple times if she had wanted me to figure it out on my own. I thought it was more likely she simply wasn't aware I had soaked up every single detail my little bird had ever written to me and kept them in the forefront of my mind. She had thought I wouldn't know her anywhere.

Her breath came out in a heavy gust, and when I sat down on the couch beside her, she shifted her body to look at me with her impossibly wide eyes.

"Okay, wow. I am terrible at subterfuge." She swiped the back of her hand over her forehead. "I really was going to tell you tonight."

I cocked my head. "I believe you."

Her hands were tiny and soft looking, always moving, fidgeting with her clothes, touching her face or hair. I warred between wanting to grab them, hold them, still them, and following their erratic path, touching every place she did. For now, I pressed them down to her lap. She sucked in a breath that shot me straight in the groin. I liked that sound even more than I expected.

"Should I start?" she asked.

"Please do."

"Were you angry when you first saw me?" Her hand turned up under mine, her fingers sliding along my palm. "Are you angry now?"

I closed my hand around hers, keeping it still. "I've been angry for a long time, Wren. But not so much now."

"Okay." She tried to move the hand under mine. When that didn't work, she used the other to tuck her already tucked hair. "I was going to come to see you in New Jersey, like I said I would, but I got scared. I thought you would think I was ugly and fat and you'd be disappointed *I* was the girl you'd been writing to and...I have a lot of baggage and my self-esteem had pretty much bottomed out at that point. So, I went down to Maryland to visit my cousin, and we went to the Swerve Tour there, a week before the Jersey show. I scrounged up all my savings and bought a backstage pass."

My stomach clenched tighter and tighter with every word that passed her little pink lips. All of this was brand new information.

"I don't know if you remember when I went to prom and then dropped off the face of the planet for a while." Her eyes lifted to mine. They were shining, but she wasn't crying. I didn't know what I'd do if she cried.

"Of course I remember." She'd sent me into a blind panic when she went silent on me. I had broken a knuckle when I punched drywall only to find a stud right behind it.

"Right." Her gaze fell to my hand on hers again. "Well, I went to prom alone. And that took major guts. I was there for a while, sitting at a table by myself, when Karthik Singh...he was my first kiss—"

"I remember that too, Wren." I knew my instincts about that Karthik kid had been right. He should have been dead the second he looked at her. He never should have had the chance to touch her, least of all hurt her.

"Well, Karthik invited me to sit with his friends. So, I did, and everything was fine. They were talking about random crushes and hookups they'd had. Obviously, I had nothing to contribute. Then the subject changed to a bet they had all made, to hook up with the person they were assigned by the rest of the group. One girl practically gagged about having to make out with David Watanabe, which, honestly, I understood. He only ever talked about his favorite serial killers and never brushed his teeth. I laughed too, even though I felt pretty awful and gross about the whole thing. But then…"

She drew in a deep breath, and everything went quiet, like the moment before a tornado touched down. The seconds prior to a nuclear explosion. The last inhale before plunging into an icy abyss.

"Then it came out that I had been a dare for Karthik. He'd never liked me, but *everyone* knew I liked him, so he used that. I'd won him twenty dollars. *Twenty freaking dollars.* That was all my humiliation had been worth to him, and he wanted me to know about it. Him and all his friends laughed in my face while they told me I was no better than the serial killer lover with foul breath. And it got around prom. Everyone knew by Monday. If it hadn't been almost the end of the school year, I would have dropped out and—*ow!* You're hurting me, Callum."

She shoved at my hand, which had tightened around hers so hard, my knuckles had gone white. I let her go with a hiss. She brought her hand to her chest to cradle and peered at me with an expression so forlorn and vulnerable, it took everything in my power to stay there and not tear my entire building down brick by brick.

Those were the kind of eyes Wren had. The kind that would make a man destroy the world for her if she told him the world had done her wrong. One glance from those oversized, liquid amber eyes, and I was on the edge of forgetting the way she'd left me alone without a backward glance.

"I'm sorry that happened to you," I gritted out. "You give me their names, I'll destroy Karthik and every kid involved."

She choked out a laugh, obviously thinking I was joking, and that was probably better in the long run. If Wren had any idea what went on inside my head, she wouldn't be sitting here allowing me to touch her.

"Please don't. I've let it go. High school isn't important anymore. I only told you that story to explain where my head was when I went backstage."

I rubbed between my brows. "I don't understand."

"I just...I don't know." She shook her head. "I don't know why I did it other than to confirm what I thought was true. That you wouldn't be into a girl like me. And maybe our relationship was only friendship for you, but it was a lot more than that for me. I *wanted* more than that with you while, at the same time, telling myself it would never, ever happen."

Her eyes flicked to mine, and my mouth flattened. I needed her to get to the point, not draw it out with questions that shouldn't have needed to be asked.

She took another deep breath, her shoulders lifting then slowly falling. "I went backstage at the Maryland show and asked to meet you. You were in a corner by yourself, drinking a bottle of water. I remember you were wearing a pair of gray trousers and a white T-shirt. Your hair was pulled back in a bun. You looked like you were a thousand miles away, and you probably were. I wanted to hug you so badly, but obviously, I didn't. Your handler or PR person, whoever she was, took me to you. She told you I wanted to meet you. I was shaking like a leaf I was so nervous. And you—" Her teeth practically impaled her bottom lip.

"What'd I do, Wren?"

"You looked through us both at first, like we weren't even there. Then the PR woman snapped at you to get your attention. She told you again I was a big fan and wanted to meet you. You looked right at me, Callum. At my shoes, my hair, my face, and you said no."

I raised my eyebrows. "No?"

She nodded. "You looked me over and told me no. You did not want to meet me."

Leaning forward, I braced my elbows on my knees and dragged my fingers through the sides of my hair. I had no memory of any of this, but it wasn't a surprise. Iris, Roddy, and Adam were good with our fans. They took pictures, signed autographs, answered questions, while I drifted along in the background. I had no interest in talking to strangers when the only thing we had in common was their love for my music. I appreciated their existence…from a distance.

"Did you tell me who you were?" I asked, even though I knew she hadn't.

"No. I didn't get the chance. You took one look at me and dismissed me. I wasn't even good enough for an autograph from you. I was absolutely gutted."

"I dismiss everyone. Stone cold, remember? How could you be surprised you got the same treatment I give everyone when I didn't know it was you? Were you givin' me a test you knew I wouldn't pass? Was that what it was, Wren?"

Those eyes of hers were more than wet. They were brimming with tears. My body tensed for the first one to spill, but she swiped them away with the sleeve of her sweater before that happened.

"Maybe it was," she whispered. "I was so low back then…the way you looked at me, like I was beneath you, brought me right back to Karthik Singh and being the laughingstock of my school. I couldn't stand for you to look at me in that way when you knew who I really was. I just couldn't do it. It would have ruined me for good."

"You should have told me." I was gruff with her, but I was having an internal battle. One side of me was so fucking angry she'd done this to us. The other side understood being low like that, feeling unlovable, outside of the norm. But rising above every fucking thing else, all I wanted was to protect Wren.

"I know. I'm so sorry, Callum. I was depressed and my life was a huge mess, more than I ever let on in our emails. I ended up making some terrible, self-destructive choices. There was no sun for me for a long time, and I convinced myself you were better off not knowing me at all anymore. I don't know how to apologize and show you how deeply I regret ghosting you. I don't think there are words for that. I don't know them if there are."

Yanking at my hair again, I stared at her, trying to figure her out, but I couldn't.

"I made up a lot of scenarios of what happened, you know. I had plenty of time to do it. They were nothin' close to this. If I had known you were within reach, I would have gone out of my mind." I huffed. "Well, more out of my mind than I already was."

"I'm sorry," she whispered.

"I thought it was me." I scoffed, almost laughing. "I guess it was, in the end. I'm such an asshole, I sent you spinning. If I'd taken one second to pay attention to a girl I thought was a stranger, I would have realized it was you."

She shook her head. "No. I won't let you blame yourself. You were my very best friend and I set you up to fail." Her bottom lip was trembling. There was a red mark in the center where her teeth had dug in. Without thinking, I reached for her and pressed my thumb against it. Her warm breath floated over my skin.

"You did do that. You were my brave girl, but you couldn't be brave for me." I took her chin in my hand, gentle in how I handled her this time. "The first time I saw you, when I knew it was you, it clicked. Of course this is what you look like. How could you look like anything else? I would never have been disappointed, Wren, but you didn't know that. You couldn't have known that."

Her lip began to tremble again. Wren wore sadness adorably. It drew me in, needing to see it up close. "No, I didn't know that, and even if you'd told me that, I wouldn't have believed it. I wasn't in a place to believe *anyone* would be attracted to me, let alone *you*."

"Why not me?"

"Because you were important to me. You meant everything. And...you're a rock star. Holy granola, don't you get that? You're a beautiful, talented rock star coveted by women everywhere you go."

Letting my hand fall from her chin, I waved her off, dismissing all but her first two sentences. "Why are you using past tense?"

"Um..." She tucked her hair twice. "Because it's been three and a half years since we've spoken. I'll treasure what we had forever, but we're not best friends anymore. Too much has happened to call us that. I don't even know if we were back then. We never said it."

"We were."

Her lips parted in an O. "Okay. We were."

At least we agreed on one thing. At least I knew I wasn't fully crazy and our relationship had actually had value to her. A dark corner of my mind had always whispered words on a screen didn't equate to anything more than what they were. They weren't a connection. They weren't feelings. They weren't real. But I knew that wasn't true. Nothing had ever been as real as Wren Anderson.

"You're still important to me."

"Thank you," she said.

I laughed under my breath. "You're welcome."

"Did you know who I was at the party?" she asked.

"Yes."

She nodded, her nostrils flaring a bit. "But you let me be with Adam."

"At the party, I didn't know what I wanted with you yet. But Adam's not gonna have you. As far as I'm concerned, no one else is."

Her hand drifted from her chest to her forehead, cupping it as her head bowed.

"Are you saying *you're* going to have me?" Her voice had gone tiny and meek.

"Yes." No sense in beating around the bush and pretending those weren't my intentions. Wren was mine. She'd been mine since she first wrote to me, even if neither of us had known it at the time.

"I don't know you, Callum. I'm not...I can't..."

I dragged her hand from her face and lifted her chin. "Don't shrink."

Her mouth twitched. "That's really strange to hear you say in person with your Alabama accent. The voice I had in my head wasn't anything like this."

I wasn't amused like she was. I didn't find humor in her telling me she didn't know me. There was nothing funny about having the image of Adam's lips touching hers forever burned into my memories.

That wasn't her fault. It was mine. I'd let that go too far, but I wouldn't make that mistake again.

"Come here." I laid my hands on my thighs, showing her where I wanted her.

Her pale brows furrowed. "What? I just got through telling you I don't know you anymore and now you want me to sit in your lap?"

"Yes." I held my hand out for her. She didn't budge. "Come here, Wren."

"Okay."

Slowly, she crawled across the wide cushion separating us. I could have scooped her up and taken her once she was within reach, but the unpracticed sway of her round, wide hips froze me in place. How could she have thought I would be disappointed that she was my little bird?

She kneeled beside me. "I'm here."

"No." My arm circled her waist and tugged her until she was sprawled against me. "Now you're here. Sit."

"I'm not a dog." Her lips were quirking again. She obviously wasn't offended by my abrupt orders.

"I know that. You're a little bird."

She perched on my legs like she was seconds from springing up and making a run for it. I kept my arm around her middle, securing her in place. She was small, but solid, every bit of her full and convex, and I liked the feel of her weight on me.

"What is this?" she asked.

"I don't like you sayin' you don't know me."

She sighed and brought her fingers up to the scruff on my jaw. "I know parts of you, just like you know parts of me. But I was able to hide a lot, and I'm certain you were too."

"I didn't hide anything."

Her eyes flared. "Well, I had no idea you were a voyeur."

"If you'd asked, I would have told you. I'll never lie to you."

"Okay."

I rubbed my face into her hand. Her short nails gently scratched my cheek, and it felt almost as good as holding her in my lap.

"What do you think of me?" I asked.

Leaning back, her brow pinched in confusion. "What do you mean?"

I waved my hand in front of my face and torso. "Do I live up to your expectations, or are you disappointed? Were you disappointed when you saw me backstage?"

Sometimes feelings eluded me. Expressions went right over my head. Subtle hints were lost on me. But Wren wore her feelings all over her face. Every thought and emotion was there, in the pinch of her brow, the parting of her lips, the flush of her skin. Right now, she looked confused and a little pissed off, with parted lips and cherry cheeks.

"I knew what you looked like, Callum. It wasn't a secret."

"But not up close. You'd never heard me speak or touched my skin. I want to know if I'm livin' up to your expectations."

"What if you're not?" The question was a challenge, but her face was so sweet and earnest, it didn't feel that way.

"Then I'll fix whatever you don't like."

She let out a short giggle. "It's that simple?"

"Why not?"

Her hand landed on my chest, barely skimming my T-shirt. "You don't have anything to fix. You're exactly like I'd hoped. Well, no. You're better." Her teeth caught her bottom lip again. I used my thumb to free it, and her eyes flicked to mine. "I'm not going to ask you if you're disappointed. I know I'm not perfect and the list of things I need to fix is stupid long, but I don't want to know—"

I covered her mouth with my hand.

"No."

"No?" she mumbled.

"No. There's no list, nothin' to fix. I like everything about the way you look and even more, I like how you feel when I'm touchin' you. You smell like the very first summer on earth, when life was fresh and clean and bright. Your hair is pure gold and sunshine, and your eyes would bring a man with half a brain and a fraction of a heart to his knees if you turned on their full power." I ran my hand up her side, skimming the side of her breast without going any farther. "Ever since I had you in my lap at the party, I've been dreamin' of gettin' you back here so I can touch more of your soft little body. There is nothing about you that's disappointing, Wren, other than you runnin' away from me for three and a half years with no plans to return."

Her throat bobbed as she swallowed hard. "No one's ever said anything like that to me."

I cupped her breast, giving it a light squeeze before dropping my hand to her stomach. "I should hope not. And if someone does after this, I will feed him his dick."

She giggled again, and I knew she thought I was kidding, but I wasn't. I'd come to a decision about Wren Anderson, and I wasn't going to waver. She was mine, and that would not change. If I had to convince her, I would. There wasn't an outcome that didn't include us together.

Her lips touched my cheek. "I thought you didn't talk," she murmured beside my skin.

"I don't, unless it's important." My fingers wove through her silky hair. "I told you, you're important to me."

"I want to believe that, Callum." Her nose nuzzled into my scruff. "Can we go slow? Just a little. There's so much we know about one another, but so much we don't."

"Does that mean you don't want me to hold you?"

"No." She shook her head. "No, I like this. But I was thinking we could maybe have the dinner you promised and not talk about shoving dicks down anyone's throat for the rest of the evening."

"I was gonna chop it up and sauté it. No shovin'."

She snorted a laugh, and this time I was actually joking, so I laughed with her. And I agreed it was time to dial down the intensity for a few minutes, so I led her into the kitchen where we made plates of Thai food. We sat beside each other on stools at the island, eating and talking about The Seasons Change. Wren had a lot of questions about touring and what it was like to be well known. I enjoyed answering her. It reminded me of her early letters, and knowing she was, at least partly, who she'd always said she was, filled me with a deep satisfaction.

It was near midnight when I buttoned her up in her coat at my front door, hating to let her go, but knowing I had to. For now.

Her fingers curled around my wrists when I got to the button beneath her chin.

"Thank you, Callum. For dinner, for forgiving me, for everything you said."

My fingers slid into the back of her hair, cupping her crown in my palm. "I need to know when I'll see you next."

Her lips flattened. "Well, I don't know, but—"

"Tomorrow."

"I have things I have to do." My fingers curled in her hair, tugging gently, but with firmness that couldn't be ignored. "Are you going to be murder-fighting again? I might be free to watch you spill some blood."

"For you, I'd murder-fight any time you want me to."

Her eyes landed on mine, so wide and open, like twin planets floating side by side, naked for all to see. The next second, her arms were wrapped around my middle and her face was pressed against my chest as she sighed. My arms responded without a clear thought from me, holding her against me, and my head dipped to bury my nose in her hair.

"This is what I wanted to do that day. I wanted to hug you so tight." Her voice was muffled, but I heard her loud and clear.

"I would have really fuckin' liked that, Wren."

Her head tipped back. Her lips spread into a tremulous smile. "I want to see you tomorrow, but it can't be for long."

"I guess I'll have to take what I can get then." I touched her lips with my fingertip. "If I kiss you right now, I won't let you go."

"Then you better not." Her tongue peaked out to lick where my finger had been. "We're supposed to be going slow anyway. This is hello, not goodbye. We have time."

"I like that." I touched my lips to the top of her head, then stepped back. Not because I wanted to, but out of necessity. "Let's go. The car's waitin'."

Downstairs, I helped Wren into the SUV then climbed in after her. She started, but quickly scooted over to give me room to sit.

"You're coming too?"

"Why not? It gives me a couple more minutes with you."

With a smile, she slid over so her thigh was aligned with mine and rested her head on my shoulder. I took her hand and stacked our palms on top of each other. We sat that way in silence for the short ride, then I walked Wren to her door.

She shoved me away as soon as she got it unlocked. "Go, before you freeze."

Chuckling, I kissed the top of her head again. "All right. Go to bed, I'll go warm up in the car."

With a wave, she stepped inside, and I waited until I heard the door lock, then I headed back to the SUV.

"Home, Mr. Rose?" the driver asked.

"In a minute." We were double parked, but it was late enough, it didn't really matter. "Just sit here unless we have to move."

I looked at the townhouse Wren had lived in with her great-aunt Jenny for a little over three and a half years. She'd moved in a month or two after she'd stopped emailing me.

Her absence had taken me to a dark place. One of despondence and self-hatred. I never blamed Wren for leaving me, even though I'd been angry at her for the way she'd done it. I told myself it had been my neediness that drove her away. I had pushed her too hard. I'd misread the situation and her feelings didn't actually reflect mine. I told myself a lot. It took me six months to shake myself out of my stupor and into action.

When I told Wren it hadn't been difficult to find her, I'd been truthful. Three years ago, I asked my cousin, James, a tech genius, to trace her IP address, which led me to her parents. They were too happy to inform me their 'slutty daughter' was living with her aunt because she was no longer welcome in their home. It didn't take much digging to track down Jenny Malkovich in Queens.

Three years ago, I sat outside Wren's townhouse in my car and saw her for the first time. Sunlight loved her. It rested on her copper hair like a halo and flushed her cheeks rosy. I'd nearly swallowed my tongue when I'd caught sight of her swollen belly. She was so short, she had been pretty much all tits and baby.

She was the most beautiful girl I'd ever laid eyes on, even with another man's baby in her belly.

Betrayal had burned through my blood that day, but once I had found my little bird, I couldn't stop watching her. She hadn't been mine anymore, and the evidence growing inside her body reminded me she never really had been.

I was there the day she brought her son home from the hospital after a month-long stay in the NICU. I'd watched her take her stroller on endless walks through her neighborhood, and I'd witnessed her sit down on park benches and sob her heart out. There were times I almost stepped in because it became too much even for me to bear, but she always pulled herself together and moved on.

Over the years, I considered taking her and keeping her. More than considered, I'd planned it in my head. It wasn't rational, but it soothed me and allowed me to keep my distance.

Wren made it easy to watch her. She was a devoted mother and student. When she wasn't in school, she was with her child. Her shadow had finally found her, and she was so busy with her life, she'd never once checked behind her to notice.

As time passed, our connection should have withered, and maybe it did on her end. My obsession calmed, but it wasn't ending. Wren was mine to protect. Always.

Helping her find a job at Good Music had been a small part of that. Putting her in my path had been another. What I hadn't expected was my own reaction to being in the same space as her and letting her finally see me. That first day, I couldn't even look at her. It took seeing her in Adam's arms to break me out of the chains that had been holding me back, and finally, after years of watching, to claim my little bird as my own.

Wren's light turned off in her bedroom. I laid my head back on the rest and closed my eyes. She was safe and secure. For now, that would be enough.

"Take me home."

CHAPTER THIRTEEN

WREN

I SHOULD HAVE BEEN ON MY WAY TO GROCERY SHOP. It was what I did on Sundays. Instead, I was stepping inside Callum's Krav Maga studio to watch some murder-fighting.

At once, I was hit by the smell of bodies and sweat and an underlying hint of lemon cleaning product. A class was taking place on the mat closest to the window, but Callum wasn't among that group this time. He'd texted he would be on the mats in the back of the studio, which was far larger than I had thought from peering inside the window.

I hung my coat on a rack in the small lobby by the door and made my way on the path skating around the mats to the rear of the studio. A swarm of neurotic butterflies filled my stomach. I was more nervous now that Callum knew who I was than I was before. That could have had something to do with the way he'd declared me to be his last night. Crazy as it was, I had liked hearing that. But holy granola, I had not been prepared for that reaction out of him.

This thing between us needed to be slow and thought out. If it had just been me to consider, I might have dove headfirst. But I had Ezra, and he was my top priority. I couldn't be a normal twenty-two-year-old running into the arms of my rock star fantasy. Especially since my rock star fantasy didn't even know my boy existed. I promised myself that would be rectified soon.

A small group was circled around a mat in the back, watching with rapt attention as two men sparred. Callum was dressed in black like he'd been last week, but now, he had padded gloves on his hands and shin guards. His opponent wore Adidas athletic gear instead of a uniform and was a few inches shorter, but he made up for it in being broad and powerful.

I stood behind a row of men in black uniforms, a knot in my throat as I watched. Callum's expression was vicious, and so was his attack. He followed Adidas around the mat relentlessly, kicking and jabbing. His opponent fought back just as hard, landing blows on Callum's torso and face.

I winced every time Callum was hit, but when his jabs landed true, I had to hold myself back from cheering. Violence wasn't the answer, but Callum might have been able to convince me otherwise.

The fighters grappled until Callum flipped Adidas over and they both went down to the mat. Callum rolled to his back, wrapping his long legs around the other man's waist and throwing punches at his stomach and shoulders.

Someone called out for them to reset. Callum and Adidas hopped up from the mat and started over. Punching, kicking, going for the throat, rolling on the ground, unrelenting in their determination to kill each other.

It was so freaking sexy, I almost couldn't stand to watch another minute.

Then, Adidas and Callum went down again, both on their backs. Adidas had his arms locked around Callum's throat and his legs were holding his waist. Callum braced his feet flat on the floor, bucking upward and breaking free of Adidas's legs, then he twisted his body around and rolled, sliding out of the choke hold. He laid on top of Adidas's prone form, fully pinning him to the mat.

My pulse fluttered wildly when time was called and they walked off the mat, letting a new pair take the center. Callum stooped to grab a towel from the floor and wiped his sweaty forehead. No one spoke to him, though more than a few people were looking at him.

I stayed half hidden, twisting my cardigan with my fingers. After everything, I shouldn't have been nervous. He had stated in no uncertain terms he wanted me, and he'd been more than pleased when I'd suggested for me to come here. But waiting for him to see me felt like the first time all over again. The horror show that was my mind kept running images of him walking right past me again.

He didn't let me wonder for long. One last wipe of his face on the towel and his eyes were on me as he skirted around the mat to get to me. As soon as I was within his reach, one long arm shot out, snagging me around the waist and pulling me into his sweaty chest.

"Why are you hidin' over here, Wren?"

Rin. Holy granola, how had I gone all my life without hearing him say my name like that?

"I was worried about blood splatter. It's so hard to get out of wool." I reached for his face, skimming my fingertips over a red spot on his cheek. "Aren't you supposed to be pulling punches?"

He leaned into my hand until I was cupping his rough jaw. "That's the idea, but I've never been the kind to be afraid of a little pain. That's why I like to spar with Gregor. He doesn't know the meaning of takin' it easy."

"So, you're telling me he beat you? Maybe I should go find him." With a grin, I moved a fraction of an inch before I was tugged back firmly against Callum.

"You really want me to kill him?"

I shook my head. "No, I don't. I'm teasing. I never thought I'd be into watching a fight, but that was..." I sighed, and Callum's lips tipped.

"Are you a bloodthirsty little bird?"

"Maybe I am."

He dipped his head to nuzzle his nose in my hair and inhaled. The pained groan that came from him landed directly between my thighs. "You smell delicious. Wait for me to get cleaned up?"

"All right. I have to go grocery shopping, so I can't really stay for long."

"Just wait, Wren." He took another whiff of my hair and backed away. "Wait."

I nodded and pointed to the floor. His brow furrowed, and he lingered, almost glaring at me, then he nodded back and disappeared into the locker room.

I did stay in that spot for a minute or two, but then I felt too conspicuous waiting in the middle of all the action, so I returned to the lobby and grabbed my coat from the rack. I had just buttoned the second to the last button when rough hands grabbed my shoulder and turned me around.

"You were gone. I told you to stay." Callum slipped the final button in place and tucked my hair behind my ear. "I thought you left."

"I promised I'd stay." His cheeks were red and scrubbed clean, his hair freshly pulled back. He'd thrown a black hoodie over his uniform, and a duffel bag was clutched in his tight fist. "I came to see you, you know. Why would I leave?"

Exhaling, he shook his head. His hand dragged down my arm to thread our fingers together, then he pushed out the door into the cold. Callum was lost in his head, pulling me along in the direction of the grocery store.

His strides were long, eating up a block in no time. I took four steps for each of his, basically jogging to keep up with him. It wasn't fun. My chest ached from sucking in the icy air, and Callum had no awareness of my struggle.

"Hey, slow down. My legs are half the length of yours." I tapped his arm at the same time I stumbled over my own feet.

He caught me in an instant, dropping his duffel to wrap me in his hold. He buried his face in my hair as he embraced me.

"I'm sorry, Wren. I wasn't thinkin'."

"Hey." I cupped his cheeks with both of my hands, bringing his face closer to mine. "I'm fine, I'm just short. I know I should've stayed where I said I would, but I wasn't leaving. I promise."

Blue eyes burned into mine, old sorrow and new desire blending so thoroughly, it was hard to tell one from the other.

"Wren," he murmured a moment before his mouth was on mine. There was nothing slow or tentative about the way Callum Rose kissed me. He took my head in his hands, tilting it to the side, and speared his tongue into my mouth. I whimpered, not because he was forceful, but from his desperation leaking into me. I felt his frustration with me and his fear I'd walk away again.

"You taste as delicious as you smell." His lips skimmed mine, nipping and sucking like we were in the privacy of his home, not on a sidewalk in Queens on a Sunday afternoon. "I'm not letting you go now."

On instinct, I bit his bottom lip, and he growled, holding me even tighter against him.

"I'm not going anywhere," I breathed.

"Come to my place." His hands skimmed down my back. If I were any taller, he'd probably be palming my butt. "Come, Wren."

Someone honked and yelled something in Spanish. I had an idea of what they were saying, and my cheeks burned, but Callum didn't even flinch.

"I can't."

"Why?" he demanded.

"It's too fast, Callum." I pushed up on my toes and kissed the corner of his downturned mouth. "Can't we just take a walk?"

He kissed me again, this time slower, his tongue dancing with mine instead of dominating it. I'd kissed exactly three people in my life, and I barely remembered the second one. I would never forget this kiss. Not only because it was with Callum, but also because I felt it all the way to my toes. He took over not just my mouth, but my entire being. That was why it was hard to pull away, but I did.

Slowly.

Reluctantly.

"We're going to end up on your fan websites. All your groupies are going to want to claw my eyes out."

He pecked my nose before pulling back. "Good. I want everyone to know you're mine." He took my hand in his and picked up his duffel. "Let's go for a walk. I've been waitin' for this for a long, long time."

This time, he tempered his pace to match mine, and since I was a foot and a half shorter than him, he had to go *really* slow.

"How long have you been practicing Krav Maga?" I asked.

"Three years, officially. I had an uncle who was in the army in Israel and was trained in it. He and I sparred a lot growin' up. He beat the shit out of me until I got bigger, then I beat the shit out of him."

"Your family's Israeli?"

"No." His small smile seemed indulgent. "He wasn't blood related. I had a lot of aunts and uncles. I can't even tell you who was a real relative."

"On your commune?"

He chuckled. "No, I didn't live on a commune. We were travelers, remember? Caravaners who followed fairs and carnivals, performing and thievin'."

Callum had told me a little about how he'd grown up, and some I'd learned through Googling The Traveling Roses. They were a group of ten or fifteen adults and an unknown number of kids who sang folk songs and lived off the grid. The adults took care of each other's kids like family. The article had made them seem like they were living a whimsical, alternative lifestyle, but Callum's depiction had hinted at something much darker.

"Do you know if they're still traveling and thieving?"

His hand tightened around mine, and he pulled me deeper into his side. "Don't know the details. I cut ties with them when I left at eighteen. My brother and sister came around a couple years ago lookin' for money."

I wrinkled my nose. "Were you close to them growing up?"

"I was, until I left. I would've given them money if they'd only asked. They didn't just ask, though. They tried to blackmail me, threatening to tell the press how I grew up."

He peered down at me, and I grinned back at him. "Did you tell them to go fuck themselves?"

He stopped walking entirely and stared at me without blinking for several hammering beats of my heart. "It's fuckin' adorable when you cuss. It doesn't even make sense comin' out of your sweet little mouth, but damn is it cute."

He dipped down and touched his lips to mine. This time, he kissed me slowly, licking my *cussin' tongue* and sucking on my *adorable lips*. When he let go, I chased him with my mouth until he was kissing me again, sighing in pure bliss.

"Yeah, Little Bird. I told them to go fuck themselves. I don't care what anyone thinks of me." He pecked my nose like he did before. "Except you."

"Did they sell your story?"

"Nope. No way they wanted to call attention to themselves."

The grocery store was in front of us, and my stomach dipped. I didn't really want to say goodbye, but I needed to get going and shop for my kid.

"Well, I think you're a good kisser and I like you." I tugged on the strings of his hoodie. "You could dress warmer, though. I think that's your biggest flaw."

"I like you worryin' about me." He started for the door of the store, and I had no choice but to follow since he still had my hand tucked in his.

"You're coming in?" I asked.

"Yeah. I'm takin' my time with you where I can get it."

Callum walked beside me while I pushed the cart, throwing in my usual produce and essentials. I hadn't brought my own cart to get my bags back home, so this would have to be a lighter trip, which was just as well, since there was no way Callum actually wanted to be here. Although, he seemed pretty content to be with me, just as he'd said. Fortunately, he didn't question me tossing in Ez's favorite snacks and cereal. I would tell him soon, but not now. Not when I'd already told him so much and was just getting him back.

When I headed toward the register, Callum frowned. "This is all you're buyin'?"

"Yeah. I didn't want to bring my cart to the studio. But that's fine, this will get us through a few days. Jenny can go during the week since her schedule's more flexible."

When I checked out, Callum tossed reusable shopping bags on the scanner without saying a word. They were the nice kind, canvas with thick handles. Out of my budget, but I didn't protest. When the total came up at the end, he nudged me aside and shoved his credit card in the machine.

"Thank you." I knocked my forehead on his arm. "You didn't have to do that."

"You're welcome." He tucked his card in his wallet, then pressed a kiss to my crown. "I did it because I wanted to. That's all."

"I know. It was very sweet of you." I also had a feeling he'd hate it if I'd fought him on it, so I didn't. It didn't feel like he was giving me charity in that moment. I felt taken care of, and my chest was warm and fuzzy.

He took three of the bags, and I carried one. The lightest one, containing eggs and bread. We walked just as leisurely back to my house, holding hands and chatting a little, but mostly quietly being together. It was everything I'd wanted with him. The perfect dream dragged from my imagination to reality.

At my door, I turned to him and pushed up on my toes to kiss his chin since that was all I could reach. He placed the bags on my welcome mat and dropped down a step so we were more level.

"Is that better?" he asked.

"Yes." I put my bag down beside his and looped my arms around his neck. "I still can't believe I'm standing here with you."

"I hope you know I'm not goin' anywhere."

"I hope you know I don't want you to. I missed talking to you even more than I realized it. But honestly, this is better. I like seeing your face when I'm talking to you."

His warm breath ghosted across my lips, then he gave me a light kiss. "I missed everything about you, Wren."

"I need to go inside."

He kissed me again, just as light. "Go."

I was surprised he didn't press me to come into the house with me. He didn't even try to carry my grocery bags. He watched me, though. He stood on my steps, cataloging my every move until the very last moment when I finally closed the door between us and leaned my back against it.

Squeezing my eyes shut, I squealed with giddiness.

"That good, huh?"

Jenny was walking toward me with a smirk. She took two of the bags from my hand while I got myself together and kicked off my sneakers.

"Better than good," I answered.

"I'm happy for you, Birdie. When do I get to meet him?"

"Soon. Maybe." *As soon as I tell him about Ezra.*

Callum didn't strike me as a kid person, but maybe he'd be a *my* kid person. Fingers freaking crossed.

———————————

Monday night, I was curled up in bed, reading on my phone, close to falling asleep, when I received a text from Callum. I smiled before I even read it. He'd sent his car for me in the morning and when I left work in the evening, but I hadn't seen him.

Callum: *Are you asleep, Little Bird?*

Me: *Almost. I was reading. Thank you for the ride today.*

Callum: *You're welcome. Did the driver tell you to expect him every day now?*

Me: *He did, which seems like too much, but I won't argue, because I have a feeling I won't win.*

Callum: *It isn't too much. I have a lot of years to make up for with you. And even if I didn't, I don't like you being vulnerable on public transportation. I want you safe.*

Me: *I know. What are you doing?*

Callum: *I was thinking about your sweet lips and the noises you made when I fucked your mouth with my tongue. I'd like to know what noises you make when I put my mouth on your pussy.*

I threw my phone across the bed with a yelp. Holy granola. This man was intense, and he made me blush so hard. But…oh, I thought I liked being talked to like that. It made me feel desired in a way I never had.

Callum: *Has anyone had their mouth there, Wren?*

Me: *No. No one.*

Callum: *Good. I'm going to eat your pussy to make up for all the years you were hiding from me. You know what you could have had for the last three years? I would have been licking you* *every morning and kissing you good night with your taste on my lips.*

Me: *I regret everything I've missed with you, Callum.*

Me: *I want to put my mouth on you too. You like to watch, so you can watch me suck you. You can tell me exactly how you like it, then I'll kiss you good night with your taste on my tongue.*

Callum: *Fuck.*

Me: *Yeah.*

Callum: *You make me want to sneak in your window and make good on this.*

Me: *Would you tie me up and gag me?*

Callum: *I'm so fucking hard right now for you. This wasn't why I texted you, Little Bird.*

Me: *But I like knowing I do that to you.*

Callum: *You make me crazy. I want to do all kinds of crazy things. Tell me when I can see you.*

Me: *Saturday night. Are you going to make good on your teases?*

Callum: *This isn't teasing. This is planning.*

Me: *I can't wait. Not just for the sexy stuff, but to spend more time with you.*

Callum: *God, Wren. You're too fucking sweet for your own good. There's no way I'm giving you up. No way.*

Me: *I don't want you to.*

Callum: *Go to sleep like the good girl you are. You have to wake up early.*

Me: *K. Good night, Callum Rose. Miss you. Xoxo*

Callum: *Good night, Little Bird. x*

CHAPTER FOURTEEN

CALLUM

SHE HAD NO IDEA I WAS BEHIND HER.

I'd gotten good at blending, though it wasn't always the easiest with my height and rising fame. Wren didn't know it, but she was used to my presence. When I wasn't touring, I always found a way to watch her at least once a day.

I wasn't a total psychopath, though. My obsession didn't involve peeking in windows or eating her trash. I didn't jack off into her stolen underwear or dream of making her into a skin suit. Watching Wren live her life soothed me. Knowing she was safe and cared for allowed me to keep my distance.

Now that I could talk to her, inhale her summer scent, touch her sweet skin, I realized I'd been starving for years. The tastes I'd gotten of Wren had only begun to sate me.

Leaning forward, my nose brushed the back of her hair. She stiffened and shuffled a step closer to the person in front of her. Wren was such a creature of habit, she'd only been at her new job three weeks and had already developed a routine. Coffee shop at twelve thirty, followed by eating her brown-bagged lunch in the park, and back at her desk by one thirty. I hadn't even had to follow her to end up in line behind her today.

"Little Bird," I whispered. "Don't try to get away from me."

Her shoulders jumped, then she whirled around, already smiling. "You scared the shit out of me, sir." Her lips spread into a wide grin, and a giggle bubbled out. "What are you doing here?"

I tucked her hair for her. "I have to head into Good Music to put some finishing touches on a couple songs. I knew you'd be here, so I came here first."

She played with the zipper on my leather jacket. "Am I that predictable?"

"Mmhmm. I like that about you."

Her eyes drifted up to mine. "I'm happy to see you. I was beginning to forget what you look like."

"Three days is all it takes?" Hooking my finger in the space between her buttons, I tugged her into me and dipped my head so I could speak to only her. "A thousand years, and I won't forget your face, Wren."

She shivered and clutched my jacket. "You can't just say those types of things to me in a coffee shop. All those times I told you in my emails that you'd made me cry, I wasn't kidding." She sniffled and rubbed her face on my leather sleeve. "The things you say, Callum Rose...I swear, you have a direct line to my tear ducts."

I had to laugh, even though she was making my chest ache. "I don't want you to cry. Never."

She nodded, still hiding her face. "Somehow, I know that."

When it was our turn to order, Wren was still pressed against me, so I did it for her, adding a chocolate chip cookie and a cup of coffee for myself. I should've been in the studio. I had only intended on a quick stop to get a fix of Wren, but now that I had her, I didn't give a single shit about my schedule.

Outside, Wren held her coffee in both hands and blew through the small hole in the lid to cool the steaming liquid.

"Do you have to go?" she asked.

"I have some time. Do you mind if I sit with you during your break?"

She bit her lip, but she couldn't stop her grin. "I don't know. My bench is very exclusive."

"I saw a pigeon shittin' next to it when I walked by earlier."

She snorted a laugh. "That adds to the ambiance. Everyone knows pigeons class up any joint."

We sat on her shitty bench. I drank my coffee. She ate her turkey sandwich. Her cheeks were pink every time I looked at her, and there was a quiver in her voice that eased the more time we sat there. Wren told me about her job and the coworker she had an odd relationship with. She named all the musicians who'd come into the building she deemed more famous than me, then checked to make sure she hadn't hurt my feelings.

I thought I knew a lot about Wren Anderson. And maybe I did. But I hadn't really grasped how kind she was. It wasn't a trait I had come across very often in my years. I almost wished she was a little meaner, if only to protect herself.

I knew dark and manipulative people who would prey upon someone like Wren. I grew up with them, learned from them, and had to fight my way out of it.

But I wouldn't change her. I'd be here to protect her from that darkness. It would never touch her.

"There's no one like you," I said.

She stopped chewing and covered her mouth with her hand. "Is that a good thing?"

"It's a fact. No one's like you."

She swallowed and wiped her mouth. "I guess that's probably true. I know there's definitely no one like you, Callum. I have never had someone say the sweetest things to me in person, then text me rude, dirty, hot messages later that night."

"Good. If someone does, tell me and I'll break his phone."

She giggled. "You mean you won't chop off his fingers and stuff them down his throat?"

I raised an eyebrow. "That goes without saying."

Wren set her lunch aside and slid closer, until her thigh pressed against mine. Her gloved hands came up to my cheeks, and she guided my face down to hers.

"You are officially invited to have lunch with me on my bench whenever you want."

I closed the narrow gap between us and kissed her hard. Her fingers anchored in my hair, and I looped an arm around her middle, nearly drawing her onto my lap. She mewled as my tongue swept past her lips to taste her everywhere. If all I had with her were stolen hours in the middle of a park in broad daylight, I'd treat my time like we were in a shadowy back alley and kiss her how we both needed. I didn't care who saw. All that mattered was Wren knowing she was still mine. She'd always be mine. And I was unequivocally hers.

The walk back to Good Music was all too short. Wren let me hold her hand, even though I knew she was worried about her coworker seeing us together. The irony was, it was Adam who spotted us. He was approaching the building from the opposite direction, and there was no hiding we were together.

Wren tried to take her hand back anyway. I wouldn't allow it. "No. He knows the deal with us."

"It's awkward for me," she murmured.

"Why? Because he thought he stood a chance with you?"

"Maybe. I don't know." Her fingers flexed between mine. "I need to get back to my desk. I can't do this at work. I'll text you tonight."

I relented, even though it went against my every instinct. "I'll be waiting."

She hurried inside, tossing a wave at Adam over her shoulder just as he arrived at the doors. He cocked his head, glancing from her to me. I crossed my arms, bracing for whatever he had to say.

"What, are you together?" he sputtered.

"We are. Why are you surprised?"

"Uh," he threw his arms out, "because I've never seen you with a girl in all the time I've known you. You're all look, no touch. Now you're, what, in a relationship? I'm sorry if I am having some whiplash here."

Before I could answer, Rodrigo appeared between us, glancing back and forth. "What's up, gentlemen? Why are we having an argument on the sidewalk?"

"No one's arguing," I replied.

Adam jabbed a finger at me. "Callum is dating the receptionist."

Rodrigo scratched his head. "You're *dating*?"

"I wouldn't call it dating." Wren and I were together. Dating implied getting to know one another in order to decide if being a couple would work. As far as I was concerned, we were well beyond that.

"They were walking down the sidewalk holding hands." Adam said it with the same incredulousness he would have if he'd caught us juggling fire or tripping nuns.

Rodrigo's wide-eyed gaze swung to me. "You were *holding hands*? Holy shit, I feel like I've missed an entire episode."

"Yeah." Adam rubbed his forehead. "No fucking kidding. I mean, I'm happy for you, man, but excuse the shock."

"Oh yeah." Rodrigo knocked my shoulder with the back of his hand. "Don't mistake my surprise for not being supportive. I obviously don't really know Wren, but from our brief meeting, she seems like a sweet girl."

"She is." I exhaled a heavy breath to loosen the knot in my chest. I really didn't want my relationship with Wren questioned. But Adam and Roddy weren't strangers, and as much as I didn't like being under a microscope, I knew their intentions were pure. "Thanks, man."

The three of us entered the building together, and I could tell they were both inspecting my little bird, who was back at her desk, blushing scarlet and sitting ramrod straight.

"Good afternoon. Welcome to Good Music," she greeted.

Roddy waved. "Hi, Wren."

Of course Adam stopped and propped his elbow on her counter. "Hey, cutie. How's reception life?"

She lifted a shoulder. "Rarely a dull moment." Her eyes were so wide, her forehead was crinkled. "How are you?"

I hooked my arm around his neck. "He's fine. He has places to be, though. No time to talk. Be good." I dragged Adam toward the elevator to the sound of Wren's shaky little laugh at my back. If I stayed in that lobby another second, I would have been dragging *her* away instead. As much as that appealed to me, neither of us could stop our lives.

Rodrigo slugged Adam hard in the arm as soon as we were on the elevator. "Don't call Callum's girl cutie, man. That's not cool."

Adam held his hands up. "It slipped out. No harm meant. I've accepted Wren is into the strong, silent type—and that'll never be me."

Roddy chuckled. "You're the loud, jackass type."

"Motherfucker!" Adam lunged at him, grabbing him in a headlock. They wrestled for all of ten seconds, then the doors slid open on our floor and it was over.

I followed them to the studio, pleased as hell with what had just gone down. My obsession with Wren had been a secret I'd kept close to my vest all these years. No more hiding, though. Those days were done. Wren was mine, and everyone we met would know.

Wren: *Hey…are you still working?*
Me: *Just got home. Are you in bed, Little Bird?*
Wren: *Yeah. You know me. I'm not a night owl.*
Me: *Early bird.*

Wren: *I rise with the sun.*

Me: *Why'd you stop going by Birdie?*

Wren: *Jenny still calls me that, but she's the only one. I just wanted to be someone new once I was out of my parents' house. Plus, Wren looks a lot better on resumes. Is it weird for you to call me that?*

Me: *I never thought of you as Birdie. You were always my little bird. But I like Wren. It's not weird for me at all.*

Wren: *I'm still getting used to having this kind of access to you...you know, not waiting for your next email for weeks.*

Me: *Sometimes days or an hour.*

Wren: *You got better at writing me back the longer we corresponded.*

Me: *Only because I wanted more of your words in my fucking inbox.*

Wren: *Well, you'll have to tell me if I'm bugging you now. I feel like I might want to talk to you all the time.*

Me: *I'll tell you right now, you will never bother me. I want all your thoughts and words as much as I want your lips and pussy. Everything. Don't hold back.*

Wren: *See? Dirty and sweet.*

Wren: *Seriously, though, don't give me free rein. You're the only man I've ever texted like this. I have no established boundaries.*

Me: *You're in luck then. I told you before, I don't even try to conform to arbitrary boundaries and standards some jackasses on the internet deemed as the appropriate amount of time in between texts. I expect you to text me when you want to. I'll do the same.*

Wren: *You might have to remind me.*

Me: *I will. What are you doing?*

Wren: *Thinking I might sleep soon. You?*

Me: *Thinking about taking you to the club on Saturday night and watching your cheeks get bright red, hearing your little* *pants, feeling you squirm in my lap.*

Wren: *And I bet you're imagining what the girl will look like...*

Me: *No. I told you what I'm thinking about. You.*

Wren: *Okay. I believe you.*

Me: *Why can't I see you before then? Friday?*

Wren: *You can see me on my bench. Friday night I'm being dragged out for drinks with Natalie, my co-irker. <- not a typo!*

Me: *Do you not want to go?*

Wren: *No, I think I do. She's inviting a couple other girls from Good Music. It'll be good for me to make friends at work. Natalie's just...well, I don't think I get her.*

Me: *Text me the address of where you're going.*

Wren: *Why? So you can stalk me?*

Me: *Just want to know where you are.*

Wren: *All right. When Natalie tells me, I'll text you.*

Me: *Go to bed, Wren. I'll see you tomorrow in line.*

Wren: *You make me smile, Callum Rose. Good night. Xoxo*

Me: *Night, Little Bird. x*

CHAPTER FIFTEEN

WREN

AUNTIE JACKIE OPENED HER DOOR WITH A BIG, white smile on her face. "Hey, Mama. Come in here. Ezra just kicked my butt at Candy Land."

I shook my head and followed her into her house, which was a mirror image to Jenny's next door. "He's a regular Candy Land shark, is what he is. He pretends he's never played, then cleans the floor with you."

Jackie was a pretty, statuesque Black woman in her forties. Single, with no kids, she worked from home for a private investigation firm doing background research and other fun stuff she wouldn't tell me. She'd moved in next to Jenny and me about a year after I did and had been a second aunt to me and Ezra.

"Hi, Mommy!" Ezra popped up from the floor with his arms straight out. I picked him up, giving him a squeeze and kisses on his cheek. Thank god it was Friday. I had missed this delicious kid all week.

"Hi, baby buddy. How was your day?"

"I made a dino and ate cakes for snack."

I reared back and scrunched my nose. "Cake for snack?" Ezra's preschool was liberal, but not *that* liberal. I didn't necessarily object to cake for a snack, but I'd be surprised if that was what he'd actually eaten.

Jackie picked up his backpack from the floor. "I didn't quite buy that story either, so I checked his daily report. Our boy had *rice* cakes for snack."

"Oooh, yeah, that makes a lot more sense." Laughing, I took his backpack from her. "Thank you for picking him up last minute today. I really appreciate it."

Jenny normally picked Ezra up from his preschool slash daycare since she got off work a lot earlier than I did, but she'd been detained by a last-minute meeting. All it took was one frantic text to Jackie, and she jumped at the chance to grab Ez for me, like always.

She waved me off. "You know it's always my pleasure. If I didn't take a break to spend time with my favorite boy, I'd be libel to become surgically attached to my laptop."

Ezra gave her a hug before bounding out the door to our house next door. As I unlocked our front door, the sensation of being watched prickled the back of my neck. I rubbed my nape and let the feeling wash over me. I was probably crazy, but I kind of found it comforting.

Ezra and I had a quiet dinner, just the two of us. He made a mess of his noodles, getting sauce all over his face and bare chest —we didn't do shirts on spaghetti nights. I soaked up his voice and his presence. Working full time and seeing him less had been an adjustment for me. I was getting used to it, but that didn't mean I liked it.

"I have three new friends, Mommy," he said suddenly.

"Oh yeah? What are their names?" I put my fork down and listened to him.

"I like Vicky, Seamus, and Javi."

I nodded. "Oh, those are nice names."

He nodded back, his little stained-orange face serious. "Do you have any friends, Mommy?"

"Oh gosh, I don't know if I have as many as you. Let me think." I tapped my chin, legitimately racking my brain. Friends weren't something I had in abundance, but I didn't want my kid to think his mom was a total loser. "Well, I have a new friend named Natalie. And...um...I have a friend named Callum too. Obviously you're my best friend."

He cackled, like me calling him my bestie was ridiculous. "I'm your baby buddy!"

"That's true. Silly me."

Jenny arrived home as I was getting Ezra into his pj's. She laid in his bed with us while we read stories and kissed his forehead good night after I did. He normally zonked right out after a long day at school, so he didn't protest when I turned out his light and closed his door.

She followed me into my bedroom and perched on my bed while I scrambled to get ready to go out with Natalie and the girls.

"Long day?" I asked when she sighed.

"The longest. I'm looking forward to a glass of wine and some Netflix." She shook her head when I held up a cardigan. "You can't go out looking like a mom, honey."

"But I *am* a mom. Besides, it's not like I'm looking for a man tonight."

"That may be true, but you don't want to show up looking all dowdy to hang out with girls who undoubtedly are going to put in some effort. Why don't you wear that dress you wore to the party a couple weeks ago?"

With no time to go through my meager closet, I tossed the dress on the bed and vaulted into my shower. I spent five minutes under the spray, leaving my hair dry since it was in good shape, and honestly, doing it was a little too much effort. I really didn't know how my planned shopping trip with Natalie had become Friday night drinks, but here we were. I'd rather be curling up with a glass of wine next to Jenny, but that was all the more reason for me to go out. I couldn't spend my life hiding and afraid of social situations.

Jenny was still on my bed when I came out. "Are you sure you don't mind me going out two nights in a row?"

"Not even a little. It's not like hanging out in my own house while Ezra is sleeping is a huge burden. I *love* that you're going out and getting a life. It thrills me."

I slipped my dress over my head and fluffed my hair. My makeup consisted of a swipe of mascara on my blonde lashes, a little eyebrow powder, and raspberry lipstick.

"Speaking of the life you're getting," she held my phone out to me, "you have a text from a man. *The* man, if I'm not mistaken."

"There's no other man."

Callum had found me in the coffee shop three times this week and we'd texted every night before bed. I was practically vibrating with anticipation for tomorrow night.

Callum: *Be good tonight. I'm on my way to dinner. Thinking of you always.*

Me: *I'm thinking of you too. I'll see you tomorrow. Have fun!!*

Grinning to myself, I set my phone down and slid a pair of hoops in my ears. While I was at drinks tonight, Callum was going to dinner with the rest of The Seasons Change to celebrate finishing their album.

My phone started ringing just as I secured the back on the second hoop. Callum was calling.

"Hello?"

"Little Bird," he breathed. "Are you mad?"

My eyes flicked to my reflection. "No. Why would I be?"

He exhaled in my ear. "Where were my hugs and kisses then?"

It took me a second to understand what he was asking, then it dawned on me. I hadn't typed 'xoxo.'

"That wasn't on purpose. I'm rushing to get ready. Jenny told me to wear the dress I wore to Benson's party."

There was a pause, then another exhale. "You looked fuckin' delectable in that dress. I'm jealous of everyone who's gonna see you tonight. But I know you'll be a good girl. You always are."

My teeth dug into my bottom lip. My stomach flipped. God, this man was something else. He had a bead on the exact kind of thing to say to make me melt into a puddle for him.

"For you I am," I replied.

"Wren." My name sounded like a sigh. "I gotta go before I decide to say fuck everything and come get you. I just needed to make sure I didn't fuck up."

"You didn't. I promise. Have fun, Callum."

"Good night, baby."

As soon as he hung up, I texted him.

Me: *Xoxo!*

Callum: *That's a lot better. I'll talk to you later, Wren. x*

"Oh, babe, you've got it bad. Look at your smile," Jenny teased.

"I know, right?" Ignoring my fluttering heart and warm cheeks, I tucked my phone and lipstick into a small purse. "I'm really trying to take it slow with him, but he's just so...he's Callum."

She snorted a laugh. "I get it. I've heard enough about him over the years to completely understand."

I sucked in a deep breath and smoothed a hand over my stomach. "Shit, I have to go."

"Go, go. Have fun. And don't worry about a single thing."

The bar where I was meeting Natalie, Marissa, and Adelaide was in the next neighborhood over from mine, a part of Queens that was becoming more and more gentrified by the minute. To my surprise, though, Natalie had chosen a low-key dive that wasn't packed with dude bros in ill-fitting suits. Some of the people inside actually looked like they might live in the area and hadn't been imported from Manhattan.

The four of us ended up tucked in a booth, sharing a pitcher of margaritas. I was sipping mine slowly since two drinks was my limit. No one wanted to deal with a hangover while chasing around a three-year-old.

Natalie was sharing my life story with Marissa and Adelaide while I listened, wondering how she knew so much about me. "So, Wren over here has a son. She's a single mommy, y'all. The dad's out of the picture, which, good riddance, I say. If he didn't scoop you up when he knocked you up, he obviously has a brain the size of a shriveled walnut."

Marissa, a production assistant in engineering I'd only said hi to in passing up until tonight, rolled her eyes. "My god, men are stupid. Does he at least pay support?"

I held my oversized glass up so it covered half my face. This wasn't my favorite topic. "A little, but I'm fine doing it on my own."

She flipped her long black hair. "Honestly, better to be on your own than putting up with an idiot for the rest of your kid's life." Her eyes widened. "Did I tell you I caught David texting his ex even though he'd promised he'd blocked her? That motherfucker."

Marissa and Natalie started going off on David, who I gleaned through context clues was Marissa's boyfriend, not that either of them bothered to tell me. The girl across from me, Adelaide, seemed just as lost. Her eyes widened, and she flashed me a cheeky sort of grin that put me at ease instantly.

She tapped my hand. "Want to go play darts? I'm absolutely terrible at it."

"Sure." Relief swept through me. A break from Natalie and Marissa was exactly what I needed. "I might be worse, though."

"That sounds like a challenge."

We took our drinks to the back of the bar where there was a free dartboard. Adelaide probably had the advantage since she was about a foot taller than me, with long, graceful arms, but I wasn't much for competition anyway.

"Are you good friends with Natalie?" she asked.

"Friends? Um…I wouldn't call us that. You?"

She snorted as she lined up her shot. "She accosted me in the hall and insisted I come tonight. She said you were lonely and needed friends." Her dart landed in the wall next to the board.

My face flamed. "Me? What?" That was…not entirely inaccurate. But fuck Natalie. Jeez, where did that woman get off?

Her hazel eyes slid to mine. "Yeah, dude. I only came because you seem nice when I pass you every day and I didn't want to leave you alone with her and Marissa."

I laughed even though I was still a little confused. "Thanks? I feel like I owe you a life debt."

She shrugged. "It's cool. I didn't have anything better to do. Natalie's daddy is loaded, so she always pays for drinks."

"Oh. Is her dad in the music business?"

Adelaide burst out laughing. It was deep and throaty, unapologetically turning heads. "Oh no, dude. Not her dad. Her *daddy*. As in, she's taken care of by an older gentleman. She's a kept woman. You know?"

"Uh, yeah. I think I do. That's…" My picture of Natalie was becoming more and more clear, yet even more confusing. That was just Natalie in a nutshell.

Adelaide threw another wild shot, then raised her eyebrow. "Not surprising, right? Don't worry, I'm not gossiping. Everyone knows, which is why I thought you knew too. Nat is proud of her crusty old man lover."

I choked on my margarita. This girl was something else. She was tall, thin, and stunning, with the mouth of a frat boy. She seemed genuine too. Like she gave no fucks what people thought of her.

My attention was pulled from her when, out the corner of my eye, a light overhead caught on a diamond earring. I turned, dread pooling in my stomach. Edwin Cruz had just sat down at a table full of his buddies, and I seemed to have caught his eye too, gauging by his slow, oily smirk.

"Oh god," I groaned and shuffled so I was behind Adelaide. "Hide me please."

"What? Who are we hiding from?"

"This awful guy from my neighborhood who thinks no means try harder. He's the one with the sharp edges and big, gaudy diamond in his ear at the table near the bathroom." Describing him made me shudder and get a creepy-crawly feeling down my back.

Adelaide subtly pretended to stretch so she could peer over her shoulder to check him out. "Oh, gag. He's way too pretty. You know he takes more time getting ready than any woman. Bleh." She looped her arm through mine. "Let's go to the bar so he can't see you because mister mans is about to break his neck trying to check out your tits right now."

There was more of a crowd around the bar area than there had been when I first got here. The pair of us tucked ourselves in between two groups. Adelaide's head peeked out over the top of almost everyone else, but I was pretty well hidden.

We stayed there for a while, yelling in each other's ears to be heard over the conversations flowing around us. Natalie swung by with another round of margaritas for us, then told us not to come back to the table because she and Marissa had invited some 'cute boys' to sit with them.

Adelaide held up her drink. "Once I finish this, I'm out. You too?"

"Absolutely." She was good company, but I was pretty much done socializing for the night.

"You probably get up early with your kid, huh?"

I nodded. "Yep. Pretty early."

She poked her lip out. "Bummer. Well, if you ever go to a playground at a reasonable time, text me. I don't get to swing as much as I'd like since an adult hanging around playgrounds without a kid gets side-eyed."

I snorted into my drink again. Meeting Adelaide tonight made all the awkwardness with Natalie and Marissa worth it.

I took a long swallow of my margarita while Adelaide started talking to the group of girls behind her about...well, something. I couldn't quite hear over the rising din of conversation and music clouding the air.

Someone grazed my back, bumping me forward. I leaned my elbows on the bar to get out of their way and set my glass down. I took a deep breath and froze. My nose and throat were coated with cloying, heavy cologne so familiar to me, I didn't even have to look to know who'd sidled up beside me.

Edwin brushed my hair aside and placed his lips right next to my ear. "Hey, mami. What are you doing here?"

"I'm leaving, actually. Sorry." *Shit, I had to stop apologizing!*

"Come on." He gripped the back of my elbow. "Stay. I never get to talk to you."

His lips grazed my ear, and my stomach lurched. I really didn't like this man.

"Back up please." I hated that I couldn't make myself sound more forceful. I felt it. In my head, I was wielding a sword and shield, releasing a battle cry that put dread in my enemies.

"Aw, mami." His hand slid from my arm to my back, tracing down my spine. "We could be good friends. The best friends. I don't know why you keep being so stuck up. I'm a good guy. I'll take care of you...in every way."

I'd had enough. His rape-y flirtation had been going on for two long years. It didn't seem to matter how many times I turned him down. He wasn't getting it, or he chose not to.

"You don't even know me," I said.

His head cocked. He hadn't heard that from me before. "I know all about you. You're sweet and shy. Some men might be turned off by that, but I think it's sexy as hell."

"What's my son's name?"

That seemed to stump him, but not for long. "Details, baby. I'll get to know him in time. He needs a man around the house to show him things."

His hand inched lower and lower until he was fully palming my ass. Bile rose in my throat, and I lurched sideways to escape him, but he only pressed closer, trapping me against the bar.

"Oh yeah, that's nice. Nice and thick," he purred like a fucking lecherous cat.

I shoved at his arm and whispered for him to stop, but he was enjoying taking liberties with my body too much to even give one iota of a damn about my reaction.

Suddenly, Edwin's head was slammed down on the bar beside me. A massive hand gripped the back of his neck, holding him immobilized.

It happened so fast, I whipped around to face the attacker, and the air was sucked from my lungs. Callum's face was etched in fury, the razor-sharp planes of his jaw and cheeks strained, his eyes narrowed into angry slits. His wrath wasn't aimed at me, but I staggered back anyway, my spine colliding with the bar.

"Don't touch her," Callum gritted.

Edwin's arm flailed, harmlessly bouncing off Callum. He changed tactics, clawing at the hand holding his nape like a vise. "Man, get off me. I'll kill you!"

"You don't get to touch her." He bent over Edwin and drove his elbow deep into his spine. "You won't have hands if I *ever* see you try to put them on her. You won't have legs if you ever try to walk close to her. I will feed your tongue to the feral cats who live in my alley if I catch you talkin' to her. You hear me?"

"You're crazy!" Edwin screamed. "Get the fuck off me. I don't want that bitch."

The people around us were watching, but no one was stepping in. They were eating up the drama instead. From the corner of my eye, I saw one camera pointed at them, but there had to be more. I just couldn't bring myself to look away from my furious man to find out.

Adelaide reached for me, to pull me from the fray, but I shook my head. I wasn't leaving Callum, even if he looked like he could tear the bar apart with his bare hands.

"She doesn't want *you*," Callum gritted out. "You see her, you turn the other way. Do. You. Hear. Me?"

Edwin's face had turned puce. He was bucking viciously under Callum's iron hold. I thought he was going to fight him or deny Callum's demand, but slowly, his arms slackened and he started to sag into the bar.

"I hear you, asshole," he muttered through a tightly clenched jaw. "Get the fuck off me. I hear you!"

With one last shove into the hard surface of the bar, Callum straightened and took a step back. Edwin immediately flipped around, hatred pouring from his black gaze. He stayed slumped back over the bar, scrubbing his flaming red face with his hand. Callum loomed over him as he rolled his shoulders and smoothed a hand over his hair, appearing completely unthreatened by the man shooting eye daggers at him.

A whimper climbed up my throat. Callum's head jerked, and his eyes landed on mine. They were icy blue, colder than I'd ever seen, but he still looked like a life raft, even if he was made of stone. I lunged for him. Not on purpose, but because my legs weren't working properly. He caught me easily in one arm, pressing me tightly to his side.

He didn't speak or assure me everything was going to be okay. Vibrations rocked his muscles, but his hands were gentle where they touched me, soothing caresses up and down my arm and over my shoulder. It sort of felt like I should have been comforting him, but right now, he seemed untouchable.

Just as he started for the exit, Callum pushed me into the random bodies surrounding us and whipped around. Edwin charged him, growling with rage. He was nearly a foot shorter than Callum. If the situation were less fraught, I might have laughed. But Edwin had anger powering him and surprise on his side. He collided with Callum, wrapping his arms around his middle, and they both went crashing to the ground.

It was over in seconds. Callum rolled and locked his arm around Edwin's throat. He whispered in Edwin's ear with a dangerous gleam in his eye. Defeat filtered through Edwin's limbs. Again, he slackened, training his gaze on the ceiling, most likely so he didn't have to face everyone who'd watched him get taken down for the second time in minutes.

Callum shoved him away and hopped to his feet with more grace than he had any right to with his impossibly long limbs. Standing over Edwin's prone form, he held his hand out to me, and I took it. I thought I heard Adelaide calling my name, but Callum swept me out of the bar before I could find my bearings or even think to turn around to tell her I was okay.

An SUV was waiting for us out front. Callum bundled me inside, following right behind me and slamming the door. The driver took off, putting distance between us and the bar. My hands were clutched in my lap, twisting the material of my dress. I was shivering so hard, my teeth clacked together.

"My coat." I turned around, staring out the back window. "I don't have my coat. We should go back. I have to have my coat."

Callum wrapped his arms around me and pulled me into his lap. Fingers stroked my hair, soothing and soft, until I tucked myself under his chin. Obviously, we weren't going back. That had been stupid to suggest. Maybe I was in shock. I certainly didn't feel normal.

"People were filming you," I whispered.

"I'll deal with it," he murmured.

"I didn't want him to touch me."

His lips touched my crown. "I know."

"Am I going home?"

"No."

"Are you mad at me?"

"No."

"Do you need a minute?"

"Please."

Because I needed a minute too, I gave it to him. We rode in silence. Callum's rhythmic stroking of my hair calmed my thrashing heart. His quiet breathing helped to bring my thoughts back in order. By the time his driver stopped at the curb outside his building, I had mostly calmed down. Well…I wasn't on the verge of a panic attack anymore, at least.

He held me close through the lobby and inside the elevator. I willed him to speak. To tell me why he'd shown up tonight and what he'd seen before he went ballistic. He said he knew I didn't want Edwin touching me, but was he being truthful? God, why did his silence make me feel like I'd done something wrong?

We stepped into his apartment, and Callum leaned his back on the door. Head tipped back, eyes closed, he exhaled a long, heavy breath. I kept twisting my dress on my fingers, watching him, unsure what to do or say.

"Please, Callum," I pleaded.

His fingers clenched into fists at his sides. Eyes flying open, they locked on mine. Chest heaving, he took a great breath.

And then he came for me.

CHAPTER SIXTEEN

CALLUM

WREN'S CHEEKS WERE COLD IN MY HANDS, her lips trembling. She was afraid, worked up, in shock. I should have let her breathe. Talked to her. Taken care of her feelings. But I was hanging by a thread over shark-infested waters, and she was dry, safe land.

My words became lost in the seconds before I saw my little bird being touched without her consent. I was adrenaline and action now.

My tongue lashed hers, punishing her for going out without me to protect her. For making me crazy. For being so fucking adorable and beautiful and everything I wanted.

My mouth drove into hers, too hard, but I couldn't pull back. Her teeth pressed into my lip, and I felt, more than heard, her whimper. My ears were muffled with the sound of my thrashing heart.

Her small hands dove under my shirt. The shock of cold skin on mine sent a jolt to my abs. Her palms flattened, moving upward, leaving paths of ice.

"Wren."

"Callum." She pushed up on her toes and chased my mouth, sipping from my bottom lip like a little hummingbird. "Callum."

God, I had to have her. It was an outright desperation I'd never experienced. A visceral need to consume her body, claim it, plant myself deep inside until we were all mixed up in each other. Until there was no Wren, no Callum, only *us*.

"I need you to be mine." I slid my hands from her cheeks to her hair, twisting it around my fist. "Show me you're mine."

This woman consumed my thoughts. Every ounce of pleasure I jerked from my body was because of her. It had been that way for years. Longer than I'd ever tell her.

We made it to my bedroom, barely breaking apart to find our way there. I flipped the lights mounted on either side of my bed on, casting a flickering, yellow glow throughout the room.

Wren fell back on the bed, her dress riding up her thighs. I dropped to my knees and ran my nose along her leg, from her knee to the crease of her thigh. I kissed the crease and tongued the edge of her black underwear. Her fingers grazed my hair and forehead, tentative and shaking. I grabbed both her hands and pressed them to my head, giving her permission to take and take, because I fully fucking intended to.

I nuzzled the wet spot on her underwear, inhaling her scent until it was a core memory that would be locked with me until my deathbed. I wanted to rip her panties off, tongue fuck her, consume her juices like dessert, then go back for more and more and more. But some restraint still lingered in the back of my mind, holding me back from devouring this girl so I didn't scare the ever-loving shit out of her with my intensity. God, I probably was already, but it was too late. I was too far gone over the edge for her.

Looping my finger in the soaked crotch of her panties, I yanked hard. She yelped in surprise and lifted her hips to allow me to slide them the rest of the way down her legs. Her dripping, pink pussy was topped by pale red curls. Glorious, puffy thing, slick with her need for me. My sweet, beautiful girl couldn't hide that desire from my prying, greedy eyes.

Her hips lifted again, searching for me, and I dove forward, letting her find me. I licked and sucked, tasting her everywhere.

My palms pressed her inner thighs open wider to give me more space to work—to bury my entire face in her pussy until I was coated with her.

My sweet little bird was rocking into my mouth, writhing on my tongue. Her moans were unrestrained, as wild and high as I felt. This was the first time I wanted to do this more than I wanted to breathe. Eating Wren was necessary for life. She was in trouble, because now that I knew, now that I under-fucking-stood how good this could be, she was now one of the fundamentals I needed to get through my day. I was gonna need this pussy on my tongue seven days a week, and she was going to have to allow that to happen.

Her cries got sharper, hips thrusting toward me. She had to be close, so close. I didn't have it in me to tease her. Her climax was as vital to me as it had to be to her. My lips wrapped around her swollen clit, sucking gently, then a little harder. She squealed and bucked, pushing my face even deeper.

Wren moaned my name as she shattered. I lifted my eyes to watch her fall apart. Her kiss-swollen lips parted, hair splayed around her head like sunrays, cheeks flushed deep pink, she staggered me.

"Oh," she sighed. "That was, that was…"

I tossed my shirt aside and climbed over her, using my grip on her hips to rotate her so I could fit between her legs. She reached for my face, tracing my coated lips with her fingertips. I dipped down, kissing her mouth, then her neck, her cleavage, sucking the curve of her breast. I tugged on her dress, grateful the material had stretch to it. Otherwise, I would've ripped it to get to more of her. The cup of her bra went with the dress, exposing her tit. Tight, pale brown nipples drew me in to suck, lick, lave. There was no universe where I would ever get tired of having any part of this woman in my mouth.

My cocked prodded her soft little belly, desperate to sink into her. I'd been patient for a long, long time, but that was through.

This little bird was mine in every way—and every part of her needed to understand that.

Pushing back on my knees, I shoved my jeans down, freeing my cock. Wren gave me her owl eyes, darting from my face to where I stroked my throbbing length in my fist. Her tongue slid along her lip, leaving a shining trail.

Falling over her, the head of my cock slid between her folds. She sucked in a breath, squirming and clenching her thighs around my hips.

"It's been a long, long time," she whispered. "Go slow."

My tip prodded her entrance and a shot of heat blasted through the base of my spine. I was in trouble. "I don't know if I can tonight, Little Bird. It's been forever for me."

She nodded with parted lips and wide eyes, tilting her hips to me, accepting what I had to give. I pushed forward once, then another time, sliding all the way home. And just like that, my brain went haywire. She was so hot. So tight. Clenching around me. Fitting me perfectly. The fantasy of what this would be like paled the face of reality. This was Wren, not some faceless woman who made my skin crawl. Wren's touch brought me light.

I backed up and drove in again, watching her expression, the bounce of her tits, bending my head so I could see our physical connection. My cock was shiny with her cream. Sinking inside her again and again was like walking through a fire after being frozen and only experiencing the heat. No pain, only relief after a thousand icy winters.

"Look at that, Wren. Watch me fuck you." I slid my hand behind her head and lifted so she could see between our bodies and watch me drive into her. "Does that feel good? Do you like it?"

She mewled, clutching at my arms and shoulders. "You're so big. I just...oooh." Her neck arched. Her eyes rolled back. I must have hit something good. The right spot. I kept at it, plunging in and out, keeping Wren trapped in bliss.

If I could have watched her and kissed her at the same time, I would have, but the call of her mouth was impossible to resist. I groaned when our lips collided, wet and desperate. Her fingers raked through my hair, dragging me closer. She was in this, just as much as I was. Answering each of my thrusts with the rise of her hips. Sliding her tongue along mine. Gripping me everywhere.

I couldn't stop. Not even for a second. I knew I was going to come soon. Too fast. Too hard. But I couldn't help myself. Not this first time. I'd be good to her next time, when I got myself under control. When I wasn't experiencing this...this perfect storm of newness, rapture, anger, and unconquerable desire.

"Can I come in you?" I panted.

Sweat beaded on her forehead. Her cheeks were perfectly rosy. It took everything in me not to spill right then and there. With wide eyes, she nodded.

"I have an IUD."

Her legs hitched higher, and I sunk into her so deep, my muscles seized and pleasure rolled from my spine to every corner of my being. Wave after wave of it, pumping through me into her in hot spurts.

Maybe I should've been embarrassed with the speed in which I lost my shit, but I wasn't. I wouldn't allow any negative feelings to intrude on my first time with Wren.

I fell to my side and dragged her with me, pulling her leg over my hip. I was still fully hard and nowhere near done with her. I tugged the other side of her dress down and buried my face between her heavy tits. She stroked my hair, arching her spine to give me more access.

"I want this to be the place I go after a long day." I kissed along the curve of both breasts, up to her neck, and nuzzled there too. My cock slid between her soaked folds, needing back inside again. I kicked my jeans off so I could feel her everywhere.

"You're still so hard."

"Need you again, Little Bird."

Her fingertips grazed my scruff. "I'm gonna be so sore tomorrow, but I think I need you too."

Reaching between us, I circled her clit. "I'll go slow this time. I'll make it better for you, beautiful girl. I just...I lost my fuckin' mind feeling you from the inside, Wren."

"You think that wasn't good for me?" Her eyes were so round and a little glazed. "I don't have much experience, but that was incredible for me. That's why I want it again...and again. And maybe again after that."

I hooked her thigh on my elbow, raising it high. "Think we can do it this way, Little Bird? Think it'll feel just as good?"

"We can try."

Her hips tipped forward, and I lined up at her entrance, sinking into her as slow as I could. Her lips found mine, and we were kissing and fucking, not quite as frenzied, but there was still an underlying feeling of desperation between us.

She'd wanted us to go slow but fuck that. We were five years in the making. I'd been waiting for her all my life.

I broke away, holding the sides of her head, keeping her eyes on mine. "Tell me you're mine."

"I'm yours." No hesitation. Maybe she'd been waiting too. Not in the same way, but waiting regardless.

Her palm smoothed down my spine to my lower back then tentatively moved to cup my ass. I did the same, taking her round cheek in my hand, squeezing and trailing my fingers down the valley.

"Fuckin' touch me. I'm gonna touch you wherever I want. Need you to know that." I dipped my head to suck on her nipple, showing her exactly what I meant. If she was mine, so was her body. Every damn part of it.

She squeezed my ass and tried to press me in even closer to her. "This is new. But I want you to touch me."

I brought my head up, running my nose along hers. "New for me too." I found her clit again, circling it with the pad of my finger. "Gonna need to make you come this time. Tell me what feels good."

"This feels good." Her hand covered mine, and she shifted it a tiny bit. "There. Please, keep doing that. *Please.*"

I fucked her slowly and circled her clit the way she wanted. Pressure was building in my groin, an undeniable need to drive into her wet heat and come deep inside her walls, but I wasn't a kid. What we were doing together was unprecedented for me, but I sure as hell knew how to walk to the edge and pull back at the last second. Wren's snug little pussy made it infinitely harder to grasp that control, but I kept the reins. Barely.

It became nearly impossible when she started to clench around me. Her pussy was so swollen and tight, I could barely move, but I was distracted by the sight of her. Her tits jiggled as she shook. Her mouth fell open to release a melody that would live in my head for the rest of my life. She cried out for me and used me as an anchor, her fingers holding firmly to my shoulders.

I followed close behind. A few shallow thrusts, and I was groaning, clutching my sweet girl in my arms, filling her with my cum until it was running down both our thighs. We were a mess, sweaty and wrapped in each other, breathing hard to catch our breath.

I let her leg fall and pulled out of her perfect heat, finally softening a fraction. I knew I could have gone again. Half of me really fucking wanted to. But I heard her when she said she'd be sore tomorrow. My greed for Wren did not override my desire to keep her safe and protected.

"Hey." Her nails scratched my jaw gently, the way she liked to do. "I want you to know I haven't been with anyone in a long,

long time. I'm clean...I mean, I was tested after that time. Are you—I mean, are you up to date on all that? I realize it's a little late to ask, but—"

I cut her off with a hard kiss. "There's nothin' to worry about on my part."

She drew back. "That means you've been tested or...?" Her eyebrows rose expectantly.

"There's no one else, Wren. There's never been anyone else. Never really wanted to before you." I took her breast in my hand, rubbing my palm over her tight nipple. "I'm gonna need to have you as often as I can. You've bewitched me like I'm Mister fuckin' Darcy."

"Body and soul?" she whispered.

"Yeah, Wren. Body and soul," I whispered back.

"But..." Her pale brows furrowed. "How can that be...? You never had...?"

I got that she was surprised, but I didn't think she should have been. I didn't *like* people. Wren Anderson was one of the few exceptions. And I more than liked her. I was obsessed with her, now more than ever.

"No, I've never." I flicked my tongue along the seam of her lips. "Now I have, and we're going to be doing a lot more of it. *A lot,* Wren."

Her brow furrowed even more. "But you go to sex clubs. And sex parties."

"To watch. I don't touch. I never have."

"Because you didn't want to?"

"No. Watchin' on my own terms satisfied me."

She went quiet, but I could almost hear her mind whirring. Maybe I should have told her, but I hadn't exactly been thinking straight when we got here. The thing was, if I'd had sex with a thousand different women, being with Wren would have still been something entirely different. It didn't matter that no one had come before her. Being inside Wren was a singular experience.

Her big eyes lifted to mine, swirling with liquid amber. "Are you sure it's not a big deal? I mean, I wish I had known, so I could have, I don't know…"

"You think anything could have been better than that?"

"No." Again, no hesitation. The corners of her mouth curved up. "Well, I think we might be able to best ourselves after extensive practice. But I wouldn't change anything about what we just did."

I ran my finger down the pinch between her eyebrows. "Me either. Stop freakin' out, Little Bird. Nothin' to freak out over."

She settled in my arms, and I pressed my nose to the top of her head. She smelled like her usual sunshine, but now, her scent was mixed with sweat and sex and a little of me.

"You think you're going to have trouble…with what happened tonight?" she asked timidly. "A lot of people were recording."

"Maybe. I don't regret how I reacted." I lifted her chin. "Does it bother you?"

"No. You protected me when I needed you." Her teeth dug into her bottom lip. "But I don't want you to have to deal with repercussions. Not for me."

"Nope." I covered her mouth with mine, kissing her hard and rough. "Don't ever say that to me. I will end the world for you."

She grinned, letting out a delicate little chuckle. "Please don't. I kind of like it here."

She always thought I was kidding about the lengths I would go to for her. Better that than her knowing I wasn't joking at all. She'd be gone faster than I could blink, then I'd be forced to chase her and follow through with my original kidnapping plan.

"What were you doing there? At the bar?" she asked.

"I think it's obvious. I came to see you."

She blinked, a small smile still curling her lips. "You couldn't go the whole night without seeing me?"

"No. I heard you were wearin' my favorite dress. It wasn't fair other men were layin' their eyes on you."

"Thank you for saying that, but nobody was looking at me."

"Baby, I had to drag a man off you. Trust me, they were lookin'." She didn't understand how pretty she was. How her sweetness and timidity drew wicked men in like moths to a flame.

"Edwin is an exception. He's been asking me out for two years. He's only interested because I keep saying no."

"Fuck. I did not hit that guy hard enough." I should have known Wren had a guy hounding her. It was my job to keep her safe. How had I missed that?

She giggled, and the dulcet sound was enough to calm me down. "Well, I know I'll never look at this dress the same again."

Wren rolled onto her back, pulling her dress over her breasts along the way. She sighed at the ceiling, her eyelids drooping slightly.

"I'm tired."

I laid my hand on my stomach. "Sleep here."

Her head turned, and something behind her eyes shuttered. "I can't."

"You can."

Chewing on her lip, she let her eyes sweep over me. "There's something I need to tell you. I planned to tell you before we did...this, but...um—"

I knew what she wanted to tell me. The topic I'd avoided thinking about. Of course I knew Wren had a child. A son. I'd seen them together a thousand times. But my brain compartmentalized that facet of her life and tucked it away, so when we were together, she was just my Wren. I didn't share her with anyone else.

"Tell me."

She sucked in a deep breath, averting her eyes. "I have a son. He's three. I know I should have told you, and I'm so sorry. It's just that—"

"Okay." I turned her head toward me and touched my lips to hers. "It's okay."

"Um…" she blinked a few times, "okay?"

"Yeah. It's okay. That doesn't change anything." I propped myself up on my elbows, dragging my finger along her cheek. She really did look tired. If she wasn't staying with me, then I needed her tucked snug in her bed. "I should take you home now."

"Oh." Her face fell, crashing straight to the ground. "Of course. I need to go to sleep. You don't have to take me. I'll get an Uber."

"Wren." I rolled on top of her and covered her mouth with my hand. "Quiet. Nothing has changed. You're tired. We'll talk more tomorrow once you sleep. *Nothing* has changed. Tell me you hear me."

She nodded, and I moved my hand to give her another kiss.

"Say it."

"I hear you. Nothing has changed," she repeated.

We both got dressed, and I gave Wren a hoodie so she wouldn't freeze without her coat. I held her close on the ride back to her house, feeling pretty fucking forlorn I had to allow her to walk away. Too bad kidnapping was off the table.

For the moment at least.

She didn't get out right away when the car pulled up to the curb. Her arms were crossed at her middle. "Will I see you tomorrow?" Her voice had gone tiny.

"Yeah." I scrubbed my face with my hand. "You will. I have a feelin' I'll have to deal with my manager, but you'll see me. We'll talk."

Her nod was sharp. "Okay. Well, thank you for rescuing me. And everything else." Even in the dark, I could see her chin tremble. "It meant a lot to me."

"Wren." Palming her crown, I drew her into my chest. "Nothing has changed."

"Okay." Her arms came around me, hugging me tight for a breath before she let go. "Good night."

I took her chin in my hand, holding her still so I could press a hard kiss to her lips. "Good night."

I watched her until she was inside, then asked the driver to stay another few minutes. I'd had my little bird completely tonight, but I still needed to sit here and peer up at her window to calm my beating heart. Old habits never died, especially when I had no intention of ever giving them up.

CHAPTER SEVENTEEN

WREN

I HADN'T GOTTEN ENOUGH SLEEP THE NIGHT BEFORE, so by seven p.m., I was dragging. It didn't help that I was in a grumpy mood and Ezra was even grumpier. We'd both been off all day. But while he blew off steam throwing toys and collapsing on the floor in a fit, I had to keep it together until bedtime—then I could lose my shit.

I was already losing it internally.

Callum had texted exactly once. At ten this morning, he said he would call or text when he could. That was it. One little 'x' at the end, but nothing else. No 'last night was amazing, I miss you, nothing has changed even after I had time to think about the bomb you dropped on me.' Nope, none of that. Not even a bossy demand.

That was pretty much the cause of my poor attitude.

My cranky toddler wasn't helping matters.

"No bath," Ezra wailed.

"Yes, bath. You have mac and cheese in your hair."

He stuck his lip out and tears collected in his lashes. "I like it. I don't want a bath!"

I kneeled in front of him, holding his belly in my hands. He was half naked, smeared in cheese and paint. If he hadn't been so damn crusty, I would have given in and skipped the bath. My boy was a mess, though. He wasn't getting out of this, even if getting him into the tub killed me.

"I know, baby buddy, but you have to." I rubbed his belly in slow circles. "Let's take a bath, then we'll read an extra book tonight."

Oh, how his chin quivered. "Jenny read me a book?"

I nodded. "Of course Jenny will read you a book. You know she loves to read to you."

He stomped his foot, but I saw the fight flowing out of him. He let me take him upstairs, even though he was crying and stiff. That was the only fight he put up.

Once I had washed his hair, he was much calmer, just as I knew he would be. Jenny popped in and sat on the closed toilet, chatting with us both.

The doorbell rang, followed by a knock on the door. I glanced at Jenny, she frowned at me. It wasn't late, but we didn't get visitors often.

"Can you go check, babe?" she asked. "I'll get Ez out and in his pj's."

"Yeah, sure." I hopped up from the floor and ran downstairs, drying my hands on my sweatshirt as I went. There was another soft knock as I approached. I peered through the peephole and gasped, then I opened the door with caution.

Callum cocked his head, peering at me through the crack. "Hey. I called, but you didn't answer."

My eyebrows lowered. "It's bath time. I didn't have my phone on me, so I—" I shook my head. "What are you doing here?"

"Told you I was comin' to talk to you today." He reached out and pushed the door open wider. "Aren't you gonna invite me in?"

Just then, my son let out an ear-piercing shriek. Callum jolted, but I didn't even flinch. I knew that cry. Ezra wasn't hurt or sad, the kid was angry and over tired.

"This is a very bad time, which I could have told you if you'd called or texted me earlier today. I need to go take care of my son." I grabbed the doorknob and tried to push the door closed, but Callum wasn't budging. "We'll talk tomorrow."

"No. Go do what you need to do. I'll come back in an hour."

Ezra shrieked again, and this time, it was followed by Jenny calling for me. "All right. Fine. An hour."

He let me close the door then, and I ran back upstairs to deal with my son. Callum would have to wait. He'd kept me waiting all day, he honestly deserved a little of the same.

Exactly one hour had gone by when he knocked softly again. Jenny beat me to the door, whipping it open and blocking his way. She'd never gotten to growl and intimidate my dates since I'd never been on one, so I was pretty sure she was trying to make up for lost time.

"Hello, young man. It's awfully late for you to be knocking on our door." She was clearly going for stern, but she ended up sounding like a mom from an '80s sitcom.

"Hello," he answered. I couldn't see him from my spot in the living room, but I heard his confusion. "Is Wren here?"

"She is. Aren't you going to introduce yourself?"

"I'm Callum Rose, ma'am." Oh, he did southern gentleman well. "Is Wren home? She's expectin' me."

I came up behind Jenny and shoved her gently aside. "I'm here."

He looked me up and down, then his eyes landed on mine. He had that stone-cold look that made him completely unreadable.

"Hey." He slid his fingers through the side of his hair. "Think we could talk?"

Jenny bumped me with her hip. "I'm going to make myself scarce." She started to walk off but turned back. "You don't need to heat the entire neighborhood, you know. Invite him in and close the door, babe."

Then she was gone, and it was just Callum and me. "Do you want to come in?"

"Yeah." He stepped up into the house, so close, my chest brushed his stomach, and closed the door behind him. Two fingers pinched the strands of hair that had escaped my ponytail. "I like your hair this way."

"Oh. Thanks." I tipped my face up. "You disappeared today and it made me feel really shitty. Now I'm in a crap mood and don't know that I can be very good company. I know I said we'd talk, but I'm tired and crabby and—"

He covered my mouth with his hand. Damn him, I had a love-hate relationship with him doing that.

"Quiet." I sort of loved it when he said that. "I told you I'd get in touch. I didn't lie. This is the first chance I've had to get to you." He let go of my mouth and gathered me in his arms to hold me flat against him. The groan that rumbled from his chest traveled directly into mine.

"Why'd you disappear?"

His nose tickled my scalp as he shook his head then he kissed my crown. "Didn't disappear. I've been dealin' with the fallout of last night."

My head jerked back, but he wouldn't allow me any more space than that. "What do you mean?"

His sigh was heavy. "Do you think I could come all the way inside and feel like maybe you're gonna allow me to stay awhile?"

"Only if you plan on offering me a reasonable explanation for not contacting me all day."

He studied me from under a furrowed brow. "Did you really believe I wasn't comin' for you, Little Bird? I left you hangin' on that thought all day?"

"Yeah, you did." I wasn't quite happy with him, but I led him around the corner to the living area anyway. I tried to sit beside him on the couch, but he plucked me right up and plopped me on his lap like I was a feather. Truth be told, when he held me like this, I felt delicate and precious, and I was quickly becoming addicted to it.

Callum stroked my hair and dragged his knuckles along my cheek. I looked at him, really looked at him, and found the shadows under his eyes, the pinch around his mouth. He hadn't had a good day either.

"I'm always comin' for you." Those words were so soft but unwavering, they settled in my chest and spread over my limbs. "I made a mistake not sending a text. I realize that now."

"Is that an apology?"

He took my chin in his hand and pressed a hard kiss to my lips. "It is. I'm sorry I didn't text. Now, I need you to tell me you're sorry for not tellin' me you needed that from me. As far as I know, the phone works both ways. You didn't check on me either, Little Bird."

Any indignation I'd had left flew away like a thief in the night. I hadn't texted, that was true. Why hadn't I? He told me he would always welcome me contacting him. I guess I hadn't believed it. Or I'd been so ready for him to ditch me when he found out about Ezra, I'd just assumed that was what he was doing.

"I'm sorry too." Leaning in, I gave him the same kind of kiss he'd given me, except when I tried to pull away, he caught me and plunged his tongue in my mouth. Callum's kiss was so hot and deep, all the ice that had been building around my heart instantly melted. "I'm glad you're here." I rubbed my lips back and forth along his.

"Yeah?"

"Mmhmm. I had a crummy day, but this makes it better." I pulled back enough to see his face. "Tell me what you had to deal with."

"I will. First, you need to tell me you remember you have to text or call when you're feelin' neglected. I will always want to hear from you. You can blow up my phone and it will be welcome. I'll only be mad if you want to text me and don't. I'll be pissed if you spend all day thinkin' I disappeared on you." He lifted my chin with his knuckle. "Tell me you understand, Little Bird."

He'd told me this once through text, but it was an entirely different thing wrapped in his arms and looking into his eyes. It was pretty impossible not to believe he meant what he said.

"I understand. I'll blow your phone up with memes every chance I get."

His answering chuckle was enough to wipe away the rest of my bad mood. "I look forward to it."

"Will you tell me now about your day?"

"Mmhmm. I spent the morning with my manager and lawyer. There are videos out and you've been identified. It makes me sick, but there's nothin' we can do to stop it. Fortunately, I'm not Iris, so my private life isn't interesting to most people."

My nose wrinkled. "They found out my name?"

"Don't worry. I'll keep you safe. I won't let any of that touch you." He squeezed my arm, then slid down to my hand, lifting it to his mouth to press his lips to my wrist and palm.

I inhaled, then let it out slowly. "Okay. What else?"

He held my hand against his cheek and closed his eyes. "I had to talk to the cops. The guy isn't pressin' charges, so it was only routine. I asked my lawyer to start the process for you to obtain a restraining order. I don't want that guy thinkin' he can ever come near you again."

The idea made me shiver. I'd never been afraid of Edwin, at least not until last night. A restraining order, though? It seemed so outlandish, but I wasn't going to argue either.

"Okay. Thank you."

"Not fightin' me?" He sounded bemused.

"No. I've seen what kind of fighter you are. I don't stand a chance."

"That's right. You don't." His mouth captured mine, tongue licking my lips then inside. It wasn't the kind of kiss I ever thought I'd have with my son right upstairs, asleep, but here I was, and I couldn't think of a single thing wrong with it.

"I had to talk to a couple reporters, give a statement." He nipped my bottom lip. "Told them I was lookin' out for my girl and that was all there was to it. I think they were more interested in Krav Maga than my life."

I giggled. "It is pretty badass."

He stilled with a curve at the corners of his lips and light in his icy blues. "I've been missin' out all this time."

"What do you mean?"

He shook his head like he was in a daze. "Being with you is a balm. I've been missin' out on this all these years. I didn't know what this would be like."

"We've both been missing out." I looped my arms around his neck. "Looking back, I'm glad I didn't meet you until now, though. I was too much of a mess before."

He sucked in a deep breath and slowly exhaled. "Because you had a kid?"

"Well, yes and no."

Okay, we were doing this. The talk I'd been putting off for as long as I could.

"When I got pregnant, I kind of dove off the deep end mentally. My pregnancy was a surprise, and at the time, I thought it was pretty much a horror show. My parents kicked me out when I wouldn't have an abortion, and then I was so, so sick. I had hyperemesis...basically morning sickness times a million. I had to be hospitalized, it got so bad."

Callum tensed up, long fingers wrapping around my arm like a steel band. "I didn't know."

"How could you have?" I laid my hand on his and rubbed. After a few seconds, his hold eased enough that it didn't hurt. "Anyway, I started feeling better for a couple months, then my blood pressure spiked. I had him seven weeks early. He was so small, and I was so afraid. I didn't want to be a mom, but I knew if I lost him, I'd die. Luckily, he was fiercer than he looked. He came home after only a month in the NICU."

That NICU stay would have ruined Jenny and me financially, but we got lucky. A charity some philanthropist ran picked my name out of a hat and paid off my entire bill. I still thought about how different my life might have looked if I had that bill looming over my head.

"What's his name?" he asked.

I chewed on the corner of my lip as my stomach twisted uncomfortably. "His name is Ezra."

Callum's gaze held steady on mine. "Why'd you pick that name?"

My nose tingled. I never pictured myself telling Callum why I'd chosen Ezra's name. "Because of the song you told me about. The one that reminded you of me."

He nodded once. "'Hold My Girl' by George Ezra."

"That's the one."

His brow lowered. "You named your son after a song that meant something to me, but he's not my kid. You got pregnant by someone else."

"I know," I whispered around the thick coating in my throat. No, I never thought we'd have this conversation. "I had sex one time. *One* time when I was drunk and sad and feeling rejected and—"

"Rejected by me?" His expression was unreadable. I wouldn't be surprised if he got up and left once I got the whole story out. It certainly didn't paint me in a flattering light.

I nodded, my mouth pressed in a flat line. "After you told me no backstage, I got so drunk, hoping I would forget. Instead, I acted like a complete idiot, lost my virginity to one of my cousin's friends who didn't give a single shit about me, and got pregnant. I felt like I cheated on you, which is probably crazy, but I was so ashamed of myself. I just...I should have emailed you at least once, but my depression and self-hatred were so intense, I wouldn't allow myself to have that small piece of you."

His fingertip traced the edge of my ear. "Is the dad in the picture?"

"Not really. I think Brian—that's his name—would have completely ghosted if he hadn't been my cousin's friend. He's met Ezra a handful of times and talks to him once a month or so through FaceTime. He's still in college, so he sends support when he can, but it's not much, and that's okay. Ezra and I are okay."

"You don't think he's gonna come to his senses and steal you away?"

I had to laugh at that, even though I wasn't certain he was kidding. "No, I don't. We're connected because of our son, but that's the beginning and end of it. Even if I'd felt something romantic for him in the beginning—which I never did—seeing what a shit father he is would have killed that a long time ago."

His sigh was heavy. I hated having no idea what he was thinking. He'd told me nothing had changed last night but believing that was difficult. I wanted it to be true more than anything.

"Okay." That was all he said.

"Okay?"

He nodded.

I frowned.

"I need you to understand that being with me is more complicated because I have Ezra and he's my top priority. Jenny helps a lot, but she's not his mom. I can't do sleepovers whenever I want or dinners after work when all I want to do is rush home and soak up the measly amount of time I have with my son during the week. I get that you might not want to deal with that, and if that's true, then tell me now. It would be better to know before we go any fur—"

Callum covered my mouth with his hand again and pressed his nose to my cheek. "Quiet, Wren. I said nothing's changed, and I meant it. I'm not leavin', and neither are you, so don't bring it up again." He uncovered my mouth and turned my face to his. "I've had a long, kinda shitty day. All I want now is to sink into you and forget every last part of it except that."

I seized up, with both desire and nerves. "I want that too, but Jenny and Ezra are upstairs, and I don't know if—"

"Does your door have a lock?"

I nodded.

"That's all we need. I can think of ways to keep you quiet. Silence is my specialty." He gripped my jaw. "I'm not goin' another hour without having you. Even if that means I drag you back to my place. Make up your mind, Wren."

"I can't leave."

"We'll stay." No hesitation.

"I didn't shave my legs today."

"Don't care." Again, he didn't even blink.

"I'm not wearing cute underwear."

His nostrils flared. "I'm gonna rip them off you anyway."

"But I—"

"Why're you makin' excuses not to be with me, Little Bird?"

"You make me nervous," I breathed.

He pressed his nose to mine. "You make me nervous too."

My stomach swooped. My heart did a crazy, twisty thing. Those were the exact words to get me to drop my barriers and give in. Callum Rose was the real deal. He was who he'd represented himself as in his letters, only magnified and infinitely more beautiful than I'd first thought.

I pushed off his lap, took his hand, and quietly led him upstairs. I could hear the faint sounds of Jenny's television as we passed her room, and the even fainter roar of the waterfall white noise I played for Ezra as he slept. My bedroom was at the end of the hall, with a bathroom between my wall and Ezra's.

As soon as the lock clicked on my door, Callum was on me, backing me toward my bed and having his way with my mouth. Cupping my face, he kissed me slow and deep. None of the urgency from earlier. None of the roughness either. His tongue slid a sensual line along mine, and his lips nipped and teased.

Callum tugged my hair down, then tossed my shirt off. My pants and underwear came off in one swoop, then I was naked and he was fully clothed, pressed flat to my front, his hands roaming freely over my back.

The groan of pure appreciation that rumbled from his chest when he squeezed two handfuls of my ass sent a rush of heat to my core and calmed my jitters. This wasn't our first time, but it was still brand new, and he was still Callum Rose, and I was the chubby mom with big tits, a pudgy belly, and...yeah, okay, a great ass. And I knew, even though he hadn't had sex with anyone but me, he'd seen plenty of gorgeous women. They probably threw themselves at him. I wasn't that. I was something else.

His lips touched my cheek, then below my ear. "Where'd you go?"

"I'm here." My fingers tangled in the short curls at the base of his hairline. "Trying to be quiet."

"No, you were thinkin'." He stepped back, extending his arms, but keeping his hands on my hips. His gaze swept over me, starting low, then working higher and higher. "Whatever you were thinkin' wasn't good. It took you away from me."

"I was thinking how beautiful you are." And that was the truth. Too beautiful for me, but I didn't want to let him go so I'd have to get over it.

His hands came to my breasts, cupping them with enough force to draw my attention. "Do you have any idea, Wren? Every fuckin' time I thought of you today, I got hard. I'd picture your sweet little body, your soft curves, these pretty tits, and my cock was ready to spear through my pants. In front of my lawyer, in front of the cops. I had to stop myself from gettin' up and walking out on my meetings to get to you. So whatever ideas are going on in your head, clear them out. You're mine, and when I have you naked, about to toss you on your bed and have you sittin' on my cock, I want your mind on me like mine's on you. Got it?"

Throat suddenly dry, I could only nod.

"Good."

Callum backed me up until I had no choice but to lie down on the bed. He shucked his clothes off, then he was on me immediately, sucking my nipples deep into his mouth. Playing with my pussy, which was already wet and swollen. Probably still a little from last night. Callum was all over me, touching me, tasting me, savoring the body I'd been worried wasn't attractive enough for him a few minutes ago. He swept me right out of that mindset, and all I could do was let him have me.

He worked his way between my legs, burying his face in my core. I had to bite my lip to keep quiet, but it was difficult, and holy granola, I didn't want to. Not with how Callum was devouring me. And stroking my sides and breasts while he worked. It felt like being worshiped. Like I was his deity and he was showing his devotion for my very existence.

It was too much, not enough, everything, everything. My neck arched, and I brought my hand to my mouth to muffle my moan. There was no holding them back anymore. Callum licked and sucked me through an eye-rolling orgasm, wringing out every drop of my pleasure he could.

I was boneless but filled with desire. When he rolled to his back, I climbed to my knees, straddling his hips. His hands landed on my thighs, and he watched me. He liked to watch, and though I wasn't brimming with confidence, he'd injected me with enough that I could give him a show.

I dragged my lips across his chest, flicking his tight nipples with my tongue. He held my head in his hands, and I explored and tasted him like he'd tasted me. My mouth watered over the ridged lines of his torso. He had tattoos, but not so many that I couldn't see his skin too. When I got to his belly button, I rimmed it with my tongue just because I wanted to. Watching his abs crunch and the small groan he emitted had me smiling against his skin.

"Like that?" He sounded pained, and it made a fresh gush of heat flood between my thighs.

"Mmhmm. I like you," I whispered.

"Then get up here and sit on my cock like I told you. I want to see you ride me."

I wrapped my hand around his length, gasping softly. He was beautiful everywhere. *Everywhere*. Smooth and long, with a little bead of moisture on the tip I licked off. His abs flexed again, and this time, he used his hold on my head to pull me up toward him. I shuffled on my knees, adjusting myself so I was hovering over him.

Callum took hold of my hip with one hand, using the other to guide his cock to my entrance. I lowered myself down, notching his head inside. Just that inch or two stretched me and made me sigh.

"Sit on me, Little Bird. Take all of me." His lids had gone low, and his tongue snuck out to moisten his upper lip. Oh, I liked that look on him.

As much as I was tempted to tease, I wanted him too badly. I rocked forward and back, drawing him deeper and deeper, until we were flush, pelvis to pelvis, and I was filled completely with Callum. My insides were reshaped to fit only him. He should have been way too big, but he was just right. The wild, almost crazed look in his eyes made me think I felt just right to him too.

"Watch me," I said.

He never took his eyes off me, though his gaze roamed just as much as his hands did. For once, I didn't think about how I looked, only how he saw me. I rode him slow at first, finding my rhythm. Callum held my breasts and hips, brushing his fingers over my stomach and where we were connected between my thighs.

When my confidence grew, I balanced one hand on his chest and started to really ride him. My skin slapped against his with each pass. It was a good sound. The best sound. My ass hitting his thighs, his answering groan. I had to shush him even though I never wanted to hear the end of his pleasure. God, it was music, and I was making it with him.

My clit was throbbing. My belly was tight. So tight, I could barely stand it. Callum must have sensed my rising frenzy. His thumb found my clit, pressing and circling in the perfect way. I fucked him harder, slamming myself down again and again, so wet and needy.

The whole time, I bit my lip, stifling my moans. I'd probably be swollen and red there tomorrow too, but I couldn't bring myself to care.

I was Callum's show, and he was ever attentive. His cock swelled inside me, and his whispered grunts rose and rose in volume.

"Callum, shhh."

He jackknifed into a sitting position, wrapped his arms around me, and buried his face in my neck. When his teeth clamped down on my shoulder, I was off, moaning in ecstasy. His hand covered my mouth, but it wasn't enough to stifle me, so I bit down on the meaty part of his palm and writhed through my pleasure. Callum grunted with me, fucking me from beneath now. Harder, faster, plunging in and out, wrecking my shoulder and neck with his mouth. He held me, and I held him until he let go, coming inside my fluttering walls.

Breathless and wrung out, I let Callum move me however he wanted me on the bed. I was on my back again, and his hands were braced on either side of my head. His mouth covered mine, kissing me so thoroughly, I forgot where and *who* I was. It was only us. Only this. His mouth. Mine. This bed. One moment.

His forehead rested on mine for a long beat, then he sat back on his heels and spread my legs wide. One finger dragged through my folds. Oversensitive and a little sore, I tried to clamp my thighs shut, but he pushed them open again.

"What are you doing?" I whispered.

He swirled his finger around the outside of my entrance. "Seein' how pretty your cunt looks with my cum dripping out of it." He plunged his finger into me. "And thinkin' I want you to keep this piece of me inside you for as long as I can."

Goose bumps rose along my skin. This shouldn't have made me feel sexy, but it did. Knowing he wanted me to carry his pleasure inside me made my inner walls clench.

Eventually, he fell down beside me and kissed my cheek in a tender, sweet kind of way. He was silent, and I was sleepy, especially when he kept stroking my back and hair. I melted and allowed my lids to lower, but each time I started to drift, I jolted awake.

"Just go to sleep, Wren," he soothed.

"Can't. I have to send you home, but this feels too nice and I don't want it to end."

His hand on my back stilled. "I'm not goin' home."

Suddenly, I was awake. I propped myself up on my elbow and frowned down at him. "I want you here, I do, but I am nowhere near ready to introduce you to Ezra. It's too early, and I haven't even begun to think of how that would even go down or how I'd explain you to him so—"

"Shhh." I raised my eyebrow, but he only stared at me, unflinching. "I'm stayin'. If you want to smuggle me out in the morning, you can do that. But I'm not gonna let you kick me out tonight when we've both been wanting to be in each other's arms all damn day."

"I don't know…"

"Wren." His fingers sifted into my hair, and he pulled me back down to lie on his chest. "I don't need to meet him right now. I'm good with it being just you and me until you're ready. This is all I need, your body tucked next to mine. I will climb down a drainpipe in the morning if you want me to, but there's no way you're gonna get me out of this bed until then."

"Fine." I shoved at his chest, even though I wasn't mad at his stubbornness. "You have to put clothes on, though."

I couldn't imagine the conversation Ezra and I would be having if he snuck into my room and found a giant naked man in my bed. I shuddered at the thought.

He groaned. "Don't want to, but if it means I can stay without having to tie you up to force the issue, then I'll throw on some pants. Give me a minute to hold you like this first."

"'Kay." I snuggled my head under his chin and draped my body along the side of his, completely content. "Just for a minute, though."

It turned out, Callum Rose was the perfect cure for a crappy day…even if he'd been part of the cause.

CHAPTER EIGHTEEN

CALLUM

THE SECOND I WOKE UP, I remembered I was in Wren's bed. Without opening my eyes, I also knew for sure she wasn't in it with me. The shower was running in the bathroom next door, so I assumed she was in there.

It must've been early. She hadn't kicked me out yet, and I was still tired as hell. That was partly because Wren and I hadn't fallen asleep until...well, it was late. But we had lost time to make up for, and no matter how many times I came, I couldn't seem to get enough of being inside her.

She couldn't get enough either. She let me bend her soft, round body in every way, experimenting to find positions we liked, then fucking missionary, because hell, sometimes vanilla was the sweetest flavor of them all. Wren never forgot where we were, though, reminding me to be quiet when I got too loud, smothering her face in her pillow when she couldn't hold back her moans. Even that part was sexy, because it was *her*. My pretty little bird who was finally in the palm of my hand. Everything I never knew I wanted.

All these years, watching from afar, telling myself she wasn't mine, that I was protecting her from a distance and I'd been missing out. Not just on her body, but on her. I smiled when I was with her. I *talked*. I didn't cringe at the sound of my voice when we were having a conversation.

What the hell had I been thinking staying away?

I knew. I'd been wrapped up in her purported rejection. Too consumed with jealousy over her being with another guy to even question why the asshole wasn't in her life when he'd knocked her up. Licking my wounds like a damn kicked dog instead of taking charge and getting my girl.

So much time we could've been together, all wasted. I fucking refused to waste another second. I'd push if I had to, but I wasn't going away.

A gentle poke on my shoulder had my eyelids flying open. Dark amber pools stared back at me from beside the bed. *Ezra.*

Shit. Wren wasn't going to be happy. To be quite honest, I didn't love the situation either. A tiny sweet-breathed boy staring at me like a puzzle before the crack of dawn. I should've climbed down the motherfuckin' drainpipe like I'd planned.

"Are you Mommy's friend?" he asked.

"I'm Callum."

Wren's son has the same color hair as her, but where hers was silky and glossy, his was a pile of wild curls on top of his head. His cheeks were just the right amount of round, and he shared her too-big eyes. The kid was cute. But maybe I thought that because, up close like this, all I saw was a baby version of Wren. It was like she'd made him without any outside help.

I liked that idea.

"Callum?" He had trouble with 'L.' In his soft, little boy voice, my name came out "Cow-um," and I don't know, maybe it was an improvement.

"Yeah. I'm Callum."

He nodded once. Decisively. Like that had sealed the deal. "You are Mommy's friend. She only has three."

"Did she tell you about me?"

He nodded again, this time smiling. His teeth were small, with gaps between, and bright white. "Mommy only has three friends." He snickered like he'd just told the funniest joke he'd ever heard, and damn if I didn't fight the urge to chuckle. "Mommy thinks I'm her friend!" He laughed even harder.

"You're not?"

"No, I'm her boy."

"Can't be her friend too?"

His nose wrinkled. "No. I'm Mommy's boy. You're Mommy's friend."

"Yeah." I rubbed some of the sleep from my eye. "I guess I am."

Or...I had been until her kid found me in her bed. Didn't know how friendly Wren was gonna feel toward me when she discovered Ezra and I were acquainted.

He looked me over, kinda judgy. "You wearing your jammies?"

"I think I forgot to put them on last night." Thank fuck I'd listened to Wren and tossed on my briefs and a T-shirt. She *really* wouldn't have liked me if her kid had seen my bare ass.

He tugged on his snug T-shirt. "I'm wearing jammies. You like them?"

I looked him over. He had some kind of dog with a fireman hat printed on his shirt. The dog seemed pretty legit.

"I do. You think they make those in my size?"

He squinted at me, like he was taking stock of just how big I was. "I can ask my mommy. She could buy some for you." Then he ran out of the room, yelling for his mother.

I rolled onto my back, breathing out a sigh. Raised the way I was, with a mishmash of families living communally, I'd been around kids. A lot of kids. I'd never been uncomfortable with them. The thing was, in the back of my mind, I thought I'd resent Wren's kid. *Ezra.* Not that it was his fault he existed, but I thought I'd resent his existence anyway.

I searched around my brain and chest, and there was none of that there. I didn't quite know how I felt about him, but it wasn't anything bad. Definitely no resentment. He was too much of

Wren for that to even be a possibility. That was a good thing, because I didn't think Wren would like me too much if I gave her kid the stink eye.

A few minutes later, Wren stepped into the room, wrapped in a towel, with bright red cheeks and wild, frantic eyes.

"Oh my god," she wheezed.

"Yeah." I sat up and swung my legs off the bed. "I met Ezra."

Her eyes flared. "Oh my god!"

"He's cute, Wren. Looks like you."

That snapped her out of her broken record stupor. Pride straightened her spine. "Right? Brian's DNA got trounced by mine."

I chuckled even though hearing that fucker's name didn't fill me with the warm fuzzies.

She approached me, standing between my legs. Gripping her hips, I pulled her close enough that I could press my face into her stomach. Her fingers trailed through my hair, and I felt her sigh.

"He should be sleeping. I think he must've heard me showering and wandered in here. I'm sorry. That had to be weird for you."

I shook my head. "He told me you talk about me."

She stiffened for a beat, then giggled. "Once. I mentioned your name once when I had to scramble to come up with friends' names so my own child wouldn't think I'm a loser."

"Are you sayin' I'm not your friend?"

Her hand smoothed over my head down to my shoulder. "You were always my best friend, Callum Rose. I'm hoping we can get back to that status. You're definitely my friend, though."

I slid up her towel to cup her butt. "Gonna work hard to get back there." I moved my face back and forth against her stomach, wishing I could pull her astride my lap and let her ride me hard like she had last night. Now wasn't the time. And I still didn't feel that resentment I'd worried I might. I was more relieved by that than I expected. Then again, not liking my girl's son was probably a dealbreaker for her.

"I have to get dressed." She poked my shoulder. "And so do you. Ezra's playing in his room, but there's no telling how long he'll be occupied. I need to sneak you out of here before he unloads a million other questions I don't have an answer for."

I didn't let her go, pulling her closer instead. "Why do you need to sneak me out? The cat's outta the bag, Wren. He's met me. I've met him. The world didn't end."

Her shoulders curled with a weary sigh. "I don't know what I'm doing here, but it seems like I shouldn't be introducing men to Ezra all willy-nilly. I don't want him confused by it."

"Men?" My fingers dug into her peachy ass. "Why plural? I'm the only man he's gonna be meeting, and that ship has sailed. He's met me, he's cool, let it be."

The corners of her eyes pinched. "You're sounding awfully presumptuous, sir."

"Mmhmm. You're mine. I'm not lettin' you go. So, there's no need to worry about Ezra meeting other men. It's me and only me. I get that you wanted to go slow, but that didn't happen, and this is the place we're at now." I rose to standing, letting go of her ass to cup the sides of her neck. "I'm not goin' anywhere, Wren, and neither are you. Not gonna hurt you or fuck up your life. Not gonna hurt the boy. Stop worryin' and get your sweet ass covered before I act inappropriately with someone's mother."

Her mouth fell open, so I bit her bottom lip. "Go, Little Bird. Put some clothes on."

I tugged my jeans on, then I sat down to watch the show that was Wren getting dressed. Her panties were no-nonsense black, bra the same. She caught me looking a few times, blushed over her shoulder at me, and shook her head like I was crazy for wanting to see her like that. She didn't understand how starved I was for this—this intimate peek into her life she gave me freely, not something I had to steal.

"Am I entertaining you?" She tossed a balled-up pair of socks at me, which I caught, grinning. "This can't be as interesting as you're making it look."

Cocking my head, I grinned and swept my gaze over her. "Like watchin' you get dressed. Bein' in your room, smellin' your girly scent all over everything, seein' you in the soft morning light, it's like I'm enveloped in Wren-world, and I'm not in any hurry to get out."

She blinked, a smile playing at the edge of her mouth. "I smell girly?"

"So girly. Like lemonade, summer sun, and pure, sweet girl. I've had dreams where all I'm doin' is smelling you and it's like fuckin' heaven."

Her bottom lip caught between her teeth right before she turned away, sifting through her closet. I approached her, pushing her hair aside to kiss her shoulder, then looped my arm around her chest and pressed my front to her back.

"You don't need to hide your reaction from me," I murmured.

"I'm not." Her head fell back on my chest. "It's just…you keep saying these things that are filling a part of me I hadn't even been aware was empty and I'm scared."

"Why are you scared?"

"Because what if I get used to it and it goes away?" she whispered. "It was okay that I was empty before. I didn't even know what I was missing, you know? But now I do, and I'm afraid if you keep filling me up the way you do, I'll get used to it. And then, one day, what if this doesn't work out and you're gone, and I have this big empty place in me I'm acutely aware of because you took such good care of me and said such nice things and made me feel so pretty and desired. What am I going to do then?"

I took her by the shoulders, spinning her around, and covered her worried mouth with mine. She gasped at first, then melted into me, giving me her lips and tongue.

Words weren't my thing. I once went fifteen days without speaking, and only broke my silence so I didn't fade away. But with Wren, my thoughts tumbled out, and my thoughts about her were overwhelmingly sweet. Maybe I should've played it cool, kept some of it to myself, but games weren't my thing either.

My forehead knocked against hers when our lips parted. "Not gonna happen. I'm not goin' anywhere by choice. If I should happen to be hit by a bus tomorrow, then I'm glad you're aware of that part of you that's been achin' to be filled. You deserve to have that. I never want you to think bein' empty is okay. Even if my ass is splat under a damn bus."

She scratched my beard and sighed. "I need to get dressed."

Reticent little bird. I guess I was just going to have to show her how out of my mind I was over her. She wasn't getting it. But she would.

As if on cue, the door to her bedroom banged open and Ezra charged inside. Ignoring his mother, he stopped in front of me and jumped up and down, poking his chest.

"Mommy, Mommy! Cow-um wants my jammies!" he proclaimed.

Snorting a laugh, Wren pulled a long-sleeve T-shirt over her head. "Really? I don't know if they'll fit, Cow-um." Her eyes flared with amusement. "Are you a big *PAW Patrol* fan?"

I raised a brow at her. I had no fuckin' clue. "The biggest."

Ezra jumped again, this time with his arms straight up in the air. "I'm the biggest!"

I smacked my forehead. "That's right. You are the biggest. I forgot."

He squealed and threw himself at Wren's legs. She laughed and rubbed his hair, all while keeping an eye on me. I'd seen them together, but watching from the outside was nothing like being in her sweet-smelling bedroom, Wren pantless, Ezra in jammies and crazy hair, hugging and happy.

"What do you want for breakfast?" she asked her son.

"Eggs!" Everything seemed to be an exclamation from him. "Cow-um can make them."

Wren laughed. "Callum has to go bye-bye. I'll make your eggs, baby buddy."

It was early Sunday morning, I had nowhere to be. I wanted to contradict her, but I wasn't about to do that in front of her kid. I didn't always understand a lot about most people, but I knew better than to get between a mother and her kid.

Ezra poked his lip out. "You gotta go bye-bye?"

I shrugged. "Maybe I can hang out for a little while. I can't cook eggs, though. Not unless you want them to be black."

His tiny nose wrinkled. "Nooo! That's yucky!"

Wren put her hands on her hips. "See why Mommy has to cook your eggs? Nobody likes black eggs."

Ezra screeched again and ran to the bed to start bouncing all over it. Kid had energy, fuck. It wasn't even six thirty in the morning.

Wren looked at me. I looked back at her. Her forehead was crinkled.

"You need pants."

She looked down at her legs, giggling after a beat. "Yeah, I guess I do."

Once she put on a pair of leggings, I got down on my knee and took a foot in my hand to slip a thick, woolen sock on. Then I traded it for the other foot, repeating the process. I stood and kissed her crown. Her forehead was crinkled again when I met her gaze.

"Go make your kid breakfast, Little Bird."

"Are you staying?" she asked.

"Yeah. Maybe you could make me a couple eggs too."

She reached out and squeezed my hand, giving me a shy, sweet smile. "I think I can handle that. As long as you're not freaked out about hanging around my kid for a while longer."

I shook my head. "Not freaked out. Wishin' I had the freedom to do dirty things to you whenever I want, but no, I'm not freaked out."

She sputtered a laugh. "Oh my god, the mouth on you."

I was still tired as hell, regretting I couldn't take Wren back to bed and fuck her until we were both sore, and unsure what to do with a three-year-old, but I plopped my happy ass down next to Ezra on the couch and watched an episode of *PAW Patrol* with him. He was a talker, that kid, so I really didn't have to do a lot, which was good. If I'd been called to do much more than watch a TV show, I didn't know that I could have kept up. I would have tried, though.

But I sat there, with Ezra's hand on my arm, catching glimpses of Wren's head as she was busy in the kitchen, and I didn't resent a single thing about this morning. Well, I could've slept a couple more hours. Maybe I was delirious, but even that didn't seem so bad.

When we were eating buttery eggs and toast, Jenny came down, giving kisses to Wren and Ezra, and shooting me a glare without any heat behind it. She fixed herself coffee and Wren sat beside me, eating her breakfast while keeping an eye on Ezra, who, it appeared, liked to throw his food to the two cats who seemed to have emerged from the ether. Lyle and Lovett. God, even the cats had great names.

Wren squeezed my leg under the table. I looked at her, her kid, and her aunt. This was family. I'd grown up never alone, always surrounded by brothers and sisters, aunts and uncles. It hadn't felt like this. It'd been strange, unconventional, and sometimes fucked the hell up. Wren's family wasn't conventional either. Teen mom, widowed great-aunt, one little boy. That was it, no one else. But it was a whole lot.

As I ate my eggs and listened to Wren and Jenny talk about nothing much but riveting all the same, I thought Wren had better like me, 'cause I liked her, liked her family, and I wasn't going anywhere.

Night fell, and I was spent. After a sunrise breakfast with Wren and Ezra, I went home to further deal with the shit show of the fight I'd gotten into at the bar. A few blogs were covering the story, and the video was circulating, but it wasn't huge news. All my *people* seemed pretty unworried by it. My bloodthirsty manager even seemed a little gleeful about the attention. What mattered to me was keeping Wren safe and her privacy secure. For now, her name was out there, but the buzz was low enough, I wasn't crazy concerned.

I picked up my phone and sent my girl a text. It'd become our ritual to end our day like this. It didn't matter that I'd spent the morning at her place, followed by her stopping by to watch me spar with Gregor, and then a visit to the grocery store. I couldn't get enough of her. Soon, I was going to find a way to have her by my side all the time.

Me: *Hi, Little Bird. You in bed?*

Wren: *Hey. Yep. You know me. Are you?*

Me: *Yeah. Someone kept me up all night with her demands.*

Wren: *Don't blame me for your insatiability!*

Me: *You think it's not your fault my dick is constantly rock hard? 'Cause it is.*

Wren: *Well, it's mutual. I don't even want to tell you how many panties you've ruined.*

Me: *Please, tell me. Better yet, give them to me so I can wrap them around my cock when I'm thinking about you.*

Wren: *Gah! I'm trying to wind down and you're getting me worked up. No more sex stuff. I'm too tired to get myself off tonight!*

Me: *Wish I was there, Little Bird. And not just because I would tongue fuck the frustration out of you. I want you in my arms when I'm going to sleep.*

Wren: *Callum Rose! That isn't helping…but yeah, I'd like that too. A lot. Let's give it some time, okay? Then we'll do that.*

Me: *Hope you mean both the tongue fucking and the sleeping.*

Wren: *I absolutely do mean that.*

Me: *Fuck, Little Bird. You're too hot. Drive me crazy. Today went well, right?*

Wren: *Yeah. Everything about today was really good. Ez was asking if you're going to be here in the morning. Love how he says your name. It's so cute.*

Me: *I kinda like it too. I spent a lot of time around kids growing up. Lots of kids. Think yours is the cutest.*

Wren: *Obviously. :) Thank you. I like him. He likes you too. He told Jenny you're going to teach him to play guitar.*

Me: *And he's gonna show me Bob.*

Wren: *I'm happy, Callum. Really happy. Are you?*

Me: *Can't you tell?*

Wren: *I think? Maybe? I've never had a boyfriend. I don't know what I'm doing. I'll probably break all the rules and read every signal incorrectly.*

I froze with my phone in my hand. My cock went rock hard, straining against my jeans. Wren was mine in my head, but seeing her calling me her boyfriend without being forced or prompted made me want to tear down the city blocks between us and claim her sweet pussy all over again.

Wren: *Crap. I probably shouldn't be calling you my boyfriend until we actually talk about that. So, maybe just ignore that.*

I dialed her number. I couldn't have her doubting me because I got too caught up in my own thoughts to reply to her.

"Hi," she whispered.

"Wren. Stop."

"Stop?"

"Mmhmm. Stop freakin' out. I told you you're mine. If you wanna call me your cock slave or your boyfriend, I'm good, as long as you're callin' me yours."

Her laugh was choked. "Cock slave? I don't know if that would fly in public. In private, though..."

"Wren."

"Yeah. I hear you. I'm getting used to this, Callum. Like I said, having a boyfriend is really new for me. You might need to be a little patient with me."

"I'll be as patient as you need."

I could hear her shifting in bed, and the soft sounds of her breathing. My cock was still throbbing. I would have given almost anything to be in that bed with her, holding and touching her warm body.

"You haven't been a boyfriend before, right?" she asked.

"No. Never. There's never been anyone else I've wanted."

She sighed. "So, I could be a hot mess at this, and you'd have no idea?"

"Yeah. Same goes the other way, though."

Her laugh was breathy and soft. "Thanks for calling me and talking me down from my mental ledge. I really don't want to screw this up."

"You won't."

"I might, but I don't want to." She yawned. "Will I see you for lunch tomorrow?"

"Yep. Wouldn't miss it. You and your shitty bench."

"I really can't wait," she replied.

"Go to sleep, Little Bird. I'll see you tomorrow."

"Good night, Callum."

Wren wasn't going to screw this up. Me? No doubt I would. I could only hope she was patient with me, because after this weekend together, there was nothing that would get me to walk away from her.

My phone rang, jerking me out of sleep. Instinctively, I knew whatever lay on the other end of the call wasn't going to be something I'd like. Nothing good came from one a.m. phone calls.

My sister's name flashed on the screen, and if I didn't answer, she'd call again and again.

"Chrys," I groused into the phone.

"Cal. Hey, honey. I wake you up?"

Chrysanthemum Claudette Rose was exactly ten months younger than me. She was one of two of my full-blooded siblings. I didn't know how many half-siblings I had. God, I didn't even want to know.

"You did. You wantin' money?"

No sense in beating around the bush. Chrys might call and act like she cared, but in the end, money was the real reason she got in touch.

"Saw your name in the news." She chuckled. "You're still gettin' in fights, huh? What'd the guy do to piss you off this time? Bump into you and spill your beer?"

I didn't bother answering. She saw the article, so she knew why I'd gotten in an altercation—and it had nothing to do with a beer.

She sighed. "It's been a long time, honey. I miss you. The only way I see you is if I read the music news. I was thinkin' about comin' to the city with Rasc. Maybe you'll have time for a visit?"

Rascal Theodore Rose was my other full-blooded sibling, and he was exactly ten months older than me. Once upon a time, the three of us had been thick as thieves—and I did mean that literally. But shit happened. I needed out of that lifestyle, to go my own way, and Rasc and Chrys got stuck. They didn't see a way out, but they'd never looked.

"How much money you want, Chrys?"

Her sigh came heavier. "Do you not want to see us? I know we're not close anymore, but we love you, Cal. We're family, honey."

My jaw clenched so tight, I heard my teeth squeaking. "Were we family when you blackmailed me?"

She made a choking sound, then cleared her throat. "That was a mistake. I would never hurt you. I don't know how to make you believe I'm sorry. We were desperate."

"I'm tired. I don't wanna play games with you. Just tell me how much you want this time."

"I saw your woman in the video. I'm glad you have someone in your life. That makes me so happy for you. Raised like we were, it isn't easy to have someone. But you...you were always the best of us. If anyone was going to rise above it, it was you, Cal."

Barbed wire wrapped around my chest. There was no threat in Chrys's words. She probably didn't even intend to imply one, knowing her. She was a good girl. A sweet girl. But desperation made people ugly, and her and Rasc knowing about Wren wasn't safe.

My hands opened and clenched, opened and clenched.

"Don't you even think about her. She doesn't exist to you. You tell Rasc the same."

"Okay," she whispered. "I'm sorry."

"Now, *how much* you want, Chrys?"

She didn't speak for a while, but I could hear light chaos in the background. I had no idea if she was still with The Traveling Roses or if she'd broken off to start some other brand of grifting. Either way wouldn't surprise me.

"I hate askin', Cal. Hate it so much, especially when you don't think of me as your sister anymore. But the RV Rasc and I are travelin' in needs some repairs. The thing is, we can't earn money unless we're travelin', but we're stuck and—"

"How. Much?" This was the last time I'd ask. The less I knew about my brother and sister, the better.

"A thousand, if you can spare it." Her voice quivered, and if I didn't know better, I'd say she sounded ashamed. But I knew better. "Maybe two. That would be even better."

"Tell me where you want me to send it. It'll be there by morning."

She rattled off the place, still sounding shaken as she spoke. I kept my walls up, heart hard, not falling for her tricks. Never again.

"Cal—"

"No. I'm sending you this money so I can get off the fuckin' phone and go to sleep. Not because I want anything to do with you. The opposite is true. You dropped a nuclear bomb on the only bridge between us when you blackmailed me. I'm hangin' up now, Chrys. I'm done."

Ending the call, I tossed my phone onto my nightstand with a clatter.

Fuck this.

After a perfect day with a perfect family, of fucking course the antichrist had to remind me of the hellhole I came from and would always come from.

My family. The very fuckin' reason why I'd never been able to have nice things.

Fuck this.

CHAPTER NINETEEN

WREN

ADELAIDE SKIDDED TO A STOP at my desk first thing Monday morning. Her mouth spread into a wide, lascivious grin, and her eyebrows bobbled.

"So…?"

I frowned at her. This was the first time she'd ever stopped at my desk, and I was more than a little confused. "Good morning to you too."

She waved me off. "Good morning, yeah, yeah. Now, I'm going to need more info about the giant Scandinavian rock star who whisked you away from the bar after going all medieval on that perv's ass. I've waited two entire days to hear this. No time for manners and social conventions. Spill, babe."

"I think he's mostly English, actually."

Adelaide's eyes goggled, and her cheeks filled with so much air, explosion seemed imminent.

From behind me, heels clacked on the floor, warning me of Natalie's fast approach. I straightened, tipping my head to the side to signal to Adelaide that she needed to go, but she was planted in her spot.

Natalie came to stand beside Adelaide, coffin-shaped nails tapping on my desk.

"Well…?" Her perfectly arched eyebrows shot up.

Adelaide elbowed her. "She wants us to say good morning before we ask her about the rock star."

Natalie rolled her eyes. "Good morning, Wren. Now, tell me what the fuck happened Friday night."

"Um…" I clasped my hands together to stop from fidgeting, "well, this guy from my neighborhood was bothering me. Really bothering me. Then Callum came in, saw it going down, and… uh, he took care of it."

Natalie rolled her eyes again, and this time, Adelaide joined her. "Are you kidding me? You're the worst at telling stories," Natalie announced. "We need details, and not about the neighborhood rat. Jesus, Wren. Get with it."

Adelaide elbowed her a little harder than the first time. "Don't talk to her like that."

Natalie's eyes lowered to her hands, and to my surprise, she seemed chagrined. Maybe she actually respected Adelaide. "I apologize. My mouth gets away from me when I'm eager. By the way, I rescued your coat from the bar and tucked it in your cubby."

"Oh, thanks. And it's fine." It wasn't fine. I didn't love this type of attention. I had to stop myself from attacking my cuticles. "Well…so, Callum and I are seeing each other. So yeah. He wasn't pleased with Edwin touching me, and he let him know."

Adelaide grinned. "Callum Rose is your boyfriend?" She seemed genuinely excited by that fact, if the way she was bouncing on her toes was any indication.

He *was* my boyfriend. I'd confirmed that last night. It was still strange to hear out loud, though.

"Yeah, he is," I confirmed. "We're pretty new, so I'm not announcing it to the world or anything—"

Natalie snorted. "Good luck. Everyone saw your video from the bar. People are interested in Callum because he's such a mystery. No one knows jack about him. Then, all of a sudden, he shows up at a bar in Queens and throws *down* over an unknown girl. Yeah, I'd say people are interested."

Adelaide rubbed her hands together. "I'm more interested in the juicy details. How'd you meet? Does he treat you like a queen? Etcetera, etcetera."

"He's nice. So nice to me. Really sweet and caring and protective." I bit my bottom lip. "I guess you know that since you were there on Friday. Anyway, we met here, he asked me out, and we just clicked. He's intense and funny and I like him."

Those were all the details they were getting from me. Our history was ours alone. Callum and I hadn't discussed how to handle that, but instinctively, I wanted to keep our story between us.

Natalie folded her arms over her chest. "I *did* tell you fraternizing with the talent is frowned upon, right?"

Adelaide shoved her before I could respond. "Oh, shut up. Go be miserable and jealous somewhere else."

Natalie stomped. "I'm not jealous. I'm looking out for Wren. She doesn't need to get a bad reputation. How is she going to move up in the company if she gets a reputation of throwing herself at musicians? I mean, not all of us can rely on nepotism."

Adelaide's cheeks reddened, and her nostrils flared. "I think I hear your phone ringing, Natalie. I'd go check it if I were you. Wouldn't want to fuck up your job, now would you?"

With a huff, Natalie stalked off, leaving me stumped and Adelaide with another wide smile.

"Wow, do I not like her," she said.

"Sometimes she's nice." I had no idea why I was defending Natalie. Girl could take care of herself.

"Yeah, well, sometimes it snows in hell. Ask Natalie. She sucked Satan's balls this morning."

I had to giggle at that, and so did Adelaide.

She leaned forward, propping her elbows on my desk. "Listen, I know you're probably all private because Callum's famous and all that. I am not offended if you want to tell me to fuck off."

"I don't want to tell you to fuck off." I shrugged. "I think I'd be private even if he weren't famous. He's my first boyfriend, so I don't know, but I think I like keeping *us* to myself."

Adelaide's eyes bugged. "First boyfriend?" I nodded. "Wow, go big or go home, huh?"

I giggled again. "I guess. By the way, what did Natalie mean by nepotism getting you your job?"

Her shoulders rolled forward, and the humor drained from her face. "My last name is Goodman. As in Good Music. Saul Goodman. That jackass is my dad and most certainly why I have a job I'm not qualified for."

"Whoa." Adelaide's dad was technically my boss, although there were probably a hundred minions between me and him. "Not a fan of your dad?"

Her lip curled. "Not so much. I hate accepting things from him. But a girl's gotta eat. I'd be stupid not to accept this job just because I don't like my dad."

I nodded. "If my dad owned a record label instead of working the night shift at

Al's Liquor Emporium, I think I'd feel the same way. No judgments."

She shot finger guns at me. "You're the best. I'm glad you have a gorgeous, mysterious rock star boyfriend, honey. You deserve it, as long as he keeps treating you like the queen you are."

I smiled at her, thinking I couldn't wait to go home and inform my kid his mother had another name to add to her friend list.

Callum was never outgoing or effusive, but while sitting beside him on my shitty bench in the ice-cold afternoon air, he felt removed. A lot farther away than his shoulder brushing mine and his hand claiming my thigh made it seem.

I put my sandwich down and sucked up the nerve to address it. "Did I do something wrong?"

His head turned sharply in my direction. "What the fuck?"

"It's just...you seem kind of miserable and I...well, I hate it. If I'm the cause, I'd like to know so I can help you not feel that way anymore."

He took my face in his hands so fast, I almost missed the movement, and jerked me into his chest. "You will never make me miserable. You are everything good and easy. I'm stuck in my head and fuckin' things up, so I'm sorry. I'm not good company today. I would've canceled, but I can't seem to go a day without seein' you anymore. I know it's selfish since I'm infecting our time together, but I can't stay away."

"I don't want you to stay away. I want you to let me make it better." My gloved fingers wrapped around his wrists. "Callum, did something happen? Is it about what happened at the bar?"

"No, it's not." His lips covered mine, tipping my head back to slide his tongue inside and deepen the kiss. He didn't have to use words to reassure me I wasn't the source of his black cloud. I felt it in every centimeter of our connection. He kissed me like I was the sunshine that broke his stormy existence. And I loved being that for him. I wanted him to lean on me and let me protect him that way—to give him back some of the care he gave me.

I would have climbed on top of him and soaked up his entire being if he hadn't pulled away, stroking my face and murmuring that we were in public where anyone could see.

"Don't want to share this with anyone, Little Bird."

There he went, taking care of me even when he turned me into a wanton floozy about to mount him in a public park in Manhattan.

"I like your kisses a little too much," I said.

His lips twitched, and I felt some of the turmoil parting. "No such thing. I want you addicted so you'll keep comin' back."

"Mission accomplished."

I scratched his beard, once again utterly devastated by his beauty. Callum Rose only became more gorgeous the closer we grew. He made me jitter with nerves, then he soothed me with his steady, unrelenting presence. When he said he wasn't letting me go, I was beginning to believe that was true. And so, even though I still thought he was far too beautiful for a girl like me, I was also beginning to believe he didn't think so. He didn't think so at all.

"Got a call from my sister last night." He grimaced but didn't pull away from me. "She was lookin' for money, even though she tried to disguise it by sayin' she missed me."

I kept stroking his face, even while my heart broke a little. He'd told me about his brother and sister blackmailing him and had shrugged it off like it didn't matter. But now, I knew him better, and I saw the cracks beneath his surface. What he felt was far more complicated.

"Is it possible both are true? I know I'd miss you if you were gone. I *did* miss you when you were gone."

His brow slanted, and the corners of his mouth tugged down. "She might miss me, but not enough to call when she doesn't need something. I don't even blame her. We grew up seein' people outside of family as marks and nothin' else. I'm outside the family now. I'm a mark to her."

My hands curled around his neck. I wished he had a scarf. Something to protect him against the harsh elements. "Did you give her money?"

He nodded. "She asked for two grand. I wired her five."

"You care."

Ice-blue eyes lifted to mine. "Don't want to."

"But you do."

"She's not worth carin' about. She proved that to me and keeps provin' it to me."

"But you do anyway."

"Fuck, Wren." His eyes squeezed shut. "We grew up knowin' nothing but lyin' and deceit. Any show of kindness from strangers, we took advantage of it. I can't even blame Chrys and Rasc for bein' how they are. It's all they know. I blame myself for the soft spot I can't seem to scrub out. The one they know exists and pounce on whenever they want."

I knocked my forehead against his, my heart breaking a little more. "As much as you try to project it, you're not stone cold. That's your brother and sister. They might have betrayed you, but I know you. You feel deeply, and you don't turn off those feelings easily."

His hands worked into my hair until he cupped the back of my head. "Wish I could. It'd be easier. I'd make a clean break and walk away."

"You wouldn't be you if you could. And I like you so, so much."

He stilled, except for his fingertips on my scalp, which rubbed me in a rhythmic motion.

"I'm not likable," he said after a minute.

"To me you are. My son likes you. So does Jenny. So maybe rethink that opinion of yourself."

Another minute passed of him rubbing my scalp and peering at me like I was a tropical oasis in the tundra.

"You make everything better, Wren. You know that? This is why I'm never giving you up. You might be addicted to my mouth on you, but I'm addicted to the way you reach into my soul and pour goodness and light in. Nothin' like it. Can't get enough." His mouth hovered over mine while my heart did a wild gallop in my chest. "I want to fuck you, Little Bird. I'm not waiting until the weekend to do it."

I nodded. The spot between my legs throbbed at those words. "I was close to mounting you on this shitty bench, so I don't think I can wait either. Come over tonight after Ez goes to sleep."

"I will. You're gonna make me be quiet?"

"Mmhmm."

"Need you to come to my place this weekend so I can fuck you loud."

Goose bumps spread down my arms. "I need that too."

His hands in my hair flexed. "This is good, Wren. Do you feel that?"

"I do. I'm surprised by how good it is, but yeah, I definitely feel it."

"Why are you surprised?"

I rubbed my lips together. "Because I don't know what I'm doing or how to be a girlfriend. I'm a single mom and you're a freaking rock star. I'm a Jersey girl and you're an Alabama boy. We started because I sent you fan mail, and we ended because I was too afraid to meet you. None of those things bode well for us, but it doesn't seem to matter, does it? When I'm with you, all of that falls away. We're just Wren and Callum. We're the friends we were in our letters, but more. So much more. And I like it so, so much. I like you so, so much. Even more than when we were pen pals. Even more than I did yesterday and the day before. I'm surprised by it because I've never had it, but I hope to all that is holy I can keep having it."

Once again, he'd gone still, but the ice in his eyes melted, leaving pure, blue fire. Finally, he drew me to him, touching his lips to mine, then the tip of my nose and both eyelids.

"Never letting you go," he murmured. "You'll keep havin' it, Wren. I came here today gutted and empty, and I am so full now, since I can't fuck you until tonight, I'm gonna have to go for a long, long run to work some of this out of me."

"That's a nice thing to say."

He grinned. Finally. "Only you would think so."

"Isn't that all that matters?"

His nose touched mine. "Yeah. All that matters."

Callum was in my bed Monday and Tuesday. We thought of creative ways to keep quiet. His favorite way of silencing me was stuffing my panties in my mouth. Second to that was giving me his hand to bite down on. He kept himself quiet by sucking on my various body parts, most notably my tits and shoulders.

I wouldn't let him sleep over, which pissed him off. He protested, but when I pulled the mom card, he couldn't say much, even though he wanted to. And that only made me like him more. It wasn't that I didn't want Ezra to see Callum with me or for them to get to know one another, it was just that I wanted to be deliberate in how I integrated Callum into Ezra's life, accidental meetings aside. I was head over heels and falling stupidly in love with Callum Rose, but when it came to my son, I'd always try to make the wisest decision. And for now, going slow seemed like the right course.

By Wednesday night, Callum was back to himself. His sister's call no longer weighed heavy on his shoulders. Something like that didn't go away, no doubt it was in the back of his mind, but it wasn't between us.

Nothing was between us.

Callum was behind me, and I was on all fours, soaked between my thighs as he thrust into me with smooth, deep strokes. He'd made me come three times already. He'd come once. We were working toward another one for both of us.

"You're so sexy like this, Little Bird." His palms trailed over the roundness of my hips and ass. Dipping his thumbs between my cheeks, he spread me, and I knew he was watching himself move in and out of me. "Look at you, taking me. All stretched out and pink. My cock loves your sweet pussy. Never wanna leave it."

I moaned into my pillow. His filthy, loving mouth sent me to the edge. "I don't want you to leave it. I like feeling you when I'm sitting at my desk. All I can think about is you."

He growled, hands moving to cup my breasts and toy with my nipples. I shuddered and pushed back, meeting each of his thrusts. He liked to be in charge, to move me how he wanted me, but once I got there, he liked it even more when I took what I needed from him. So, I swiveled my hips and fucked myself on his cock, panting into my pillow, wanting to scream his name, knowing I couldn't.

"Fuck. Jesus. Fuck." He went harder, rocking me and my entire world. I held on, bracing my hands on the headboard, and he grabbed my hips. Callum didn't go easy on me. I never wanted him to. "God, your ass, baby."

My back arched, half to put on a show for him, half because I just couldn't help it. Callum had given me a gift, and he didn't even know it. When he had me this way, taking me like he'd cease living if he didn't, I felt powerful. Beautiful. Desired beyond measure. That was seeping out of the bedroom into my life.

While I was filling his soul, he'd been building up my self-confidence, brick by brick, orgasm by orgasm. I noticed myself lifting my chin higher, making eye contact for longer than a glance. And I asked for what I wanted.

"Harder, Callum." My fingers bent around the top of my headboard, bracing for what was to come. "I need you to go harder."

"I always give you what you need. You know that." His big hand pressed between my shoulder blades until my face and shoulders were flat on the bed. Then his knees knocked mine wide, and his arm threaded around my belly, nearly lifting me off my knees so he could get to me.

He handled me roughly, pounding me with fervor. I needed it. Loved it. Craved it. Callum could toss my round body around and drill me into a wall if he so chose. He made me feel delicate and treasured in life, but in our bedrooms, he turned me into his own personal sex kitten, and there had never been anything better.

"Fuck, Wren, fuck. You gotta come, baby. I need you to get there. Feel you clampin'. You're close, baby. I wanna get you there."

My arms were limp, but I managed to wend one under my belly and press two fingers against my throbbing clit. That was all it took to set me off. My mouth opened, and I screamed my release into my pillow. Callum kept going, riding me through my climax, thundering toward his.

"That's gorgeous, Little Bird. Need to have you in my bed so I can hear all your noises. I want your cries bouncin' off my walls." He swelled inside me, and I was a quivering mess beneath him, taking him as best I could without any bones left in my body.

Suddenly, he pulled out and rolled me onto my back. My eyes flared, but his were steady on me. His fingers wrapped around his cock, pumping it over me.

"I wanna come on you. On your tits. Your belly. Wanna see it painting you," he gritted.

I nodded and reached out to cup his balls while he fucked his hand. "I want to see it too. Make me messy, baby."

The cords in his neck were strained, muscles on his arms and belly taut. He was close, so close, and my inner walls were clenching all over again in anticipation. Everything we did was still so new, and I hadn't seen Callum erupt yet. I hadn't known until that point how badly I wanted to watch.

His free hand roamed over my belly, squeezing my sides and working his way to my breasts. He rolled my nipple between his fingers and groaned. Not loud, but I felt it between my legs.

He jerked and grunted, biting down on his lip as the first spurt hit my skin. His fist closed tight around his cock, pumping it furiously while he came all over me. And it was…hot. So hot, I had a mini orgasm of my own, panting and writhing on the sheets.

Callum finished and sunk back on his heels between my parted legs. Now, his eyes were the ones to roam, tallying the cum he'd gotten on me. I propped myself up on my elbows to look, and it was…even hotter than it had felt.

I ran a finger through the puddle beside my nipple, and Callum groaned like he was being tortured. My eyes flicked to him, and my breath caught in my throat.

"Keep goin', Little Bird. Explore. Let me see."

Always wanting to give him a show, I did as he asked, moving my fingers over the spray of cum on my breasts and stomach. I swirled it around and rubbed it into my skin, and Callum just watched, holding his still-hard cock in his hand. I wasn't sure he even breathed.

I lifted a finger to my lips, sucking the tip inside, and let out a soft gasp. I did it again, finally tasting him like I'd been wanting to.

"Mmm." My eyelids fluttered. "I like that."

"Shit," he growled. "I can't…I can't stop."

He was over me, then inside me, fucking me like a maniac, frantic, frenzied, and I hung onto him for dear life. I'd never, ever been wanted this way.

We were limbs and sweat and kissing and biting. There was nothing pretty or neat. It was pure need, bouncing back and forth between us. He held me close, and I had him even closer, circling my arms and legs around his body.

When we came, we came together, moaning into each other's mouths.

Finally, Callum fell to the bed beside me, bundling me in his arms. I was limp and sweaty, needed a shower more than anything, but I wasn't going anywhere. He nuzzled my neck, touching his lips to my skin to leave gentle kisses.

We lay tangled like that for a long time. Callum, being sweet and affectionate, me, lost in my thoughts. He noticed, turning my face toward his.

"Where'd you go?" he asked.

"I'm here."

"Body, yes. Brain is off on an adventure. I need you here with me."

I sighed and reached for his face. He caught my hand, leaving a kiss on the inside of my wrist. "Is this enough for you?" I asked.

His scowl was immediate and fierce. "What the fuck, Wren? Why would you even think to ask me somethin' like that after what we just did?"

"No, no, god, that didn't come out right. I meant, I know you like what we just did, what we've been doing, but is it enough? You're used to sex parties and clubs, not keeping quiet in a small townhouse. Like...do you want to be kinky? I don't know..." I bit my lip, my entire body going up in flames. "Do you want more?"

"Wren...I was used to fucking my fist before you. You *are* my more."

"But...don't you like to watch?"

He sifted his fingers through my hair. "I like to watch, yeah, but you give me that. And kink? Yeah, I'm into it. I wanna try all you're willing to try. I'm gonna fuck all your holes eventually, but I can't seem to stay out of your sweet, perfect pussy long enough to contemplate that yet. What is this about? Am I not givin' it to you good enough?"

He asked me that last part with a subtle smirk on his lips. He *knew* he was giving it to me more than good enough. I couldn't imagine any woman had it better in bed than I did. It certainly couldn't be common to be fucked the way Callum fucked me. If that were true, the civilized world would come to a standstill because no one would bother to get out of bed.

"I'm just thinking and wondering. That's how I am, you know."

His smirk slid into a grin. "I know. But you gotta tell me what else is on your mind."

"Well...I think I like to watch." Oh yeah, I was on fire. Every word I pushed out doused the flames in gasoline.

Callum only chuckled. "My little bird wants to watch?" His nose grazed mine. "Why didn't you say? I'll give you anything you want."

I lifted my eyes to his. "I only want it if you do too."

He exhaled through his nose. "I want to make you hot. I wanna fuck you while you're hot from watching other people fuck. So yeah, I want it too. I'll take you to the club." He caught my chin. "But, Wren, I'm gonna need you to sleep at my place after. I need all night, and I need you loud."

I nodded. My tongue felt too big to speak. Callum just said whatever the hell he wanted, and it was both refreshing and disconcerting as hell. Sometimes, I didn't know how to respond. Other times, like now, I simply wasn't able to.

He raised a brow. "Yes to everything?"

I nodded again, and he laughed. "Well, all right, Little Bird. I cannot fucking wait to wake up beside you."

I pushed my face into his neck and hugged him as tight as my short arms could. After asking him to take me to his sex club and telling him he could do anything he so desired, kinky or otherwise, to my body, my beautiful, crazy man couldn't wait to wake up with me.

How? How did I get so damn lucky?

And more importantly, how did I keep it?

CHAPTER TWENTY

WREN

I DIDN'T KNOW WHAT I WAS MORE NERVOUS FOR: spending my first night away from Ezra or spending my first evening inside a sex club with Callum. It was a true toss-up. The insane fact that this was my life and something I was actually contemplating had not escaped me.

Ezra and I had an extra-long snuggle session before he went to bed to make up for the fact that I wouldn't be home in the morning. Jenny was there, so he really didn't seem to mind. I was crumbling to pieces...just a little bit.

As I fretted by the front door waiting for Callum to pick me up, Jenny took my hand and slapped it. Not lightly either.

"Relax, Birdie. The world won't end because you miss a morning with Ezra."

I huffed and smoothed my hands over my silky red dress. Despite my best efforts to avoid her, Natalie had corralled me during my lunch break and taken me shopping, leaving Marissa to man my desk. Fortunately, it was the one day this week Callum couldn't meet me. Double fortunate, I found this dress— and it was *hot*.

"I know it won't. My son will be just fine without me, and I don't know if that makes this easier or harder."

Jenny snorted. "He's not graduating college, babe. You still get to wipe his snotty nose and tie his shoes."

I laughed. "Thanks for the perspective." Headlights illuminated the street, stopping in front of our house. "That's Callum. I'll see you in the morning. Call me if you need me. I'll be close and—"

She smacked my butt. "Get out, girl. Don't come back until at least noon tomorrow."

I had no choice but to leave when Jenny physically shoved me out the door and slammed it behind me. Seeing Callum on the sidewalk at the bottom of the steps made it that much easier not to turn back.

He took my hand as soon as I was close enough, pulling me into his body and wrapping me tight. I didn't comment on his leather jacket being too light for the cold. Well, I couldn't anyway, not with his mouth covering mine so thoroughly. His hands slid into the sides of my coat to my backside, cupping it in his palms and groaning.

"What are you wearing?" He practically grunted at me.

"A dress."

"I can feel your skin through it, baby. I don't know if I'm gonna let you out of the car."

I grinned, pleased with myself, and more than a little turned on. "We have to get in the car before you can trap me in it."

"First, tell me you're wearing panties."

"I'm wearing panties."

He pulled back to frown down at me. "I don't believe you." His hand curved around my ass. "All I feel is you."

I shrugged. "They're very small panties."

He groaned again, gripping my butt hard enough to bruise. "Neither of us are gonna be able to walk by morning."

I lifted my eyes to his, fluttering my lashes. "Promise?"

"Trouble," he gritted out. "Nothin' but trouble."

Eventually, he let me get in the car, and eventually, we arrived at the club. The outside was nondescript. Nothing boasting sex shows or arrows pointing to the door with the words "Kink Inside" in neon.

Callum held my hand tight as he led me into the club. At first glance, we were entering a high-class bar. Low lighting, plush seating, faint, rhythmic music in the background. The bar occupied one side of the space, and there were several well-dressed patrons around it.

Callum slipped off my jacket and his, handing it over to the coat check. Then he led me a few steps away, stopped, took a step back, and swore under his breath.

Then he swore louder. "Fuck." His icy eyes were on fire, trailing over my exposed shoulders, my deep cleavage, the red satin of my dress skimming my lower body until it stopped a couple inches above my knees, my sky-high heels and red toenails. I wasn't always confident, but I knew I looked good tonight.

"I wore this for you," I purred. Yeah, I purred. Callum brought that out in me.

"I have no words." He stepped into my space again, drawing me to him with a hard jerk. His lips landed on my shoulder. "Fuck," he groused.

"You sound grumpy."

"I'm pissed, Wren. I know you're not gonna let me drag you out of here, so I'm gonna sit here with a hard cock all night until you finally take mercy on me."

"You're right, I'm not. But you have me *all* night, and you can do anything you want with me...later."

He stared at me for a long time, his chest rising and falling rapidly. He was hard against my belly. His fingers on my back were digging into my spine. I reached up, stroking his beard the way we both liked. At the last second, he caught my hand and kissed my wrist the way I *loved*. Then he took my hand in his and continued leading me into the main area of the club.

"Drink?" Callum asked.

"Yes." My jitters were flaring high. I needed something to soothe them so I could actually enjoy myself.

I *really* wanted to enjoy myself.

Callum wrapped his arm around my torso, settling his hand just beneath the curve of my breast, and walked me to a table set against a wall. I sat down on the velvet bench, giving me a clear shot of the room. Callum remained standing.

"Stay here, but look around. I'm gonna make arrangements for us and I'll come back with drinks." When I licked my lips, he bent down. "Everyone saw you come in with me. They know you're mine. No one will bother you."

I nodded, and with one last look, he crossed the room, heading back to the bar.

At second glance, it was obvious this wasn't any old club. A St. Andrew's cross took up the center of the small stage at the front of the room. Two men sat at a table, each with women kneeling at their feet. Leather seemed to be the most popular fabric for clothing, lace coming in a close second for the women. And if the visuals hadn't been enough of a hint to the type of place this was, the stir in the air would have given it away. Nothing overt, there was just a sexual vibe that couldn't be ignored, like heat waves coming off asphalt.

A silver-haired man approached my table, stopping right in front of me. "I know you," he announced.

My breath caught in my throat. I knew him too. "Oh, hi. It's nice to see you." It really wasn't. Benson Martin had given me the creeps the first time we met, and that hadn't waned.

His eyes traveled over me, paying special attention to my breasts, which were pushed up high and on display beneath the deep V of my halter dress.

"Oh, it's very nice to see you again, peach. You look even more beautiful and ripe than the last time I saw you." He helped himself to the bench beside me, only leaving a small space between us. "Did Wainwright leave you all alone? In a place like this?"

I tried to scoot away subtly—why I was trying to spare his feelings, I didn't know, I just was—but he was watching me too closely for me to make a run for it. He hadn't done anything wrong, I just didn't love him being there.

"I'm not with Adam."

"Oh?" He cocked his head. "Who brought you here, beautiful?"

I rubbed my hands on my legs, stopping myself from searching Callum out. If he were anywhere within sight, he'd be beside me, removing Benson from my space.

"My boyfriend." That was all I was offering.

Benson laughed, his shiny white teeth gleaming even in the dim light. "A taciturn little peach, hmm? I like a woman who keeps things private. I find it freeing." He draped his arm across the back of the bench, behind my head. "Tell me, what was your favorite part of my party?"

My chin had begun to quiver, but I clamped down on my lip to stop it. I wasn't afraid of this man, not in this space at least, but I was uncomfortable and had no desire to continue this conversation.

"As you said, I'm private. I'll keep that between me and my partner." I barely kept the tremble out of my voice, but I managed.

Benson found me amusing, laughing once again. "I suppose I did." He dipped his head at the same time his arm came around my shoulder, cupping my bicep. "This boyfriend of yours, does he share? Because I am very much interested in finding out your secrets, peach."

I shook my head hard. "No, no he doesn't. I don't either."

"Aw, come o—"

Benson was gone before he could complete his cajole. Callum leaned over him, Benson's shirt in his fist, pressing him into the bench.

"You touchin' my woman, Martin?" he growled.

"Fuck, Rose, get off me." Benson Martin tried to push Callum away, but that wasn't happening.

"What makes you think she wants her hands on you?" He shook Benson hard, until his gleaming white teeth rattled. "I *know* she told you she was with someone. I didn't have to hear her to know that's how this went down."

Callum's words were slow, low, and dripping with threat. He hadn't heard what I'd said to Benson, but he had no doubt in me.

"Take it easy. We were just talking."

Callum braced a knee on the bench, right between Benson's legs, and got even deeper into the other man's face. "You were touchin'. I know you know better. That woman is mine. *I* say who can talk to her. *I* say who can touch her. *I* say who can look at her. You were not given that privilege."

Benson stopped struggling and held up placating hands. "You're right, you're right. You have a treasure. I messed up."

Callum grunted in acknowledgment, and in a movement that seemed far too easy, reared back and yanked Benson to his feet. "I'm gonna let go of you, and you're gonna walk away. You will not look at my woman without my permission. You'll forget she exists unless I allow you to remember. This isn't a discussion. We're done here." Another tooth-rattling shake. "You feel me, boy?"

"Yeah, shit, I feel you. I hope you feel me when I tell you you're not welcome at my parties any longer."

Callum released him with a violent shove. "Don't need your parties. Got everything I need and more right here in a pretty red dress. Go fuck yourself."

Benson Martin's hands balled at his sides. "I liked you a hell of a lot better when you didn't talk, asshole." He stormed off, grabbing a statuesque blonde and dragging her along with him toward the exit.

Callum was a stone statue, facing away from me. Just as I'd felt the vibrations in the air when we entered the club, he was disrupting the air with his rage. I stood, walking around to his front and laying a hand on the center of his chest. He stared at me, nostrils flared. I circled my arms around his middle, my head taking the spot my hand had vacated. It took a moment or two, then Callum was holding me tight, bending down to bury his nose in my hair.

"I shouldn't have left you."

I shook my head. "I'm fine. I promise. He was creepy, but he didn't do anything bad."

"He was touchin' you. Do you know what I wanted to do when I saw that?"

"No," I murmured. "I'm okay, baby."

He went on like he hadn't heard me. "I would have killed him if I wouldn't have been taken away from you after."

That was a scary thought, but I wasn't afraid of him. "You didn't, though. I'm safe, and he got the message."

Cupping my face with both hands, he tilted my head side to side. "You're okay?"

"Yes, baby. I'm just fine, but I really love knowing you'll protect me like you do."

His brow pinched then settled. "I like when you call me baby. No one's ever done that."

"Good. That's my thing for you." I lifted onto my toes to touch my lips to his. "I'm just as possessive over you, you know."

His lips twitched. "That isn't possible, Little Bird. Not possible at all."

"Watch me the first time a groupie throws her panties at you. I will...talk very sternly to her under my breath."

That broke him. He laughed and tipped my head back so he could cover my mouth with his in a deep, thorough kiss I felt all the way to my toes. No doubt we were being watched since

Callum had made somewhat of a spectacle of us and he was only continuing it, but for once, I didn't mind.

He pulled back, his gaze searching me. "You want to stay?"

"Yeah, I do." I smoothed my hands up and down his back. "Do you?"

"Mmm. I have a private room arranged for us."

"Okay," I whispered. "Let's go."

The room Callum took us to was small and cozy, with a sleek leather couch, low tables, dimly lit sconces on the burgundy walls, and not much else. That was because on the wall facing the couch was a large window, and beyond that window was another room, and in that room was a couple, standing by a bed.

Callum cupped my nape and directed me to the window. "They can't see us. All they see is a mirror."

"But they know someone's watching?"

"Yeah. They get off on it."

The woman was pretty, with full curves and silky black hair. She was older, maybe in her forties, but well kept. The man was tall, with lean muscles and smooth, bronze skin. He couldn't have been older than his midtwenties.

He was undressing her slowly, kissing each piece of skin he revealed. Her head was tossed back, pink lips parted as she enjoyed him. They were soft with each other, careful and sweet— so unlike the way Callum and I were with each other.

"Do you like this?" he murmured beside my ear.

"I do. They're different from us."

His hand flexed on my neck. "Jealous?"

"No. I love how we are." I leaned my head back on him. "But I like watching them."

"Turned on?"

"Since the second I saw you tonight."

His erection skimmed my lower back. "Sit down on the couch. I've been needing to get my hands on you since *I* first saw *you.*"

I didn't sit down on the couch. Callum placed me in his lap, but first, he pulled up the back of my dress so my bare ass was seated directly on his crotch. He laid a palm on the center of my back, bending me forward, and took a long perusal of my red, lacy thong. While he did that, running his fingertips along the material that disappeared between my cheeks, my eyes were on the other couple.

She was down to her underwear, the man in his briefs. He carefully folded down the cup of her bra and sucked her beaded nipple into his mouth. Her fingers combed through his black hair and down his shoulders. He moved to her other nipple, running his tongue around it in tight circles.

Callum squeezed my ass and spread my cheeks apart, then he tugged on my thong, wedging it into my soaked pussy. I couldn't help the moan that fell from my lips, and for once, I didn't try to keep it in.

"I had all these ideas. Things I wanted to try." Callum's arm banded around my shoulders, and he pressed me against him. "But all I can think of now is havin' your pussy on my face, dripping into my mouth."

"Oh." My thighs would have clenched if he hadn't lifted my dress in the front to cup between them. My eyes went wide as the man laid the woman down on the bed and ran his tongue from her throat to her belly button. "I want that too."

Callum helped me take my dress off, and with a look of pained regret, divested me of my underwear then reclined on the sofa and settled me over him, so my thighs surrounded his head. He grasped my hips, drawing my pussy to his eager mouth.

A month ago, I would have blushed at the very idea of sitting on a man's face, let alone *this* man's. The first time Callum told me where to park myself, I tried to insist my thighs would smother him.

"Do I look like I'm jokin' with you, Little Bird? Pussy on my mouth. Now."

"But I don't think girls like me do that..."

"What? Beautiful girls with delicious, dripping cunts? Women whose bodies are the kind of soft a man could lose himself in and be fuckin' happy to be gone?"

"Um..."

"Be quiet, Wren. No more talkin'. Watch me eat you then tell me girls like you don't do that. Tell me."

After that, when Callum asked me to sit on his face, I complied without hesitation. And because I was luckier than I had any right to be, he asked me often. *Often.*

He ate me hungrily. He went at me hard, almost vicious, licking and sucking. He didn't sip, he gulped and devoured. My eyes threatened to close, but the couple on the bed caught my attention. I rode Callum's gorgeous face as the man worshiped between the woman's thighs. Her back arched as his tongue speared into her, thrusting in and out slowly. Her face was a picture of bliss. She loved what he was doing just as much as I was going out of my mind with Callum's relentless tongue fucking.

In my head, they were watching us too. Seeing the differences between us. Finding us just as hot and erotic as I found them.

I came hard and fast, my entire body seizing into one violent spasm. My nails clawed at the arm of the couch, and it was all I could do not to go tumbling to the ground. Callum held me tight to his face, eating every drop I gave him. Keeping me safe from the fall, always, no matter how deep into pleasure we both were.

The woman's mouth fell open, and her fingers laced with her partner's as she came. He licked her through her climax, then kissed her thighs and belly as she lay panting.

Callum kept going, grunting as he ate me, and I went off again, screaming this time. I couldn't stop myself. And I didn't care who heard. My beautiful man did wild and crazy things to my body.

I needed him. I needed him so badly, I could taste the desire on my tongue.

I scrambled off him to the floor and ripped his jeans open, releasing his swollen cock. Without a second's delay, I wrapped my lips around him and sucked him just as hungrily as he'd eaten me. The guttural groan I wrenched out of him went straight to my head, making me dizzy with pleasure.

Callum let me suck him for a while, stroking my hair and cheeks as I took my fill. I was no expert, but god, I just needed this with him so badly. And he liked it. I knew he did, from the sounds he made no effort to tamp down. From the strain in his abs and his barely controlled grip on my head.

"That's enough, Little Bird."

Ignoring him, I sucked him all the way to the root, savoring every inch. He groaned and sat forward, gripping me under the arms.

"Enough, Wren."

He pulled at me, and I whined, keeping him in my mouth until he popped out. Then I was straddling his lap, and he entered me in one powerful thrust. His mouth was all over my breasts, sucking my nipples deep. Tossing my head back, I cried out, in pain, in ecstasy, both at once.

He controlled me, holding my hips and shoving me down on him at the same time he surged up, again and again. His lips were red and swollen from his time between my thighs, brow pinched, beads of sweat at his hairline. Callum was beautiful, and he was mine. Only mine.

"I'm gonna come, baby." I didn't know why I told him. He had to feel me fluttering around him.

His eyes shot to mine, and one of his fingers found my clit, circling it so expertly, it was like he'd been doing it for years instead of weeks. I detonated then, looking into his eyes, his cock buried so deep in me, I nearly felt it in my chest. The couple was probably fucking behind us, but I was so all about Callum, they only crossed my mind for a second before they were forgotten and it was just me, soaring through bliss.

Callum jerked me to his chest, his face in my throat, powering into me from beneath. Then he moved, flipping me onto my back, one knee hooked over his arm. He went at me, working in deep, pounding into my very being with his. I cried. He grunted. Our skin slapped. It was loud, messy, perfect. Then he reared back, his throat arced and exposed, and something like a roar shot from his parted lips. My hips were in his hands, and he rutted into me until I was filled with his liquid heat.

Panting, he fell over me, and I turned my head to the window, curious. The window was shuttered, a screen over it, so it was just Callum and me. He'd closed it when I wasn't looking, and for reasons I couldn't explain in words, that filled my chest with warmth.

"Shit, Wren." His mouth was on my skin, not kissing really. Just there, like he couldn't stand to be anywhere else.

"Yeah." I nuzzled my face in his throat. "You closed the window."

He tipped his face to mine. "They were distracting me from the real show. My beautiful girl so tight on my cock I could barely move. Those tits bouncin' in my face, red cheeks, pouty lips. Best show I've ever seen."

"Does that mean you don't want to watch anymore?"

He shook his head. "Fuck no. If bringin' you here gets me all that, we're gonna keep doin' it. Not every day, think it might kill me, but I'm gonna need more of that from you."

I nodded, grinning happily. "I'd like that."

"Anything you want, it's yours. You know that, right?" He peered down at me with an unwavering, intense gaze, waiting for my answer.

"I'm getting there."

That was the honest truth. I'd never been given a thing in my life besides love from Jenny and Ezra. It'd been a hard road, getting where I was. And I thought, if I held on to Callum's offered hand, it could be smooth going from here. It would take me some time to trust and believe I could really have something like that and it would be so easy and perfect in the long run.

"Get there." His nose slid along mine. "Now, I'm takin' you home."

CHAPTER TWENTY-ONE

CALLUM

I'D BEEN AWAKE FOR A WHILE, watching my sweet little bird sleeping in my bed. Wren clutched the sheets under her chin, her pale brows furrowed. Even in her sleep, she had a lot going on in her mind.

She was a beautiful sight to wake up to. This way, I could take my time perusing her. First, I studied the copper hair spread on her pillow. The silky strands of gold, red, and orange swirling together to make the prettiest color I'd ever seen. Her lashes were long and blonde, fanning out on her cheeks, which were dotted with light copper freckles. Her brows were the same color as her lashes. But it was a secret only I knew, because during the day, she wore makeup to darken them both. I liked knowing I was one of the few who'd seen her this way.

Fuck knew she was the only one who'd seen most sides of me. Wren was inside me, had been for a long, long time.

My years of watching her from a distance had never prepared me for what it was to know Wren up close. Weekly reports on her activities didn't tell me what her skin would feel like under mine. That she smiled in the last moments before she fell asleep. That she murmured in her sleep but never moved from the position she started in. Those reports I received were the surface of her, they were not who Wren was.

This girl in my bed was the real. She was the Wren from her letters times a thousand. If I'd given us a chance, I would have fallen for her without our history.

The fact was, I never would have given her a chance. We wouldn't be here if not for our letters. We'd still be history if I hadn't started watching her. If I hadn't interfered in her life from afar, all that we were building wouldn't exist.

If I was asked whether I felt guilty for not cluing Wren in on all I'd done for her and the time I'd spent watching her, I'd answer no. Without qualms or hesitation. Wren was mine, and I was hers. How we got here didn't matter. What mattered was I'd rip apart the very fabric of the universe with my bare hands and reshape it if I had to in order to keep her.

Amber eyes fluttered open, and when they focused on me, her small, pink lips tipped into a grin. "Stalker."

I combed the hair from her sleepy face. "You like it."

She let go of the sheet and scooted into my arms. "Maybe I do."

"I like wakin' up to you, Wren."

She tucked her face in my throat, but I felt her smile. "I like it too, Callum. Everything about it except knowing it has to end."

My hands roamed her warm little body, naked under the sheet. I couldn't get enough of the soft slope of her belly or the dramatic curve of her hip. I liked to trace those rounded lines over and over, sometimes with my fingers, others with my tongue. Wren protested once when I touched her stomach, but only once. I made her understand there was *nothing* about her I didn't find sexy. Fuck, I spent my days apart from her half hard picturing what she looked like when she rode me or how her ass moved when I took her from behind. There was no hiding that body from me. It was scored into my memory for all time.

"You need to hurry home, or can I keep you here a little while longer?" I slid my fingers along her slit, her legs opening to give me access.

"Seeing as it's the ass crack of dawn, I think we have time." She nipped at my neck. "I'm a little sore, though, baby."

I rolled her onto her back and slid my nose along hers. Her cheeks were flushed already, just from the idea of me inside her.

"I can go slow." I pecked her nose. "I'll be gentle and take care of you."

Her breath came out in a gasp. That was it. The promise of taking care of her was all it took to turn my little bird on and get her ready for me.

I took my time with her, my sleepy girl. Her skin was so warm and soft in the morning, I couldn't keep my mouth off it. By the time I slid inside her, she was pliant and soaked. Her arms wrapped around me as best they could from beneath me. I cradled her head to my chest and went slower than I ever had with her.

And I thought, this was what I wanted my mornings to be like. All my mornings. Watching my beautiful girl, then having her. Making slow, lazy love until we were smiling and happy and filled up to face whatever the rest of the day had in store. Even if it was media bullshit, work hassles, a grumpy kid, any of it. This would fortify us.

I needed this.

"Callum," she whispered. "You feel so good."

I kissed her forehead and cheek, held her close, slid in and out with gentle ease. Her plush thighs anchored my hips to her, and the rest of her body arched into mine.

"Need you, Little Bird. All the time."

"I need you too," she answered.

We went on like that, fucking slow, whispering, holding one another, until it became too much. Too good. I rocked into her harder, and she took it, raising her hips. I never stopped holding her, even as I drove into her with force. She was wrapped around me, kissing the skin she could reach, sighing and moaning my name.

When I came, she did too, and it was something else entirely. We got lost together, writhing like one body, clutching onto each other as we flew high. God, she was beautiful when she came. Nothing better than Wren letting herself go and having not one care in the world.

After, we showered and got dressed. She frowned at me when all I wore was a pair of sweats, telling me I'd catch my death from the cold. My little bird wore a sweater that was so long, it almost reached her knees, fleece leggings, and thick, fuzzy socks. I liked it because she looked sweet, but also because her sweater kept slipping off her shoulder and I got to kiss that bare skin when it did.

I made bacon and toast for breakfast. Wren chopped up strawberries and bananas. She couldn't sit still and let me serve her. I got it, her instinctive need to take care, so I didn't complain even though I wanted to give her the morning off.

We sat side by side at the counter eating our breakfast. This was our first time doing that, and it drove a small stake through my chest thinking it might be a long while before we could again. That just wasn't fucking acceptable to me.

I tossed my toast down and wiped my mouth with my napkin. Probably sensing the sudden change in me, Wren stopped eating and swiveled in her chair to look at me.

"I need to wake up with you. This has to happen more often." My brow pinched. "I won't ask for every night yet, even though that's what I want, but I need you in my bed or me in your bed at least every weekend."

"Um..." Her eyes darted around. Her fingers twisted in her sweater. "I really can't ask Jenny to watch Ezra overnight every weekend. It wouldn't be fair to her, but I also don't want to leave him so often. That's not to say I don't want to sleep with you. I have loved everything about last night and this morning. It's just more complicated than that."

"So don't ask Jenny. Bring Ezra with you."

She flinched, like the idea was so surprising, it had hit her like a physical slap. "Really? You'd want him here?"

"Of course. If it means havin' you here, hell yes."

"I'll have to think about it. I mean, where would he even sleep? He's particular and—"

I took her hand and pulled her off the stool, tugging her through the living room, down the hall, to the first bedroom, two away from mine. I pushed the door open, then I pushed Wren inside. I followed, wrapping my arms around her shoulders from behind and resting my chin on her head.

"He'll sleep in here."

The room was sparsely decorated, but it was painted pale blue, with a full-size bed in the center. A matching nightstand held a lamp that looked like a globe. A framed picture of the last TSC album was hung above the bed. Striped blackout curtains draped from rods over the window.

"Wow, okay. This is a really nice room. I'm not sure how he'd feel, but—"

I covered her mouth. "Don't say no. Not yet. Our morning is goin' too well for me to hear you say no. If he needs to get comfortable here, bring him over to hang out. I'll pick up some toys, fuckin' PAW Patrol and the like, make it a cool place to hang, and see what he thinks. I know you two come as a package, and I'm gonna do everything in my power to earn that package. Hopefully with a sexy little bow on your half."

She laughed behind my hand, then twisted in my arms to face me. "I'm going to cry, baby." Her eyes were shining like that was true. "That is incredibly thoughtful and sweet. Ezra would completely dig hanging out here, *especially* if there are PAW Patrol toys. And this room is sweet too. I think he'll like it, once he gets a feel for the place."

I didn't mention I already had rails for the sides of the bed tucked in the closet. Wren knew I was slightly off-center, she just didn't know how far off, and it'd stay like that if I could help it.

"I hope like hell he does. I need you to know, I'm so far in with you, I'm not gonna find my way out." I held her face in my hands, stroking a cheek slowly with my thumb. "I also need you to know in a couple months, I'm gonna be on the road touring, so this time we have is really fuckin' precious."

She swallowed. "I forgot about touring."

"Yeah. It's nothin' like when we were writing to each other, but I will be gone for a couple weeks at a time, at minimum."

Another thing I wouldn't bring up was I intended for Wren and Ezra to join me on the road eventually. I knew myself well enough to realize I wasn't gonna be sane if I had to be away from her that long. That topic would come up soon, but not today.

"I don't even want to think about it." Her fingers wrapped around my wrists. "We'll have to start writing notes to each other again."

I sucked in a breath through my nose. "You know, I never stopped. Each year on our anniversary, I wrote you an email. One on your birthday too. I didn't send them, but I couldn't let the date go by without marking it in a way."

Her forehead hit my chest, her mouth following. "Callum," she murmured. "Baby."

Her arms were wrapped so tight around my middle, we were close to merging as one. I felt her tears on my skin and the tremble traveling through her body.

"I didn't mean to make you cry, Little Bird."

"I know." Her fingertips dug into my back. "I'm sorry I'm being such a weirdo and crying all over you. It's just…it kills me to know you were thinking about me, about us, and left wondering. I still hate myself for doing that to you."

I dipped down to put my mouth beside her ear. "I can't say I didn't hate you for a while for doin' it too. But now, we're buildin' what we're buildin', and I don't feel bad about any of it anymore. I've let it go. In the back of my mind, I might wish I'd had you the last three years, but I'm sure as hell not pining over that lost time when I have you standin' right in front of me now."

"Okay," she rasped. "You're right."

Her head tipped back, and a smile curved her lips, even as tears sparkled in her big, owlish eyes.

"Damn right I am." I swiped a tear away. "If you ever want to read the emails I never sent, they're on my laptop. Just turn it on. You'll find them in my Wren folder."

"You have a Wren folder?" She was full-out beaming now.

"I do. I saved all our emails."

Just like that, her head fell against my chest again and another sob broke through. "Oh my god, you're killing me, baby. Just killing me."

"Never knew you were a crier."

"I'm a crier and a laugher, and when I get pissed, I'm a yeller."

"When I make you come too."

"Yeah," she giggled. "You make me yell a lot."

I only had her for a couple more hours before she had to return home. I hated letting her go after the sweet as hell morning we had...and the hot as hell night. The only reason I did was because I knew, without a doubt, I'd have her back. Soon, when the time was right, I wasn't ever going to let her leave me again.

Adam kicked my chair. "What's up, man? Haven't seen you in ages."

I kept my head still as a woman brushed my nose with powder. "Doin' my thing. You?"

He rolled his eyes. "Doing your thing? Is that code for spending quality time with your girlfriend?"

It was. Like I had told Wren, this downtime was precious. I sucked up every single second of her time and attention I could get. I needed it. I liked her more than any other human on the planet, and when TSC went on the road, I was gonna need this time stored up so I didn't give in to temptation and tuck my girl in my luggage.

It'd been almost a week since the night at my club. A couple days, it'd been too cold to sit outside on Wren's shitty bench, so my driver circled the block while my girl and I sat in the back seat and she ate her lunch. Weather wasn't gonna keep me from her. I parked my ass in the car for her morning and evening commute too and wound up spending most nights in her bed, sneaking out at sunrise. No more Ezra incidents since the first one, though Wren seemed less and less concerned about it. So much so, she'd brought Ez to my place for dinner twice this week. He hadn't slept there yet, but that was coming soon.

Iris's head jerked up from her phone. "Callie has a girlfriend?"

Rodrigo plopped down in her lap even though he had fifty pounds on her. "Keep up, bestie. Callum's dating the cute little receptionist from Good Music."

Iris's eyes bugged out of her head. "No fucking way! That adorable, shy little thing who told me our chorus was a pile of shit and she was absolutely right? That one?"

"Wren," I confirmed.

The makeup person studied my face for a second, nodded once, then moved on to Adam in the chair beside me. That kid was all kinds of shiny. She'd have to use gallons of powder to make him camera ready. And he needed to be camera ready, since we were about ten minutes away from recording an appearance on *The Nighttime Show*, debuting our first single from the album we'd recorded a few weeks ago.

Iris snapped her fingers. "Wait one second. The rumors have been swirling, but you know me, I ignore that shit. Were you, my Callie-Cal-Cal, in a bar fight? Because I heard that story and told Ronan it had to be patently false. My Callie doesn't go to bars unless there are whips and chains on the walls, and he most certainly doesn't make a spectacle."

Rodrigo leaned his chin on his fist. "Who knew Ronan was a gossip?"

Iris grinned wide, showing the gap between her front teeth. "Ronan is all the things. He has his ear to the ground and always knows what's going on with my people. He didn't tell me Callum has a lady, though. Major oversight on his part." Under her breath, but not too far under, she muttered something about Ronan being the one who'd end up tied to the bed tonight.

Roddy batted his lashes. "So, Callum, do tell. What made you come to blows in a place where your ass got recorded?"

I lifted a shoulder. "Didn't think about cameras. Someone touched my girl, I took care of it."

Iris fell back in her chair and fanned her face. "Wowza. I like that for Wren. Protective Callie, who knew?"

Adam raised his hand. "I did. The man nearly ripped my head off for looking at his girl."

The glower I shot him said all I needed to say. He'd done a lot more than look at her, and he needed to forget that ever happened. The memory of his lips on hers needed to slide right out of his mind.

Iris crossed her leather-clad legs. "Where's your head at with touring, now that you have a woman? You were my main man, Callie. Even when the other two fools—I love you guys, but you drive me bananas—can't get their acts together, I can always count on you to be ready to perform. Are you still here with us? Are you going to be good going on the road?"

I shrugged. "Don't know what I don't know. I'm not gonna be happy bein' away from her. But that's somethin' I'll work on in my own time. I won't bring that on stage."

Her eyes narrowed. "You never bring personal stuff into the band. I'm just going to say this now and let it lie, because I know you hate being the center of everyone's attention like you are right now. Ronan will be with me most of the time when we're on the road. Hope will be with Roddy. If you want Wren with us, then she's with us. If you need to fly home between shows, we'll make it happen. I'd prefer to have adorable Wren with us since there aren't enough girls around here, but I want you happy, Cal. I want our band to rock the shit out of our shows too. So—"

"She has a kid."

Iris stopped speaking. Adam jerked away from the makeup artist to twist around in his seat and face me. Roddy straightened, his eyebrows up to his hairline.

"How old?" Iris asked.

"Three."

"Cute?" Roddy asked.

"Fuckin' adorable," I confirmed.

Iris grinned. "Look at you, all paternal and proud."

"She has a kid?" Adam seemed perplexed by this.

"Yep. Ezra."

Iris crossed her arms over her chest and flicked her fingers. "I know tours aren't exactly ideal places for small children, but we're all settling down—"

Adam coughed. "Speak the fuck for yourself, madam."

She rolled her eyes. "All of us are settling down except legendary groupie-magnet, Adam Wainwright." She flicked her fingers again. "*Anyway*, the kid is welcome. *Ezra* is welcome. I'm just putting that out there. When the time comes, we will hammer out the details."

I dipped my head. "Thank you."

I didn't say more, but that acceptance meant a lot. Because I did plan on bringing Wren and Ezra around my band. I did want them to attend shows and spend some nights on buses with me. If I had pushback from my bandmates...well, if it came down to a choice, I knew the one I'd make, and it wouldn't make me happy.

But right now, I was happy.

A producer stuck their head in the room, inviting us to follow them to the stage. The audience was live, the broadcast wasn't.

The appearances, interviews, autographs, paparazzi, the fame, it all got old. But this, heading to the stage to play with the three people I'd lived through some of the shittiest, happiest times in my life with, this never got old. The seasons were always changing, but the desire to blow down the house with our sounds never, ever went away.

CHAPTER TWENTY-TWO

WREN

EZRA THREW HIMSELF THROUGH THE DOOR WITH A SCREECH. "COW-UM! Cow-um's house!" Then he threw himself at Callum's legs. "Hi, Cow-um."

Callum's big hand patted Ezra's small head gently. "Hey, Ez."

"I'm gonna play." Then he was off, making himself at home in the living room. We'd been here two times for dinner, and he'd already claimed the blue room as his, even though I didn't think he quite grasped what a sleepover would mean. Callum had loaded a couple bins with toys for him, so as far as Ez was concerned, this was the coolest place he'd ever been.

I stood in the doorway grinning, balancing a box of pizza. "Delivery for Mr. Hottie McRockstar."

Callum cocked his head, his mouth twitching. "Hottie McRockstar?"

"I'm assuming that's your alias when you're traveling. You know, so your groupies don't find you and boil bunnies in your hotel room."

His eyelids went heavy as he looked me over. We'd seen each other only a few hours ago, but he was looking at me like he was hungry for the sight of me.

"Don't think that's what groupies do in hotel rooms, Little Bird."

"Well," I lifted my pizza and one eyebrow imperiously, "I wouldn't know."

His chin dipped. "Is there any reason you're still in my hall, holdin' a pizza, talkin' about groupies, and not kissin' me? If there is, I'd like to know."

I shoved the pizza at him, which he took with one hand, then threw myself at him much in the same way my son had. He had to bend for me to reach his lips, but this had become automatic now. He bent. I raised. We collided.

Callum didn't do anything without intensity, and that included kissing. Even though we were standing in his wide-open door and my son was in the other room, his tongue swept into my mouth, his hand gripped my ass, and he devoured me.

"That was nice," I murmured against his lips.

"More than nice."

He took my hand, kicked his door shut, and pulled me into the kitchen. From there, I spied on Ezra playing with some of the toys Callum had bought for him.

"I can't believe you bought him insects."

He put the pizza down on the counter and circled his arms around my shoulders. I loved when he did that, because when he spoke, the vibrations traveled through his chest to my back, landing right in the lockbox I kept inside me for Callum's words. The way he made me feel was far too big to even attempt to contain, so for now, it was the words.

"You told me he liked creepy-crawly critters, I bought him creepy-crawly critters."

"Yeah," I whispered. "You remembered something I said offhandedly weeks ago about my son. That is a big reason I'm so gone for you, Callum Rose."

His arms tightened. "He's a part of you, and I would do any-fuckin'-thing for you. That means I'd do any-fuckin'-thing for him."

I breathed a sigh. This man. The goddamn man. He had made it utterly impossible to go slow and ease into things. He was gorgeous and irresistible, and even though I knew me having a kid at least partially freaked him out, he rolled with it as smooth as butter.

"Speaking of, two things happened since I saw you, which I wanted to update you on." I turned in his arms. He frowned down at me, his brow pinching the way I liked.

"Need your face." He scooped me up like a pile of feathers and plopped me on the counter, bringing us closer to being eye to eye. "Better. Tell me what happened."

Before I could, his lips were on mine again, his tongue spearing into my mouth. This kiss was even more thorough than the last, and now, I was able to hug him with both my arms and legs. He kneaded my hips and wrecked my mouth with the most perfect, deep kiss.

All too soon, he pulled away, raising his head to peer in my eyes again. "Now, tell me."

I giggled, but it came out with a sultry, breathy quality I'd never heard myself make.

"I've decided in my next life, I'm coming back as a celebrity. The average woman gets harassed and stalked and maybe even beat up by a man, and a judge shakes his head and calls it a misunderstanding. You make some calls, probably pay your attorneys big bucks, and in less than a week, I have a restraining order against Edwin. Your lawyer, who apparently is my lawyer, called me on my commute home to inform me of this and told me she'd email me the specifics. It was right before I got home, so I haven't even had time to really process it, but—"

His fingers curled around the nape of my neck. "It's a good thing, Wren. Means if he fucks with you, a judge *can't* call it a misunderstanding. Gives you a layer of protection and lets him know you're serious about him stayin' away. I don't care much for bein' famous, but I will squeeze every advantage I have to keep you safe."

I rubbed my palm along his chest. "I'm not mad about it. Promise. I am hoping he'll receive the message loud and clear. I was just in awe of the power of celebrity and all it can accomplish in such a short period." My head fell where my hand had just been. "Thank you, baby."

He touched his lips to my crown. "You never have to thank me. That's my job."

"I'll swoon if you keep this up." I swatted at him. "Stop it."

"Never."

I tipped my head back. "Can you see what my child is doing? Is he destroying your living room?"

Callum glanced over my shoulder. "He pulled a cushion off the couch. He's usin' it to jump on and make one of his insects fly."

That made me smile. "He's fine?"

"He's fine," he confirmed.

"Okay." I brushed his hair behind his ear. "The other thing that happened is related to the first thing. Ez and I ran over to our favorite bodega to get cat food for Lyle and Lovett. Mr. Sulaimani informed me Edwin is banned from his store. Banned, Callum. I didn't want to ask him if he'd seen the video of the fight because he's kind of religious and I didn't want to insult him by asking him that. But he must have, right? Because it's sort of sudden for him to make that decision. He's seen Edwin asking me out a hundred times over the years and he always kind of chases him off, but he's never out and out banned him."

Callum jolted. "I never knew he asked you out hundreds of times."

"Of course you didn't. We weren't together when most of it was happening. It wasn't ever anything like last weekend, though. It doesn't matter anyway. Hopefully he's as done with me as I am with him."

He took my face in his hands. "You'll tell me if somethin' else happens."

Not a question. "I'll tell you."

His nose dragged along mine. "There was a time when you got hurt and I couldn't protect you. All I could do was wait for you to email me and tell me if you were okay or not. We're never gonna go back there. Anyone bothers you, makes you uncomfortable, scares you, hurts you, I'm here. I'll take care of it. You don't have to worry. That's on me now. You got it, Little Bird?"

I exhaled through pursed lips. "I think so. I'm getting there."

His nose gently tapped the end of mine. "Get there. This is your reality." Lips touched mine. "Now, I'm gonna feed you and your boy."

I grinned. "Always taking care of me."

"Always."

The three of us settled on the floor in front of Callum's couch with our slices of pizza and, in Ezra's case, plenty of napkins because my child was basically a monster when he ate.

This wasn't a regular dinner. No, this was an occasion. We were here to watch the recording of The Seasons Change on *The Nighttime Show*. Through our separation, I'd carefully avoided watching any of their appearances. My heart just hadn't been strong enough to take it.

Now, my heart was threatening to burst from my chest as Callum fast-forwarded to the right place in the show. This was silly, really, to feel nervous about seeing my boyfriend on TV— something he'd filmed the day before, mind you—when he was right beside me and my child was cuddled on his other side. He was no longer the stone-cold giant on the stage. He was the warm, affectionate man who, more often than not, shared my bed.

My heart wasn't getting the message. I was nervous as all get-out while Ezra was practically flying out of his skin with excitement. He didn't grasp what Callum's job was, nor did he understand fame. What he knew was his new buddy Cow-um was about to be on the same TV where he watched Bob Ross and *PAW Patrol*, and *that* was a big freaking deal.

"All right, everyone ready?" Callum held the remote with his finger poised on the play button. Ezra shrieked, and I nodded. The lump in my throat was too big to fit any words around.

Iris strutted onto the screen, looking gorgeous and intimidating. The camera panned over the band, sweeping past Callum, whose face was impassive and glorious. Ezra put down his pizza and climbed into Callum's lap when the music began. He leaned forward, resting his chin on his pudgy fists. His eyes were wide, reflecting the images on the TV. My boy was a talker, but he'd been struck silent as soon as he saw Callum.

As for me, the music they were playing filled my ears, but my eyes were on my two boys. Callum had frozen when Ezra plopped on him. His arms and shoulders were as stiff as a corpse. As the moments passed, his limbs relaxed, until his arms formed a loose circle around Ezra. And then he turned to me, caught me staring, and jerked his chin at my kid. My breath caught. If he wasn't happy about my son being in his lap...well, I'd deal. It wasn't right to expect Callum to automatically be comfortable with him. But that wasn't to say I wouldn't be a little disappointed.

A second later, a wide grin broke out on Callum's face, and all my worries vanished. I smiled back, ruffled Ezra's hair, and ran my fingers along Callum's scruff. He caught my hand, kissed my fingertips, then kept it in his lap, right beside Ezra's little body.

When the song was over, Ezra asked for Callum to play it again. I leaned in, my chin on Callum's shoulder. He turned to me, so close, all I could see were his icy blues.

"You like?" he murmured.

"You guys changed the chorus."

His eyes danced. "Yeah. You said it was a pile of shit."

I snorted. "I don't remember those words coming from my mouth."

"Somethin' like that." His nose nudged mine. "You like, Little Bird?"

I nodded. "Very much." I liked the music, the night, the man. All of it.

Ezra whipped his head around, a scowl pulling at his features. "Be quiet, Mommy! I can't hear the music."

I snorted a laugh but covered it up with a cough. "Can you ask Mommy in a nicer way? I'll be happy to lower my voice if you can be polite."

I could tell he was torn between manners and missing the show, but Callum paused it and placed his palm on top of Ezra's curls.

"What'd Mommy say, Ez?" He said it so low, so gently, I would have thought he was a parent himself.

"I'm sorry." Ezra's lip quivered. He did not like to be reprimanded, no matter how gently, which I understood, because who did?

"I forgive you, baby buddy," I answered immediately. "Don't you just love Callum's band? Isn't it cool he gets to be on TV and play music?"

Ez nodded. "Like Bob."

"Yeah." Callum slid his hand down the back of Ez's head. "Like Bob, only I'm not even close to bein' that cool. I can't even paint."

Ezra twisted all the way around in Callum's lap and cupped his cheeks. "Bob can teach you, Cow-um."

"Oh yeah? I'm up for tryin'. Your mommy told me how much you like to paint, so I got us some art supplies. Thought maybe we could trade. I show you my guitar, you show me the ways of Bob."

Ezra giggled hard. "The ways of Bob. What does that mean?"

Callum laughed too. "I don't know, bud. I thought you were gonna tell me."

Ez shook his head. "I don't know!"

"You know, there are a couple Bobs I like too."

Ez's eyes went round. "More Bobs?"

"Ever heard of Bob Marley?"

"Is he your friend?"

Callum chuckled. "No, bud. He's this chill, talented musician. I'll play you some of his music later. I think you'd like it."

"When I'm taking my bath?"

"You want to listen to Bob Marley while you're takin' your bath?"

Ezra nodded hard, sending his curls tumbling. "Yeah. Bob and bath!"

"All right, bud. Bob Marley and bath. Next time, I'll tell you all about Bob Seger."

My heart wasn't even bursting anymore. It had exploded and was now dripping off the walls of my chest. Real gory scene. They'd have to burn the whole place down to set it right again. There was absolutely no recovering from my son and my love laughing and chatting with each other like it was as natural as breathing.

After pizza, Ezra got to take a bath in Callum's deep soaker tub. He insisted Callum sit in the bathroom while he did this, which was fine, since Callum had to play DJ for him. My son was entranced by Bob Marley. It should have come as no surprise that his favorite song was "Three Little Birds". It was a fantastic song, but also, wasn't that the way this life worked? Everything was connected, even Bob Marley and Callum's nickname for me.

When he'd fully turned into a prune, I got Ezra out of the tub and into his jammies. Callum met us in the blue bedroom, which had changed since the first time I'd seen it. There were rails on the bed, just like Ezra's at home. There was a stoplight alarm clock on the nightstand, again, just like Ezra's at home. Last, but really freaking not least, the picture over the bed had been switched out.

Ezra spotted it a millisecond after I did, and the calm he'd achieved during his bath was obliterated. He scrambled onto the bed and stood staring at the picture while his entire body vibrated and he clutched his hands under his chin.

"Bob," he whispered.

Callum put a knee on the bed beside him, staring up at the landscape painting iconic to Bob Ross fans everywhere. "I thought you might like havin' a Bob hangin' above you when you sleep over."

Ezra was silent, but his eyes were moving a mile a minute. I kneeled on the other side of him and wrapped my arm around his middle.

"Whatcha think, baby buddy? Do you like this room?" I asked.

He looked from me, then to Callum, and he leaped. Not at me. No, I was chopped liver next to my big ol' rock star of a sweet, sweet man.

Callum caught him, cradling Ezra's small body to his.

"Thank you, Cow-um. I love my Bob. I love it."

"You got it, bud." Callum's eyes met mine over Ezra's head. They were softer than I'd ever seen them. My boy had that effect. And maybe, I was a little surprised his pureness broke Callum down the way it did, but I liked it. Oh, I really liked it.

Then, Ezra further clenched the remnants of my damn exploded heart by asking Callum to lie with us while I read him a bedtime story…which he insisted Callum choose.

So, the three of us laid in Ezra's bed for the night, and it felt… natural. Way too comfortable and sweet. It scared me, the way I loved every second of it. It scared me the way Ezra seemed to love every second of it too.

After two books, Ez was flagging and said he was ready to go to sleep. Callum gave his head a pat, and I kissed his cheeks and gave him a mighty squeeze. I left him there, looking so small and peaceful in that big bed. Callum was waiting for me in the hall.

Without saying a word, he wrapped his arms around me, holding me against his chest. I held him back, resting my cheek over his heart.

It was early still, so we ended up back in the living room. Callum lay on his back, his head propped on a couple pillows. He positioned me on my side, my front plastered to him, my back to the cushions. My arm was draped over his middle, his was around my shoulders. Our legs were tangled, and it was so damn comfortable and easy, I didn't know what to do with myself.

"He's lucky," Callum murmured.

"I know he is. I try really hard not to be my parents."

He shifted so he was looking at me. "Even when you corrected him, you were so gentle. Not used to that, Little Bird."

"I can't imagine being harsh with him."

"Lots of parents are more than harsh with their kids, even when they're tiny like Ez. You and I both know that."

"Yeah."

His fingers trailed along my arm. "You know what I was doin' when I was three? My mama had this grift that worked like a charm. She'd walk around with a big pregnant belly and me by her side. I carried a bag of oranges and I'd sell 'em to people at fairs and on the street, depending on where we were. She liked takin' me out more than Chrys and Rasc because I was quiet and didn't fuck her shit up. Plus, I was kinda cute. Not as cute as Ez, but cute."

"That doesn't sound so bad." But I knew it had to be worse than that, and I almost didn't want to hear it.

His fingers kept trailing, nice and slow. "She wasn't even pregnant. Belly was a fake to garner pity and make quick green. She'd dirty me up before takin' me out. Sometimes that came from rubbin' dirt on my face, other times, it came from not bathin' me for days. So, I was filthy, sad, draggin' around, sellin' those oranges. People felt bad for me, for her, so they'd buy an orange for five bucks. It wasn't the worst thing to happen to me, not by a mile. But the fact that I was three and can remember it, clear as day, says a lot. I can still feel the blisters on my feet from walkin' for miles in cheap, plastic shoes that were fallin' apart. She had a set amount she wanted to make each day, and we'd stay out until she did. It'd be hours, Little Bird. I'd get sunburned, dizzy from the heat, and she'd keep tuggin' me along."

"Shit," I breathed.

"Yeah. Shit." He rolled to his side and touched his lips to mine. "That's what I know. So, when I say Ezra's lucky, I mean it. Seein' you together, the way you're so damn good to him, that's a balm to my battered soul. 'Cause the oranges? They're so small in the grand scheme of the things I saw, the events and trauma I lived through and walked away from. Knowin' Ez will never experience anything like I did is a bridge over the chasm of my childhood."

"You're such a good man, Callum. You could have stayed down in that dirt, but look at you, baby. *You* pulled yourself out of it. *You* rose above it. I hate that you had to rise above anything, but you did. And you stayed good and kind and gentle through all of it."

"Nah, I'm not good."

"You are to me. You are to my son."

He exhaled slowly through his nose. "I always will be. You can't leave me, though. Not after givin' me this taste. You can't walk away."

"I don't want to, baby. Keep being good to us, and there's no reason I'd ever walk away."

He nodded, but that furrow appeared between his brows again. "I don't know how to be normal. I've got a lot of shit in my head I'm probably never gonna work out. Don't think I'll ever like many other people. I'm gonna be possessive of you in a caveman sort of way. I've got kinks I'm always gonna need to indulge in with you. Sometimes I get dark and disconnected, though it's better when you're around."

I interrupted him. "I know all this, baby. Why are you telling me this like I don't know you?"

His fingers sifted through my hair, pushing it off my face. "Because, even with all those reasons I should let you go, all the bad in me I'm well aware of, I'm not walkin' away. I won't ever. *Ever*. And I'll always be good to you and Ez, even if I get some things wrong."

I cupped his cheek. "My eyes are wide open with you, Callum. I know you. You were my best friend for a long time, and now, you're the person I'm closest to besides Jenny and Ez. I don't know all your stories, but I know *you*. I'm not scared of your dark because I have plenty of my own. I want to share your kinks. I understand what it's like to disconnect. I know you, Callum. I know you."

"Yeah," he sighed, laying his forehead on mine. "You sure as hell do."

We held each other, touching, kissing, whispering. It was sweet, and then it was hot. My leggings disappeared, followed by my panties. Callum's pants were lost sometime in there too. He lifted my leg over his hip and slid into me smoothly. And I thought, no matter how many times we did this, I would never get used to the stretch and fullness I felt when I took him. He filled me up to the brim and then overflowed.

He took my breath away, and I was addicted.

We were rarely face-to-face when we were together like this because of our height difference, but I had to make a note to use this position more often. I couldn't tear my mouth from Callum's as he moved inside me. We were packed tight on the couch, the cushions behind me, Callum in front of me, and I loved it.

Something had shifted between us tonight. My need to be close to Callum couldn't be sated. Our chests were flush, he was inside me, but it wasn't enough. My arms wrapped around his neck, and I shoved my face in his throat, kissing his heated skin. He groaned, circling me with his arms so tight, I could barely breathe, but that was okay. Barely was still breathing. I was alive, more alive than ever before, even with the wisps of breath I could inhale into my lungs.

"I'm your shadow, Little Bird."

"I know." I mouthed his Adam's apple. "You promised you'd come."

"Always knew it'd be me."

I hadn't known. I'd wanted it, hoped for it, but never believed I could truly have this.

Slow and steady transitioned to hard and needy. Callum hooked my leg with his elbow, tilting my hips so he could work his way even deeper. His pelvis ground into mine, and I clung to him through it, kissing his skin while he took utter control of my body.

And that...that loss of control without an ounce of panic drove me over the edge, Callum following seconds later. He lifted my face from his throat and kissed me wet and deep while pulsing inside me.

I broke the kiss, panting. "You have to stop or I'm going to need you again."

He huffed a laugh. "I'm still inside you."

My lashes batted. My inner walls clenched. "You've created a monster."

"That was my plan. Get you hooked on my cock so you'd stick around."

"It worked."

Chuckling, he gave my ass a squeeze and groaned as he pulled out. Then he took me to bed, though not before stopping by Ezra's room to check on him. And when he stood beside me, peering down at my sleeping boy, he sighed.

He *sighed*, over the sight of my son, asleep in his bed.

If I hadn't been slip-sliding into deep before that moment, that would have done it. There was no coming back from this with Callum. He might have planned to get me addicted to his cock, but more than that, I was addicted to *him*.

CHAPTER TWENTY-THREE

WREN

"NEED YOU IN MY BED WHEN I GET BACK, Little Bird."

"I need to be there too."

"I'm gonna be selfish and ask to have you to myself."

"Jenny can watch Ez. I miss you."

"Fuck, I wanna feel you sayin' that against my skin."

"Then I wouldn't miss you anymore."

"Need to feel it. Need it."

"Then I'll say it."

Two weeks had gone by since Ezra's first sleepover at Callum's place. We'd done another sleepover the following weekend, then Callum was gone. He'd been out in LA for the last week, shooting music videos and making appearances. By the middle of the week, we were both aching for each other.

I had to think it was a little easier for me because when I wasn't working, I was with Ez and Jenny. When Callum wasn't working, he holed up alone. I knew that because the second Ez went down for the night, Callum called me and stayed on the phone until I fell asleep, even if I was watching TV with Jenny or doing some cleaning. He wanted to hear me and be present with me from the other side of the country.

Jenny judged at first. And yeah, it was intense and might've seemed strange, but that was Callum. He needed the connection we had, and maybe he realized I needed the reassurance that, even though he was gone, I was still at the very forefront of his mind.

But now, he was back, and after a reunion that involved me jumping on him the second he'd opened his door to me and him kissing me so hard and for so long, my lips were puffy and tingly, we were going to a party.

A party!

Saul Goodman, CEO of Good Music, technically both our bosses, was hosting a party for some of his artists at his penthouse. Callum promised he had to go, be seen, and then we could make our exit. Back to his place, back to bed, our introverts' paradise.

I stood in his bathroom, touching up the makeup he'd kissed off. My dress was slightly rumpled from being rucked up around my waist when he fucked me on the kitchen counter five minutes after I walked through the door, but I liked that. It was like a secret between us.

Callum wandered in, yanking his shirt over his head. He had a fresh one in his hand, but he stopped behind me, running his hands over my hips and sides, watching me in the mirror. His hair was mussed from my fingers dragging through it, and I liked that even more than my wrinkled dress.

"Hi."

His chin propped on my head. "Hey, beautiful girl. Almost ready?"

"Almost." I raised a brow at his bare chest. "Are you changing clothes?"

"Just my shirt. My girl turned into something of a hellcat and ripped the collar."

I whipped around with wide eyes. "No. Did I?"

He grinned. "You did, Little Bird. I'm gonna frame that shirt."

"Well, maybe if you'd taken it off—"

"So you'd rip my skin apart instead?"

I giggled. "I'd never hurt you and—" I stopped speaking.

"Wren?" Callum tipped my chin with his knuckle, trying to catch my eyes, but my focus was on his chest. Specifically, the tattoo that hadn't been there when he'd left New York last week.

"What is that?" I breathed.

He actually looked down, as if he didn't know what I was referring to. "Oh yeah. I got a new tattoo when I hit LA. My guy is based out there. I hit him up when I'm there and lookin' for ink." He dipped down and touched his nose to mine. "Speak, Wren. Do you like it?"

On his chest, right over his heart, was my name inked in black. Written in flowing script, the W had wings and looked like a little bird taking flight. There was nothing subtle about this design. There was nothing abstract about his intentions in getting this tattoo. He had my name on his body. Permanently.

"You didn't tell me you got this," I whispered.

"Wanted to show you in person. Do you like it?"

I brought my hand up to touch it but stopped myself. Callum caught my wrist and placed my palm over the tattoo.

"It's almost a week old. You can touch it as much as you want," he said.

My eyes finally flicked to his. "This is intense."

He flinched, but only slightly. "It is."

"You're intense."

His nostrils flared. "Not a surprise."

"No." I shook my head. "It's not."

"I need you to answer me. Do you like it?"

"I don't—" He stiffened when my eyes fell back to the tattoo. It was pretty. The lines were crisp. The design was clever. Almost sweet, especially among Callum's harsher, more Gothic tattoos.

No, it wasn't almost sweet. It was the single sweetest thing I'd ever seen. The shock was wearing off, replaced by tenderness. I leaned in and touched my lips to the skin beside the W, just in case it was still sore. Callum groaned and cradled the back of my head.

"I like it," I murmured into his skin. "I missed you, baby."

He curled around me to hold me in his arms. "Never gonna get enough of you. I needed you under my skin for everyone to see. But you were already there. Always been there."

"Same for me, Callum."

"Not freakin' out?"

I breathed a laugh. "I did for about a second, but I got over it really fast." And slipped even deeper with him.

We left a few minutes later. If we'd stayed a second longer, we would have ended up in bed. Once we were in bed tonight, we weren't leaving.

And we had a party to attend.

Bodyguards checked our names on the list and allowed us to enter Saul Goodman's palace. The lights were dim. Music and conversation filtered through the air. The grand, open living room wasn't packed, but it wasn't empty either. As we wandered through the crowd, I recognized face after face. This party was a groupie's wet dream.

Callum and I stopped at one of the bars—*one* of the bars! There were multiple freaking bars—and continued wandering with drinks in hand. I nearly spilled mine when I heard my name shrieked from behind me.

"Wren Anderson, oh my god!"

Callum and I swiveled around, finding Adelaide Goodman stomping toward us with an old, bulldog-faced man on her arm. I really hoped that was her dad and not her date.

"Hey, Adelaide." My smile was genuine. She was a ray of absolute sunshine day after day, always stopping by my desk to gossip and shoot eye daggers at Natalie. I had definitely added her to my list of friends. "I didn't know you'd be here tonight."

"Same, girl." She and her old man stopped in front of us. "Dad, this is my work bestie, Wren Anderson. She's an angel and brightens up the lobby every day. Wren, this is my dad, Saul. He'll probably tell you to call him Mr. Goodman because he's a dick like that. And Dad, I'm one-hundred-percent sure you know Callum Rose, Wren's towering, hottie boyfriend."

Saul Goodman didn't even flinch at his daughter's evaluation of him. "Welcome to my home, Wren." That was all I got, which was fine. Saul didn't give off the best vibes. I wondered how Adelaide could have possibly come from him. "Callum Rose. What a pleasure to have the recluse of The Seasons Change in my home."

Callum tipped his head and pulled me flush to his side, his arm wrapping around my back. "Thanks for having us. This'll count as my once-yearly sighting."

Saul boomed with laughter. "No one told me you were funny, Rose."

Callum stared back impassively. I filled the silence with a giggle.

"He makes me laugh. Always," I said.

Adelaide's eyes rounded. "Oh yeah, he seems like a real jokester." She extricated herself from her dad's arm, then tucked her arm in mine and began walking. I had no choice but to follow her, Callum with me since we were attached. "Anyway, I spied the rest of TSC near the hors d'oeuvres. Rodrigo was stacking crab cakes on his plate six deep. I grabbed one before he cleaned us out of them, and they were exquisite. Chef's kiss and all that jazz."

"Oh. Well—"

"Look!" She pointed to the area near the floor-to-ceiling windows. "There they are."

Heads came up as we approached. Iris with a tall, impressively wide man in a spectacular suit, Rodrigo and a beautiful woman with a sheet of black hair, Adam between an adorable woman with apple cheeks and wavy brunette hair and a silver fox I recognized as Dominic Cantrell, rock legend. All of them watched with rapt attention as we joined them.

Adam was the first to speak. "Fuck. I don't believe my eyes. Is this real life?"

Iris stepped forward and pecked me on the cheek. "What my rude friend means is hello, we're happy as hell to see you, Wren." She motioned to the man behind her. "This is Ronan Walsh, my man. Ronan, say hello to Wren."

The man, who made Callum seem small, reached out a hand, which I shook. "Nice to meet ya, Wren." Holy granola, he had an Irish accent. Swoon.

Callum tugged me away from him, and I swore he growled under his breath, even as he tipped his chin to Ronan.

Next, I met Rodrigo's girlfriend, Hope, who was something of a world-famous DJ. Plus, she was insanely hot. Then Adam kissed my cheek and whispered, "Hi, cutie," to which Callum responded by shoving his shoulder. Adam didn't look upset for even a second, but that was probably because he'd been intentionally pushing buttons. He threw his handsome head back and laughed his ass off. Callum's mouth twitched.

Adelaide was still mixing it up with Iris like they were old friends when I was introduced to Claire, the woman with the apple cheeks and wavy brown hair, and her husband, Dominic, who was even more intimidating up close. Until he looked at his wife, then everything about him softened. There was a definite age gap between them, but it didn't seem to affect the deep love they had for one another. Just meeting them minutes ago, it was already obvious.

Swoon again.

Callum and I were talking to Dominic and Claire about their baby, Georgia—well, I was talking, he was holding me as close to his side as humanly possible without slicing himself open and inserting me beneath his skin—when Rodrigo drifted over and draped an arm over Claire's shoulders.

She nudged his ribs with her elbow. "What's up, boo?"

He grinned and nudged her back. "I'm here to ask Wren a question."

"Is it inappropriate?" Claire asked.

"Have you met my girlfriend? She'll kick my ass if I even think of asking an inappropriate question."

Claire held her hand out, gesturing to me. "Then ask."

I took a long pull of my drink in preparation.

Rodrigo's eyes alighted on me. "What did you think of the tattoo?"

Just when I thought it was impossible, Callum held me tighter. I breathed easier, though. This was a question I could answer.

"It was a big surprise, but I really love it."

Roddy grinned. "Yeah? 'Cause I went with your man when he got it and tried to talk him out of it."

I tilted my head to lean on Callum's arm. "I'm glad he didn't listen."

"What's the tat?" Dominic asked.

My tongue darted out to moisten my lip. Claire, I was comfortable with. Dominic made me tongue-tied. Fortunately, Roddy spoke up for me.

"Cal's got Wren's name over his heart. It's a pretty sick design, but yeah, it's her name."

Claire smiled at me, and her cheeks pinkened in the sweetest way. "If you both like it, that's all that matters, right? Callum obviously knows you better than Rodrigo."

Roddy crossed his arms, faux pouting, which was funny on his tattooed, muscle-bound frame. "Wren and I go way back. She almost took your best friend spot."

Claire slapped his arm. "That's not nice. We have matching tattoos. I think my spot is pretty firm."

I laughed. "You have matching tattoos?"

Claire and Rodrigo showed me their wrists, and yeah, they both had a tiny moon and sun in black ink. It was cute and made me think maybe I'd want to get Callum's name on me. Someday. Not now. Not soon either. But maybe someday.

"*We* don't even have matching tattoos," Dominic groused.

Claire rubbed the center of his chest. "I have your lyrics on my skin and in my soul."

His eyelids lowered, and the look he gave her was so heated, I had to glance away. "Yeah, you do," he murmured.

Adam shoved himself into our circle. "Are you talking about the tattoo?"

I waved him off. "The topic has been covered. I love the tattoo, it's not the kiss of death, etcetera."

He folded his arms over his chest. "Well, all right, Wren. I like the way you shut me down and put me in my place. I like that for my boy."

Hope shimmied in between Adam and Roddy. "Someone put Adam in his place?"

Rodrigo wrapped his arm around her shoulders. "Wren told Adam he was being dumb."

My cheeks flamed. "I definitely didn't say that."

Callum stroked my hot cheek with his thumb. I peered up at him, and he was already watching me, the corners of his mouth curving.

"Hi," he whispered.

"Hey, baby," I whispered back.

"Well..." Iris pushed Adam aside to join our circle, "that's new. My Callie's a sweetheart."

I tore my eyes from Callum to grin at Iris. "He is. The sweetest heart."

Sighing, she threaded her fingers through Ronan's hand. "Okay, so are you going on tour with us or what? You and your son are invited, and I can't see Callum surviving an entire summer without you. He was practically crawling out of his skin the entire time we were in LA."

"Oh, well, I don't think—" I shook my head. "I have a job and —"

Adam made a face. "You should quit and tour with us. It's a lot more fun than sitting at a desk."

I laughed. "I have no doubt about that. The thing is, maybe you forget what it's like to be a regular person, but we have bills and student loans. *Mountains* of student loans. Quitting my job, even if it's not as fun as touring, isn't really an option."

Callum stiffened beside me, and I instantly felt bad. We hadn't talked about what it would be like when he went on tour, but of course I'd thought about it. In my dreams, maybe I'd pictured Ez and me on the bus with him, riding down long stretches of highway. But that was just a dream.

"Responsibilities are boring," Adam quipped. "Your first mistake was going to college."

"Higher education, boo, hiss!" Roddy added.

That made me laugh again, even distracted by the man beside me growing stiffer by the minute.

"We're leavin'," Callum barked.

My head snapped to the side to look at him. "What?"

"Now, Wren." There was something in his command, a tone I hadn't heard before, that put me on edge. I nodded, never taking my eyes off his.

"Okay. We can leave."

He jerked his chin at his friends, his bandmates. I got the chance to wave goodbye and glimpse their shocked faces before he pulled me along with him. Not too fast, though. Even in whatever strange state he was in, he remained mindful of my short legs and high heels. When we got to the coat rack by the front door, he carefully slipped mine on me, then buttoned it up to my chin like he always did.

In the elevator, I squeezed his hand. "What just happened?"

"We'll talk at home." His eyes were on mine, and the furrow between his brows might have been six feet deep.

"I don't like you dragging me out of a party without an explanation."

Nostrils flaring, he cupped my jaw. "We will talk at home, Wren."

"Fine." I didn't like it, but I wasn't going to fight him, not when he had clearly dug his heels in and nothing I could say would get him to lift his feet. "We'll talk at home."

I couldn't wait.

CHAPTER TWENTY-FOUR

CALLUM

I WAS FUMING, and I had nowhere to direct my anger. How the fuck could I murder student loans that shouldn't have existed?

I had taken care of that for Wren back when I found her. She'd deserved to go to college, even if her plans had gotten waylaid by having Ez. And since I couldn't give her money directly, I had a lawyer—one of my many, many shady relatives—draft a letter to her great-aunt Jenny telling her the fifty-thousand dollars she was receiving was from a fund for widows of fallen police officers she mistakenly hadn't received when her husband died years earlier. I assumed, wrongly it turned out, she'd pay for Wren's schooling.

Yet, here she was, three years later, buried under debt. Debt she should not have had. Debt that would keep her tied to a job she barely liked and not on the road with me where we both knew she'd rather be.

My parents would be ashamed of me. My grift had had far too many holes. They'd taught me better than that. Always look at a grift from every angle because what could go wrong inevitably *would* go wrong. I should have looked at it from every angle. At the time, I was blinded by emotion at finding Wren, and clearly, I hadn't been thinking straight.

I did a hell of a lot better when I paid off her hospital bills.

Wren allowed me my silence. Inside my apartment, after locking us up tight, I turned her to me and unbuttoned her coat.

She turned away and allowed me to slide it from her shoulders. I hung hers up, and mine followed.

She walked to the kitchen while I did this, and I found her there drinking water from a glass. Her eyebrows raised, but she didn't ask. I felt her anger, and I didn't like it. She was my soft girl, my sweet girl, the girl I wanted to make happy every second of her day. It killed me to be the cause of her anger.

She placed the glass on the counter, but kept her fingers curled around it. Her tongue darted out to lick a drop of water from her upper lip.

"I don't care your reason, dragging me out of that party the way you did was not okay."

She wasn't yelling, even though she'd once told me she yelled when she was pissed. Maybe she wasn't as angry as I'd thought. Then, she went on, and it was worse.

"I'm so embarrassed, I don't know if I'll ever be able to look any of your bandmates in the eye again. You know better than anyone how difficult social settings like that are for me. I thought I was doing well. I truly did. Then you dragged me out like I was a tantruming child, and I really need to know what I did wrong to deserve that treatment."

I reached for her, but she held up a hand. That wasn't acceptable, so I snagged her hip and tugged her closer. I gave her space, but not so much that I couldn't keep my hands on her.

"Callum...I need you to speak." Her hands lay gently on my chest. "I need you to explain this to me so I can understand."

If I dropped to my knees and tongue fucked her, she'd forgive me and forget tonight. I'd make her come as many times as her body could take and she'd melt. My sweet little bird would fall over me, into my arms, and I'd have her again.

She was shoving me now, huffing at my silence, pushing my hands away from gathering her skirt. My eyes met hers, and the wetness pooling there staggered me. My chest caved in like I'd been hit with a boulder.

"Wren…"

She let go of my hands to swipe at her cheeks. "If you're not going to say anything, I'd like to go home."

"No."

"I don't want to, but I'm not going to let you do what you did without explanation."

"You don't take you away from me. You gave me you, and I'm keeping you."

Her breath hitched. "You claimed me without asking."

I dipped my forehead to hers. "Don't pretend you didn't let me."

"If I'm yours, you need to take care of me."

I stilled, her dress bunched in my fists. She was right. She'd given herself over to me, trusting me to be careful. She hadn't known I'd been caring for her from afar for years. But I'd failed her. I couldn't right my wrong from three years ago, but I could fix what I'd trampled on tonight.

"You were perfect tonight, Little Bird." I opened my hands to slide my palms up her sides. "So brave, walkin' into a room filled with strangers. You don't even have to speak. Your smile speaks for itself. I was in awe, having you by my side."

Her body trembled. "If that's true, why did we leave?"

I took her hand, using her fingers to unbutton my shirt, then slid it inside, over her name on my skin. "This week apart from you was difficult. Almost impossible. I don't want to repeat it. But this summer, we're goin' on tour, and there's no avoidin' that. In my head, I've been picturing you and Ez ridin' along with me. Maybe not the whole time, I know the road isn't the easiest for a little guy, but at least part of it. But in one second, that hope was smashed to bits. You shut it down as soon as Iris brought it up."

She shook her head. "We haven't even talked about that…and it's months away. You can't know you'll want me with you then."

My fingers wrapped around her jaw, tipping it back so our eyes were locked. "I know. Don't doubt that for one second. You are my one. You are my only. That won't change."

She whispered my name, and the tinge of fear in her expression killed me. It fuckin' killed me because I wasn't afraid of anything except losing her.

"I can't quit my job." From the firmness in her words, she believed there was no bending.

"I'm not askin' you to do it today."

Her fingers dragged back and forth on my skin. "But you're going to ask, and I'll have to say no. I will hate every second you're gone, but we'll find a way to make it work. Other people do it and—"

I yanked her against me, eliminating the space I'd allowed her to have. "I'm not other people. *We're* not other people."

"I know we're not. If it was just me, I'd consider it, but I have to make the right choice for my son. You know that, baby. I can't be irresponsible."

"I'll take care of you. You just have to let me."

She stiffened. "Callum—"

"Tell me where to send the money. The loans will be taken care of tomorrow."

"Why would you do that?"

She seemed truly perplexed, and it didn't make sense to me. I'd told her from the beginning she was mine. I'd done nothing but show her that was true.

Instead of answering, I asked, "Did I get a fresh slate with you?"

Her head jerked, but her body remained tight in my arms. That was my choice, not hers.

"What do you mean?"

"Are you holdin' the way I hurt you backstage all those years ago over my head, or did I get a fresh slate?"

"I'm not holding it over your head," she whispered.

"You sure?"

Her big eyes got even wider. I could see the world inside them, but I could not read her thoughts. That maddened me.

She took her time answering, worrying her lip with her teeth. Then, after an eternity, she shook her head. "I'm not holding it over your head. You have a fresh slate."

"Then why don't you trust me?"

"I do." This was automatic. No thought given to her answer. I liked that.

"Then trust that I am never walkin' away from you. I tell you I'll take care of you, so I will."

"Can you let go of me? I can't think when I'm in your arms."

My hold on her tightened. "No. You're *not* walkin' away either."

"Take my hand then. Keep it in yours. Just let me breathe for a second."

Though reasonable, I balked at the suggestion. She could think in my arms. I knew damn well I thought better when she was there.

But Wren and I were different. If she asked for two feet of space, that wasn't unreasonable. I wouldn't give it to her, but I *would* give her one.

My arms fell away, but I wove my fingers through hers as soon as they did. She sighed. I was inches from bundling her against me.

"Can we go by the windows? I want to look at the lights." My little bird peered up at me, and she looked so lost, my heart thrashed with panic, as if she'd been physically harmed. But no, it was just me, making a mess of us.

I took her to the windows. My views were worth shit, but I guess she didn't much care. She leaned her forehead against the pane while I stood behind her, loosely holding her hips.

My dick wasn't pressing against her back. She had space.

"Let me pay the loans."

Oh yeah, I was fuckin' terrible at space.

She huffed a short laugh. "Callum, come on." Her head turned to the side, so I took the opportunity to dip down and touch my lips to her cheek. Her lashes fluttered, then she spun to face me. "We haven't been together long enough for me to allow you to do something so big for me. That's crazy."

"It isn't crazy. When you love someone, you take care of them. I love you too much to let you struggle. I have the resources, and I want to give them to you. If you don't let me, I'll find a way to do it anyway. It's happening."

Her lips parted. Her chest rose in a heave. "Callum!"

"No. I'm done fightin' about this, Little Bird."

She slapped my chest, right over the tattoo, and I couldn't say it didn't sting just a little.

"You can't just tell me you love me so I'll do what you want." Her cheeks were blazing. If I thought she'd been angry before, it didn't touch what she was now.

"Why not?"

"Because...because..." She shoved at me again, releasing a frustrated cry. "Because I have loved you for almost as long as I've known you existed, Callum Rose. I've wanted you to love me for just as long. But...but...I don't want it this way."

The tension in my muscles relaxed, even as Wren huffed and squirmed in my hold.

"I love you, Wren." She stopped moving. Her face turned up to mine. "I might not have loved you from the very beginning, but I caught on quick. I fell for your words on the screen, but once I saw you, knew you, there was no gettin' up. So yeah, I love you. And yeah, this might not be perfect, but I'm an imperfect man. I mess up, but I won't mess up lovin' you."

She whimpered and fell against me, circling her arms around my waist. "I love you too."

"Yeah. I got that," I murmured into her hair. "I'm so fuckin' honored you're givin' that to me. I need you to let me give back to you."

Her hands dragged up and down my back, then clamped around my waist again. "Don't use your love against me."

"I'm not. I treasure it. I'm only tellin' you what I need. Takin' care of you is a requirement for me. I won't be able to rest knowin' you're struggling. That's part of me lovin' you."

"Let me think about it."

"My answer's not gonna change."

"Then let me wrap my mind around it." She kissed my chest. "I'm sorry I slapped you. I shouldn't have done that."

With a groan at her sweetness, I bent my knees, gripped her under her ass, lifted her off her feet, and walked her to the couch. I sat with Wren straddling my legs. Her hands cupped my jaw, then she leaned forward, grazing my lips.

"Wren."

"Hmmm?"

"Need more of your mouth, Little Bird. After all that, I have to have it."

Her mouth came to me, a smile curving the corners. We kissed and touched, whispered promises—not the big ones on the tip of my tongue, but small ones, easy ones to keep and accept—and I was content.

At peace.

Wren hadn't agreed to what I wanted—no, *needed*, but she would. I'd make sure of it.

CHAPTER TWENTY-FIVE

WREN

I WAS...RESTLESS.

I should have been content. And in a way, I was. Callum and I had spent the night and a good portion of the morning in each other's arms. He loved me like I'd never been loved.

That was huge. Vital. I wish I could say it was everything, but it wasn't.

I was still uneasy about what had gone down at the party. His reaction had stirred something in the back of my mind I didn't quite grasp. It wasn't until he walked out his door to pick up breakfast for us that I really examined my doubts.

His presence was consuming, and part of me wondered if that was purposeful. If he never let me go, how could I take a step back and really look at our circumstances?

I hated that I was having doubts. My love for Callum was so deep, it had settled in my bones. It wasn't something that would go away. I knew that from trying to shove it in a box the past three and a half years. I hadn't been able to move on then, and I knew it would be impossible now. That was why I hated these doubts.

With a sigh, I picked up his laptop and turned it on. I hadn't read the emails he had sent me every year, and it seemed like now might be the time to do that. I needed that lifeline in the moment to remind me who we were together. Who we'd always been.

His screen was a chaos of icons, and it made me smile. Callum's apartment was so spare, there was hardly anything in it, so it surprised me to see his busy screen. But it was him, and I liked him a lot.

I found the icon with my name after searching for a moment. I dragged the cursor to it, but something else caught my eye.

A folder with the name of the private investigation firm my neighbor Jackie worked for. That niggle in the back of my mind grew. I couldn't stop myself from clicking on it.

Immediately, I wished I hadn't.

Bile rose in my throat.

My name was everywhere. Dates, times, locations, reports on my life. I could only skim the words, but they went back three years. Three years! My eyes blurred with tears. My stomach churned. I didn't understand it, but I hated it. God, I hated it. So much, I tossed the laptop to the ground and leaped away from it like it was a cockroach skittering across my kitchen counters.

I was in my pajamas, but I didn't stop. *Go. Run. Escape.*

I grabbed my purse, stuffed my feet in my shoes, threw on my coat. Then, I was gone. Racing down the elevator, through the lobby, into the harsh winter morning.

I bent in half on the sidewalk, half blind with panic. I couldn't stay here, in front of Callum's building, not when he'd be back any minute. I had to get out of here. My home was safe. I needed to be there, to think, to try to understand and wrap my mind around what I had seen. What Callum had done. What he'd been doing for three years without my knowledge.

My legs moved swiftly once I decided where I was going. I huddled in my coat, eyes on the ground, and plowed through the bitter wind. It felt good, even as it sliced at my skin. It woke me up, cleared my head, helped me order my thoughts.

By the time I'd arrived on my block, my plans had changed. Instead of going to my house, I knocked on the door beside it.

Aunt Jackie answered a moment later, ushering me in without questioning my appearance.

She smoothed her hands over the sides of my hair. "You're a mess, baby."

I nodded, my eyes watering. "I feel it."

"There has to be a story that led you to knock on my door looking like a ghost. You want to tell me?"

I nodded again. "Do you think I could sit down for a minute?" I was all kinds of wobbly now that I'd stopped moving.

She jumped back and motioned for me to walk ahead of her. "Come in, come in. You want coffee?"

"Yeah." I plopped my butt on her couch. "I think I need it."

"Okay. You wait here. I'll be right back."

My phone had been vibrating nonstop the last ten minutes. I knew it was Callum freaking out over my absence. The last thing I wanted was for him to come here and pound on my door, demanding answers, and that was the first thing he'd do.

I scanned over his panicked messages without taking in the words, then I typed out a succinct reply.

Me: *I'm home and safe. I don't want you coming here. We will talk, but I need time. If you come to my house and upset Ez or Jenny, that answer will change. I need you to respect that. I will be in touch soon.*

His reply was immediate. He'd obviously found the laptop and knew why I'd left.

Callum: *I need to explain.*

Me: *And I will let you, but what I need is some space.*

Callum: *Give me a time.*

Me: *No. It doesn't work that way. I will contact you when I'm ready.*

Callum: *You are not taking you away from me.*

Me: *I don't know what I'm doing, which is why I need space.*

Callum: *You told me you love me.*

Me: *That was before I had all the information.*

Callum: *You still don't have it. I'll explain.*
Me: *I'll text you. I'm turning off my phone now.*

Jackie handed me a mug and sat beside me. She sipped her coffee while I sipped mine. When I found it wasn't scorching hot, I took bigger gulps.

"Are you going to talk?" Jackie asked.

"Callum Rose."

Her sharp intake of breath was all I needed to hear. She hadn't been kind to me and Ez out of the goodness of her heart. Aunt Jackie was no benevolent neighbor. I was a job to her. Nothing more.

"What do you know?" she asked cautiously.

"I know you're being paid by him to be my friend." I was trying so hard to be tough, but the hitch in my words proved I wasn't doing a great job.

Her shoulders curled inward. "Oh, baby, no. That isn't true. Not at all."

I lifted a hand. "Then tell me what *is* true, Jackie. Because right now, I feel like everyone's been lying to me and I don't know what's real anymore."

A sob broke through, but only one. If I let loose the well of sadness gathering in my chest, I'd never stop. And I couldn't give in to that. Not when my little boy was right next door, waiting for me to come home with a smile on my face.

"I'm bound by confidentiality, Wren, but—" she cut herself off and looked away, rubbing her mouth roughly. Then she turned back, determination lighting her gaze. "No. I'll tell you as much as I can. I won't have you walk out of here thinking I don't care for you and Ezra, because that just isn't true."

I choked on another sob. "Okay. Then tell me."

He came in the dead of night. I wasn't at all surprised to hear the creak in the hallway, and then, a moment later, my bed dipping under his weight. His long, cold body curled around my back, his arm like a steel band wrapping around my middle.

We lay there for long minutes. He knew I was awake since I curled my fingers around his. As time ticked by, his jagged breaths smoothed out, and the tautness in his muscles eased. I felt him melt into me, weighing me down into the mattress.

"Growing up, I hung out with Jenny whenever I got the chance. You don't know this about her, but Jenny is a big movie buff. She goes to the theater whenever she gets the chance and has a long list of favorite films. So, when I hung out with her, naturally, we'd watch a lot of movies."

Callum had frozen in place, listening to me speak so hard, he was barely breathing.

"One of her favorites was *The Truman Show*. I don't know if you've seen it, but I've watched it a dozen times. There's this guy, Truman, and he has a picture-perfect life...or so he thinks. It turns out, everyone in his sweet little town is an actor and his life is a TV show. None of it's real. His friends are being paid to be his friend. It's all fake. His job, his wife, even his home is being controlled by the man behind the curtain."

Callum's hand flattened on my stomach. "Wren."

"I think you understand where I'm going with this. I've been on *The Wren Show* for the last three years. Aunt Jackie, Mr. Sulaimani, and god knows who else, have been looking out for me because they're paid to do so. And you...you knew who I was for years and never said anything. Not a word, Callum. I ached for you, my heart broke missing you, and you were *there* the whole time. I have always felt someone watching me, but it didn't feel scary, so I let it go. God, I shouldn't have let it go."

Jackie didn't know everything, but she told me what she *did* know. Callum had hired the PI firm to find out information on me and my neighbors. When the townhouse next to Jenny's became vacant, Jackie had needed a place to live, so she moved in. Her job was to keep an eye out for me, nothing more, and she only reported if anything was amiss, which it very rarely was. She had promised me she watched Ez because she loved him, but I didn't know what to believe anymore.

Mr. Sulaimani at the bodega had also kept tabs on me. I didn't know what he'd been paid since Jackie wasn't aware. I only knew I'd never look at him the same way again.

Jackie hadn't known everything, but I felt she'd been as forthright as possible. Just like Mr. Sulaimani, I didn't know if I'd see her the same after this.

After minutes of silence, Callum spoke. "Mr. Sulaimani had been savin' money to pay for an immigration lawyer to help get his mom here from Yemen. He didn't want shit to do with watchin' over you for me until I offered to pay all the legal fees. She's comin' in the spring."

I nodded in the dark, pinching my mouth tight to stave off more tears.

Wasn't that just Callum to do something so good for an entirely selfish purpose? I wanted to be angry, and I was, but I couldn't be mad at Mr. Sulaimani. Not when his precious mother was finally going to be able to come to America.

"Did he give you my college papers?"

"Yeah."

"Why?"

"I wanted more of your words."

A knife to the gut. How did he do that? He made me ache for what we'd lost even while I was desperately angry at him.

"Couldn't you have spoken to me? I would have given you words."

His hold on me tightened to the point of suffocation, but I didn't fight. This might've been the last time I allowed his arms around me, so I'd drown in him, just a little.

His cool lips touched the back of my neck. "You remember where you were three years ago? You'd shut me out of your life and were pregnant with another man's baby. I didn't think I'd be welcome to speak to you, and I'm sorry, Little Bird, but it took me a while not to want to roar when I saw your big, gorgeous belly."

Another stab, right next to the first one. If the tables had been turned, I would have been devastated. I got that, I truly did. I understood why he hadn't come forward then, but *three* years had gone by and...nothing?

"Why didn't you walk away?"

"Couldn't. I should've, but you were mine. You were my little bird and I couldn't walk away from you." He nuzzled my nape. "Loved you then. Love you now. Always will. Your shadow found you, it just took you a while to know it."

I jerked, pushing at his hand. "You were *hiding* from me."

"I thought I'd be able to let you go. If I could see you livin', happy, that would be enough."

A third wound, to match the other two. I'd been disposable one too many times. The suggestion that I might've been to Callum was almost too much to bear.

"You were going to let me go?" Oh, I sounded pathetic now. Like a lost little girl. I hated myself for it, but I'd felt nothing but lost the entire day.

He kissed my neck again. "I don't know why I ever thought that. I want you happy and livin', but I need to be the source of that happiness, and I need to be livin' right beside you."

I couldn't go there. If I took in his words, I'd break. The only thing holding me together was my simmering anger.

"You've been manipulating my life from behind the scenes this entire time."

His forehead pressed against the back of my head. "I've been takin' care of you."

"You're a liar."

"Not a liar. I'm a lot of things, but not that. If you think back, I've never lied to you. Told you I was obsessed. Told you I was stalkin' you. Told you I knew who you were. If you'd asked me when I'd figured it out, I would have told you the truth."

"Did you pay my NICU bills?"

No hesitation. "Yes."

I sucked in a breath. That was bigger than I could wrap my head around. "Thank you."

"You don't need to thank me. I'll do anything for you." He stroked my belly, slow and methodical. "Sometimes I thought about takin' you. What it would be like to keep you for myself."

"That's crazy," I rasped.

"I know it is. I'm only admitting this so when I tell you not to thank me, you'll understand why. I'm not a good man, but I'll be unfailingly good to you. You might not understand my actions, but I'm always thinkin' of how to make your life better."

If I thought too much about the magnitude of what he was admitting and everything that had been revealed, I'd have to leap out of this bed and scream the walls down. This was too big, too much, too everything.

If he was in a truth-telling mood, I'd ask more questions. If nothing else, I'd leave today behind with answers to everything I'd wondered.

"Why were you angry about my student loans?"

He exhaled through his nose, heating my skin. "Jenny got fifty grand for widows of fallen officers, yeah?"

I knew why he was asking immediately. "That was you?"

"I didn't anticipate her not helpin' you. I made a mistake."

"She did help me. Not with tuition, but with Ez. She was able to cut her hours down at her job so she could watch him while I was in class. That money was huge for us."

I felt him relax. "I would've given more." His fingers stroked my stomach, tracing the curve he couldn't seem to get enough of. "Didn't have it at the time. I gave you everything I could. I've got a lot more now. It's yours. Say the word, and all that I am is yours."

"I don't want your money, Callum. I just want—" I clamped down on my lip.

"Me? Us?"

That was what I would have said yesterday. Right now? I wanted yesterday back.

I twisted my head, then my body. No more speaking to the ether. I needed to see his face while he whispered his crazy.

"It doesn't matter what I want. You manipulated me and my situation, and now you've broken into my home when I asked you for space. I'm not okay with any of that. I missed you for three and a half years, and you've been there the whole time… and that kills me. Maybe even more than Auntie Jackie and Mr. Sulaimani. I don't know, I don't know. I can't make sense of it. This isn't good. It's not right."

"The job too." His thumb traced my bottom lip.

"What?"

"Helped you get your job too."

My eyes fell shut. Maybe I didn't want to see his crazy. "Callum, you can't do things like that. You can't be here, you can't watch me, you can't!"

"Why? Because you think you're not supposed to like what I've done, or because you really believe it? I didn't harm you. I'd cut off my limbs before I ever hurt you. I've been helpin' you and watchin' over you. I gave you the distance I thought you wanted while keepin' you safe."

"Callum…" I groaned, suddenly exhausted and even more jumbled than I'd been before.

"I love you, Wren. It might be a psycho kind of love, but it's pure and it's true."

"What if I don't want a psycho kind of love?" I squeezed out.

"The thing with this kind of love is you really don't get a choice. It's yours."

I laid my head on his shoulder, not because I'd forgiven him or lost my anger, but because I was spent and there had never been a place I'd felt safer than in his arms. Even now.

"I can't talk anymore."

"Sleep, Little Bird." He pulled me into his chest, laying his head on mine.

"You need to go."

"Not goin'."

"I'm very, very angry with you."

"I know. I'm still not goin'. I gave you space today, but that's done. You sleep. I'll keep talkin' to you when you're rested. Tell you more. Explain it all. But I'm not goin', so you need to stop askin'."

"This isn't okay," I whispered.

"I'll make it so it is."

I believed he would be relentless in his pursuit to make it so.

Sleep shouldn't have come so easily, but I'd spent the day with my mind whirring and my heart cracking. The emotional dervish that was Callum Rose had exhausted me to my bones. And dammit, my body slotted against his far too perfectly to even pretend to deny.

I closed my eyes. Callum kissed my head. I fell asleep.

CHAPTER TWENTY-SIX

WREN

THE BED BESIDE ME WAS COLD WHEN I WOKE UP. The level of disappointment I felt at that discovery staggered me. I didn't allow it to level me. There was no time for that. Ezra would be awake any minute if he wasn't already. There was breakfast to make, laundry to do, shopping for the week...no time for my broken heart.

I threw a sweatshirt over my pajamas, washed the sleep out of my eyes, and gave my teeth a quick scrub, then I peeked in Ezra's room. He wasn't in there, but Jenny's door was still closed. My heart thumped.

Where is he?

I took the steps in a hurry and heard my son's sweet voice coming from the kitchen. Another voice answered him back.

My heart thumped again at the sight of them.

Ezra was sitting on the kitchen counter, his hands over Callum's as they mixed something in a big bowl. They were speaking quietly, laughing at some inside joke I couldn't hear. Ez's hair was crazy like it always was in the morning. Callum had swept his back in a bun.

I stood there on the periphery, allowing them this moment. How could I end it? I didn't want to, that was for sure.

Callum's blue gaze found me, and a slow smile broke out on his gorgeous face. Shadows may have loved him, but *I* adored him in the light.

"Mornin', Mama." His morning voice was gritty, and it hit me right between the legs.

Ezra found me next and he gasped. "Mornin', Mama!"

I laughed, trailing into the kitchen. "Oh, are you Southern all of a sudden?"

His face scrunched. "What's that?"

I shook my head, still smiling at my boo. "Nothing, baby buddy." I peered into the bowl. "Hmmm...let me guess what you're making. Is it snot sandwiches?"

"No!" he yelled.

"Oh, silly me." I kissed Ezra's forehead. "I bet this is... hmmm...pancake batter."

He nodded so big, his head flew around his head in a cloud. "Cow-um's making them. I'm helping him."

I narrowed my eyes on the man himself. He smiled back at me as though we weren't right in the middle of something very serious.

"I woke up to a little boy pokin' my nose this morning. You were still out, Ez was wide awake, so I thought we'd hang out until you got up. He showed me the basement."

Ezra giggled. "Cow-um was scared of the spiders."

My eyes went wide. "You showed him the spiders? Oh boy."

"I got scared, but I didn't run," Callum supplied. "Now, we're makin' pancakes, so go sit your fine ass down while the boys do the cookin'."

"Don't say ass," I whispered.

Callum chuckled and went back to mixing. I didn't know what to do. I needed space, to think, to sort out my feelings, but I couldn't make a scene in front of my kid, and I already knew Callum wasn't going to leave if I asked politely. I didn't *want* to have a scene with Callum anyway. I wasn't a scene making kind of girl.

So, I went into the living room and sat on my fine ass. What I didn't do was relax. Any peace I'd gained from a *really* good night of sleep had already been burned through—and it was only seven thirty in the morning.

When I was called to the table for breakfast, I hadn't sorted through a single one of my thoughts. But Ezra was happy, and Callum...well, he seemed to be too. He grinned at me as I took my seat, and the crinkles around his eyes made my heart thump once again.

He liked this. Being here, hanging out with my boy, making breakfast. Crazy, silent, obsessive, strange Callum Rose was enjoying the hell out of being part of this ordinary, stunningly beautiful life I led.

Callum slipped his hand under my hair to cup my nape. "Sleep well?"

I sighed. "Yeah. Better than I expected."

"Good." He shoved a forkful of pancake into his mouth.

Ezra filled the space with stories about preschool then he wanted to hear a Bob Seger song. His resounding opinion was that Bob Marley was his second favorite Bob to Bob Ross. Bob Seger was a distant third.

Jenny came down after breakfast and wrangled Ezra upstairs to get dressed and give us some privacy. She didn't know what was going on, but she knew something was up. I probably hadn't been in top form the day before.

I wouldn't tell her because she wouldn't understand. Not that I did, but she *really* wouldn't.

"You need to go home, Callum," I whispered.

Because he was Callum Rose, he didn't do what I asked. He took me in his arms instead, and I wrapped mine around his waist.

"I liked bein' here this morning, lettin' you sleep while me and Ez cooked. Not something I could have predicted I'd like."

I nodded against his chest. "I know you liked it. But you still need to go."

"After you had him, you used to go on long walks with the stroller. Sometimes you'd sit down on a bench and cry your heart out." I went stiff. I remembered those walks all too well. "I got close to talkin' to you then, but you're Wren. So fuckin' strong. You'd pull yourself together, get up, and keep movin'."

I banged my forehead against him. "I wish you'd spoken to me. Maybe not in the middle of my crying jags, but before or after."

He took my chin in his hand and tipped my head back. "I love you, Wren, but you have to know you left me out in the cold. *You* abandoned me. You can be angry or freaked out that I watched you for so long, but I do not accept you being angry at me not speakin' to you when you made it clear with your silence you were done with me."

My mouth fell open to refute him, but he cut me off.

"Knowin' what I know now, of course I wish I'd approached you. I look back on the last three years and see the time I wasted. I can't get it back, but I'm not gonna waste the time we have now. So, when you tell me to leave, give you space, I'm buckin' against that with all I have. I've given you space, and I'm done with that. I'm done with it, Wren. I will come clean on every detail of my obsession with you. You ask me anything, I'll tell you, though you pretty much know it all. What I won't do is give you up. I will not allow you to be mad at me for keepin' my distance when I did it because I thought that was what you wanted. We were apart for the last week, and I hated every second of it. That's enough of that."

He patted his chest, right where the tattoo was. "You're on my skin, under it, in my bloodstream. This is it, Little Bird. I'm here now. The last three years are done and gone, and we can't retrace our steps. We can only move forward, and there is no way in hell I'm movin' forward without you. I *love* you."

I swallowed down the feeling of my heart trying to escape from my throat. "I need to think. I can't think when you're here.

You're just…in my face. You're saying all the right things, but I don't know if they're right because they make me feel good to hear or if they're actually right."

He cupped my cheeks, dipped, and brushed his lips over mine. I whimpered, and he went in again, kissing me longer, deeper, but not hard. Still gentle, so gentle.

Then he stepped back, leaving me staggered all over again.

"All right, Wren. You can have today. I won't be in your face, but I'll be in touch. I need you to respond when I text or I'll be back to make sure you're okay." His eyes narrowed on me, like he didn't quite trust me to follow that request.

"All right. I'll respond."

His hands flexed by his sides. He stared at me for a long moment, his chest rising and falling in great heaves. Then, he nodded, turned on his heel, and headed for the door. I followed right behind him, all the way outside to my stoop, the bitter winter air cutting straight through my sweatshirt.

Callum took a step down, then he spun around, yanked me to him, and kissed me hard. His tongue slipped between my lips, tasting every inch of me. I clawed at his chest, desperate for him to stay right here, needing him to disappear so I could function.

His shirt was bunched in my fingers. One of his hands slid under my sweatshirt to my breast, the other cupped my throat. Our mouths were fused so tight, his air became mine. Mine became his. I loved him, completely and irrevocably. Only the smallest fraction of me wanted him to leave, but I had to listen to that fraction.

But his mouth, his kiss, I'd never been kissed this way. That was because he loved me, was obsessed with me, couldn't get enough of me. I was the same when it came down to it.

The sound of a truck rumbling by broke us apart. Callum took me by the shoulders and gently pushed me toward my open front door. I turned right back around in the doorway. He gave me another long look, his brow crinkled and mouth curving down in displeasure.

And then, he was gone, leaving me reeling.

That night, I laid in bed alone. I hadn't done much thinking, but I was calm. My anger had ebbed. Now, I was just confused and tired.

Callum had texted me three times during the day, just checking in. My replies were succinct. That was it, and it felt colder than his silence.

He could be silent with everyone else. The world could think of him as stone cold. But with me, he was always warm and open.

My phone chimed, signaling I had an email. I sucked in a breath when I saw it was from Callum. I hadn't checked my old email address in three and a half years, since I last wrote to him. He'd sent this one to my current address.

I opened it, my heart firmly lodged in my throat.

Little Bird,

I don't know if you got the chance to read the emails I wrote to you over the years. I don't think you did. I'm not sending you this to guilt you, but for you to understand how I felt when you were gone.

Here you go. This is everything. Read them or don't. I hope you do.

I fucking miss you, Wren. Not even 24 hours and I'm close to climbing up your drainpipe to take a peek at you.

Callum

I didn't know if I wanted to, but I did know I had to, so I opened the first email he sent me after I'd disappeared.

Little Bird,
No crying over me. I won't allow it.
Someday, I'm going to make you believe you're everything I've said about you. You're not going to doubt it, even for a second. Those voices that have made you feel like you weren't amazing will be drowned out.
Don't be scared. I'm not scary. I'm just a big, weird rocker who wants to be beside you.
We're doing this. So fucking soon, we're doing it.
I'm staying sane solely for you.
Callum

Once I started, I couldn't stop, so I read the string of emails he sent when I didn't reply. Each word, each letter, dripped on my skin like battery acid.

Little Bird,
Where are you?
Did my last email get too intense? Lost in the ether?
Talk to me.
Callum

Birdie,

I need you to reply. Did something happen? If meeting is too much, I get it. We'll wait. I'm not going anywhere. I need to know you're okay. Why aren't you replying?
Callum

Fuck, Birdie, where are you? Just talk to me.
Callum

He sent twenty emails over the next month. Each one got more and more desperate. The last one came on the day we had planned to meet, and it absolutely broke me.

Wren,
Even after a month of silence, I looked for you. I thought you'd show. We'd laugh at whatever the misunderstanding was that kept you from emailing me. We'd be awkward and stumble over our words but happy as hell we got up the guts to meet.

Didn't happen. And you know what? I'm hoping like hell this is your way of telling me to fuck off. Because when I think of the alternative, that something's gone down in your life that's so bad you can't get to your computer, I feel like I'm going crazy.

I can't keep doing this. I won't write you again, but I'm here. I'm open to hearing from you. Even if you need to tell me to fuck off, just please fucking tell me. It's the not knowing that's killing me.
Callum

I couldn't read anything else. The other emails would have to wait for another day when I was stronger. I curled into a ball and let myself feel all of it. How I hurt Callum by disappearing. Threw away the most important relationship I'd ever had from fear. His confusion. His loss. His desperation. The time we lost because I screwed up in a huge, magnificent way.

I took it in, and it was an ice pick to my gut. I did this. I was afraid, and I destroyed something perfectly beautiful.

The fact that Callum had the capacity to love me after the way I fucked up so royally was a testament to who he was. He called his love psycho, and maybe it was, but it was also forgiving and generous.

I didn't know what to feel about his manipulations. I knew I wasn't okay with it.

I also wasn't the same person I'd been back then. Depression and anxiety had been like living, breathing monsters on my back, and for the most part, I'd learned to cope. I had my son, finished school, grew the hell up. The time I was taking from Callum to sort myself out wasn't running away, even if that had been my first instinct. My thoughts and emotions had been far too jumbled to make a decision.

But it was clear now what I wanted—what I'd always wanted.

Me: *Will you be in the car with me in the morning?*

Callum: *I wish I could say yes. I have to do some radio interviews beginning at the crack of dawn. I'll be there on your way home.*

Me: *Okay. I'd like to talk.*

Callum: *I'll come over.*

Me: *No, baby. I'm about to fall asleep. I want to be clearheaded. You want to have dinner with us then we'll talk when Ez goes to bed?*

Callum: *So fucking bad.*

Me: *Then that's what we'll do.*

Callum: *Need to hold my girl.*
Me: *Let's do the talking thing first.*
Callum: *Gonna hold you in the car. Second I see you.*
Me: *All right, baby.*
Callum: *Go to sleep, Little Bird.*
Me: *I am. Good night. Xoxo*
Callum: *Love you. Sleep well. x*

CHAPTER TWENTY-SEVEN

WREN

WINTER WAS BEGINNING TO THAW IN MANHATTAN. The air was still crisp, but it wasn't as biting. I loved it, though. I'd be sad when it started to get warm. There was no way I would be spending my lunch hours in the park under the beating summer sun. This girl was not built for the heat.

As I approached Good Music at the end of my break, I was lost in the warm sun and the cool air, optimistic, and more than looking forward to tonight. A young boy and his pregnant mother were stopped on the sidewalk so I had to dodge around them. My eye caught on an RV double parked, and I shook my head. They were going to get a ticket. And who brought an RV to the city?

"Oh, I'm sorry," the woman called from behind me. "We got in your way."

I turned back to smile at them. "Don't worry for a second. Have a good day."

The little boy waved. His blue eyes were so big and round, I couldn't help waving back. His mother's head jerked to the side, then so did mine. But it was too late.

A man the size and shape of a wall wrapped his arms around me, plucked me from the sidewalk, and shoved me into the RV. I tripped over my own two feet onto a threadbare bench anchored to the floor.

"Wha—?" I rose to my feet, but the man shoved me down again. He was gentle about it, but I still slammed on my butt since he was nine feet tall with arms like tree trunks.

The pregnant woman and her son hurried through the door, then the wall-man slammed it shut, locked it, and threw himself into the driver's seat. We were moving a moment later.

"What are you doing?" I cried. "Who are you? Wha—?"

The woman brought her finger to her lips and shushed me. It shocked me so much, I actually quieted. Then she squatted in front of the boy, ruffled his hair, and smiled. "Go up to the loft and put on your headphones. Watch your show, okay?"

He nodded, eyeing me for a split second, then climbed a ladder to a narrow loft above the driver's seat. The woman spun to face me when the boy was safely tucked away.

"I'm not going to hurt you," she said.

"Just kill me?" Oh god, why would I even suggest that? I was terrible at being kidnapped.

"No, of course not." She actually laughed, as if that was so silly. Then she sat down on the bench, a foot of distance between us. "My name is Chrysanthemum. The man drivin' is my brother, Rascal. The boy is my son, Sparrow. He has a bird name like you."

My eyes rounded. "You know who I am?"

She mimicked my expression. "I don't look a little bit familiar? Even the eyes?"

Hers were icy blue, and her hair was a pale blonde. She was tall and lanky, even with the round belly. The man had been just as blond and icy, but not even close to lanky.

"Are you related to Callum?" I breathed.

She clapped once and grinned. "You got it. When we were little, they called us the trips. Rasc got big, I got girly, and...well, Callum got gone, so our triplet days ended. But we looked just alike for a while there."

Any other day, I'd love to be hearing about Callum's life from his sister. But not this day—not when I'd been shoved in an RV and driven god knows where.

"Where are you taking me?"

Her smile dimmed. "Oh, we're not goin' anywhere. Rasc is just makin' circles so we can talk uninterrupted. I told you, we're not gonna hurt you. This meetin' is just to say hi and talk. Cal won't take my calls, and I *really* need to talk to my brother. I'm hopin' I can appeal to your heart and you'll ask him for me."

My skin prickled when I thought of what Callum's reaction to this would be. I knew he wouldn't take kindly to it, and I really didn't want to be the messenger.

I'd play along with anything if it meant I'd get out of this RV. I hadn't glanced around much, concentrating on my captors instead, but from what I saw, it was old, but spotlessly clean. Everything should have been replaced years ago, but the floor wasn't sticky and the air smelled like lemons. So at least I didn't have to worry about being infested with bugs when I left here. I just had to worry about actually getting the chance to leave.

"Why do you need to talk to Callum?"

She might have said she wasn't going to hurt me and they weren't taking me anywhere scary, but the windows all had cardboard over them and she *had* sent her kid away. I didn't trust this woman, and I was terrified of the wall-man in the front. I'd play along, though, if it meant I'd escape with my body parts intact.

"Well," she laid her hand on her rounded belly, "I'm havin' a baby in two months. The dad abandoned me, tellin' me he didn't believe the baby's his." Her eyes misted, and it jabbed at me. I knew all too well what it was like to have a baby with a man who shirked his duties. "He knows damn well he forced himself on me."

Her voice caught, and tears slipped down her cheeks. And I... well, I was affected. This situation was terrifying, but I was human. Seeing her in pain, with her big belly, knowing what she had coming, it made me raw for her.

"I'm sorry," I rasped.

Her eyes connected with mine. They shined like the sky on the sunniest day of the year. So blue, they were almost unreal. And they were so incredibly sad. Still, she forced out a half smile.

"His parents offered to help—I guess they know what kind of man their son is—but you see, they're all the way out in California. Rasc and me have been workin' odd jobs, but the RV broke down and it's expensive to fix a vehicle this old. We spent all our money on makin' the RV run. If we can just get to Cali, we'll be golden, but funds are short. I'm hopin' Callum will help us one last time so I can have my baby near her grandparents. They don't have much, but they'll watch her and Sparrow while I work and we can live with them. We won't have to be stuck in the RV anymore."

"That'd be nice." I was thinking about Jenny and what a lifeline she'd been for me. How I wouldn't have survived without her. And then I remembered what a lifeline Callum had been and I hadn't even known it.

"Yeah." She smiled through her tears. "Sparrow can have a real bed. He can get enrolled in school. It'd be real, real nice. We just gotta get out there. Lorraine and Mike can't afford to loan us much, so we're a little desperate. I know it isn't right, grabbin' you and scarin' you, but Rasc and I didn't know what else to do. So, I'm beggin' you right now to ask Cal to help us. And I'm throwin' myself at your mercy, askin' for your forgiveness. *Please*, Wren. Ask him to call me."

I nodded, seeing so much of myself in her. She was breaking my heart with her sad blue eyes that reminded me so much of Callum's.

"I'll ask him. I'll try to make him understand." Reaching out, I laid my hand on hers. "I know you grew up rough, but you're making things better for your kids, and that's so commendable. I think Callum will help you, but can I ask that when you call in the future, it's just to check on him. Don't call when you need something. Call because you love him."

Her head jerked back as if I'd surprised her. "Um...okay. Yeah, you're right. I should definitely do that." She stood up and cupped her mouth. "Rasc, we're good."

The vehicle slowed a minute later, then pulled to a stop. Chrys tipped her chin to the door. "You can go now."

"Oh, okay."

Flustered, I smoothed my hands over my coat and climbed to my feet. My knees were wobbly, and it felt like all the blood had rushed out of my head.

Chrys followed me to the door, crowding me like she was in a hurry. "You'd better shake a tail feather," she said from behind me. "Cops catch us double parked, we'll have even bigger worries."

She swung the door open and gave my shoulder a sharp nudge. Lightheaded, knees knocking, I stepped out, and it was clear right away I'd misjudged the drop. Time slowed, and even though it was a few feet, it took forever for me to hit the ground.

When I did, I wished I was still floating.

The snap was audible. Nausea rose in my throat immediately. Horns honked, someone cursed a few times, then the rumble of the engine vibrated the pavement where I was curling into a ball.

Someone rushed toward me. Then another someone. I saw feet, men's dress shoes and women's spiked boots.

"Wren? Oh my god, Wren! Ronan, lift her up." Iris was here. Why was Iris here?

A strong hand curled around my arm, and my vision went black. Someone screamed so loud and high, windows must have shattered. *That was me. I screamed. Oh god.* The hand retreated right away. Another hand drove through my hair, stroking me gently, shushing me.

"Wren, honey, Ronan needs to help you up. Is anything else injured?" Iris asked.

"I don't know. I don't think so." I cradled my wrist to my chest. I'd never broken a bone, but I had no doubt I'd broken this one. The snap would forever be ingrained in my mind.

"Come on, love," Ronan cooed softly as he took me under the elbows. "Let's get you up and take care of you."

He got me standing, holding me against his broad frame. Iris was there too, stroking my hair and looking me over. That was when I saw we were right in front of Good Music. Natalie had run out of the building. She was watching from the entry, worry crinkling her brow.

Then I was ushered away. Iris sat beside me in the back of a plush SUV while Ronan sat beside their driver, Bill. He drove like I had a life-threatening emergency instead of a broken wrist.

"Want to tell me who shoved you out of that RV?" Iris asked.

"I don't know if I was shoved—"

"You were shoved, girl," Ronan barked. "And they drove off, seeing you lying there. I hope that wasn't someone you consider a friend."

I shook my head in disbelief. "That was Callum's sister," I whispered, and Iris gasped. Bill's eyes shot to the rearview mirror. Ronan twisted in his seat, scowling ferociously.

"I'll call him, tell him what happened." Ronan picked up his phone, but I slapped his seat.

"Please don't. He'll be so angry, especially if he doesn't hear it from me. I have to make him understand what happened."

Ronan's eyes narrowed. "If you don't tell him you were shoved, I will. Iris will too. We both saw as we were leaving Good Music. There's no denying that. He needs to know."

"He'll be so angry," I whimpered.

"Good." Ronan's nostrils flared. "If he wasn't angry his sister injured his woman, I'd be worried."

I couldn't fight with him. I already had one domineering man in my life, I didn't need to take on another. Plus, the adrenaline in my system that had been dulling some of the pain was ebbing, and the sharp ache took all my concentration to breathe through.

Ronan charged into the emergency room, securing me a bed faster than he should have been able to. Iris stayed with me as I spoke to the doctor and was waiting for me when I got back from my X-ray. It all went so fast, action blurring around me. I'd been to the emergency room before, and it was never like this. I didn't mind the special treatment, though. Not in the least.

Fortunately, I didn't need surgery even though my break was fairly serious. I was wrapped up in a hot-pink cast, given instructions and a prescription for pain meds, and sent on my way. All of this took several hours, getting dangerously close to the time Callum would pick me up from work.

Ronan loomed at our backs as we walked out of the hospital to Bill's waiting SUV.

"Can you text Callum for me?" Iris nodded, poised with her phone. "Tell him I'm with you but I'm coming to his place."

"Got it, honey bunny."

I worried my bottom lip with my teeth. "He's going to lose his shit."

"Yeah." Her eyes, which were a rich blue, found mine. "Do you want me to stay with you when we get to his place?"

"No, thank you. I'm not afraid of him. I'm just scared about what he'll do."

She canted her head. "You think he'll go after them?"

My chin dropped to my chest. Dread rose within me. "Pretty sure he will. They're his brother and sister, so I don't know what he'll do, but I don't think he'll see reason."

Iris climbed into the SUV, and I followed. Ronan stood at the door, looking us both over.

"I'll stay with you." His nostrils flared. His mouth had gotten tight. "If he needs to go after them, I'll go and make sure nothing gets out of hand."

I nodded, and he closed the door.

As we drove, Iris leaned closer to me. "A few months ago, I was in that same hospital."

I turned to her. "I remember reading you were attacked."

"Yeah." Her hand went to her stomach. "I still have the scars."

"I'm sorry."

Her smile was sweet and sympathetic. "I thought I was okay after. I'm a tough girl, you know? But sometimes it still haunts me. I picture the knife, my attacker's crazed eyes, and I feel like I'm back there. I know your experience wasn't the same as mine, but I'm here if you need to talk to someone who understands, honey bunny."

My chin quivered. Iris was a beautiful, famous rock star. She *was* a tough girl, and she looked it. Her boyfriend was a massively suited bodyguard, walking intimidation. Both had been kinder to me in the last few hours than people I'd known my whole life.

"Thank you," I squeezed out.

She rested her hand over mine, even as her chin quivered a little too. "Of course. You're Callie's girl, that means you're my girl too."

I bit down hard on the inside of my cheek to stop my tears. I would cry later, and it would be a flood, but it wasn't time yet.

Now, I had to get to Callum and make him believe I was going to be fine.

CHAPTER TWENTY-EIGHT

CALLUM

PHONE IN HAND, I paced at my open door.

Wren was coming. Iris was with Wren. Ronan too.

Something was wrong.

They wouldn't say, but I knew. Why else would she be with Iris? She should have been at work, but she was coming here.

My stomach tightened. I was sick with worry. They'd be here any second. Any second, I'd have the answers. But that didn't make it easier. That did not relieve the knots in my gut.

I saw Ronan first. He strode down the hallway from the elevator. When he met my eyes, there was nothing but stone behind them. He stepped to the side when he arrived at my door. First, Iris came into view. The smile she gave me wasn't one of happiness.

My gaze bounced to Wren. At first glance, I couldn't find anything wrong with her. I took her in, swept her from head to toe, and stopped at the sleeve of her coat hanging loose at her side.

"What happened?" I addressed Ronan.

Wren rushed forward before he could answer and threw herself into my chest. I backed into the apartment with my little bird in my arms. Ronan and Iris followed.

"What happened?" I asked her, softer this time.

"I had an accident." Her head tipped back, and I was relieved to see she wasn't crying. I'd seen enough of Wren crying to last a lifetime. It gutted me every single time.

"Are you hurt?"

She nodded, then shrugged her coat off, dropping it to the floor. "My wrist is broken." She showed me the hot-pink cast extending from her hand up her forearm. "I didn't need surgery, though."

I kissed her fingertips, wishing on all that was holy I could take her place. I'd snap all my bones to repair Wren's one. My Wren was broken, and this was one thing I couldn't fix.

In my periphery, Ronan crossed his arms over his suited chest. "You need to ask her how she fell."

I focused on Wren, locking eyes with her. "How did you fall, Little Bird?"

She rubbed her lips together and tried to look away. I snagged her chin in my fingers.

"Eyes, Wren. Start speakin' or I'll ask Ronan."

A sigh fell from her lips. "I met Chrys and Rasc today. She... um, kind of lured me into their RV and trapped me there so she could talk to me. She's pregnant, and the father—oh, it's awful. He forced himself on her and left her with nothing. But his parents are willing to help her, they just need to get to California. She needs to talk to you. I told her I'd ask you to call. They let me go, Callum. They barely touched me."

I turned to stone. My hand fell to my side, clenching tight into a fist. "They touched you?"

Iris laid her hand on Wren's shoulder. "Honey bunny, you need to tell him everything. He has to know how to deal with this."

I stared hard at my girl, waiting to see how much worse this could get. As of now, Chrys and Rasc were dead to me, but they were going to hurt first.

Wren's breath went ragged. "I think they're really desperate. They weren't thinking clearly, and maybe they didn't see any other way out of their situation."

Ronan cleared his throat. "I'll say it since Wren is trying to protect them. Iris and I were leaving Good Music when the RV pulled up. The door swung open. Wren was standing there, holding the sides. The woman behind her gave her a hard push, and Wren fell to the pavement. The drop wasn't high, but she wasn't prepared. Her wrist nearly snapped in half."

Black. Ice. Fury.

My fist plowed through the wall beside me. But it wasn't enough. A roar ripped through my chest the second time my fist met drywall. Nothing would ever be enough. They were dead. They were both dead. Not to me. To the world.

"They touched her." I grabbed Wren's fingers, holding up her casted arm. "They hurt what's mine. No one touches you, Wren. No one."

Iris came toward me. "Callie, calm—"

Ronan pulled her back, tucking her behind him. "Do you know where they are?"

My shoulders straightened. "I can find them."

He nodded. "I'm with you, brother. I won't let you take this on alone."

My chin jerked. "You carryin'?"

Ronan stared back at me. "I am."

A wail from my girl. A whimper from Iris. They didn't like the direction this was going.

"Callum, baby." Now the tears were leaking down Wren's perfect cheeks. "No, baby. Stay with me. I need you. You don't have to help them, I understand, but don't go. Please don't go."

I was already gone. In my head, I was ripping my brother limb from limb. My sister...well, my sister would be taken care of too. This would not stand. No one should dare lay their hands on my little bird. Since they did, they were going to wish they never had.

I strode through the apartment, grabbing my keys and phone. Ronan held Wren back, but through my haze, I saw her struggling against him. Pleading, begging, crying for me. She didn't understand this part of me. The side of me that grew up rough and raw, with criminals and the lowest of the low. Justice would be served, and it wouldn't be through *proper channels*. Rascal and Chrysanthemum were going to receive a clear message that what they did today was unacceptable.

Wren threw herself at me, and I yanked her into my arms, holding her tight. "I know you don't want me to go, but, Wren, I gotta do this. It's in my blood to do this."

She gripped my shirt as best she could with her cast. "Don't do anything that'll keep you from coming back to me. If you do, I'm not writing you letters in prison."

I dipped down, getting in her face. "I'm not goin' to prison, but we both know that's not true anyway. You forgave me for stalkin' you. You'll forgive me for protecting you how I need to." I kissed her hard, wet, as deep as she'd let me. "I'm comin' back, Little Bird. Wait here for me. I need to know you'll be here for me."

She let out a tearful, pitiful mewl, but she promised she'd wait. That was all I needed. I could walk away, take care of the business that had to be taken care of, knowing I'd be coming back to my girl.

Ronan's driver, Bill, took us to a Walmart parking lot in New Jersey. The beat-up RV was parked crooked at the edge of the lot. As soon as we pulled up, Rasc lumbered out the door, crossing his arms over his chest. He'd been expecting me. Had texted me their location himself. He knew what was coming.

I was out, moving toward him with a crowbar in my hand. "You touch my girl?"

He held his hands up. "It's not like that, Cal. We ain't hurt that girl. Just needed to talk."

"You touched my girl. You *hurt* my fucking girl." The crowbar connected to the side of the RV, and it crumpled like the tin can it was. "Tell me why I shouldn't do that to your fucking head, Rasc. Tell me!" I pounded into the RV again, unleashing my rage there first. If I started on Rascal, he wouldn't walk away.

"Jesus, Cal. What the hell?" He took a step back. "You gonna hit your own brother?"

"Yeah, you fuck." I dropped the crowbar and charged him. My brother was a big motherfucker, but I was beyond my body's limitations. Rage and righteous indignation powered my limbs, and I took him down to the pavement. Rasc had had some of the same training I'd had when we were kids, but he'd gotten soft and slow. My fist powered into his cheek, and his arms were seconds too late to block it. His head shot to the side, spittle flying out.

Commotion in the form of Chrys went on behind me, but I was laser focused on the asshole who'd once been as close to me as another human could be. I'd held on to that, even after they'd burned the bridge between us. This was me letting go. The last of my connection to my siblings disintegrated into a bloody mist as I pounded my fury into Rascal's flesh.

"What the fuck were you thinkin'?" I screamed in his wounded, leaking face. "That's my woman! You know you don't touch other men's women. You know this, Rascal!"

He'd finally gotten his arms up to protect his face, but I was straddling him, legs locked around his waist, raining blows wherever I could reach. He wasn't fighting back because he knew. He fucking knew he'd done wrong and there was no defending it.

He was bloody, swelling, limp, but breathing and conscious when I hopped off him. He stayed down, right where I wanted him. I could have killed him. I had it in me. But that would take me away from my little bird, and that was not an option.

Bill had my back, and Ronan was containing a snarling, snapping Chrysanthemum. Gone was the sweet, good girl she'd been growing up. A hard life had whittled her down to an angry, rotten core.

"I always knew you were crazy, Cal! Look at you, no amount of money's gonna make you normal." Ronan held her by the waist, and still she tried to get to me. I knew my sister well enough to know she'd claw my face to shreds if she could. She'd rake her claws over the world before admitting she was wrong.

"I might be crazy, Chrys, but at least I'm not you." I took her face in my hand, smushing her cheeks. "You broke her wrist. You shoved her out of this worn-down vehicle like a piece of trash when you were done with her."

Her eyes narrowed. "I didn't push her."

Ronan jerked her hard. "You did, girl. Saw it with my own eyes. That sweet woman of Callum's tried defending you, but there's no defense against what you did. You fucked up, love. No comin' back from this."

She tried to slam her head backward, but Ronan easily dodged her attempt. "Fuck both of you. I'll go to the press. I'll tell them everything about how we grew up. Tell them my brother is mentally ill. You're not stone cold, you're crazy."

I tilted her head back and forth, examining this monster that bore my sister's face. She hadn't always been so damned hard, but life hadn't been kind to Chrys. She hadn't done much to help herself either.

"You're not gonna tell anyone." She hissed, but she didn't deny it. "You're a Traveling Rose as much as I am. That shit doesn't fade. We don't tell our secrets. We don't go to the cops."

Her eyes were slits now, but she didn't deny one word.

"You're gonna leave and not come back. My well has run dry as far as you're concerned. The second you approached my woman, you lost me for good."

Rasc sat up on the ground and spit a puddle of blood next to him. "Timmy's with us, Cal. He's inside the RV."

"I heard. You're makin' a fine example for him."

Chrys groaned and jerked in Ronan's hold. "Don't talk about my son. You don't know anything about the life we're givin' him. You've never even met him."

"True." My nostrils flared. "Now, I never will. I'm done with you. You are no longer my brother and sister. You come around again, I don't know you. You talk to Wren, look at Wren, approach Wren, I will not stop her from callin' the police. I happen to know both of you have warrants out. Don't think they'll let you keep that kid of yours when you're rottin' in a jail cell."

Chrys screamed like I'd scalded her, but I hadn't said anything she didn't know.

"We just need some money, brother. Didn't mean to hurt her," Rasc said.

I glared at him. "Now you've got nothin'. We're done here."

We were gone, driving away from my bloodied brother and bawling sister. I didn't feel any better, but the message had been delivered. They might be back, they might not. But I knew down to my depths they wouldn't try anything on Wren again. Chrys might want to, but Rasc got it. He knew he'd done wrong, broken the code. He'd put a stop to any schemes on Chrys's part when it came to my girl. I could breathe easier now that that had been imparted.

I felt Ronan's eyes on me. "Are you good?" he asked.

"I'll be good when I'm back home."

He shook his head and clucked his tongue. "I didn't think you spoke."

Turning to the window, I knocked my forehead against it. "Only when I have somethin' to say."

I'd spoken. I'd said enough. Now, it was time to hold my girl.

CHAPTER TWENTY-NINE

WREN

IRIS WAS THE ONLY REASON I stayed sane for the two and a half hours Callum was gone. She stayed, talked to me, urged me to call Jenny and ask her to keep Ez overnight. Iris and I FaceTimed with them too, and that pulled me further out of my stupor.

And then I explained to Iris how Callum and I had started five years ago. She listened to all of it and remembered the time period after I left when Callum became even more removed from the band than he ever had been. That made me sad.

But mostly, we stuck to the good things. I discovered Iris truly loved Callum. She didn't know him the way I did, but then, I didn't know him the way she did.

We bonded over our shared love for Callum, and then over our mutual experience of being attacked. Because as time ticked by, I admitted to myself that Chrys and Rasc had hurt me. They'd forced me into their vehicle, terrified me, and yeah, Chrys *had* pushed me to the pavement. Admitting that out loud had sent me into another wave of sobs.

By the time Callum and Ronan crowded through the door, I had calmed down and cried all my tears. I rose to my feet, and in seconds, Callum snatched me around the waist and bundled me against him. He cupped the back of my head, his body curling around mine, holding me close. I held him back, breathing in his

Callum smell, weak with relief he was here, he was standing, he was mine.

Sometime while we were holding each other, Ronan and Iris made their exit. After forever, I pulled back and tipped my head so I could examine Callum's face. It was unmarred, no cuts or scrapes or bruises.

"You're not hurt," I whispered.

He dipped his head to press his mouth to mine. It started sweet but turned deep and hot in seconds. I clung to him while he took my mouth. He clung back just as fiercely.

Finally, he eased his mouth away, breathing heavy and hot on my lips. "No, I'm not hurt."

"Rasc and Chrys?"

He exhaled. "Rasc can't say the same. Chrys is fine."

"Good. I was worried about her."

"She doesn't deserve your worry." Anger laced his words, but I knew he wasn't angry at me. He didn't want me to spare any worry over his sister, but as a mom, I couldn't help myself.

"Well, I guess I'm worried about the baby. She looked like she's due soon."

He stilled for a beat, then his mouth tipped into a small smile. "She's not pregnant, Wren."

"She is." My eyes went wide. "It's kinda hard to miss her big belly."

"Remember the story I told you about the oranges and my mom?"

It took me a moment to recall the story. And then I did. And it dawned on me. I'd been played. Of course I had. "Belly was fake?"

He nodded. "She was raised by the same mama I was. Fake belly always gets you more money. Grifting's in our blood."

"Was that really her son? Sparrow?"

He sighed. "Yeah, that's her boy. Name's not Sparrow, though. I'm thinkin' she made it up knowin' you'd appreciate the bird connection. Kid's name is Tim. She got knocked up by a married guy. Took ten grand from him and hit the road."

"I feel dumb for falling for that."

"You're not dumb. You're just so good, you don't see the bad."

I squeezed his arm. "Are you okay? I know you're not hurt, but this can't be easy. What they did to you—"

"All I felt was anger. I'm done now."

I sucked in a breath at the finality of his words. "That easy?"

"It's that easy because they have been settin' fire to our relationship since they knew how to strike a match. This has been goin' on for years. It sounds cold, I get it, but I'm ice for them." He cupped the sides of my head. "Me turnin' off my heart to Chrys and Rasc doesn't mean I'd ever be able to do that to you. You aren't them. The only match you'd light is one to keep me warm."

That was the most true thing he'd ever said.

He backed me to the couch and pushed me down gently, then he lay down with me, putting most of his torso on mine, his head on my chest. I was crushed into the cushions by his weight, but I liked it. My good hand came up to stroke his hair. Callum's arm looped around me, and he held me tight.

Then we were quiet for a long time. Stroking and hugging. He kissed the curve of my breast every minute or two, moved his big hand over my stomach just as he liked doing, but he seemed to need this. To hold and be held. I guess I needed it too. My wrist ached. My heart hurt a little too. Even if Callum didn't say it, what happened with Rasc and Chrys couldn't have been easy on him.

"I *do* want your kind of love, Callum," I whispered.

His roving hands stilled. "My psycho love?"

"I don't know if I'd call it that."

"What would you call it?"

"I read the emails you sent me after I disappeared. I saw what I did to you. You forgave me and helped me and watched over me even though I ripped you apart. I can't be angry at that. Maybe I should be, but I'm not. I'm *honored* you care for me so intensely."

He propped himself up on his elbow and dragged his fingertips down my cheek. "I won't stop. I couldn't back then, and that was before I knew what it was like to have you."

I reached up and scratched his beard. "I've never believed I could be loved or even liked in a real way."

He growled at me, which made me laugh softly. He'd always defend me, even from my own self-doubt.

"When I had my space to think yesterday, I realized the kind of love you give me is what I need. I don't question it because you are completely up front and blunt with your feelings for me. It might be too much for another kind of woman, but for me, it's perfect."

He scowled at me. "Then you should know mentioning me loving another kind of woman doesn't make me happy. There's no other kind of woman. No other women."

I nodded. "I know. Stop frowning at me, baby."

His scowl deepened, and I giggled. His thumb traced the edges of my smiling mouth. "You know I don't connect with people. It's never been easy. With you, it always has been. Even behind a screen. I learned to love when I met you, Wren. The way I love you was shaped and molded for you. I won't love anyone else because I only know how to love you."

My eyes trailed along his face then back to meet his. How anyone could ever think this man was cold was a mystery to me. He didn't need to wear a coat in the ice-cold winter because he contained the warmth of the sun inside his core. And maybe it only burned for me, but to me, it was impossible to miss.

"You can watch me, Callum."

His scowl finally faded. "Oh yeah?"

"Yeah. Just don't keep anything from me."

"I have no interest in keepin' anything from you. I'm here because I want to spend my life with you. Livin' life with secrets sounds like hell."

I smiled wide. "I love the way you think. Your mind is beautiful."

He dipped down, grazing his lips along mine. "You're beautiful, Little Bird. I was coastin' before you. You woke me up. One email from you and life flipped. I didn't know you were mine yet, but it didn't take long for me to catch on to that."

"You're mine too, Callum. Do you know that? I didn't want to leave you when I did."

His nose touched mine. "You got Ez. We both grew up some. I regret the pain, wish I had the time with you, but I'd never erase what happened because we're here now."

"Yeah," I whispered. "We're here now."

Running out of words, we kissed. Callum was careful with me, so careful, but his need was as palpable as mine. He shifted to the side, rucking my dress up, cupping my core. Still kissing me, plunging his tongue deep into my mouth.

He was still so careful when he pushed my panties down my legs and touched me between them. He wasn't broken in the same way I was, but my hands were gentle on his skin and in his hair.

Hips fitted between mine, Callum entered me like a soldier coming home from a long war. Finally inside, relief and joy marked plain on his face. His sigh was sweet on my lips. We moved together, slow, getting reacquainted.

We kissed and slid into each other without speaking. We had said all there was to say for now. Callum loomed over me, and I rose to meet him. My baby. My beautiful, beautiful man. He was mine, and I didn't question it. Not when he was inside me, not when he was beside me, not even when he was only notes on my screen.

His strokes became harder, longer, hitting so close to the end of me, I mewled. That made him grin, which made me laugh. And then we were both smiling and making love, and it was one of the most perfect moments in my life. I was broken. Callum's knuckles were bloody and swelling. We might've both been a little crazy, but our love was pure. And it was lasting.

We came together, because it was that kind of night. This time, he rolled us both to our sides and snuggled me under his chin. That was perfection too.

I wrote love notes on his arms with my fingers. He rested his palm on my butt. Every minute or two, he kissed the top of my head. *Perfect.*

"I can't go all summer without this," I murmured.

His breathing stopped. "Yeah?"

"I believe you'll take care of me. So yeah, I'll quit my job and come on tour with you. I'm bringing Ez, so it has to work for him too—"

He untucked my head and stared down at me. "Everything I feel for you extends to him. We'll make it work for him."

I nodded. "I know you will."

"It's gonna be good, Little Bird."

"The tour?"

His thumb dragged along my bottom lip and chin. Icy blues met my deep ambers. "This life I'm givin' you. It's gonna be good."

I held his face, making sure he saw me and heard what I said. His sole focus was on me. He was listening.

"That's the thing, baby. It already is."

He exhaled. I breathed him in. He smiled. I did too.

"Yeah. It already is."

WREN

EZRA WAS CRANKY AS HELL, and I was done. A long day followed by an even longer evening had me exhausted and needing to put my feet up like nobody's business. But my son was covered in paint and dirt and I didn't even want to know what else. He needed a bath, no matter how bad my back hurt and how good the damn couch was looking.

Sometimes parenting was pure bullshit.

I loved Ezra with everything I had and everything I was, but yeah, pure bullshit.

"I hate baths!" My sweet angel turned overtired demon wailed at the top of his lungs. Luckily, the condo we'd moved into last year had walls made of cement so our neighbors couldn't hear his screams. They definitely would have thought a child was being murdered if they had.

Jenny missed us living with her, and she never said it, but I was pretty certain she was enjoying her empty nest and living the single life again.

I tried to bend down to lift Ezra from the floor, but my back twinged sharply on the way, and I gasped. A warm, wide hand gripped my bicep, pulling me upright. Stormy blue eyes were on my face.

"What are you doin'?" Callum asked, not quite happy with me.

"Trying to get Ezra in the bath. Obviously."

"Attitude, Little Bird." He pushed his thumb between my pinched brows to smooth them out. "Go sit down. I'm on Ez duty. From now on, baths are mine."

"No bath!" Ezra kicked his feet up and let them fall heavily to the floor. "I'm clean. I don't need a bath."

Callum crouched and scooped Ezra off the floor like a little doll. Ezra didn't stop whimpering, but he immediately went limp in Callum's arms, whining but not trying to get free. That was because being in Callum's arms was one of the top three places in the universe.

Callum pressed his nose in Ezra's curls and made a face. "Wow, little man, you're smelly. I think we should get you in the tub. You can do some scrubbin', and I'll be the music man."

"'I Shot the Sheriff'?" Ez sniffled.

"You pick the songs, I play them. Deal?" Callum and Ez walked off together, leaving me with a warm chest and a tingling nose.

I'd been getting those kinds of feelings over and over for the past two years. Callum didn't joke around about wanting a life with me. Six weeks after the incident with Chrys and Rasc, we were engaged. Two months later, we got married in the park near Jenny's house.

The ceremony was small and simple. Perfect for us. The Seasons Change were in attendance, as were a few friends, including Adelaide and Natalie, and some people from the neighborhood. Mr. Sulaimani brought his family. His mother sobbed when she met Callum and didn't stop thanking him for a good five minutes. Jackie helped me pick my dress. Jenny walked me down the aisle. Ez was happy to be there and annoyed with his suit, but damn, had he looked cute.

Instead of sitting down, I went to the fireplace where there was a picture of the three of us from the wedding. Callum had one arm around my shoulders, and he held Ezra in his other arm.

He'd worn a suit too, and damn, had he looked handsome. I still got butterflies when I looked at this picture.

The one next to it made me smile in a whole different way. With a tour bus as the background, Ez and I were at the center. Callum was on one side, looking at us instead of the camera. Rodrigo had his face scrunched up, cracking Ezra up. Adam gave the camera bedroom eyes. Iris was tucked tight in Ronan's arms. That summer tour was one of the best times in my life. Iris's sister, June, had come along to nanny for Ezra when I needed it, giving me the chance to go to most of the shows while Ezra was tucked away sleeping on the bus. We'd traveled, and I'd gotten to go to places I'd always wanted to. We'd had fun, and bonded, and laughed more than I'd ever had.

Callum had made it good, just like he'd promised. He'd kept all his promises, taking care of Ez and me in every way. Callum understood on a visceral level what it meant for a child to have a safe, secure home, and he gave my son that in spades. He gave it to me too.

And so, it shouldn't have been a surprise when Ezra started calling Callum daddy. It had been, and I hadn't quite known how to react except run to my closet and burst into tears.

Callum found me hiding. "What's that about?"

My arm flailed in the direction of the door. "He called you daddy."

He wrapped me up and held me against his chest. "Yeah. I heard that. Fuckin' cool."

"He's got Brian. I don't even know if he's allowed to call you daddy."

"Brian's his dad. He's also a piece of shit. If he wasn't, Ez wouldn't be callin' me daddy."

I choked back a sob. "You are his daddy, you know."

He dipped down and kissed my head. "Know it, Little Bird. He's my boy."

Brian had been miffed for half a second when Ezra referred to Callum as daddy on one of their calls. The calls that had begun to fade and fade. And a year ago, when I approached Brian about allowing Callum to adopt Ez, his hesitation had lasted even less time than he'd been miffed.

Now, Callum really was Ezra's daddy, and Ezra really was his boy. It had already been true, but now, it was official. We were the Roses. I liked to call us The Stable Roses. Callum laughed when I said it, so I thought he liked it too.

My boys had moved from bath time to bedtime. A lot had changed over the last two years, but Ezra still loved his stories. And Callum, my Callum, was a master at it. These days, I'd been downgraded to spectator. I didn't even mind, because that meant I got to watch them together.

By the time I made it back to Ezra's bedroom, story time was in full swing. I stood in the hall, giving them their time, just the two of them. Callum was telling him a story about an old married couple who'd adopted a million cats. It made Ez laugh, and from the inflection in Callum's voice, I could tell he was smiling.

At the end of the story, Ezra was quiet for a beat, then he started talking. "Are you and Mommy going to get old?"

"One day, a long, long time from now, yeah. That's the plan."

"Then you'll die?" he asked.

My heart stopped. Five-year-olds asked questions about every damn thing. Sometimes they were funny, and sometimes they made me want to curl into a ball because I wasn't wise enough to know how to answer.

"That's right. That's called the circle of life."

I peeked in the room. Callum was stretched out on his side next to Ezra. My son had grown like a weed, but he still looked so tiny next to his dad.

Ezra reached out and picked up a piece of Callum's long hair. He toyed with it between his fingers, then tipped his head back.

"Are you scared of that?"

Callum shook his head. "No. Not at all. You don't need to be either."

"What happens after you die, Daddy?" Ezra didn't sound worried, only curious.

Callum hummed and rubbed his scruffy chin. "Some people believe in a thing called heaven. I'm not too sure about that. I'll tell you what I wish could happen."

"Okay." Oh, this boy was entranced. So was I.

"In a long, long time, Mama and I are gonna get old and die. And then, we'll turn into trees, standin' side by side 'cause you know I couldn't get by without bein' next to Mama."

Ezra giggled. "I know!"

"You know Mama always gets cold so she bundles up. Well, when it becomes fall and it's time to drop our leaves, I'll hold on to mine as long as I can to keep her warm. And when it's windy, I'll use my branches to shield her. When it gets too hot, I'll be her shade. In the spring, I hope I'll blossom first so I can give them to her. But we both know her blossoms are gonna be the most beautiful. That's what I want to happen when we die."

"Yeah. I want to be a tree too."

"One day, a long, *long, long* time from now, you can be a tree with us. And in an even longer time, us Roses will make a whole forest."

"Can the baby be with us too?" Ez asked.

"In a very long time, far, far in the future, yeah, the baby will be there too."

Callum caught my eye and motioned for me to come to them. I crossed the room, emotion choking me. Ezra reached for me, trying to hug my belly but getting nowhere because it was just too damn big now. So, he gave his sister a kiss instead.

"You're gonna be a tree, baby."

I combed my fingers through his damp curls. "I love that idea, baby buddy. How about let's enjoy life right now, though?"

"Okay, Mommy."

We tucked him in and said good night. Callum followed me to the bedroom. His arms were already out when I flung myself at him. He knew what he'd done to me, the monster.

He took me to bed, making me lie down alongside him. He cupped my belly and stared into my eyes. I stared back, blinking away the tears. I would've cried over the tree story even if I hadn't been pregnant, but damn, it'd hit me like a Mack truck with the addition of my daughter growing inside me.

"What's my tree going to do for you?" I asked.

"Exist." No hesitation. That was his answer.

"Your tree's going to protect mine, shade it, shield it, keep it warm, and mine's just going to exist?"

His hands were so warm as they worked their way under my shirt to touch my stomach. I was due in a month, and Callum had only grown more obsessed with my pregnant body the bigger I became. Not just sexually—although there was a hell of a lot of that—but he loved feeling the life he'd help plant in me. He whispered secrets to our daughter and sang her songs. He loved her big and openly, just like he loved me and Ezra. God, I was lucky. And fortunately, this pregnancy had been much, much smoother than Ezra's.

"There's no 'just' to your existence. In this life, you've given me The Stable Roses. You've given me a son, and soon, a daughter. I'm awake because of you. I'm loved without strings. I'm understood and taken care of. You've given me purpose and a home. And one day, when we're trees, our roots are gonna be so entwined, I couldn't live without your existence. So, when I say exist, that's what I mean."

"Okay," I rasped.

He kept staring at me and stroking my belly. Our baby kicked and rolled under her daddy's hand. We smiled at each other. And I got it. I understood what he meant because I felt it too. Our roots were already entwined. This home, this family, this love, this life, we'd given it to each other.

And it was beautiful.

So, one day, we'd be trees. If we were lucky, it would be a long, long way away.

DO YOU WANT MORE OF THE SEASONS CHANGE? Grab Iris and Ronan's story, Falling in Reverse!

mybook.to/FallinginReverse

Ronan Walsh.

Delicious Irish accent. Built like a slab of marble. Infuriatingly controlling.

My new bodyguard...

All I want is to rock hard with my band, The Seasons Change, and finally live my life exactly how I please. No one telling me what to do, no constraints, total freedom.

Too bad I've managed to piss someone off.

Crazed fan or bitter ex, it doesn't really matter, since the result is the same. My wings are clipped and I'm strapped to a bodyguard with steamrolling tendencies and a disdain for celebrities.

Everyday I spend with Ronan is a battle. For control. For independence. And most unexpectedly, with my own willpower.

Because Ronan doesn't just want to protect me. He wants me in his bed too, and ceding my control to Ronan is more tempting than I ever imagined.

But I'm Iris Adler, a fierce-to-my-bones rocker. If Ronan Walsh really wants all of me, he'd better be prepared for the fall.

PLAYLIST

"ARCADE" DUNCAN LAURENCE
"IDK You Yet" Alexander 23
"Silence" Marshmello, Khalid
"You broke me first" Tate McRae
"Skinny Love" Birdy
"I Wanna Be Your Slave" Maneskin
"Bloom" The Paper Kites
"Penpals" Sloan
"Remember That Night?" Sarah Kays
"Are You With Me" nilu
"Changes" Hayd
"Happiest Year" Jaymes Young
"You" benny blanco, Marshmello, Vance Joy
"Cigarette Daydreams" Cage the Elephant
"Hold My Girl" George Ezra
"Shy Away" Twenty One Pilots
"Hate Myself" NF
"Stone Cold" Demi Lovato
"Walked Through Hell" Anson Seabra
"Three Little Birds" Bob Marley
"Make You Better" The Decemberists
https://open.spotify.com/playlist/48b4DaNZNVQoIuCiee7jI
P?si=e34d2f3a21c346d8

JOIN MY READER GROUP, The Sublime Readers, and find out about new releases, cover reveals, and other book news before anyone else. Plus, it's just a fun place to be!

https://www.facebook.com/groups/JuliaWolfReaders

Sign up for my newsletter and receive Rodrigo and Hope's whirlwind love story, Cool for the Summer, for free!

https://www.subscribepage.com/coolforthesummer

ACKNOWLEDGEMENTS

THIS BOOK WAS INCREDIBLY FUN TO WRITE. I LOVE MY JOB, but some books are more like pulling teeth to get the words out. And sometimes I have to dig incredibly deep to imagine how, for instance, a gorgeous, brave and badass rock chick would think and react. But two awkward introverts? Hell yes, sign me up. I know all about that! I loved giving Wren and Callum their person. Who doesn't want to find the one who truly gets them?

Speaking of people who get me, I always have to bring up my girls, Alley Ciz and Laura Lee. They both taught me the value of voice memos and finally converted me to making them. Brainstorming with them gives me author life.

Thank you to Kate Farlow for making the cover design process easy and fun. I always look forward to our appointments because I know I'll be squeeing over what you make for me!

Thank you Amber, for keeping The Sublime Readers going and a fun place to hang out. And thank you to my PA, Jen, for keeping me organized and making pretty graphics! I would be lost without the two of you picking up my very long slack.

I need to give a big shout out to one of my favorite BookTokers, Kristie, AKA read_between.the_wines. Her relentless passion plus her creativity when talking about her favorite stories are a true gift to the romance community! If you don't follow Kristie on TikTok, why not? You're missing out!

ABOUT THE AUTHOR

Julia Wolf is a bestselling contemporary romance author. She writes bad boys with big hearts and strong, independent heroines. Julia enjoys reading romance just as much as she loves writing it. Whether reading or writing, she likes the emotions to run high and the heat to be scorching.

Julia lives in Maryland with her three crazy, beautiful kids and her patient husband who she's slowly converting to a romance reader, one book at a time.

Visit my website:

http://www.juliawolfwrites.com

ALSO BY JULIA WOLF

Never Again

The Sublime

One Day Guy

The Very Worst

Want You Bad

Fix Her Up

Eight Cozy Nights

Printed in Great Britain
by Amazon

82184707R00200